4-24-06 C

By Bread Alone

By Bread Alone

Sarah-Kate Lynch

LARGE PRINT

This large print edition published in 2004 by
RB Large Print
A division of Recorded Books
A Haights Cross Communications Company
270 Skipjack Road
Prince Frederick, MD 20678

Published by arrangement with Warner Books

This book is a work of fiction. Names, characters, places and
incidents either are products of the author's imagination or are used
fictitiously. Any resemblance to actual events or locales or persons,
living or dead, is entirely coincidental.

Publisher's Cataloging In Publication Data
(Prepared by Donohue Group, Inc.)

Lynch, Sarah-Kate.
    By bread alone / Sarah-Kate Lynch.

        p. (large print) ; cm.

    ISBN: 1-4193-1847-0

1. Bakers and bakeries—Fiction. 2. British—France—Fiction. 3. Loss
(Psychology)—Fiction. 4. Married women—Fiction. 5. First loves—Fiction.
6. Large type books. 7. England—Fiction. I. Title.

PR9639.4.L96 B9 2004b
823/.92

Printed in the United States of America

In praise of kooky houses, long-lost loves
and the much-maligned carbohydrate

By Bread Alone

PROLOGUE

The moment Esme's espadrilles hit the smooth stone floor deep down in the heart of the tiny *boulangerie*, she knew that up until then she herself had only been half-baked.

The sweet, sharp scent of sourdough bread cooking in an oak-fired oven wended and whirled around her unsuspecting senses and unleashed a hunger inside her she had not known existed. It hit her so hard she could barely breathe.

The air was hot and thick with the promise of life's simple and not-so-simple pleasures. She could feel that. She could smell it. She could taste it on the tip of her tongue.

Bread. Yes, bread. *Pain au levain,* to be precise, the specialty of the house. Never mind the baguettes, the croissants, the chocolate or custard pastries after which she had so recently hankered. Compared to just one crumb from the sourdough *boules* baked not ten feet away from where she stood they were nothing, nothing but sand, dry and gritty, in the memory of her taste buds. No other paltry pretender could ever hope to measure up to the beauty of those fat round loaves with their thick crunchy crusts and shining, soft flesh.

Esme licked her glistening lips, her mouth watering. She had been eating the bread up there in the outside world for a week now and was well past the stage of being addicted to its taste but had only dreamed, literally, of getting this close to the heart of it all. The atmosphere was overwhelming. The air cloaked her in its moist, sweet arms, and soothed the fluttering in her chest. She wanted to lie on that warm, worn floor and stay there forever, sleeping. It felt like home, only better. Like heaven, only closer.

Here, in this ancient overbaked room carved out of golden stone and hidden underground above a lazy kink in the Dordogne River, was where it all began. And the beginning was the key, as she was soon to learn, because the secret to sourdough was its starter, the *levain*, the living, breathing, bubbling mixture of the past and the present that was added to every batch of flour and water to turn it into the future. For nearly two hundred years the starter in that hot, heavy room had been breathing life into sourdough *boules* and no other bread in the southwest, the whole of France, the rest of Europe, anywhere in the world, tasted anything like it.

The bulk of each loaf was made from wheat grown in the surrounding fields, freshly stone-ground not a mile away and mixed with water from the river that wandered and wound below, and there was nothing very special about that, anybody could get that. But its soul, its essence, the spirit of its utter delectability was nowhere near so easily captured. That came from the faintly foaming *levain* and it drew its flavor from the past, from the crusty ancient walls themselves, from the sun that warmed the *boulangerie*'s yellow-striped awnings, from the faint scent of lavender that meandered down the stairs from the window boxes in the street, from the golden haystacks that sat squat and solid in the surrounding pastures, from the generations of bakers who had borne it, fed it, nurtured it, shared it, loved it.

Later, when Esme knew more, much more, and her hunger was being sated, repeatedly and not entirely by bread, she found herself drawn to the starter where it lay, breathing and vital, in the bottom of an antiquated wooden bin waiting to give life to the next family of *boules*.

Now that she knew what magic it worked, she was thoroughly spellbound.

For without the starter, *pain au levain* was not *pain au levain* at all, just a lifeless, dull and rather mucky mixture.

But add that potent starter to that same limp combination, gently mix in salt from the marshes of Guerande, then give it time, a little warmth, the firm heel of a baker's hand, more time and, finally, some heat, some real heat, and voilà!

Esme knew what it was to be lifeless and dull, never more so than when she stepped into that hot, salty, sweaty little room. At nineteen years old, lightly freckled and chastely English, she was more keenly aware of her missing ingredient than ever. She was ready to rise. All that was missing was the baker's magic touch.

Near the end—although of course how near she had not known—she lifted a cool jar of the precious *levain* close to her face and breathed in its tangy, intoxicating tones.

"To think," the baker murmured in his deep, low, chocolate-covered voice, "there will be some of you and me in the bread you bake, Esme."

Sheer joy and sourdough, from that moment on, would be forever tangled in her mind.

CHAPTER 1

Fifteen years later, seventy feet up in the Suffolk seaside air, Esme was juggling quinces. She'd been carrying an armful of the oversized yellow fruit from the fruit bowl to her kitchen sink when she'd tripped over the dog and the whole lot had gone flying.

She lunged forward, grappling with the air, and caught a couple, but in the process kicked one that had fallen to the ground so hard that it bounced off the baseboard and hurtled down the stairs.

In a house that was six stories high, with the kitchen at the top, this was far from ideal.

"Bugger," she said as the remaining quinces wibbled and wobbled around her ankles, making Brown jump and skitter as Esme danced her way over to the stairwell. The runaway quince, she could hear, had made it down the first eight steps, hit the landing wall, then bounced down the next eight. It was large and not quite ripe and made something of a hullabaloo.

"For God's sake, Brown," she complained as the dog scrambled behind her on the polished floorboards, panicking and spreading the quinces further. She headed down the stairs, the stomp of her no longer fashionable clunky clogs adding to the din.

Slowing on Rory's level to take the next flight of stairs, she felt the unexpected sensation of Brown's nose slamming into her rear end and all but knocking her down them.

"Do you mind," she admonished. "If you're not under my feet you're up my arse, you annoying bloody creature!"

"I beg your pardon?" the voice of her father-in-law harrumphed from below. For a man with two artificial hips and a wonky walking stick, he could move surprisingly quietly, Esme thought, sort of like a panther crossed with a snail. But gray.

"Henry!" she replied, her features fighting a grimace. Henry occupied the first floor of the House in the Clouds and rarely ventured up this far. He had his own bathroom and kitchenette down below and shared a sitting room on the next floor up with the rest of the family, although the younger Stacks hardly ever used it.

"Sorry about the racket," she apologized, descending toward his voice, "but I tripped over Brown and dropped a quince, then the silly creature rear-ended me. You don't have it down there, do you? The quince, I mean?"

She rounded the corner and saw that the bruised and battered fruit was indeed lying at Henry's feet, leaking slightly.

"You wouldn't think they would travel so far, would you?" she chirruped, stopping a few steps above him. "Or so fast for that matter. Perhaps we got it all wrong about the wheel. Perhaps it should have been quince-shaped."

Henry looked at her as though she were speaking a foreign language. It was a look she quite often noticed on him, but before she could even wish that she had shut up earlier and saved him the bother of being annoyed, Brown pushed right past her, scuttled down to the quince, sniffed it, turned, lifted his leg and peed on it. Esme gaped wordlessly as splatters ricocheted off the wall and onto Henry's brogues which, it being Friday and Henry being a creature of habit, would have been cleaned approximately one hour and nine minutes earlier.

Henry, understandably surprised, temporarily lost control of his walking stick and staggered slightly, stumbling into the wall and knocking a portrait of his late wife off its moorings.

"For goodness' sake," he rasped, puce with irritation, still leaning into the wall but attempting to right himself. "Don't just stand there, *do something.*"

Brown backed slowly toward the next flight of stairs, his tongue lolling out of his mouth, his eyes on Esme as he waited to see what the something might be.

"Well?" Henry asked again, flicking dog urine off his foot with as much vigor as any seventy-four-year-old with barely a real bone left in his pelvic region could. *"Well?"*

In the blink of an eye the House in the Clouds was alive with the clatter and bang of six legs crashing down many wooden stairs as Esme lunged past her teetering father-in-law and gave chase. Onward she lurched and downward, Brown's fat shiny rump always just out of reach as she skidded through her and Pog's story, slid past the sitting room, leaped down to Henry's level, then took the last flight to the ground floor two steps at a time.

For an animal that could spend an entire day slumped in front of the fire staring at a plate of shortbread, he could move pretty damn quickly when he had to. Cornering, however, was not his strong point, and in the tiny entrance hall his chubby, brown body skidded and smashed into the occasional table, sending it and a vase of glorious red roses crashing to the ground. Still steaming ahead, he aimed his bulk squarely at the cat door and dived through it, the tip of his tail disappearing just as Esme reached out to grab it and pull it clear off his wretched body.

The cat door rattled shut and the house was once again silent. For a moment. Then Henry's stick tap tapped across the floor above.

"Well done," he called stiffly. "I'll get a mop."

"Oh, will you ever lighten *up,*" Esme heard Granny Mac call caustically from behind her closed bedroom door in her fifty-a-day Glaswegian dockworker lilt. "You'll give yourself a heart attack with all your pissing and moaning, you silly old *goat*."

Esme froze. She looked at the door of her grandmother's room, then up at the ceiling. She had heard, clear as day, she was sure she had, but had Henry? The house seethed for a moment as nobody moved and nothing more was said, and then Henry's slow tap-shuffle tango heralded his retreat to the broom closet for cleaning equipment.

Esme blew out a lungful of air and decided to ignore what she had just heard. She could not afford to lose it this morning. She had quinces (two dozen) to paste, windows (twenty-eight) to wash, stairs (seventy-eight) to vacuum and a feverish son (four and a half) who was a worry at the best of times but never more so than when he'd had a bad night's sleep. He was passed out now on a beanbag in front of a Bob the Builder video but that would not last forever.

Turning to confront the destruction, Esme caught sight of herself in the hall mirror. Her reflection told a story she did not want to hear. Clear green eyes stared back at her with a fraught expression. She had done an awful job, if a job at all, of taking off her makeup the night before and so had black blobby lashes with smudges below them. The chic chignon she had imagined she had constructed atop her head earlier that morning was neither chic nor a chignon. In fact, her mad

9

copper-colored ringlets looked like a large ball of ginger wool that had been ravaged by angry kittens. She had lipstick on her chin, something crusty on her nose and only one earring. She gave the impression of having been very recently caught in a hurricane.

Her shoulders sagged as she took in her reflection. Was every life as chaotic as hers? she wondered. Did she invite more disorder than the next person? More catastrophe? The slapstick comedy of the peed-on quince rolled away to expose the dangerous slick that lurked just below Esme's surface. At this, her mind snapped shut, her eyes slid off their mirror image. Today was not the day to contemplate the heartache that would swallow every second if she let it. Now was not the hour to confront the tragedy that had ripped her family to shreds then so heartlessly reshaped it.

Instead she would just take that relentless pain, that torturous memory and wring it out, squash it down, suppress it the way she had every day for the past two years until it no longer consumed her but just hid inside her, deep and dark, small and hard.

That way, she could keep going. That way she could continue to put one foot in front of the other, to breathe in and out, to cook and clean and laugh and smile as though her worst nightmare had stayed just that instead of coming true and chasing her to a new life in a different place, a place where every nook and cranny was not haunted by the consequences of that dreadful day.

And by and large it had worked, these past two years, that wringing and squashing. She had survived. Pog, her husband, had survived. Rory, their son, had survived. Separately, they had all survived.

Esme stifled a hiccup of grief. Wring it out, she urged herself. Squash it down. Hide it. Put one foot in front of the other. Keep going.

But this past month had been hard. Even she could see it in those clear green eyes. And it was getting harder.

Her husband, Pog, at that same moment, was sitting at his desk three leafy, curly streets away thinking exactly the same thing.

It was now thirty-three days since Esme had baked a loaf of bread and he didn't know how to get her started again. His lips were dry, his stomach churning as he contemplated the store-bought sandwich sitting bleakly in front of him. He poked it with a freshly sharpened pencil. It was yesterday's bread. No question. It had no bounce. No allure. No joie de vivre. It was not begging to be eaten. It was just sitting there quietly suffocating its own sweating stuffing of overcooked eggs and undercooked bacon.

Of course he had tried to talk to Esme about the baking; it worried him beyond comprehension. He knew what sourdough meant to her. But the day Dr. Gribblehurst came out of Granny Mac's room casting his gloomy forecast Esme had stopped. And at Pog's first attempt to confront this, he had seen the panic in her eyes, and backed away. How, he asked himself, could he talk to her about bread, about Granny Mac, when there was so much more that needed talking about? Over the past two years the unspoken words between them had been covered up and buried and a thick comfortable quilt had grown across the top of their lives, concealing the chasm that beneath the covers grew deeper and deeper.

He should have been stronger from the beginning, he knew that now. He should have forced the issue, no matter how painful, but the truth was that he did not want to be the one to scratch the scab off Esme's wounds because he was afraid he would never be able to staunch the resulting flow.

Everybody thought she was so carefree, so happy, so strong, so resilient—why, she even thought that herself—but Pog knew otherwise. And he wanted to help her, God knew he wanted nothing more, but he did not want to push her, to break her, to open the fine, delicate cracks he knew had invaded her hardened outer shell ever since that terrible, terrible day. He could not, would not, do anything to risk losing her, his gorgeous, garrulous, glutinous wife. She was all that had kept him going since then. She was all that kept any of them going.

His stomach gurgled hungrily but the pasty preservative-laden offering in front of him held all the allure of a Wellington boot. Listlessly, he poked a straight line of holes clear through the sad little sandwich and tried not to hear Mrs. Murphy making appointments for him out in the reception area.

He needed Esme to bake, was desperate for it. Esme's bread not only begged to be eaten, but demanded it. You simply could not be in the same room as her sourdough without licking your lips and instantly realizing it was exactly what you felt like eating. No, more than that. It was exactly what you had been missing.

Pog tried to remember the exact smell. But thirty-three days without it and already it was a fading memory. The saltiness he could get, the sharp apple and vinegar tang he could recapture. But that sweet, warm indescribably delicious mouthwatering element that stamped it as made every step of the way by Esme's soft and supple hands? Gone. Unbelievably gone. Just like the delectable, crusty, fleshy loaves themselves.

Esme's soft and supple hands at that very moment were back in the House in the Clouds reaching up and wrangling her wild, red curls. "Snap out of it," she commanded herself, leaning in toward the mirror and rubbing at her eyes to clear the black rings. She moistened her lips to give them some gloss, wiped the slash of pink from her chin, scratched at the whatever-it-was on her nose and smiled. It was a well practiced and convincing enough performance to spur her on to the job at hand, which was cleaning the mess on the floor. Pushing the jagged pieces of the spindly broken table aside with her foot, she crouched down gingerly in a puddle of smelly vase water to start picking up the shattered pieces of crockery. The vase had been a wedding present from her brother-in-law Milo, the son who'd chosen a proper wife and then cleverly vacated to New York City. Breaking it would no doubt be another black mark against her as far as Henry was concerned. She knew he found her flighty and unsuitable and it must stick in his craw something wicked, she thought, trawling halfheartedly through the muck on the floor, that he was stuck under her roof through no fault of his own, other than badly investing his life's savings and ending up near penniless, to all intents homeless and without hips in good working order.

She reminded herself that he had every right to be in a permanently bad mood and felt a twinge of guilt for owning a dog that would urinate on such newly cleaned brogues.

"Hello-o!" She heard her grandmother's musical burr ring, as clear as a bell, from behind the closed bedroom door. "I said, hello-o-o!"

Esme stood up, pushed the remaining jumble on the floor toward the wall, and cocked her head to one side. Rod Stewart seemed to be softly rasping about some seventeen-year-old knocking on his door.

The singing was definitely on the outside of her head, and seemed to be leaking out from Granny Mac's room. She moved over and pressed her ear against the door. Her grandmother's favorite singer was crooning that the young strumpet could love him tonight if she wanted, but in the morning she had better be gone.

Gingerly, Esme opened the door and slipped into the room. It was dark, just the way Granny Mac had always liked it. She shook her head to rid herself of Rod and shuffled in the dim light toward the window, reaching out as she approached it to pull back the curtains.

"Hey, you, *Hot Legs*!" the voice of her grandmother suddenly filled the room. Esme spun around and found the old woman's eyes twinkling at her beadily from the end of her bed. The room smelled suddenly and strongly of cigarettes. Cheap ones. Embassy Regal. Granny Mac's favorites.

The hair stood up on the back of Esme's neck. "Granny Mac!" she breathed with disbelief as her eyes grew accustomed to the dimness and sought out the unwavering, challenging gaze of her grandmother.

"Aye," answered Granny Mac, "amazing, isn't it, at my stage in life?"

Esme blinked, said nothing for a moment, then blinked again. Feelings tumbled inside her, searching for a slot. Disbelief, fear, anger, delight:

All clamored for space. "Granny Mac," she said again, on the spur of that moment deciding to suspend her disbelief in favor of embracing her delight. "You've been smoking!"

Her grandmother, her wrinkles in the drab light dissolving and blurring on her crinkled cheeks, simply cackled.

"I don't understand," Esme said. "I thought that . . . Well, how could you? I mean, for goodness' sake. You really ought not to . . . It's just that, well . . . I thought you had, you know, you were definitely . . . Oh shit," she said suddenly. "I am having such a strange day." She sniffed the room again. There was definitely cigarette smoke in the air. And Rod Stewart.

"Well, turns out there is a quick way to give up smoking," her grandmother said, "but I don't know that I can entirely recommend it."

Esme stood and contemplated the bed. She should not allow this, she knew that, of course she knew that, but how she adored her Granny Mac. And how she needed her! How she had always needed her. Without Granny Mac all the wringing and squashing in the world would not have kept one foot in front of the other since their move from London to the House in the Clouds. She was Esme's savior. She always had been. And perhaps she always would be. Who was Esme to argue with that?

She threw her hands in the air and plonked herself down on the end of the bed, wriggling backward until her back met the wall. She looked in her grandmother's direction and willed the blackness to stop smudging that much loved face, to snap it into focus. "You know, I was just thinking about where I wanted to live," she said, ignoring just about everything, "and I wonder if perhaps it is in here with you, maybe just for a few days. I could smoke cigarettes and read *Hello!* magazines and spy on Gaga and Jam-jar next door. It would be just like the old days."

Gaga and Jam-jar were the ancient neighbors who despite rather oddly living in a windmill were perhaps the straightest two people in Christendom and loathed Esme and her eccentric tower of relatives with a passion. The appropriately named assortment of Stacks, according to Gaga and Jam-jar, lowered the tone.

"You'd have to go out and get the *Hello!* magazines for a start," Granny Mac said. "I'm dying for want of fresh dirt on poor Fergie."

Esme felt a hot flush of devotion sweep through her. "I thought you could never forgive her," she said, "for wearing that shocking hat to the Queen Mother's funeral."

"Och, did you have to remind me about the Queen Mother? It upsets me greatly these days to hear about dead people, Esme. Spare a thought for them, will you?"

"Well, I think it was the Queen Mother." Esme tumbled forward. "But you never know with those Royals, do you? I mean, I never saw the body. It

17

could have been anyone. Did you know that Princess Diana has been seen working as a show-girl in Vegas? They might have carried the real Queen Mother out of Clarence House in a bedpan for all we know. She might be living the high life in Blackpool spending all our hard-earned taxes on slot machines and horses."

Granny Mac seemed thrilled with the possibility. "It wouldn't be such a bad life," she said. "I might try it myself."

"Oh no, Granny Mac, I need you here," Esme said, a little too desperately, because even though the chances of her grandmother actually moving to Blackpool were close to nil, stranger things had happened, were happening. "I really, really do. You can't possibly know how much."

She felt Granny Mac's eyes boring into her in a way she knew meant she wanted to know how much. She sighed.

"I'm losing it," she said, simply, with a shrug of her shoulders. "I'm bloody losing it. I mean, look at me!" A ringlet, as if to back up what she was saying, suddenly sprang out of her hairclip and bounced in front of her face.

"This past month, Granny Mac, you know, since"—she struggled for words that would not upset her grandmother—"since Dr. Gribblehurst and everything . . ." She was silent for a moment, searching for the right approach.

"Nothing feels right anymore. I don't know what I'm doing. I don't know why I'm here. I don't know anything. It all feels dark and fuzzy and strange. I feel like I'm starting to unravel and I don't know why and it's bloody terrifying."

"You do know why, you soft lass," her grandmother said. "You just don't want to face it."

Esme felt fear clutch at her heart. Was this what she wanted to hear?

"It's not that I don't *want* to," she said. "It's just that I can't. It's too soon."

"But if you wait much longer," her grandmother argued, "it will be too late. And maybe not just for you."

"Don't," Esme pleaded. "Just don't." The room, apart from the barely audible lamenting of Rod Stewart, fell silent.

"Well, what about that miserable old stoat upstairs, then, eh?" Granny Mac switched the subject to one of her favorites: Henry. "Is he still getting up your nose?"

"No more than I deserve, I'm sure," answered Esme, relieved at the change in direction. "I mean he's a bit septic and I don't seem to be able to do anything right but that's nothing new."

"Have you considered a London telephone directory to the back of the head?" offered Granny Mac. "Or a frozen leg of lamb, which you then proceed to serve up for dinner, or a bottle of wine?"

"I've thought about the wine," Esme admitted, "but only drinking it. I hadn't really considered the murder weapon potential."

"Och," her grandmother said, disgusted. "You're not trying hard enough, Esme."

Esme poked her errant curl back into her topknot. She was trying as hard as she could.

"Esme!" The sound of Rory's anxious cry filtered through from the top floor of the house to the bottom. Waking up was not Rory's best time. He suffered terrible nightmares, poor lamb, and the thought of what he dreamed about to wake up so angry and lost and lonely chilled her to the bone.

"Esme-e-e-e-e," he called again, his voice sifting through the layers of the house to find her. No matter how hard she had tried to get him to call her Mummy, he only ever referred to her by her name. Gaga and Jam-jar found it criminal.

"Is the wee boy okay?" Granny Mac asked gently.

"He's fine," Esme said, heaving herself off the bed, loath to leave the coziness of Granny Mac's company. And in truth, he was doing pretty well. The psychologist he saw every couple of months in London seemed pleased with his progress and his speech was truly astonishing. For a boy who had not spoken a single word until the day after his fourth birthday, at which point he debuted with "I'd rather have a chocolate biscuit, if it's all the same to you," his command of the English language would put most grown-ups to shame. "Truly, Gran," she said. "He's just tired, that's all. Honestly, he's fine. You don't need to worry about him."

"So, it's just you, then," Granny Mac said. "That I need to worry about."

Esme smiled into the darkness of the foul-smelling room. "Oh, I don't know," she said softly. "I'm feeling better already."

"Is that so? Well, may I be so bold as to ask if that was a quince making its way down the stairs with such enthusiasm just before?"

"How could you possibly know that?" Esme was stunned.

"Es-meeeeeee," Rory howled from above.

"A quince, Esme, of the quince variety? At this hour of the morning when you would normally, I am sure, be putting a loaf of your delicious sourdough bread in the oven?"

"Blame Doctor bloody Gribblehurst," Esme burst out. "It's all his fault."

"Well, it's you who bakes the bread Esme. Or not, as the case may be. And now is not the time to let go of what is dear to you. Now more than ever you should be clinging to it."

"I just haven't had it in me," Esme said despairingly. "I just couldn't . . . I just can't . . . It just went."

"Well, just get it back, lassie. Just get it back."

And with that Rory roared so loudly that Esme could bear it no longer, and to the retreating strains of Rod Stewart, she slipped out of the room and headed up the stairs.

As she clumped past Henry's room she saw that all signs of the recent quince-flavored disaster had disappeared. He would be cleaning his brogues again, no doubt, his schedule thrown out most inconveniently. She clenched her buttocks, not because she was thinking of her father-in-law, but because her friend Alice, who was addicted to personal trainers, had told her that combined with climbing the stairs ten times a day, it constituted proper exercise.

By the time she clattered up the last set of steps to where Rory lay pink and flushed under his favorite blanket in a corner of the kitchen, she was puffing and wheezing like an old steam engine and wishing he was old enough to know CPR so he could practice it on her.

And her bum hurt. These were the ramifications of living in a house with seventy-eight internal stairs, but every time Esme looked out the window of the top floor in her nutty tower she remembered why it was all worthwhile.

She scooped up her small, sticky, sobbing son and held him tight against her chest as she looked out across the scattered rooftops of Seabury village, over the tips of the leafy green oaks, across the lake—or the Meare as the locals knew it—to the waters of the cool North Sea lapping at the pebbly shore and trying moodily not to glisten in the watery sunshine.

She rocked Rory, quietly shushing him back from despair, and thought back to the dreary, gray, London afternoon when she had only too happily abandoned her own thriving publishing empire to drag Pog away from his office and up to the Suffolk coast to look at the house of her dreams.

"But it's not even a real house," Pog had moaned, aghast.

"Leave it out," Esme had teased, "you're an architect—you're the last person who would know what a real house looks like."

He did have a point, she'd agreed at the time, in that it was a highly unusual dwelling, but that was what appealed to her. They wanted to escape their city lives, didn't they? They wanted to start anew?

"But couldn't we just get a sweet little cottage by the sea?" Pog had asked. "Like normal people?" But they were no longer normal people—recent unimaginable events had changed that—and Esme wanted the House in the Clouds not in spite of its oddness, but because of it.

"But the whole village is not quite right," Pog had complained, his face crumpled with worry. "There are all these corners where there should be straight lines and far too many turrets and towers."

Esme agreed that the village was from the Not-Quite-Right Shop—as Granny Mac would say—but that only endeared it to her further. The whole settlement of Seabury had been dreamed up a hundred years earlier by a wealthy landowner who wanted to custom make a fairy-tale holiday resort for "nice" people like himself.

He'd gone a bit overboard, it had to be said, on

reviving the spirit of the Tudor Age, long since past, and so the town sported more than its fair share of inappropriate wooden cladding, heavy beams, curved roads and quaint if entirely unnecessary corners.

And over this eccentric collection of homes and gardens loomed the House in the Clouds, a giant dovecote, its tall slender stalk painted black and peppered with tiny white windows, and the big square room on top a deep, delicious red with pitched roofs and views of almost everywhere.

"I mean even normal-sized dovecotes are pretty bloody barmy," Pog had continued to grumble. "But one that's seventy feet high? That you *live* in?"

That theatrical landowner of yore had originally devised the house to add, rather dramatically, to the landscape but more important to disguise the town's water supply, 30,000 gallons of which was once kept in what was now the kitchen and family room.

"Disguise?" Pog had nearly fainted when Esme revealed this detail. "He *disguised* his water tower as a giant dovecote?"

"Yes, that's why there's a windmill in the backyard," Esme had answered, as though that made any more sense. When it came down to it, she told Pog, the house had spoken to her, in words that only she could hear.

"Like chocolate?" he had suggested, rather gloomily.

24

"Like chocolate," she'd replied, "only bigger."

The House in the Clouds had been the antidote Esme thought she needed to the life she knew she could no longer live, her escape from the torment of tragedy, and Pog, because all he ever wanted was for her to be happy, had soon relented and the entire Stack clan had decamped.

So, it could be infuriating to get down to the car and realize she had left the keys on the kitchen table high in the sky above her, but mostly Esme had adored her tower and the higgledy-piggledy town it came in.

"Where's Mrs. Brown?" Rory whined into her neck as his hot little body clung to her. "I want Mrs. Brown."

Esme kissed her son's thick, curly, bright orange hair and resisted the urge to tell him that Mrs. Brown, as he had originally christened the dog, had been savaged by angry cave bears and would never be coming back. Not as a dog anyway. Possibly as a potted plant but definitely not as anything with a bladder.

"Where's Mrs. Brown?" Rory continued to sob dramatically. "Where's my friend, my only friend." Esme shushed and rocked her son. The floor was still covered in quinces, the kitchen counter set up and ready for paste-making.

She caught a whiff of Rory's sweet, cranky little boy breath and kissed his nose, but at this he twisted away from her and out of the corner of her eye she saw his shadow wriggling across the kitchen cupboards and felt a clamp deep in her stomach, an inexplicable mixture of sadness and secrets and unshed tears.

At that moment a gentle sea breeze blew in through an open window and nudged open the pantry door so the sun, like a torch beam on an inky black night, sought out the stone jar that sat smugly on the floor, its contents quietly bubbling and roiling. You may have given up on me, it whispered into the morning air. But I have not given up on you.

CHAPTER 2

Granny Mac had always loved Rod Stewart. Rather bizarrely for a thrice-widowed matron in her sixties, she'd once even had her hair cut in a blond "shaggy" just like his. Each of those late husbands had had their own Rod signature tune and the merest hint of "You're in My Heart" could always be relied on to conjure up her last, Jerry O'Brien.

On a good day the most mild-mannered, polite and caring of men, on a bad day he had a mouth like a sewer rat and a contempt for Granny Mac's Catholicism that bordered on psychotic, given she was not herself a Catholic.

"Jesus was a faker, a fraud, and Mary was a hussy," he would roar at Esme and her grandmother from the safety of his armchair, his eyes roving wildly around in his head and his dyed black hair sprouting out spookily around his bald patch.

"Son of God, be damned!" he would spit, grabbing at the crème de menthe, which was all he drank.

"Did you get that, Esme?" Granny Mac would

ask her granddaughter as they hid in the hallway on either side of the open sitting room door. "Did you get the bit about being damned?" Esme would studiously write down every word, although the spelling on some of his curses truly stumped her.

When the poor man awoke in the morning with a raging headache, green teeth and enough remorse to fill an entire hemisphere, Granny Mac would be sitting on the bed staring at him and would call immediately for her granddaughter.

"Off you go, Esme," she would say, at which point Esme would take out her notebook and start reciting his obscenities of the night before.

"'Fuck the pope,'" Esme would read from her notes in her sweet schoolgirl voice, "'and the blessed virgin too even though we all know she wasn't really a virgin.'"

Jerry O'Brien would lie in his bed and weep as Granny Mac's eyes bored into him with the fervor of a Texas oilman. For the next month he would be the picture of sobriety until the demon de menthe got hold of him again and the whole process was repeated.

"God knows how often he'd have hit the bottle without the treatment," Granny Mac would say for years afterward. "Men! It's a wonder the lot of us aren't lesbians."

She had loved Jerry O'Brien deeply, however. He was the best of all her husbands, she often told Esme, when he wasn't rat-arse pissed. Her first two husbands she had hardly missed at all but by the time she lost Jerry O'Brien she could not keep melancholy at bay because by then she was also minus a daughter, Beth, Esme's mother and a perfect example of why misery and MacDougall women made such bad company.

Beth, never a sturdy creature, had found marriage, motherhood, adultery, divorce, life in general far too heartbreaking a business to continue contemplating and so had slipped away one wet London lunchtime, sung softly to sleep by a pharmaceutical lullaby. And so, as per clearly written instructions, her estranged mother was sent for and cried rare silent tears all the way from the bleak windswept shores of Gairloch to the hustle and bustle of St. John's Wood, where she was introduced, for the first time, to her five-year-old granddaughter.

Esme, sitting on the floor of a neighbor's flat, her flame red hair impossibly jolly as she ate cold baked beans out of a can, had looked at her and smiled. And so began their life together.

Despite its grim beginnings, it had been a good arrangement. Beth knew this. Granny Mac knew this. Esme's father, long since emigrated to New Zealand and remarried with twin daughters, knew it. Even Esme knew it.

Very quickly Granny Mac and her charge, who somewhere along the line adopted the family name, became as thick as thieves. Esme, for the most part, delighted in having a guardian who thought homework a sick joke and after-dinner mints the perfect sandwich filling. Their lives were full and happy and they were both better off than they had been before.

And then Esme, aged ten, had come bursting through the door bearing Jerry O'Brien, sheepish and shy, saying she had found him at the bus stop having watched him narrowly miss the alleged 11:07 to Camden and he seemed in dire need of a cup of tea. Granny Mac thought all her Christmases had come at once.

How she loved that silly old man, with his badly dyed hair, ridiculous foibles and utter devotion to the two of them. He was her reward, she had assumed, for having a mother and a daughter who had chosen to desert her. Oh yes, misery was a curse, all right.

Granny Mac had been abandoned as a child herself by a mother unable to keep waking up to a world she judged too harsh for her own gentle soul. Granny Mac carried with her this fear of such sorrow but never came close to feeling it herself until she lost Jerry O'Brien. After just one short year of happiness, it had seemed too cruel to bear. And for the first time in her life, she had let down her guard and watched from outside herself as the family hex crept in and filled her pockets of happiness with black, sticky ooze.

It did not last long.

Esme rescued her.

Even at the age of twelve she had known that with a bottle of whisky, a lot of dark chocolate and all the Rod Stewart hits of the late 1970s, they would pull through. And they had.

So now Granny Mac's sole purpose on earth was to concoct a mixture that could similarly rescue Esme. And she would.

"You had better be bloody kidding me," Esme breathed into the phone later that evening, quinces pasted, windows washed, stairs gleaming, son in bed, large glass of Chardonnay in one hand, phone in the other. "Jemima Jones is getting her own column?" she asked Alice incredulously. "In the *Sunday Times*? *The* Jemima Jones. *Our* Jemima Jones?"

"Oh, Es," moaned Alice, nestled in her threadbare armchair in her run-down Shepherd's Bush flat. "I knew you'd be upset but I've been dying to call you all day. There's a sort of build-up story about her in the paper today."

"They gave her a column!" Esme squawked again. "In the *Sunday Times*! But why?"

"Because she has reinvented herself as a society superwoman, that's why," Alice answered. "I have the paper right here. Can you bear to hear it? It is appalling, Es, honestly, you'd better get a bucket because you will be sick, I promise you."

"Read it to me," Esme commanded. "Is it really bad?"

"Repellent."

"Get on with it, then!"

"'*Married with three young children,*'" Alice started, "'*Jemima works tirelessly—*'"

"'Works tirelessly'?" Esme was appalled. "There's been some sort of a mistake. It's definitely not the Jemima we know."

"That's nothing," said Alice. "Get a load of this. '*Jemima works tirelessly as a volunteer for Princess Diana's landmine charity and is a permanent fixture on guest lists at London's most salubrious society events.*'"

"'A permanent fixture'?" Carpet is a permanent fixture. She's just a cocktail-guzzling leech," cried Esme. "She's probably screwing all the husbands!"

"And sons, by now, I should imagine," Alice added, "but that's not all. '*An accomplished equestrienne and exhibited painter, Jemima devotes—*'"

"'Accomplished equestrienne'? Oh, bring me that bucket!"

"Esme, you're going to have to stop interrupting me because there is another whole paragraph of puke-making bilge still to go."

Esme bit her lip.

"'*Jemima devotes,*'" Alice continued, "'*what little spare time she has to promoting a revolutionary Harley Street clinic specializing in removing disfiguring scars from children injured in war-torn hot spots throughout the world. She is heralded among the fashionistas as the Woman Most Wanted to Wear Their Clothes, which is why all eyes are on her new column, which starts this weekend in our Style section.*'"

Esme was flabbergasted. "I just don't know where to start," she said. "That woman! Removing disfiguring scars from children in war-torn hot spots? Only if she gave them the scars in the first place, the horrible witch. Is it definitely her?"

"It's Jemima all right. There are photos to prove it. She's dressed up like there's no tomorrow, Es, Botoxed for Africa and so thin you can almost see right through her. It's disgusting."

"In other words," Esme said between gritted teeth, "she looks a million dollars."

"Well, it could be the airbrushing." Alice sounded unconvinced.

"Oh, I can't bear it. It's so unfair," Esme erupted. "Just when my life turns to complete and utter horseshit, up pops Jemima sodding Jones being extra sodding fabulous for the ninety-ninth sodding time in a row. It's intolerable!"

Once upon a time, Jemima Jones had worked for her. Years before, in her career days, Esme had plucked her from nearly a hundred interviewees, all in various degrees of desperation, to be her assistant on *TV Now!* magazine. Jemima had been totally inexperienced and lacked even the slightest academic achievement (if you didn't count winning the Leggatt Cup for kindness to guinea pigs in her final year at school) but had been bright and funny and clearly willing to learn. Esme, her editor, had fostered and mentored the young and seemingly naïve newcomer until she happened upon her one night at a champagne bar in Soho smiling coquettishly and whispering into the ear of the witless group publisher.

Jemima had giggled girlishly at work the next day that he was an old family friend and Esme had nothing to worry about, but a week later Esme had been notified, by memo, that Jemima was being promoted to group publishing assistant, effectively becoming her boss.

Alice Watson had been the *TV Now!* receptionist at the time. It was where she and Esme had met.

"Can you believe the snake-hipped little slattern?" Esme had hissed over a sneaky chocolate bar in the photocopying room as she waved the memo in her friend's face. "What a bitch!"

"Now, now," Alice had counseled. "Be nice, Esme. She's just getting on like the rest of us. Good luck to her, I say."

She was not to say it for much longer. Alice had been thrilled with the *TV Now!* job, her first since leaving school after falling pregnant to an Afro-Caribbean DJ who had neglected to mention the perfectly nice wife and two children he kept just at the end of her street.

She'd been sidelined by her middle-class parents and had struggled alone to bring up her son, Ridgeley, but her fortunes had changed, in more ways than one, when she found work. Suddenly, she not only had money to spend but had broken a fairly substantial sex drought with a bicycle courier called Fred. He was six feet tall and made of muscle, didn't mind that she had a son, that he was called Ridgeley, that she couldn't afford babysitters. In other words, he was perfect. Or so she thought until one morning not long after Jemima's promotion when she opened the stationery store in search of staples and instead found Fred's bare buttocks jiggling furiously as he shafted the new group publishing assistant, legs akimbo, atop a stack of pink photocopying paper.

"That snake-hipped little slattern," she blubbed to Esme, spraying half-chewed KitKat over the copier. "I hope she gets hit by a bus and dies."

An enemy was born, but her star had continued to rise and its brilliance had outshone the both of them. She had gone on to launch a string of women's magazines, some with moderate success, others less so. Whatever she did was done with a great hiss and a roar and a lot of media coverage, but the industry was full of lesser mortals who bitterly bore the imprint of Jemima's stiletto heels on their backs and shoulders, and Alice and Esme were two such pincushions. Within six months of Jemima's promotion, *TV Now!* had folded, leaving the two of them gob-smacked and jobless. For Esme it was a blow, but her CV still stacked up well enough. For Alice, however, the market proved flooded already with single mothers short on skills and the ability to do overtime.

She'd been in the same dreary job—answering phones for an overbearing tax consultant only ever referred to as Nose Hair—ever since. Her son was now a recalcitrant teenager, her Visa card permanently blown out, her diets always a disaster and her search for the perfect man constantly turning up ones someone else had thrown away earlier, and for good reason.

They had been through a lot together, Esme and Alice, and while ninety miles of choked highway and tangled country lanes now separated them, they talked nearly every day for at least half an hour and continued to be each other's lifeline.

"I should be over Jemima by now," Esme said, worried.

"You are over her," Alice replied. "She's still on the same old merry-go-round that you stepped off, after all. And she can have it and stick it up her arse, if there's any room, given that she already must have to carry most of her internal organs in her handbag because there certainly isn't any space inside her body."

Esme laughed, or tried to, but news of her old rival had thrown her, and Alice could tell.

"Look, Esme, I know you are going through a rough patch and it's hardly surprising. But don't go getting cold feet about where you are and what you are doing just because it's hard. Everywhere is hard. Everything is hard. You know that."

"Dashing out a society column once a week doesn't sound hard," Esme pointed out ruefully.

"Yes, but imagine removing disfiguring scars from children injured in war-torn hot spots throughout the world? You think that's easy?"

"The way Jemima does it, by mobile phone while she suns herself on a yacht in the Mediterranean, I'm sure it is."

"Oh, Esme," sighed Alice. "Do you really think you want Jemima's life? Just getting your hair that straight would kill you. Life in the city is hell and full of bitches just like her. You should be happy with what you've got—a madhouse in the middle of nowhere teeming with people and complemented, I think you'll find, by a dysfunctional goat, a rum bunch of chickens and some very angry bees."

Esme grimaced. She hadn't the heart to tell Alice that the chickens were no longer rum. The chickens were no longer, period. One had been eaten by a neighboring something or other (never fully determined, initially suspected to be Jam-jar although he turned out not to have his own teeth) and the other four had seemed to die of natural causes shortly afterward—and she wasn't ruling out fatal bee stings. Her animal husbandry was already the topic of much mirth as far as Alice was concerned. Things that she didn't want to live proved to have extraordinary survival skills (rabbits, tadpoles), and things that she desperately needed (chickens, goats) either died or refused to produce what she'd initially got them for.

"You'll come right, Esme," Alice was saying. "Just give it time. And I don't know why I am trying to make you feel better about living in the country because I would far prefer if you were back here in London with me. We could go out and get totally bladdered on ridiculously overupholstered cocktails and sing Wham! songs all the way home in the cab." She sighed, perhaps at the memory of doing just that, many times over. "Anyway, why did the dog pee on the quince? You never got around to telling me."

Esme moved toward the refrigerator, tucked the phone under her chin and poured herself another glass of Chardonnay. She took a deep gulp and felt the wine's buttery warmth slide all the way down to the pit of her stomach and nestle there, happy. Perhaps she should be drinking more, she thought.

"I don't know," she answered out loud, thinking about Brown's bad behavior. "It's been tricky lately, what with one thing and the other. Rory's, well, just Rory. You know. Poor darling boy. It's not been easy for him and Henry's as crotchety as hell. Oh, hello, darling!"

She smiled as Pog's footsteps finally turned into Pog himself. "Hello, beautiful," he mouthed as he collapsed into a kitchen chair on the other side of the table.

"So quince paste then," Alice was saying into the phone. "That's great, Es. And so soon after that innnn-teresting zucchini relish." She paused, uncertain how to proceed. "How's the baking, then, girl? *Ou est le pain?*"

Pog had not been the only one confused and unsettled by Esme's failure to turn out her famous sourdough *boules*. There had never been anything magical about sourdough, as far as Alice was concerned. But when Esme stopped baking, something definitely disappeared and it worried her.

"What do you care?" Esme asked with a rehearsed lightness. "And if you must know, Mrs. Gladstone from down the lane liked my zucchini relish so much she wants me to donate my entire stock to the village fair next month."

"They're probably going to use jars of it for targets on the coconut shy," Alice teased, relieved at having got this far without upsetting the apple-cart. "Or have it in the tunnel of horror as the gooey muck you plunge your hands into." She decided to venture further. "You know you could always, oh I don't know, bake bread for the fair, Es."

Esme balked; she had been unequivocally unap-proachable on the subject of her breadlessness, but Granny Mac's advice had been ringing loudly in her ears all day. She thought of the jar of starter, winking at her. She closed her eyes and willed herself to speak. "Well, it's just for me, Alice," she said. "For us. I mean, it's not for everyone. I couldn't mass produce it. It's personal."

There was a small silence.

"It *is* just for you?" Alice risked.

"As a matter of fact, yes. Or it's about to be. Again." Esme glanced over at Pog.

"Oh, Esme," Alice spluttered. "I'm so pleased. That's great news."

"Excuuuuse me," Esme protested. "Is this not the woman who usually says 'It's only bread! Get over it! It's the staff of bleeding life. People put butter and jam on it and eat it'?"

"I'll never say that again," Alice vowed, "I promise. My mocking days are over. I won't even mention, for as long as I live"—she adopted a phony French accent—"your deescovery of, 'ow shall I say, the *joy of bread*, with Louis, international man of mystery, deflowerer of young Engleesh girls and possessor of the world's most enormous—"

Esme laughed loudly into the phone in a drowning-out sort of a fashion. "You are a horrible, dried up old harridan and I hate you," she said. "And you really shouldn't say things like that about my lovely husband, Pog, when you know he holds you in such high regard."

Pog raised his eyebrows as she had known he would. "Just messing," Esme mouthed back at him, pointing at the phone. "Anyway," she continued to Alice, "enough about me, tell me what's happening with that ungrateful layabout Ridgeley. How's he getting on?"

Alice sighed and made an exasperated noise. "Well, his school life is officially over," she said. "The principal finally invited him to leave and never come back and nothing I can say will change his mind, and anyway, I don't know if I could get the little shit to go back there even if he was allowed to. He says he's been out job hunting but there's no evidence of any, you know, *job* as a result."

Esme laughed. "Give the boy a break, Alice. You remember what it's like to be sixteen, don't you?

40

You'd already shagged half of Chiswick by the time you were his age."

"Yes, exactly," said Alice. "And look where it got me. Remind me to repeat this conversation when Rory is a teenager, will you?"

Pog sat at the kitchen table and watched his wife prattle, aching with relief to see her acting more like her old self. And if his ears had not deceived him, she had been joking about bread. Could this mean . . . ? He dared not believe that something as simple as a few words from Alice could bump her out of this recent frightening new level of unhappiness. But he was sure he could once more see a flicker of the light that had so recently gone out in her and it did his poor heart good. But he would not make a fuss, he resolved. He would say nothing and simply hope that one day soon the house would smell the way it was supposed to, of crust and comfort.

Once Esme said her good-byes, always a protracted affair, and put down the phone, Pog abandoned his chair and came up behind her, kissing the back of her neck as he sighed into her skin.

"You smell good enough to eat," he said, nuzzling her.

"It's not me, silly," she laughed, pulling gently away from his embrace and reaching into the oven for a fragrantly bubbling coq au vin. "It's your lordship's favorite supper."

"Jolly good," Pog enthused, rubbing his hands

together and sitting at the table again. "So, how was your day?"

"Well, if you have a chance later tonight," his wife replied as she spooned wine-rich gravy onto his plate, "you might like to talk to your father about how your charming dog demonstrated his pent-up emotions on his shoes this morning."

"Oh," he said, sliding down in his chair. "It's been one of those days."

Esme put a steaming plate of food down in front of him and ran her fingers through his messy brown hair. It was lusciously thick and grew in a hundred crazy directions, which she loved, especially when it was collar length as it was now. At six feet three he towered above her, so when he sat she loved to fiddle with him. He had the loveliest face of any man she had ever known. Not rugged or classically handsome, necessarily. Just lovely. He had big brown eyes and smooth long cheeks and the sort of teddy bear good looks and gentle soul that made all women want to be married to him.

"Hugo Stack," she said using his given name, not the nickname no one could remember how he came by, "every day is one of *those* days. But if peed-on quince is as bad as it gets, then I suppose I should think myself lucky."

"Peed-on quince?" Pog asked her, bewildered. "Is that French?"

Esme laughed and her husband let the sound he loved chase the tension and trauma of a long day's work and worry out of his bones. She poured him some wine and they clinked glasses, each thinking their separate thoughts but both smiling at the shared triumph of making it through another day.

I can do it, Pog thought, as he watched her lick a fat drop of rich, red juice from the corner of her mouth. I can do it, as long as I have her. So what if he had to spend the rest of his life designing Tuscan loggias for persnickety pensioners instead of award-winning skyscrapers for international conglomerates. It was just work. And in fact, he liked it more than he thought he would. Business was good. The phone had rung off the hook ever since the day Mrs. Murphy had hung the Architect sign up outside the office in Seabury's main street.

Whoever would have guessed that this particular pocket of Suffolk was in such dire need of so many renovations? It seemed every second house needed a solarium or a spa room or a new kitchen or a second story. And his clients were actually a breath of fresh air compared to the suits he had dealt with in London. Here, nobody shouted, few changed their minds, they all paid their bills and without exception made a good cup of tea. It was different but it was good. He could do it. As long as he had her. As long as that light kept flickering.

When the alarm went off at six the next morning, Esme's eyes sprang open. Her heart was beating too quickly and her wrung out, squashed and dangerous nugget was expanding inside her, crushing the breath from her lungs. Bread, she forced herself to think, bread. She lay there and waited for the word to soothe her and it did. Bread. She closed her eyes again and thought about that jar of starter, panting in her pantry. How could she have denied herself its comfort these past weeks? What had she been thinking? The nugget started to shrink again. Her fingers rippled as if already working the dough. She took a deep breath and slipped out of bed, shivering.

Pog rolled over into the warm place she had left and smiled to himself. In the bathroom Esme slipped on the purple fluffy slippers that everyone but she hated and swapped her white linen nightie for a tank top and faded pink cotton cardigan and her old faithful jeans with the ripped knee and the soft denim that curved in all her favorite places.

She stuck her hair up in a haphazard arrangement on her head—the chic chignon would have to wait yet another day—and scuffed quietly up to the kitchen, eschewing the light switches and instead rummaging for the matches and lighting her strategically placed collection of candles in a dozen different points around the room.

She stood for a moment in the quiet predawn just to take in the mood her kitchen took on with its sexy, subtle lighting. How dark it had been without her candlelit mornings. Out the window the Seabury lights twinkled below her, the sea beyond shimmering virtuously in what was left of the moonlight. She pulled open the pantry door and dragged out her bin of bread flour, stone-ground especially for her at the watermill in nearby Pakenham, then reached for her scales and favorite jug, all sitting, ready and waiting, as though she had never abandoned them. She measured the flour, breathing in that wheaty smell of almost nothing, almost everything, then poured it into a big caramel-colored ceramic bowl and added good old Suffolk tap water.

Then she picked up her jar of starter and slowly lifted its lid, unleashing, bit by bit, its sharp, tangy perfume. Granny Mac was right. Now was not the time to let go of what was dear to her. Now was the time to cling to it. She drank in the smell— oh, how she had missed it!

She weighed out what she needed of the foamy elixir, added it to her bowl of flour and water and plunged her hands into the mixture. It was cold and her hands reddened as they worked their way through the separate ingredients, swirling them around the bowl, rubbing them between her fingers, getting them slowly started on their journey to being something much better.

For five silent minutes she mixed the flour and water and starter in her hands. The effort chased away the early-morning chill and she felt her body start to warm. Other bakers used a mixer or electric dough hook but not Esme. She wanted her hands on that concoction, she wanted to feel every particle transform.

Finally, when the mixture had stopped being separate ingredients and become a solid, silky mass, moving around the inside of the bowl in one single smooth ball, she lifted it out onto her wooden counter and let it sit while she fed the jar of starter. She added equal parts flour and water to replace what she had taken from it and to nourish it for the next day. Clearly Pog had been doing this in her absence, for the starter was alive and kicking despite her having abandoned it. How had he known she would come back to it when she herself had not been sure? This past month of mornings she had woken up and felt nothing but desolation . . . the pull of sourdough bleak in its absence, her reason for getting up dearly departed.

And then Granny Mac from out of her Embassy Regal ether had barked her instructions and here she was back where she belonged, elbow deep in sourdough and thanking God that she had so often bored Pog with sermons on her starter. Thanks to them, he knew what a voracious appetite it had. Forget to feed it and it would shrink and discolor, she had often told him, meting out its punishment by baking nothing more than a flat, dull biscuit. But cherish and nurture it and it would grow and flourish, rewarding all and sundry with the resulting riches: fat, happy loaves, well risen and delectable.

46

She put the jar back in the pantry, almost sorry to lose sight of it, then threw a handful of sea salt flakes into her mortar and ground it with a heavy pestle, releasing the faraway scent of seashore violets from the marshes of Brittany as she did so. She could always smell them, even if no one else could. And this morning they smelled more heavenly than ever.

It was not a quick process, making her own sourdough. Once she had mixed the dough to her satisfaction, she would leave it sitting for two hours to rise, then she would knock it back, shape it into a loaf and coddle it into the linen-lined willow basket where it would gently rise for another three hours before she baked it to eat for lunch.

In the meantime there was work to be done. This second working of the dough was what made the difference between the ordinary and the sublime. It was Esme's favorite bit. She lost herself to the familiar rhythm of her breadmaking.

She added the salt to the plump ball sitting roundly in front of her and started rolling it slowly with one hand on the well-worn bench. Around and around she pushed it, gently but firmly, the palm of her hand pressing down and sweeping it around in the same wide circle each time. She felt the crunch of the salt tickling her palm and worked her hand hard down on the mixture, sweeping and circling, sweeping and circling, until it started to feel less moist, less sticky, less crunchy and more satiny and elastic to her touch. Inexperienced bakers would probably have added flour by now, finding the dough too clingy and wet to work with, but Esme knew that moisture was the way to make her bread dance on the tongue. Her fingers tingled at being back in their natural habitat. She swept and circled, swept and circled, feeling the texture change under her fingers. Around and around on the counter, she worked the dough, around and around.

How it comforted her. How it calmed the turmoil within. How it rolled back the years, sliding back over the hills and dales of time, flattening the pain and clearing the way to her sweet, seductive past.

CHAPTER 3

She had been nineteen and ripe for the plucking when she and her best friend Charlie Edmonds had skipped the inevitable disappointment of a London summer for the tiny village of Venolat perched above a horseshoe loop in the Dordogne River in southwest France.

Actually, Charlie would have preferred to holiday in more popular Provence or, even better, on the glitzy Riviera where, he told Esme, they could both probably find aging overtanned husbands with more money than sense and live the life of Riley for the next who-knew-how-long.

The only down side, Esme often thought, of having a gay best friend was that they were often in competition for the same boyfriends and she always, but always, came off second best. Charlie seemed completely irresistible while Esme considered herself more of an acquired taste.

Anyway, she and her light smattering of corn-flake-colored freckles were not on the lookout for a leathery octogenarian and so were pleased to be headed for the slightly less glitzy side of France. Granny Mac had taken her to the Dordogne three years before on the proceeds of a major Bingo win despite having said her whole life that she could never visit a country where the women carried dogs in their handbags.

Granny Mac was very old-fashioned when it came to handbags. She had seven of them, all in different shades of 100 percent vinyl but the exact same style, and she never left the house without one slung over her forearm just like the Queen.

Inside her bag was always the same collection of essentials: her change purse, two handker-chiefs, her glasses case, a lipstick—always worn away to the same alarming point no matter what its age—a packet of barley sugars, her bus pass and a signed copy of a photo of David Hasselhoff, the American actor from *Baywatch*, whom she had bumped into at Marks & Spencer on Oxford Street in 1987.

What had inspired Granny Mac to book plane tickets to Bordeaux Esme had never asked, but delighted with the outcome they both had been. They'd taken a mind-numbingly expensive taxi ride to the charming falling down Château de Roques near the beautiful wine-growing region of St. Emilion and promptly fell head over heels in love with the area: Granny Mac because it rained the whole time, which made her feel at home, and Esme because its lush green elegance and slow-moving river appealed to her fairy-tale sensibilities. It looked, she had believed, like rural France ought to look. Ancient towering bridges over looking-glass waterways; rolling green plains and happily oversized hay bales; silent sand-colored villages with washed-out sea-colored shutters. She had loved every inch of it.

And Granny Mac, a meat and three-veg stalwart from centuries back, had astounded them both by developing a robust appetite for snails and foie gras. They had promised faithfully that they would go back every year but, according to Granny Mac, Nancy Bowden from Swiss Cottage had invented a swindling system that had kept anyone other than the evil wench herself from enjoying any success on the Bingo cards. There'd be no more trips abroad, Granny Mac had said, until Nancy's varicose veins and nonfilter cigarettes combined to get the better of her.

"The overbronzed old-timers will just have to wait," Charlie said gloomily as he and Esme sped through the narrow country lanes of the southwest three years later. "Trust the Old Boy to have a house in the bit of France no red-blooded young man would be seen dead in."

"You bloody well will be seen dead here if you don't stick to the right-hand side of the road," Esme said, her knuckles clenched and white from clinging to the dashboard. "Your driving is giving me piles! And shut up, anyway. You're lucky to have a father with spare houses."

Charlie's father was "something in finance" and wore a smart suit, spoke in a posh accent and seemed to be in possession of a never-ending supply of things that had only just recently "fallen off the back of a truck."

In the time Esme had known Charlie, these included a white Volkswagen Golf, four state-of-the-art dishwashers, two racehorses and a sixty-foot yacht called *Demelza*.

She had driven at least 2,000 miles in the Golf, had watched one of the dishwashers be installed in her grandmother's apartment, won three pounds forty-seven on the chestnut and burned her nose sailing one rare fine day aboard *Demelza*.

She never quizzed Charlie too vigorously on the subject of what in finance his father exactly was because she knew for a fact that Charlie didn't really know. As he was a decent bloke with his own unique but unbending set of morals, if he found out what it was his father exactly was and it wasn't good, his abuse of the benefits thereof would be severely stymied.

Their trip to France fell off the back of a truck like everything else after the subject of their summer vacation came up one night over drinks with Charlie's father and his new girlfriend, a six-foot-two-inch lingerie model aged somewhere around twenty and going by the name of K'Lee.

Charlie liked to have Esme around when his father's girlfriend *du jour* was exhibited because he swore that in the past when he had met them without a witness on hand nobody afterward believed his true accounts.

K'Lee was a good example of the girlfriend a

stout, balding, wealthy fifty-something would invent for himself had she not saved him the bother by being a cocktail waitress at his club. The night she was introduced to Charlie and Esme, she arrived wearing three-inch heels that had her towering and teetering over the lot of them and a dress (more of a dishcloth, really, as Charlie pointed out later) made of what looked like a bunch of fishnet tights clinging tenaciously to each other over the rise and fall of her remarkable curves. Her shoes and the length of her legs seemed to put her crotch at eye level to everyone in the room, but then she did not appear to be wearing underwear so most eyes were on that area anyway.

Esme, who had been wearing her traditional black with black and lots of it, was mesmerized. Charlie was, too. Mr. Edmonds himself acted as though she was a perfectly normal specimen.

"Get K'Lee a Campari with Diet Coke and a scoop of vanilla ice cream, will you, Charles," he instructed at one stage. Esme had hooted with laughter, assuming this was a joke, but when no one else joined in she scurried into the kitchen and there was Charlie, hunting out the ingredients.

"This is nothing," he had said, shaking his head as he plopped the ball of white ice cream into a glass. "He had one that only drank retsina with freshly squeezed carrot juice. You should have seen her, Es. She was bright orange. And very hairy."

Charlie loved dissecting these meetings afterward but never showed anything at the time other than gallons of his customary politeness and charm, poured on liberally in equal amounts.

"Do you think that is the problem?" Esme had quizzed him after one particularly memorable night out with Mr. Edmonds and a very tired and emotional Croatian opera singer. "Maybe he's trying to shock you or something."

"Good Lord, no," Charlie said with great confidence. "He doesn't give a toss what I think. He just thinks they're all perfectly normal."

"But compared to your mother they are anything but," Esme argued. She knew from photos that Charlie's mother was exactly the sort of woman you would expect to be married to a stout, balding, successful fifty-something whereas the rotating door introducing her replacements produced a cast of most unlikely possibilities.

"Oh, Mummy was normal on the outside," Charlie had said. "But inside she was completely wacko."

"Please don't call her Mummy," Esme had said. "You know that makes me think you are going to grow into one of those men who gets dressed up like a giant baby and has some dominatrix dressed like a nanny feed you whisky out of a bottle."

"I say!" Charlie had said. "They do that? Now *that* sounds like fun!"

This particular night Esme had to agree that Mr. Edmonds was certainly not acting as though K'Lee was anything but run of the mill.

"Esme and I are just trying to decide what to do with our summer hols," Charlie said, handing the girl her drink. "What are you up to, then?"

"I've got a modeling contract in Germany, actually," K'Lee answered, "and I'm hoping to get into a summer school in Koln. I have a degree in German but I've spent bugger all time there so . . ." She poked at the blob of melting ice cream in her glass with one long bloodred nail and smiled at them.

Esme was busy quietly choking on her dry white wine but Charlie as usual was seamlessly smooth.

"Well, we need to brush up on our French," he said with a guilty grimace, "so Esme and I are thinking of France, ourselves."

"Is that right?" said Mr. Edmonds. He had spent most of the evening on the phone and nobody had noticed that he had joined them again except perhaps K'Lee, whose left buttock Esme noticed his hand now grasped. "We've just come into a property in France, as it happens," he said. "Some little town I've never heard of on the Dordogne."

Esme thought briefly about asking for a definition of "just come into" but decided against it.

"You two could always go and check it out for me," Mr. Edmonds said. "Tidy it up, get it ready for resale, something like that."

And so fibbing to save face in front of a far-brainier-than-she-looked model produced for Charlie and Esme the perfect plan for an ideal summer, the only problem being that neither of them really spoke French.

Esme had a good excuse—she had only learned it for a year before giving it up in favor of sewing classes. Charlie, however, could not say the same. He had studied the language for five years and claimed to have even passed exams in it yet seemed restricted in his vocabulary outside the subjects of food and drink. This, though, they agreed, would probably not be a problem in any event.

They arrived in the village one sweltering July afternoon after the tortuous drive from the airport in a car that had all the buttons for air-conditioning but not the temperament-protecting feature itself.

Charlie, who was a horrible driver at the best of times, was even worse thanks to a terrible hangover courtesy of a very late and eventful night out in the West End. He was tired and cranky and Esme was frazzled, too, being somewhat racked with guilt and anguish at leaving Granny Mac alone for so long. The two had never been separated for more than a week and she knew it was silly but she felt wretched nonetheless.

"What say she gets savaged by wild geese or attacked by an ax murderer?" she wailed to Charlie, who was short on sympathy for anybody other than himself.

"For God's sake, Es. She's probably desperate for you to get out of her hair so she can go on a shagfest at the local Sainsbury's. Stop worrying and open the back windows, will you, I am boiling."

This was not exactly what Esme wanted to hear and anyway, as she pointed out, there was nothing in Granny Mac's historical behavior that would lead one to think she would hide her shagfests from her granddaughter.

"I've lived through three successful courtships, a very happy marriage and half a dozen lesser suitors," she pointed out. "I know what very old people having sex sounds like and, as you well know, on one occasion, what it looks like."

"Oooh," cooed Charlie, cheering up instantly. "Tell me about Sailor Bill, go on!" But Esme refused to be drawn into repeating the story of catching her granny at it with a "visitor from abroad" whom she had met, apparently, in the St. John's Wood library at the Scottish Cuisine section, which was small but attracted a dedicated, as it turned out, following.

By the time they found the signs to Venolat they had stopped saying much and Esme was looking dreamily out the window, entranced by the luscious greens and golds and burnt oranges of the countryside as they whisked through it.

It all looked vaguely unreal, as though a clever painter had hijacked her dreams and was racing ahead of her, wildly repainting the landscape from whatever it truly looked like to the exact tints and textures of her imagination.

She sighed. If only everything she dreamed of could come to life in such a way. Every*one*.

"Hurrah!" trilled Charlie. "We're nearly there."

A sign to Venolat pointed them upward, away from the rolling green pastures and onto a narrow leafy lane that clung to the side of a substantial hill as it wound its way sneakily heavenward.

"One more corner and I swear I am going to be sick," he groaned five minutes later, looking pale, but Esme shushed him quiet as the car rounded a corner shaded by a canopy of ancient trees and emerged into one of the most beautiful places she had ever seen.

The road they had driven up had been partly carved into rock that had hung over them, shielding the village from their eyes as they approached. Now, though, the town sat prettily and proudly in front of them, as if pleased with the secret of itself, and allowed them—but only just—entry via a road that was barely wider than their steaming Renault.

"Charlie," breathed Esme, "it's gorgeous!"

To their left stood a church, pale yellow and majestic in the afternoon sun, while on the other side of a sunny square a sad bronze soldier stood in front of a stone memorial to men the village had lost. Farther up, on either side of the narrow road, two-storied houses leaned over them, their milky sea-green shutters framing window boxes heaving with flowers.

Esme wound down her window and drank in the smell—lavender, definitely, and jasmine, she was sure, plus the smell of plain hot summer and maybe coffee, too.

"Where did he say it was?" Charlie asked, his bad mood dissolving.

"He said turn left at the fountain and ask at the *auberge,* whatever that is," replied Esme, repeating what Mr. Edmonds had told her.

"I think it's like an aubergine," said Charlie, "but bigger."

At that point the road widened and they found themselves in a tiny square with a fountain bathed in sunlight and serenely trickling water. To their right the lane took them through an arch and obviously out of the village again; straight ahead, the road on the other side of the fountain—even narrower than it had been before—wound farther up the hill, and to the left was another lane with, perched on its corner, quite the prettiest bakery Esme had ever seen.

Its corner door faced out toward the fountain and was sheltered from the sun by a yellow and white striped awning above which read the simple word *Boulangerie.* The window boxes on either side of the building were painted the same shade of daffodil yellow and bulged with red geraniums and miniature lavender bushes.

The shop was closed, yet Esme could swear she smelled the sweet yeasty aroma of fresh bread being baked still lingering in the air.

"Coming up, one *auberge,*" Charlie said, lurching to a halt just past the bakery at a small hotel covered in vines and discreetly signposted.

"An *auberge* is a hotel?" Esme asked, getting out

of the car and looking at it. If Mr. Edmonds's flat turned out to be a pigsty, it certainly looked like somewhere nice to stay as an alternative.

"One that sells aubergines, I think you will find," Charlie said with authority, striding inside.

The two of them emerged five minutes later with the key to the apartment, which was apparently just around the corner, and a table for that night booked at the *auberge,* which, it turned out, was a restaurant that served a fixed menu, perfect for a linguistically challenged pair such as themselves.

They wedged the car in a three-point maneuver into a tiny parking space, pointed out to them by the *auberge* proprietor, and unloaded their excessive baggage from the trunk.

"Follow me," Charlie said, leading Esme back up the lane and turning through a stone archway, which emerged into the private courtyard of a three-story building with dark varnished shutters.

Stopping at double-shuttered doors, Charlie dumped his bags and unlocked them, then unlocked the French doors behind and entered a cool, white hallway. To the left were old, worn stone stairs leading upward and straight ahead was a sort of living room with a cavernous double bedroom going off to one side. It was simply but sweetly furnished and deliciously cool.

"My room," said Charlie. "It will be getting most of the traffic so it might as well be on the ground level."

Esme slapped him on the arm. "How do you

know?" she said. "I might turn out to be the biggest strumpet Venolat has ever seen, bringing home a swag of Frenchmen every night myself."

"Es," said Charlie patiently, "if you brought home one it would be a bloody miracle."

Charlie never tired of the subject of Esme's chasteness. He had done more than his bit, he felt, over the five years they had known each other, to help her in her efforts at being deflowered, but at nineteen, she remained deeply embarrassed by her virginal status yet too much of a romantic, in the absence of a suitable knight in shining armor, to do anything about it.

"I'm waiting for the right one," Esme reminded him grumpily. "I'm special, remember?"

"Special, all right," Charlie said, heading up the stairs. "Hark, is that a *National Geographic* photographer I see ahead? They'll be writing a story about you next, Esme. You're an endangered species."

They arrived on the first floor, which housed a long dark oak table and eight chairs and overlooked at one end the little lane through which they had just driven. At the other end was a kitchen so rich in appliances they doubted they would use even a fifth of them, and to one side shuttered doors led to a terrace. From there Esme looked back down to the glorious green valley below and the lazy loop of the river that meandered through it.

"We're in heaven," she said happily. "God bless the Old Boy, Charlie! It doesn't need a thing done to it. Look—it's glorious! We can just swan around and eat cheese and drink wine for the whole lovely summer."

Charlie shrugged and picked up her bags, then continued up more stone stairs to the top floor, which led them to an attic bedroom complete with an enormous armoire, en suite bathroom and a four-poster bed draped in mosquito netting.

"Well, if you can't get lucky with a room like this," he said, "there's no hope for you."

He dropped her bags on the floor and they both flopped on the enormous bed, staring in silence at the ancient wooden fan rattling gently above them.

"Charlie," Esme said, turning to him. "I've got a feeling that this is going to be the best holiday ever."

"I thought I had that feeling, too," said Charlie, "but it turned out to be gas. Bloody champagne cocktails, I tell you."

"You and your emissions! Honestly. Is that all you ever think about? I'm talking about, you know, the big deal. I'm just so ready for it."

"Gagging for it is the expression, I believe," said Charlie. "Do you think he's going to be big and black and hung like a farmyard animal?"

"No!" Esme answered. "Although maybe. That would be pretty good, wouldn't it? But I don't know. I won't know until I see him."

Charlie sighed and closed his eyes as the throbbing in his head fell into perfect time with the fan above. "Esme, you are such a sap," he said. "You're never going to find him if you're going to wait until he rides up on his white charger and asks you to oil his armpits. You should just scrape the bottom of the barrel, like the rest of us."

"No, no, no," protested Esme. "I want him to be sulky and moody and dark like James Dean in *Rebel Without a Cause* or Marlon Brando in *On the Waterfront.*"

"Marion Brando *now*, I can imagine," Charlie said rudely. Esme whacked him.

"Or a young Paul Newman," she sighed. "Wouldn't that be nice?"

"Too right," he agreed. "If a young Paul Newman turns up, I may just have to fight you for him."

"Not fair," said Esme firmly. "You can get anyone you want. You know perfectly well that a young Paul Newman, hetty or not, wouldn't choose me if you were an option."

"That's not true, Es. It's not people choosing you that is the problem. It is you choosing them. You're too fussy by far. You're waiting for the fire-works and whistles and bangs and it's not like that, really it isn't."

Charlie did not have a romantic bone in his body. To him, love and sex were the same thing and it was all about location. If you could get it wherever you were, you did; otherwise, who cared?

"It's not like that for *you*," Esme corrected him, "but I am different. I don't want to do it jammed up against the cigarette machine with a head full of E in some poxy nightclub that smells of wees."

Charlie, his eyes still closed, smiled at the thought of such a thing.

"But who says that some silly Frog is going to be more special than that anyone else, Es? That chap from the bank I fixed you up with, for example, Gordon?"

Gordon had been the latest in a succession of highly improbable friends with whom Charlie had tried, unsuccessfully, to pair Esme off.

"That horrible toff?" Esme squealed. "He wore a cravat, Charlie! And he was scared of touching doorknobs. He probably would have run away screaming if I had tried to hold his hand, let alone sleep with him."

"I always thought there was something funny about him," Charlie agreed. "I mean the cravat on its own was a worry but together with the door-knob thing . . ."

Esme laughed. "It's not funny, Charlie," she said, although it was. "I mean it's one thing to be young and as pure as the driven snow but I am nineteen now. It's going to start getting sad soon."

Charlie opened his eyes and turned to her on the bed. "Well, if it gets really bad," he said, in all seriousness, "I'll give you one to save you from embarrassment, but I've only done it once with a woman and I'm not sure I know the ropes."

"You did it once with a woman?" Esme asked,

amazed that this had not come out sooner. "I thought you've been gay since you were two."

"I have been," Charlie assured her, "but this bloke I went to school with had a sister, Phoebe, who I swear was the most delightful fourteen-year-old you ever saw in your whole life." He smiled dreamily at the memory.

"Fourteen?" squealed Esme. "With a girl? You randy little toad."

"*She* was fourteen," Charlie said. "I was only thirteen. We got off together one weekend when I was staying at their house and I must say I liked all the bosomy bits—just not much else. Strange, really. Anyway, I mean it, Es. If it's just something you want to get over and done with so you can get on with the job of being a normal girl, then I will do it for you, although I will probably have to drink a lot and possibly have a picture of the young Paul Newman in front of me as well."

Esme leaned over and kissed him in a sisterly way on the cheek. "You really are a true gentleman," she said, "in a creepy and perverted way, but still, I thank you for your kind offer and the Paul Newman thing would probably help me, too. However"—she sat up and started to untangle one side of her mad head of hair—"I am going to wait for the real thing."

Charlie sighed. "If that's the case," he said, "we'd better start drinking now."

Many, many hours later, she was slipping home through the empty streets of early-morning

Venolat, breathing in the warm, still air and trying her darnedest to get Bob Marley's "No Woman No Cry" out of her head.

She and Charlie had started the night quietly with a mouthwateringly delicious three-course meal and a bottle of *vin de pays* at the *auberge*, before discovering a tiny bar hidden in the back-streets while exploring their neighborhood on the way home. There they had happened upon a rowdy bunch of Canadians who had then hooked up with an even rowdier bunch of Dutch tourists, and the night had ended at around four with Esme deciding that the very tall accountant from Toronto with thick spectacles and teeth that could eat an apple through the bars of a chair, as Granny Mac would say, was not her knight in shining armor.

By then she felt like she had drunk all the *vin* in the *pays* and was ready for her bed. Charlie, though, had other plans and so Esme bade them all farewell and headed home.

The outside air cleared her head and once she had shaken her curls free of the stench of everyone else's cigarettes, that dreary detritus of the big night out, she felt exhilarated to be out and about in the silence on her own.

On her own. The sound of her slim black plastic-soled designer–look-alike sandals slapping the cobbles beat a solitary tattoo that bounced off the walls on either side of the lane. On her own. It would have been nice, Esme allowed herself to think, to go home and make love until the sun came up with some adoring man who would feed her chocolate Häagen-Dazs in the morning in between stealing kisses of the mole she had and hated just below her left collarbone.

The toothy Toronto bean counter was not that man, of that she was pretty sure. Perhaps she was wrong about being ready. Venolat was quite small, she had come to realize, and it was possible she had already met every single person who lived there. She slipped into the square and walked quietly over to the fountain, perching on the side of it and trailing one hand in its cool clear water.

So, she had been wrong. She stared dreamily into the pool, watching the ripples ebb and flow with the trailing movement of her hand, and all of a sudden the most delicious smell wafted gently around her curls and invaded her senses as though it had been waiting for her to sit down and be still so it could take full advantage.

Esme lifted her face to the moon and breathed in deep and long. Of course, the *boulangerie*! Bread was being baked as she sat there and smelled it and for some reason it seemed like a gift, just for her. She turned slightly, hidden by the shadow of the fountain, and looked toward the *boulangerie*, where now she could detect a faint light coming from a doorway behind the counter.

She closed her eyes and breathed in again, savoring the sweet, sharp, tangy, yeasty fragrance drifting around her. How different from trolling the bread aisle at Waitrose trying to find Granny Mac's favorite white sliced toast bread with added preservatives! If it couldn't last ten days without going stale, Granny Mac wasn't interested.

The squeak of a rusty hinge and the slap of timber on timber tugged Esme out of her reverie and she opened her eyes and leaned forward slightly, peering around the fountain but still hidden by its shadow. At first she thought she was dreaming or that it was the wine, or the moonlight or that sweet, sour smell tricking her somehow so she blinked hard and counted to three but when she opened her eyes again what she saw took her breath clean away.

Leaning against the door, lit from behind by the light sneaking through from the back of the *boulangerie* and from the front by the glow of the moon, flour graying his black curly head, dark eyes concentrating on rolling a cigarette, one knee out as his foot rested against the wall, was the man of Esme's dreams.

How she knew this, she could not say. She had known she was ready but even in fairy tales the princess didn't just happen on her prince in the village square. She had to fight for him, or he for her. Yet Esme knew, just *knew,* by the trembling in her knees and the butterflies in her stomach and the delicious dry craving in her mouth, that this was the man she had been waiting for. It was a feeling like no other she had ever experienced.

The fat-faced cherubs were nowhere to be seen,

arrows were not flying around her head, there was no heavenly chorus trumpeting in the air around her. But harps of a different kind were definitely being strummed. Deep down inside, Esme's strings were being pulled.

Staying as still as a statue, scared almost to breathe in case the moment dissolved, she rolled her bottom lip between her teeth and was surprised at the saltiness that rushed her mouth. Her senses, it seemed, were on red alert; her taste buds stood at attention.

Sitting there in the shadows, staring, she felt a shivery tingle start in her groin and swarm up to her heart, which greeted it with big, pounding pulses, as though it had never properly beaten before. It ached. Truly ached. And then it sent the shivery tingle on its way through every ventricle, every vein, every tiny capillary, to Esme's cheeks, where they branded her with the mark of someone in the first stage of a very dangerous desire.

The man (or was he a boy?) languidly lifted the rolled cigarette to his lips, the tendons in the arm she could see rippling under his smooth brown skin. Then he slowly ran his tongue along the line of glue on the top edge of the cigarette paper and when he got to the end, he lifted his gaze and shifted it to Esme.

Already frozen, she tried to stop her blood from flowing. Surely he could not see her. And if he could, what was she supposed to do? Suddenly move and act like she wasn't spying on him or stay stock-still in case it was the fountain he was looking at and not her? Why, oh why did she not know what to do?

A floury black curl, she noticed, despite her panic, had sprung forward from his left temple and dipped over his forehead, tickling, it seemed, the corner of his eye. He shifted his gaze back to his cigarette, pulled a lighter out of his pocket, brought the roll-your-own to his lips and lit it, her heart missing a beat as she watched his whole beautiful face bathed momentarily in the light from the flame. He inhaled deeply, enjoying every moment, then slowly removed the cigarette from his lips and dropped it to his side. He shrugged, she was sure—it must have been to himself—and then lifted his head and slowly, slowly, slowly, smiled a smile so deep and dark and dazzling that for a moment Esme felt dizzy and thought she was going to swoon.

And up until that point she had been quite skeptical about the whole business of swooning, believing that it was an imaginary condition applying only to fainthearted Barbara Cartland characters with their corsets done up too tightly.

But sitting there on that still-warm smooth stone lip of that trickling fountain outside that beautiful bakery with the rich, dark eyes of this completely delicious stranger burning a hole right clear through her, Esme felt on the verge of collapse. She felt like she had been emptied of every feeling she had ever had to make room for something entirely wonderful and new. Something very powerful. Something *passionate*.

It was the moment she had been waiting for all her life.

And it was so ridiculously romantic and unbelievably Mills & Boon that for a moment she doubted herself and him and it, and the swooning feeling evaporated. In its place, though, remained that strange emptiness, a bit of nausea and a hard little gem of certainty that something special was indeed happening.

The man, boy, vision, whatever he was, looked away from her, took another drag from his cigarette and slipped his free hand into the pocket of his low-slung pale linen pants. He was bare-chested and she could make out the ridges of his ribs and the beginnings of his hip bones. The harp in her nether regions strummed itself again. Then, to her delight, he started to whistle, softly at first, the volume slowly building. Esme didn't recognize the tune, didn't need to. The smell of the bread, the look of this man, the tune on his lips . . . Esme's sensory perception reached overload and a buzzer went off in her head. This is not a dream, she thought. This is really happening.

Quietly, she stood up and stepped out of the shadows. The man of her dreams looked up again, saw her, and the whistle died away on his lips as his eyes feasted on her and slowly gave way to that dazzling, dizzying smile again. He lifted one hand in what could have been a casual hello, could have been beckoning her to him. And Esme, who suddenly recognized within herself the most excruciating longing—couldn't believe she hadn't noticed it before—took one small step in his direction, the moonlight dancing off her ringlets as she did so.

The moment was so magical she thought that she, who like her grandmother so rarely shed a tear, was going to dissolve into them.

But then, the moment was shattered.

"Bloody hell," Charlie's voice rang out from behind her. "The Dutch are a forward bunch, aren't they? Three in a bed I can handle, but five? I'm English for God's sake."

He hiccupped noisily, the sound of his boots unevenly scuffing the cobbles heralding his unwieldy condition. "What the fuck is pastis, anyway? I don't know. Bloody disgusting. Es? What are you doing?"

Esme had swung around just for an instant at the sound of Charlie's voice only to find that when she turned back to the *boulangerie,* her vision was gone, the sound of timber on timber ringing sadly in the still night air. The dream had melted in front of her, like a watercolor lying in the rain: one moment a landscape of staggering beauty, the next a gaudy puddle fast disappearing down a black, bleak drain.

The light in the bakery's back room seemed dimmer. The moonlight had lost its oomph. She had to struggle to recall the smells that only moments ago had filled her head, leaving little room for anything else.

Charlie staggered up to his friend, who was standing palely riveted to the ground, her green eyes huge in her lightly freckled face as she turned to stare at him with barely disguised horror. Even in his drunken stupor he could tell that all was not well.

"I say, Es," he said. "Are you okay? Whatever's the matter?"

Esme turned and looked toward the bakery door but the vision was definitely gone. The black, bleak drain had claimed him.

"Bread," she said feebly, willing the vision to come back. "Look." She pointed gormlessly toward the *boulangerie*. "They're baking it. Can't you smell it?"

Charlie, unsteady on his feet, sniffed the air. "God, don't talk to me about food, I feel sick as a dog," he said. "What's pastis, anyway? Revolting. Come on, Essie, let's go home."

Esme wanted to stay where she was and wait for the boy in the bakery to come back out again. But it all seemed so quiet. So still. Maybe she had been dreaming. It all felt very strange. Charlie staggered and hiccupped again and she realized that perhaps home was the best direction in which to go after all.

Lying in her bed some time later, though, her head still buzzing with red wine and blue cheese and the events of the night just passed, Esme could not get the baker boy out of her mind. It was silly, she knew, to lie in one's bed and warm oneself up with the memory of one look—no, she told herself, two—and a couple of smiles from a total stranger, if it had even been she he was smiling at.

But what a guilty pleasure it was to assume the smiles were intended for her.

And such a smile! Esme stifled a groan as she rolled over in the big fairy-tale bed and thought about that one black lock of hair licking the corner of the baker boy's eye. She imagined reaching out and tucking that slick of dark hair back behind his ear. She imagined leaning in toward him and kissing the space where the curl had been. She thought about her warm, moist lips, brushing the end of his eyebrow and tracing a trail with her tongue down his cheek to his mouth.

She tasted his tongue, for a moment, in her dreams, then let her unconscious mind turn to the promise of his hands in places no one but herself had ever been.

CHAPTER 4

Six boyfriends, one husband and ten pounds, mostly around her middle, later, Esme sat at her kitchen table high in the clouds quivering with repugnance as she ogled Jemima Jones's inaugural Diary.

It was Sunday morning and she had sent Pog to the Meare Tea Shop to get the paper as soon as he had awoken even though the last thing in the world she wanted to do was read it. It had sat first on the end of her bed, then in the clothing hamper, then on the kitchen table, then in the rubbish bin, then on the kitchen table again.

Pog, witnessing all this and weighing up what it meant, had quickly vacated to the garden shed, leaving Esme seated at the table, glaring at the Style section. Finally, she snatched it up and shook it open only to see Jemima smiling enigmatically out at her, looking blond, wrinkle-free, girlish and gorgeous. She had never felt more like punching anyone in her whole entire life.

As I kissed my darling boy Cosmo good-night on Friday, she read, *he looked up at me and said, adorably: "Are all the other mummies as beautiful as you?"*

Esme tossed the paper down on the table again. Her hands itched to do something. She checked the kitchen clock; she had knocked back her bread nearly an hour before. She could start the second rising a few minutes early.

Pog, although not saying anything, had clearly been delighted at the appearance of a freshly baked *boule* at lunch the previous day. He had eaten it as though he had never eaten anything before, and Esme herself had woken that morning with a flutter of something that wasn't, as had become the norm, dread. It was good to be back at the kitchen bench.

She poked her tongue out at Jemima and moved to where her dough was sitting plumply in its bowl, glistening with the olive oil she used to keep it from sticking to the sides. She picked the warm smooth ball up in her hands and laid it carefully on the counter, then, using both hands, gently massaged it into the right shape and let it sit while she sprinkled a handful of flour on the surface next to it.

With one deft movement she turned the dough over, dipped it in flour and gently dropped it into the waiting linen basket. It was not the real thing, not French and not made of willow, but over the years Granny Mac had perfected the art of making pretty good alternatives using breadbaskets and old linen tea towels.

The dough sat smugly in its mold. It would rise in its own good time. Esme tidied the kitchen, then went back to the table and picked up the paper again.

I was dressed in gold Calvin Klein with Jimmy Choo heels, she read, *ready to go to the Dorchester for one of my charity dos, but at that moment I felt like curling up beside my son and simply lying there in his bed all night, soaking up his adoration. How my heart ached for him as I handed the* au pair *a story book (*Kitchen Confidential *by Anthony Bourdain—Cosmo is an aspiring cook!) and slipped out the door.*

She slapped the paper back down and got up to make herself a cup of tea. Cosmo? As in the magazine? She tried to quell her irritation. *Kitchen Confidential*? How old was this child?

"All right there, darling?" she asked Rory, who was watching *Shrek* for possibly the hundredth time. Like most mothers, she had sworn no child of hers would ever sit plopped in front of a TV for hour after hour, but her son had woken up in an impossible mood and she could not face the consequences of hiding the remote control.

Rory didn't answer her. Did adorable little Cosmo watch videos and ignore his mother? she wondered. Or did Cosmo bring his mother breakfast in bed, then iron her satin robe and throw rose petals on the ground in front of her as she made her way to the bathroom? She sipped her tea, sighed and flopped back into her chair.

It's not easy being a superwoman as I am sure many

of you appreciate, Jemima chittered. *A working mother can be torn in so many different directions that the days just seem to pass in a blur. Why, one day you are sitting there in your Nicole Farhi coat and pony skin ankle boots and the next thing you know it's spring and you've barely darkened the door of Harvey Nichols. I am lucky that my husband, Gregory, who's in banking, helps out a lot at home by engaging the services of two nannies, a cook, a driver and a gardener. It makes it easy to slip away and meet our social commitments without denying our three delightful children any of the attention they so richly deserve.*

"Bitch!" Esme breathed, dropping the paper again. She could not bear to read another word. "'Three delightful children,' my armpit."

"You're not supposed to say bitch unless you're talking about dogs," Rory said from his beanbag. "Granddad says so."

Esme felt shame add itself to the cocktail of feelings churning inside her.

"Sorry, sweetheart," she said, getting up and going to the fridge to fix his morning tea, "but sometimes it really is the only word that does the job."

Rory stood up, turned off the television and sat at the table, reaching for the packet of cereal Esme had ready for him. He liked toast first thing and cereal later on. Nothing could persuade him to reverse the order. "Who's a bitch?"

"Just a woman I used to work for who was once

very mean and horrible to Mummy and who is probably going to be the next Prime Minister," Esme replied sweetly.

"What happened to Tony Blair?" Rory asked, through a mouthful of food. "The prat."

Esme looked at him pouring extra sugar on his breakfast, his carrot-colored hair luminescent against the muted creams and whites and pale blond wood of the top floor.

"Rory," she said moving around the table and sitting down next to him, "you do know that grown-ups can do and say things that little children can't, don't you?"

"Yes," said Rory. He kept eating, unfazed.

"So you must also know that you can't repeat things we say about people, especially if they are mean or horrible things, because you might not understand exactly why we are being mean and horrible in the first place."

Rory shot her a look of withering proportions.

"Mrs. Monk says people who are mean are usually sad inside and you should feel sorry for them," he said, wiping his chubby little hand across his mouth. Mrs. Monk was Rory's nursery teacher and a self-righteous old battle-ax if ever there was one, but Rory liked her and Esme tried very hard never to say anything mean about her.

"Is Mrs. Monk wearing her brown wig this week," she asked her son, "or the red one?"

Rory thought about it for a moment. "It's a new one," he said. "It's sort of silver. It's nice."

He really could be very sweet, thought Esme, smiling indulgently and catching Jemima's eyes where they lay on the table.

"Rory," she said, "do you think Mummy is beautiful?"

Rory lifted up his bowl, drank the milk out of the bottom of it and shrugged his shoulders, saying nothing.

"More beautiful than Mrs. Monk, maybe?"

"Mrs. Monk has a mustache," Rory answered her. "Everyone is more beautiful than her. She just has nice wigs."

"Well," continued Esme, "compared to the other mummies then. Am I as beautiful? More beautiful?"

Rory looked at her as he pushed his chair back. "The other mothers have got shinier hair," was all he said. He picked up the honey jar and spoon Esme had ready on the bench and held them up at her. She toyed with refusing to move until he gave her the right answer to the question but decided that would be churlish, as would pointing out that curly hair never shined like straight hair. It was a reflection thing.

"Come on," Rory said, and they made their way downstairs and out onto the lawn where, joined by Brown, they trekked over to the wicker gate behind the house and stood looking mistrustfully and from a safe distance at the beehive.

The bees swarmed furiously in an angry cloud around the blue-and-white-striped hive that Pog had paid a fortune for and spent an entire weekend painting so it would match Esme's garden, which grew rich in blue irises, lavender, roses and hydrangeas. The bees were all part of her dream of serving up a country breakfast with fresh baked bread, farm-laid eggs and lazy spoonfuls of thick, brown honey, fresh from their very own backyard.

So far, she had only managed the bread. The chickens had refused to lay and then died, and in the six months that they had had the bees, only Pog had got closer than ten yards away from them, and on that spectacular occasion he had been stung sixteen times before retreating almost in tears as Esme had looked on in hysterics from the garden gate. A small amount of research—which they would have been better off doing before buying the bees—revealed they were nowhere near equipped to harvest honey. The routine of coming down with a jar and spoon had been borne out of simple curiosity.

"Bees, Dad!" Rory shouted this Sunday morning across the lawn in the direction of Pog's shed. The door opened and Pog's head poked out.

"Be careful, you two," he called, then shut the door again. Esme considered the shed. They had six stories of house, yet Pog, she knew, preferred this drafty little shack. She'd only been in there a handful of times. It was dark and cold and full of boxes and tools and jars of dirty fluid sprouting paintbrushes. Pog had a sort of nest at one end with a chair draped in an old oilskin and a filing cabinet piled high with ancient paperwork. An old apple crate provided a surface for his electric kettle and tea supplies. The whole place smelled funny, decades of garden fertilizer fused into the walls, she supposed. On each occasion she had gone in there Pog had acted peculiarly, as though she was trespassing, so once she'd seen that it wasn't a den of pornography or a crack house she had left him to it.

"A man needs a shed," he said, whenever she complained about the amount of time he spent there. And to be honest, she couldn't begrudge him his own little space; in most regards he was the perfect husband: handsome, kind, loving, understanding, generous, gentle. She thought fleetingly, as she stood there considering the dark, lonely shed, of the way she rolled away from him under the covers of their bed these days, and guilt scratched at her. There really was something very wrong with her. Here she was with all the ingredients of a perfect life sitting separately on the countertop of her future, yet now, more than ever, she seemed incapable of combining them. Was the past destined to forever poison whatever was to come?

"What makes them so cross?" Rory asked her, and she turned her attention again to the bees buzzing furiously around their home. Brown, too, still on his best behavior since the quince-peeing incident, turned to Esme for the answer.

"I'm buggered if I know, actually," Esme

answered them both, forgetting that buggered was another word she didn't want Rory using in front of Mrs. Monk. Again. "I've given them everything bees should want. They've got that lovely hive. I've seen worse places in *Elle Decor*, for goodness' sake. There are flowers blooming everywhere you look and trees drooping with crab apples and quinces so pollen shouldn't be a problem. I don't know what's wrong."

"Perhaps they don't want to live in a hive that looks like a house," suggested Rory thoughtfully.

"What makes you say that?" Esme asked, watching him watch the bees.

"Perhaps they want to live in a hive like in Pooh Bear," he said. "You know, sort of shaped like a pinecone but with ridges going around." He looked balefully up at her. "They might not know that that's their home. They might think they're lost." He looked again at the angry bees. "Or kidnapped."

Esme looked at his little pale face with its screwed up frown. His freckles seemed enormous, as though they were floating in clear water above his skin. Would she ever know what was going on in that dear, sweet little head of his? Would she ever stop fearing for him? The love she felt for him, and the flicker of anguish that always accompanied it, vibrated right through her.

"I don't think bees have very big brains, darling," she said warmly, resisting the urge to squeeze him, knowing he hated it. "In fact, I am sure I have read somewhere that kidnapping is definitely not an issue in the bee kingdom. Actually, I believe bees don't even have a word for it. Did you know that? But you could be right about the hive. Perhaps we should try and find a pinecone-shaped one. What do you think?"

Rory handed her back the jar and spoon.

"Don't care," he said. "Don't like honey anyway." This was true. He never had liked honey. He only came with her because he didn't want to miss another major attack. Please, Esme silently begged the bees, please just calm down and let us come close. Please let something go right for me today. But somehow the buzzy little bodies sensed that most of the family preferred marmalade and so stayed irate.

Rory turned and started toward the house, but before he got far, thought of something else and turned back to her, Brown as ever glued to his side. "It's not true," he said, with a slightly accusatory tone, "about bees not having very big brains. They haven't got very big bodies and their brains actually take up quite a lot of room." He squinted at her and stuck out his jaw slightly, as if waiting for her to argue with him even though he was plainly right.

"When you were little, you used to believe everything I said," Esme heard herself say petulantly.

"Henry got me a book on bees from the library," her son answered. "I know stuff for myself now."

"Yes, well, I'm right about them not having a

word for kidnapping," Esme called after his small retreating back. He was going, she knew, to seek out Henry, who might be permanently grumpy with her but was the picture of patience and devotion with Rory, who in turn adored him. She supposed she should feel grateful, and she did, mostly.

She traipsed up the stairs to make sure her son and father-in-law found each other, then snatched the *Sunday Times* from the kitchen floor and tripped back down to Granny Mac's room, only remembering to clench her buttocks on the last five steps.

The stench of Embassy Regal hit her the moment she opened the door into the gloom; Rod was waking up Maggie May because he thought he had something to say to her.

"I haven't got long," she said, taking up her position on the end of the bed. "You would not believe what a disgusting mess Rory's room is and I haven't done any laundry for days. There's a pile on our floor that looks like something from an old episode of *Dr. Who*, Granny Mac. It's practically composting. As for the garden, well, the veggie patch needs napalming and I am long overdue for goat-pooh patrol. That wretched thing has the fastest bowels of any creature I know, including my husband and son and that's saying something."

"Well, if you can't squeeze me into your busy schedule . . ." Granny Mac huffed.

"Don't be silly," protested Esme. "I'll always

make time for you, goose. Look." She rustled the newspaper. "Jemima Jones's first column. She's got a boy called Cosmo who's asked her if all the other mothers are as beautiful as she is."

"Gay," Granny Mac said matter-of-factly. "Gay, gay, gay. What else does she say?"

"'*Juggling family and career is an issue with which many British families struggle,*'" Esme read in a simpering voice, "'*and we are certainly no exception. The only difference for us, really, is that our children are quite mature and of above average intelligence in their demograph so we can explain to them, without tears or tantrums, why Daddy never comes home before bedtime and often still isn't there in the morning.*' Oh, that sounds healthy.

"'*But back to our precious little four-year-old*'—he's only four?—'*and his adorable question. When we got home from the Dorchester, where can I just say Camilla was looking positively glowing (what is it that Charles gives her?), I snuck into his room and looked at him curled up in his tiny replica of Michael Schumacher's Ferrari.*' Oh, couldn't afford the real thing, then?

"'*I had met so many women that night,*'" Esme read on, "'*from all walks of life, rich and poor, short and tall, natural and frosty-tipped, and it had struck me at one point as my mind wandered while talking to Cherie (yes, that one!), that despite our differences, we are really all the same. We're all trying to hold together the fabric that makes up our lives, be they grand or oh so simple.*

"'"*Yes, Cosmo,*" I whispered to my precious sleeping

son. "Yes. All the other mummies are as beautiful as me. In their own special ways.""

Esme dropped the paper into her lap, her head thumping against the wall as she stared at the ceiling. She could read no further.

"What the hell is she on about?" asked Granny Mac. "'The fabric that makes up our lives'? I thought it was a society column not a bloody sewing circle."

Esme shook her head, misery seeping out of every pore.

"Esme!" Granny Mac said sharply. "What is the matter?"

"I don't know," Esme answered unhappily. "I just don't know. But I feel wretched, Granny Mac. Wretched." Her voice caught and she fought to control it. "I've been so good up until now. So strong." She stopped. "And I've been baking again just like you told me to, which has been glorious, my goodness, just glorious. It's made a difference. It really has. I mean the blackness has gone."

"But?" Granny Mac prompted.

"But still I have this terrible feeling. Oh, I don't know." Esme sought the right words. "It's like I've got a great big itch somewhere inside me but I can't tell where so I can't scratch it but I can't concentrate on anything else while it's itchy. Have you ever felt like that, Gran?"

"Well, I had flea bites once," Granny Mac retorted, "from a particularly unpleasant cat called Pam that came with your Granddad Mac.

87

Calamine lotion was the thing back then, I believe."

"I'm trying to tell you my deepest darkest thoughts and calamine lotion is the best you can do?"

"And you think your deepest darkest thoughts are so fascinating? I've not a clue what you're on about with your scratching and your itching, Esme. If you want me to help you, you have got to help yourself, and spouting nonsense about bloody eczema for God's sake is getting us nowhere."

It was no wonder Rory liked Shrek, Esme thought. The caustic green ogre probably reminded the poor child of his great-grandmother. She abandoned any attempt at argument.

"I just want to be the old me," she said, simply, instead. "I want to go to charity dos at the Dorchester and drink fru-fru cocktails with Cherie Blair and have good old-fashioned uncomplicated fun." She sighed. "But everything is just so horribly tainted with what's happened to us that I can't imagine ever escaping it. I can't imagine ever being that old uncomplicated Esme ever again."

"Och, Esme." Her grandmother was not entirely sympathetic. "She wasn't so hot, that girl."

"Granny Mac!"

"Well, it's time you started facing facts, lassie. You can't be her again. She's gone. It's true, what's happened to you has made you a different person. We none of us can go back and undo what's been done, Esme. We just have to live with the consequences and find a way to move forward despite them."

"Well, don't you think I have been doing that, these past two years?" Esme was stunned. "Other people would have just melted into the ground and disappeared and God knows most of the time that's what I wanted to do but I didn't. I have moved forward, I have kept moving forward."

"And this past month?"

"This past month is your fault," Esme cried. "You know it is. I can't do it on my own. It's too hard. It's too lonely."

"Oh, not doing enough for you, am I? Well, I'll get up and dance a highland fling then, how about that? Never mind two strokes and the recent devastation of pneumonia."

Esme ignored this, rustling the *Sunday Times* furiously instead. "Well, Jemima Jones isn't helping, I can tell you that for nothing. Turning up with three delightful children, a brand-new career and not a single bloody crow's-foot in sight."

"You're going to blame this conniption on Jemima Jones?" Granny Mac asked incredulously. "Oh yes, that works. That works really well. Good job. Brilliant." A deep sigh permeated the room. "You know, you can point your finger any which way you like, Esme, but I think you know that if your bread isn't rising, you need to look at your ingredients."

Esme was silent.

"There are weevils in your flour, lassie."

"There's nothing in my flour, Granny Mac."

"I'm telling you, there are weevils."

"This has nothing to do with weevils!"

"It's all about weevils."

"Well, I don't want to talk about weevils."

"Well, you shouldn't expect to start feeling better until you *do* talk about weevils, Esme, and in the meantime don't come in here wasting my time with your incessant moaning."

The room pinged with unfamiliar tension. Rod's "Sailing" faded into the background and the smell of cigarettes slithered out through the cracks in the wallpaper.

The *br-rr-ing* of the telephone upstairs shattered the ensuing quiet and Esme pushed herself shakily off the bed, landing with a thump on the floor. She snatched the *Sunday Times* and fled the room without a backward glance.

"Don't worry, Henry," she called, taking the stairs two at a time. "I'll get it."

She slid into the sitting room on the third floor—the spilled vase water from the quince incident had rendered the ground floor phone line unusable—and grabbed the receiver on the eighth ring, gasping into it: "Esme Stack!"

"I will never get used to that ridiculous name," a voice crackled down the line. "Really, Es. There was nothing wrong with MacDougall."

"Charlie!" Esme cried, delighted. "My God, I can't believe it. Where are you?"

"Still in Honkers, darling, but not for much bloody longer. I'm on my way home—can you believe it? Never mind SARS, I never did get the hang of chopsticks, confounded things, although I've developed quite a taste for snake meat. And skin for that matter. I'm practically all reptile these days, inside and out."

Esme laughed as Charlie's nonsense washed over her. "Oh, Charlie, it's so good to hear from you, I can't tell you," she said. "I really can't."

"Well, seeing me in the flesh ought to give you even more of a thrill," he said modestly. "I'm flying in on Tuesday and I thought I might come out to the deepest, darkest countryside for the weekend and stay. Check out the good life, Felicity Kendal and all that. Eat some organic wasabe or whatever it is you have there and maybe grab a glass or six of dandelion wine."

Esme assured him she could provide alcohol from a totally synthetic source and food that had definitely been genetically modified and put the phone down, tingling with anticipation at the thought of his visit. Something had gone right! Charlie did not have a sensitive bone in his body but had been blessed with the gift of good timing. If one needed a shoulder to cry on, he was no help at all, but if one needed someone to make them laugh and forget for a moment that they needed a shoulder to cry on, he was.

She heard voices on the floor below her, followed by Henry's tapping and shuffling.

"We're going outside," he called in his gruff voice.

"Right-oh," Esme called back. She flopped back in her overstuffed armchair and contemplated the Style section, yet again. Could she stomach more Jemima? Could she keep away? Why did she feel so drawn to details of a life that only made her feel more inadequate than ever about her own? It was sick.

She turned to page two. What was little Cosmo doing now? she wondered. Bringing peace to the Middle East and curing cancer?

"Oh, fuck you, you silly cow!" she said churlishly, throwing the paper on the floor and kicking it away.

"I beg your pardon?" a voice said from the doorway. It was, of course, Henry, with Rory standing beside him.

"She said 'bitch' before, too," Rory informed his grandfather.

"That's entrapment," protested Esme. "I thought you were outside! A person can swear to themselves, can't they?" Henry and Rory looked at each other but said nothing. Esme rolled her eyes. "I'm sorry, I'm sorry. What's up?"

"Hugo has suggested a walk on the beach before lunch," Henry said in his tight, clipped voice.

"What a good idea," Esme said, going over and ruffling Rory's curls and throwing a smile at her father-in-law in hope of defrosting him. "I'll have the bread baked and the soup heated and sitting downstairs in the garden by the time you come back." Rory shot her a strange look, then picked up his grandfather's hand and led him downstairs.

"She likes bread more than the beach," he said as they crossed the lawn to Pog's shed. "But that's okay." Henry said nothing.

Pog, on hearing their approach, emerged, his face falling when he saw Esme was not with them.

"She's getting lunch," Henry said, and the three male Stacks, along with Brown, headed out the gate and down the leafy lane toward the unnecessarily winding road that led past the Meare to the beach.

Seabury was a village made, literally, for sunny Sundays such as this one. The Meare was peppered with brightly colored boats being rowed, with varying degrees of skill, by a holidaying couple here, a squabbling family there, as the local swan population did its best to stay aloof and avoid collisions.

The sky was as clear and blue as it could possibly be, the sun warming the giant oaks around the lake and sending Chinese whispers rippling through their leaves.

"Lovely day for it." Mrs. Coyle smiled at them as she cleared a picnic table outside the Tea Shop of scone crumbs. "Mrs. Stack not joining you, then?"

"Busy in the kitchen," Pog said ruefully, raising his eyebrows, and the four of them turned to look at the House in the Clouds, rising out of the trees, stiff-backed and standoffish from this angle.

"No rest for the wicked, eh?" Mrs. Coyle winked. "I hear her vegetables got away on her again this year. Had a carload in here yesterday talking about them. Couldn't shut them up!"

Pog smiled and the Stacks kept walking.

Esme was summarily regarded as the kinkiest gardener in all of East Anglia. Nothing came out the way she expected it to or even where she expected it to. Her zucchinis had scandalized Gaga and Jam-jar by all growing in the shape of giant phalluses complete with bollocks that were apparently some sort of fungal parasite. A coachload of Americans had actually stopped to take photos of them and they'd been featured on the local TV news channel. Only one artichoke out of the hundred that she planted grew, and she had been so proud she had not picked it. The Goat had got to it first, eating it in an overnight rampage that also saw one of Rory's Wellingtons shredded and gobbled and excreted in unsightly piles around the property.

When they reached the warm pebbles of Seabury Beach, the Stack males took off their shoes and socks. Rory, thrilled by the temperate breeze, the sparkling blue ocean, the earsplitting barks of his overexcited Labrador, ran up and down splashing in the shallow waters of the shoreline, waving his arms and shouting to himself. Henry and Pog sat on a wooden bench at the foot of the sand dunes and watched him.

"Your mother never cared for the beach," Henry said, out of the blue, totally astonishing his son. "Made her fret. The waves, you know, coming and coming, never stopping or some such nonsense."

She'd been gone nearly twenty years yet still it hurt Henry so much to think of Grace that usually he simply couldn't. Usually, he kept his memories of her locked in a vault in his mind where he managed to contain all the painful emotion he preferred not to confront.

His sons, he knew, had suffered as a result of his inability to share his grief. They had lost a mother, after all, and the two of them only in their early twenties. But he had lost his wife, the love of his life, his reason for getting up in the morning. How could he console his sons when all he wanted to do was howl with rage at the injustice of it all, to shake his fists at God or whoever had planted Grace's faulty genes? He'd left his boys to sink or swim.

Milo, his firstborn, had swum, finding strength in his career and his marriage to, rather sensibly Henry felt, a fellow broker with a no-nonsense hairdo and good childbearing hips. They were settled in America now, doing everything according to plan, safe and happy and no trouble to anyone.

Hugo was a different creature, always had been. Dreamy, soft, more like Grace, he supposed. He'd swum too but perhaps he had floundered a little, was floundering still.

Henry thought of Esme and his jaw clenched. His first impression of his daughter-in-law-to-be had not been a good one. She was right to think he considered her flighty and unsuitable. It had been a cold, winter night at his old house in Kent, and Hugo had turned up all bright-eyed and pink-cheeked with this jittery, bubbly, brassy redhead dressed ridiculously in fake fur and men's shoes. She'd been nervous and had drunk too much champagne, embarrassing herself by blurting out, untruthfully, as it happened, that she was abandoning her so-called career in journalism to make bikinis out of run-over cat skins.

He'd had trouble warming to her after that. They chafed at each other like mismatched cogs, always missing the connection. She talked too much, and Henry, especially in the absence of Grace, was not a talker. He felt trampled by Esme's enthusiasm. All it served to remind him was how his own small well of ebullience had long run dry. It had not helped when poor health collided with reduced circumstances, and Henry, thanks to a run of bad investments handled by his neighbor's son-in-law, a trust fund manager with a well-disguised gambling problem, had had no alternative but to sell his Kent cottage and settle his debts.

Esme, he knew, had been distressed beyond measure at his obvious loss and embarrassment, insisting he move in with them as she was dying for want of a decent house-sitter. Hugo had been more fretful than she, and he had even overheard his daughter-in-law sternly reminding his son that this was what families were for and if they could look after Granny Mac, who was rude and insolent, they could certainly look after a gentleman like Henry.

But his pride was hurt, his dignity mulched, and he had not had it in him to accept her kindness. Through all they had suffered, he had held himself at bay and he did not like himself for it. But there was no going back. He was trapped in his own grief and remorse and could not claw his way to freedom. He did not know how to rebuild the bridge between himself and the next generation.

"I didn't know that," Pog said, eyes on the horizon, confused and awkward in such uncharted territory. "About Mum. And the beach."

Henry said nothing. He wanted to reach out further, but it was simply beyond him. He looked across the pebbles at Rory, his bright red hair pinging off the blue sea behind him as he ran through the surf, white foamy chunks flying in the air in front of him.

And his heart, which nursed such pain and bitterness, swelled with love for the boy. Rory he would not disappoint.

CHAPTER 5

"Ijust can't stop thinking about her," Esme was saying the following Saturday, as she took refuge in Granny Mac's room waiting for Charlie to arrive. "She's got three children all named after magazines! There's dear sweet lovely little Cosmo, then there's a boy called George Quentin—or GQ—who loves mathematics and is going to be in banking, and the eldest is this poor little creature called Marie Claire who is going to be a model once she loses her puppy fat and gets her ears pinned back and her teeth straightened. That poor little girl, Granny Mac. Imagine having Jemima for a mother."

"Esme, will you stop banging on about Jemima Jones. Honestly. You're doing my head in."

"But, Granny Mac, it's just that—"

"It's just that nothing. Leave the poor woman alone."

"The poor woman? Oh, I'd like to have her problems!"

"You can't face your own problems, Esme, let alone anyone else's."

"Stop picking on me!"

"Stop asking for it!"

Esme was stunned. In the twenty-nine years since she and Granny Mac had moved in together, they had never argued. In fact, they rarely disagreed on anything. In Esme's teens, they even had a running joke picked up from an interview with an aging rock wife and her daughter that they were "*practically* sisters." Quite a ridiculous notion between one generation and the next, totally barmy between one generation and not the next one but the one after that.

Only once had they had an even slightly hurtful exchange, and that had been after thirteen-year-old Esme had been teased at school about not having parents, but rather a dowdily dressed eccentric old woman who picked her up in a motorcycle and sidecar and gave her peppermint chocolate sandwiches for lunch.

"You don't like the sidecar?" Granny Mac had asked her weeping granddaughter, amazed. "Well, a bus ticket or two can fix that pretty quickly. Is there anything else?"

"Yes," Esme sobbed. "Don't argue with the teachers about how clever I am. I'm not that clever. Normal mothers tell their daughters to buck up their ideas, they don't tell them to ignore the teachers because they don't know what they're talking about."

"Well, excuse me," Granny Mac had said. "What terrible, terrible problems you have, Esme. I wonder would you be better off in the home for unwanted ginger children?"

Esme's tears had dried and she had sniffed loud and long at this suggestion. It had hurt her to be mocked by her peers at school and had felt better to share that pain with her grandmother. But once it was expunged, she could see that having a guardian who drove a motorbike and put chocolate in sandwiches and thought you were brilliant was not really undesirable at all.

She was one out of the box, was Granny Mac.

"Well, if you're going to be like that," Esme sniffed, "I'll leave you to your own devices. I don't know why I'm sitting here in this dark smelly room talking to you in the first place. It's ridiculous."

"Oh, cheer up. It's nothing that a lot of expensive therapy won't fix," her grandmother quipped. "Although I've always been, as you know, personally myself, a great believer in the healing properties of the prune."

"That's not funny about the therapy, Granny Mac," Esme said, standing up and turning to leave.

"Aye, and I'm not joking about the prune juice either," a voice chirped drily behind her.

Outside the room Esme bumped, literally, into Henry, who was returning from dropping Rory off for his regular playdate with Annabelle Ashton, the only child his own age in whom he showed the slightest bit of interest. Henry looked over Esme's shoulder and she reddened as Rod's insistence that tonight was the night squeaked out from beneath the door.

"You should do something in there, you know," Henry said gruffly, starting up the stairs. "Open it up. Let some fresh air in."

"Shut your CAKEHOLE!" Esme distinctly heard Granny Mac roar from behind her bedroom door, but the meaty growl of an expensive car chewing up the gravel outside seemed to drown her out.

Esme bustled outside in a swish of petticoats, her doubt temporarily in remission, to see Charlie sitting in the driver's seat of a black Audi convertible gawking up at the House in the Clouds.

"Bloody hell, old girl," he cried, impressed. "It's positively phallic. Did Hugo choose it or did you?" He pushed his expensive sunglasses up on his head and flicked his eyes over her as she ran toward him.

"You look fantastic as always," he said, jumping out of the car and squeezing her in a fierce hug, mock spitting her hair out of his mouth. "God, it's good to see you, Esme."

Esme pulled back. "You're looking pretty bloody gorgeous yourself," she said. His hair was long and blond-tipped and fell boyishly across his forehead, the neatly tanned skin around his eyes only just beginning to pucker and crinkle. He looked, it struck her, like a younger, taller, more handsome version of Hugh Grant. "Is that Prada?" she gaped. "Head-to-toe? My God, you are a loss to the heterosexual world, Charlie!"

"But darling," Charlie said with a wicked grin,

"I am a gift to the other side. Try thinking of it that way."

"Still beating them off with a big stick, eh?" teased Esme. "Is there a big chunky gold medallion under that shirt? Shouldn't you be undoing a button or six and getting your chest wig out?"

Charlie laughed and put one long arm around her shoulders so she could nestle into his armpit where they both knew she fit. "Now are you going to ask me in or up or whatever you do to get into this monstrous abode—or not? What on earth compelled you to move to this creepy little town, Es, it's like something the brothers Grimm might have dreamed up, all twisty and windy and things not the right size."

Esme laughed. What was it with men and Seabury? The great lumps seemed so threatened by anything slightly imaginative or out of the ordinary. She ignored Charlie's question and gave him a grand tour of the property, starting with the dysfunctional pets and unconventional vegetable garden.

To her amazement, he seemed quite excited by the prospect of Pog's shed.

"You mean it's just for him and no one else?" he asked, impressed. "Sounds smashing. And does he spend much time in there?"

"He's usually in there all weekend," Esme told him. "But he's got some big project on the boil at the moment so he's at work today." She realized she had been so distracted by her own anxiousness that she had not asked Pog exactly what his project was. He'd been working a few Saturdays lately, she supposed.

The crunch of tires on gravel turned her attention to a van load of elderly people from a retirement home two towns to the south as it pulled up in the lane on the other side of the garden fence. A common enough occurrence, Esme carried on, pointing out where the world's largest pumpkins grew as the retirees snapped happily with their cameras; but Charlie was agog, especially when Gaga came out of the windmill and started shouting and waving a tea towel.

"What the hell is going on?" he wanted to know.

Esme wrinkled her nose and grimaced at Gaga. "She's lost her marbles, poor thing," she said. "Thinks the twinkie-mobile is coming to get her so she throws a hissy fit every time she sees one."

Gaga's shrieking reached a frightening pitch.

"Shouldn't you do something?" Charlie asked, wincing.

Esme shook her head. "I tried once and half of my face ended up underneath her fingernails. Jam-jar will come and get her soon. He's deaf, so it takes a while."

Sure enough, as they watched, an ancient figure in a ratty cardigan wearing Coke-bottle lenses appeared behind his angry shriveled wife and wrestled her inside.

The old folk in the van clicked their shutters madly and Esme steered Charlie toward the house. "Don't laugh," she said. "That will be me and Pog one day."

She bypassed Granny Mac's room with a swift, dismissive wave, took him in to say hello to Henry, who treated him with polite deference, then gave him lunch in her kitchen—sourdough and home-made minestrone—which he wolfed down while claiming to feel queasy at the view from the top of the House in the Clouds.

After that, she forced him to walk with her to the Ashtons to get Rory, who had done four paint-ings, all of them solid masses of very dark brown. He had not spoken a word, according to Peggy Ashton, since he arrived, but had eaten a hearty lunch and stood there placidly as bubbly, blond, blue-eyed Annabelle threw her arms around him and kissed him good-bye.

Charlie seemed at a loss as to what to say to the little boy as they strolled in the sunshine back down the lane to the house. They had not met before, Charlie claiming at news of Esme's preg-nancy to be allergic to small children and backing this up soon after by decamping to the other side of the world. He and Esme had met occasionally over the years for cocktails, usually vanilla daiquiris, during his visits home and had kept sporadically in touch by phone and by mail but he had never before seen her domestically in situ.

"So, is Annabelle your girlfriend, then?" Charlie finally asked, reaching down and patting Rory on the shoulder as they meandered toward home.

Rory squinted up at him. "No," he said.

"Never too young to start though, eh?" Charlie joked.

"Start what?" Rory asked.

"Start having girlfriends, silly," Charlie answered.

Rory looked at his mother.

"It's small talk," she explained. "It doesn't really matter. You just sort of go along with it to be polite."

"Thank you very much," Charlie cried indignantly.

"Well, there is no point asking a four-year-old about his *sex* life, Charlie," Esme hissed.

"If it doesn't really matter, why would you want to talk about it?" Rory asked.

Esme laughed and Charlie turned to her. "It's the body of a small boy," he said, "but the words of an old Scottish woman." He broke off, suddenly embarrassed. "I'm so sorry, Es—"

"So sorry nothing," Esme said, breaking into a trot, despite the almost unfeasibly high heels, and grabbing Rory's hand. "Come on, darling. I think I saw gaudily wrapped gifts in the back of Uncle Charlie's sports car."

The gaudily wrapped gifts turned out to be something of an icebreaker in the Rory-Charlie relationship department as three of them turned out to be guns. The House in the Clouds had up until then been a weapon-free environment—all the books said that was the right thing to do—

but actually Esme was relieved to see that her son reacted the way any other small boy might react: by getting quite pink in the cheeks and instantly shooting everything including her, the sheep, the bees, Brown and even Henry, who feigned disgust but was secretly impressed at the authenticity of a World War I tommy gun.

The gift-giving did not stop there, either. There was a Paul Smith shirt for Pog, which Esme knew her husband would never wear even though it would look fantastic on him, and for her Charlie had bought a bottle of Must de Cartier *parfum* and the body lotion (of course, he remembered) she no longer bothered to buy herself. On top of that, he produced two bottles of Cristal and one of the fattest joints she could ever remember seeing—but then, it had been a while.

"Sorry, Es, but I'm only here for the night," Charlie informed her as he cracked open the first bottle of champagne as soon as the presents were unwrapped. "The Old Boy's made plans for me and I can't really wriggle out of them. You know how it is."

"Oh, Charlie," Esme cried, disappointed. "I thought you were staying longer. There's so much catching up to do. I don't even know what you're doing back here. I don't know anything. Can't you stay at least another night?"

Charlie put on his strict, older brotherly look and handed her a glass. "Come on, Es," he cajoled. "Don't make a fuss. Can't be helped and all that.

We've only got one night so we'd better make it a good one, eh?"

Esme felt schoolgirlishly put out. "Well, I can't get started on the bubbly this early," she said, shaking her head at the champagne and refusing to take it. "I have old people to feed and small children to bathe and put to bed."

Charlie picked up her hand and curled it around the glass. "Don't be so silly," he said. "I'll come back again. Next week if you want me to. I'm based in London now, you know, for the rest of my working days if I can manage it. Don't make me feel guilty, Es, you know I'm no good at it."

Esme thawed slightly. "I'm making you feel guilty?" she asked, impressed, taking a firmer grasp on the champagne flute. "You're losing it, you big jessie!"

Charlie smiled his movie-star smile and charged his glass. "That's more like it," he said. "Now have a drink for God's sake, a man could die of thirst out here in the country."

Pog got home, just before eight, exhausted after spending the day in a series of very dull informal meetings with different members of the local council, which had, much to his own surprise, awarded him the contract to beautify Seabury's wobbly main street. It had taken them nearly six months to decide he was the right man for the job, and now they wanted plans and costings within three weeks. By the time he trod home, Charlie and Esme had drunk both bottles of champagne and smoked half of the enormous joint.

They were lying on their backs on the floor in the sitting room, laughing hysterically. Pog quelled the whisper of loneliness that licked at him: He loved to see Esme laugh, after all. He loved to see her happy. He wished it was he who had her rolling on the floor in hysterics but if it was Charlie or nothing, he'd take Charlie.

"Where's Dad?" he asked after shaking hands with the man and accepting, slightly perplexed, the Paul Smith shirt with which he had just been presented, noticing, as he put it on the sideboard, that it was a size too small as well as being purple, the only color in the world he truly detested.

"I think he went to the pub," said Esme, sitting up and wiping the tears of laughter from her eyes. "There was a small amount of irritation at having a noisy guest in the house," she continued as Charlie started to laugh again, "followed by a flow of condescension with a smattering of contempt forecast for tomorrow." Charlie was howling. Pog smiled and Esme felt instantly sober and guilty and mean. It wasn't Pog's fault Henry was cranky. And her husband looked tired and awkward. It was not her intention to exclude him. It was never her intention to exclude him.

"Rory's in bed asleep," she said, suddenly more sensible. "I think he has a new best friend."

She looked at Charlie, who smiled winningly up at Pog from his position on the floor.

"Well, I think I'll join him," Pog said. "Dad, at the pub, I mean. Help him get home. Let you two catch up. Does that sound all right, darling?" He smiled at her again, and Esme felt almost over-whelmed by an urge to fold herself into his arms and say all the things she knew he needed to hear from her.

"Charlie's only here for the night," she blurted out instead. "Just the one."

Charlie started laughing hilariously again at this, clutching his stomach as he rolled around on the floor.

"He has to be admitted to a psychiatric ward tomorrow morning for immediate testing," Esme continued. "As you can see he's not quite right in the head."

"As long as it's not catching," Pog said pleas-antly, noticing that Charlie's untucked shirt as he rotated on the rug had ridden up to reveal a tanned rock-hard belly rippling with muscle. "I'll see you later," he said, feeling the porkpie and jelly doughnut he had had for afternoon tea swill accus-ingly around in his own rather more spongy stomach. "Have fun."

As his footsteps on the stairs faded away and the front door clicked distantly shut, Charlie sat up and attempted to compose himself. "What appalling behavior," he said, drying his eyes with the sleeve of his shirt. "No wonder the poor chap thinks I am a complete imbecile."

"Don't be silly," Esme said, standing up

unsteadily and holding out her hand to her friend. "That's not why he thinks you're a complete imbecile." Charlie groaned and let her help him to his feet.

"Truly? He thinks that?" he asked.

"Oh, for goodness' sake, shut up," chided Esme, heading up the stairs. "He thinks nothing of the sort. Pog's just not like that. He's far too nice. Jesus, but there are a lot of stairs in this house. Come on, Charlie. The kitchen is a bomb site. I'd better go and tidy it up before Pog comes back and decides to start being like that." They clattered together up the stairs and into the kitchen, where Charlie collapsed onto a chair and Esme surveyed the devastation she had created making Rory a chocolate cake for his tea.

"Blimey, what a hovel," she said as she started clearing the bench. "Did I do this?" The dishwasher gaped meanly at her, its freshly cleaned innards glinting and reminding her what a slovenly housewife she was for not emptying it earlier. Slowly and carefully, so as not to break anything in her partially inebriated state, she removed its contents, before filling it up again with the trashy remains of her earlier baking.

After wiping the counter clean, she started excavating in the freezer for something to feed her family the following night.

"Hurrah!" she crowed, finally finding a leg of lamb underneath a spilled open bag of frozen peas and a box of half-melted ice lollies.

"There's homemade mint sauce in here somewhere, too," she muttered, pulling a bit of ice out of one of her curls and diving into the freezer again. "You should have seen my mint, Charlie, how it grew! I think NASA astronauts could see it from space." Shuffling old margarine containers around she finally found the right one, plucking it out with a triumphant look and holding it up for Charlie to see.

He was staring at her with an unreadable expression.

"What is it?" she asked, wiping imaginary fluff off her nose and checking her hair with her hand to make sure nothing jellied or minced or past its use-by date was stuck there. "Don't look at me like that!"

Charlie shook himself out of his thoughts. "I wasn't looking at you like anything," he protested.

"Yes, you were," argued Esme, suddenly remembering she hadn't fed her sourdough starter its evening meal of flour and water and reaching into the pantry for the jar. "You were looking at me as though you'd never seen me before."

Charlie laughed. "No, I was just thinking, that's all."

"Thinking what?" Esme insisted, hugging the starter to her chest, one hand on the lid.

"Thinking how amazing you are," Charlie said softly, "that's what."

"Amazing?" Esme repeated. "Me?" It was not

what she had been expecting him to say. She started to slowly twist the lid off the starter.

"Yes, you silly girl, you," Charlie said. "After everything you've been through, you still seem so, I don't know, happy."

"Happy?" The top of the jar popped off at just that moment and the pungent sweet and sour tartness of the ancient mixture hit Esme square in the face. *Happy?* In that instant, the mists of the past fifteen years fell away and she saw herself, clearly, standing in that little French bakery, wrapped in a soft sheet of cocoa-colored linen, cherishing every drop of the baker's sweat as it mingled with hers and quivering with the joy of being loved.

That was happy.

She dropped the jar on the kitchen counter and the memory vanished, leaving her breathless and terrified.

"Esme?" Charlie said, alarmed. "What's the matter? Are you all right?"

"Happy?" she gasped at him. "You think I'm *happy*?"

Charlie was confused. "Well, yes, in a Nigella Lawson sort of way, out here in your country birdhouse defrosting dead animals and growing the world's rudest pumpkins despite, you know, everything that's happened."

An ache so deep she could not tell where it came from rose through Esme's chest and erupted in the form of a violent sob. She threw herself down on the kitchen counter and to her own and Charlie's horror, started to weep.

"Oh, Lord." Charlie leaped from his chair. "Esme, what's the matter? Should I get someone? Esme, please. Are you all right? Shit, shit, shit. Should I get Pog? Oh, Esme."

"I'm a bad mother," sobbed Esme, "and an awful wife and a horrible daughter-in-law. And then there's Granny Mac, oooh, Granny Mac . . ." She wept loud, rare tears, heartbroken, into her arms, only vaguely aware of Charlie's awkward attempts to comfort her.

"I'm so sorry," Charlie said as soothingly as he knew how. "I should never have said anything. You're not at all amazing. Of course you're not. I'm so sorry, Esme, it's the pot or the booze or something. You're not happy, I can see that now. How could you be? Bloody stupid of me to suggest it. God, what an oaf. What a pig. An insensitive pig. I could just kick myself, really I could. Lord! What's the matter with me? Could be jet lag, I suppose, although I have been back five days, or is it four, and I did have a cold last month that took a bit of getting over—"

Esme lifted her tearstained face and turned to look at him. "Are you quite finished?" she asked, her voice gluey with grief but her tears drying.

"Oh hell, yes." Charlie jumped back and wrung his hands uselessly. "Yes. Totally finished. Completely. Utterly. Oh, Esme. What can I do?"

"You can give me a hankie," Esme sniffed. "And

stop fluffing." Charlie pulled a silk handkerchief from his pocket with lightning speed and thrust it at her.

"Here," he said. "And consider all fluffing as of this moment one hundred percent stopped. Finito. Kaput."

Esme laughed and blew her nose.

"I'm sorry, Charlie," she said, so sadly that Charlie stepped closer and took her in his arms, holding her tightly, wishing he knew what he could do to make her feel better and swearing to himself that if he knew what that was, he would do it.

"You're a good mother," he said, her ringlets tickling his chin. "And a good wife. You really are. You and Pog are the perfect couple."

"I'm not," Esme said, pulling away and handing Charlie back his handkerchief. "We're not. I mean, we were, and I do love him, I love him with all my heart, I really, really do, but I just don't know if we can bounce back to where we were, Charlie. There's just so much water gone under the bridge."

Her sinuses clear again, she caught a whiff left lingering in her kitchen of her sharp, tart starter and felt another pang of longing for the simplicity of the past.

"But of all the people I know, Esme, you deserve the most happiness."

"Yes, well," she said, as tears threatened to fall again, "I'm starting to think that maybe I had my chance at happiness, Charlie. And maybe I'm not going to get another one."

"Of course you will, Es. You must see that."

"I don't know what I see these days," she said. "The only things I'm sure of seem locked in the past where I can't get to them. I mean, what say my big chance at happiness is back there somewhere. You know, in Venolat."

"In *Venolat*?" Charlie asked incredulously.

"Yes, Venolat," Esme answered in a whisper.

"Oh, Esme. Not Louis. Not *still* Louis? After all these years?"

"Yes, Charlie. Still Louis. After all these years."

CHAPTER 6

When morning came to Venolat and woke Esme by sending a shaft of burning light through the shutters to hit her square in the right eye, she woke with a start and thought instantly of breakfast.

She took a shower and went downstairs, trying to ignore her throbbing headache. Charlie was sitting outside on the terrace sunning himself and drinking orange juice out of a plastic bottle. He looked gorgeous. Not at all like someone whose liver was shrunken and black and whose lungs were tarred and sooty.

"Good morning," he said chirpily. "Caught up on your beauty sleep, then?"

Esme smiled and ran her fingers through her hair, as if there was even the remotest possibility that anything other than the strongest, most foul-smelling chemicals could ever straighten out its wayward kinks.

"I thought I might go to the bakery," she said, "and get us some breakfast. What do you fancy?"

Charlie sat up excitedly in his wrought iron seat. "Oh, yes please, mistress," he said in his best public-schoolboy voice. "Something with custard and something with icing, if you'd be ever so kind."

"Charlie, we are in France, not a Merchant Ivory film," she said, grabbing the juice from the table and drinking out of the container herself. "And unless I am mistaken I don't think France is especially known for its icing and custard. I think it is better know for its . . ." She looked at him encouragingly.

"Dressing?" Charlie proffered.

"Apart from that."

He looked blank. "Don't tease me, Esme, I'm not feeling very bright this morning."

"Bread," said Esme. "French bread. And croissants. And brioche and—"

"Fine, fine, fine, yes of course," Charlie interrupted. "Anything you like as long as it's food. I'm starving."

Esme picked up her purse and trotted down the stairs, stopping to inspect herself without admitting that was what she was doing in the hall mirror by the front doors.

She had on an antique white slip dress she had bought at Portobello market especially for the holiday. Its thin lacy straps sat daintily on her shoulders, showing off her long neck and passable collarbones (mole included) and containing beneath its fine filmy cotton her braless nineteen-year-old bosoms, which sat pertly but not brazenly and were really only obvious if you were particularly looking for them.

The gentle film of freckles across her pale shoulders suited the dress, as did her loud, long mass of spiraling hair. Because she had always had pre-Raphaelite looks, she had never wanted them. Because she had always had pre-Raphaelite looks she had always wanted to look like Michelle Pfeiffer in *Dangerous Liaisons* or the girl with the black shiny bob in the Swing Out Sister video. This was perfectly normal, she knew that. Everybody with straight hair wanted curls and everybody with curls wanted straight hair and no one, but no one liked their own legs, although Esme secretly was very fond of her own feet. She had straight medium-length toes with good nails and nice bones, and serious shoe salespeople adored her.

This morning, though, Esme was amazed to find, as she surreptitiously glossed her lips before heading out the door, that she suited herself from head to toe. She couldn't remember when or if she had ever felt that way before.

Being ginger and freckly had not always been considered a winning combination, but Esme had to admit that the older she got the less she minded it. In fact, every now and then she even let herself be pleased that she didn't have mousy brown hair and a peaches and cream complexion because they were a dime a dozen. As a little girl, being different—in so many ways—had been painful, but as she approached adulthood she found herself appreciating her uniqueness, embracing it even.

Her looks, she thought, were perhaps, finally, coming into their own. Her own.

She slipped outside into the burning morning sunshine and headed toward the *boulangerie,* her stomach quivering with something she thought must have been the results of too much foie gras— although a voice inside her head kept whispering to her that it could be something far more serious than that. Something appetizing but not edible. Something mouthwatering but hard to digest. Something deliciously, delectably hopeful.

As the whisper got louder and the bread shop got nearer, however, her footsteps slowed. What was hope doing filling her head on an innocent trip to the bakery anyway? she thought. It was ridiculous. Childish. And this was only a routine visit to the local *boulangerie,* wasn't it? She was hungry, for God's sake. But for what? "Oh, get a grip," she said loudly to herself, frightening a little old woman tottering toward her with a large paper parcel, bigger than her head, smelling strongly of bread.

"Oh," Esme said, smiling apologetically when she saw the woman's expression. "*Je suis,* um—" but the word for sorry, having been on the tip of her tongue, decided it was happy to stay there and so she finished off instead with a limp, *"Bonjour,"* and the ancient matron sped up to a near scurry and shuffled past without further eye contact.

"Je suis désolée," Esme called after her, suddenly remembering the wonderfully apologetic term and

putting all the effort she could into shouting it at the bent old lady's back. *"Je suis désolée!"* The object of her apology disappeared around the corner and Esme was left outside the *boulangerie* door.

It was silly not to go in, she told herself. She needed to get breakfast. That was it. Simple as anything. This was real life, after all, and not a fairy tale. She was going to the bakery to buy some bread. End of story.

She pushed open the door of the *boulangerie* and almost swooned again at the smell. It was so, she couldn't put her finger on it—inviting, maybe? Comforting? Satisfying? No. Enticing? Perhaps. She closed her eyes and sniffed. There was yeast and warmth, a soupçon of something spicy like cinnamon, a sweetness she couldn't place and the inevitable tartness of salt; in fact she could have sworn that the heady aroma bore telltale traces of the coast.

Behind the counter, which was currently unmanned, row upon row of big, brown, round loaves sat side by side on wooden racks, staring out at her like smiling faces. There was no other bread in sight, not a baguette to be seen, just the fat round loaves, a basket of croissants and a bell. Esme felt herself shiver as she picked it up and gingerly rang it, the small sound seeming deafening to her, given what she thought she could well be soliciting by ringing it.

She stood there for a minute but nothing

happened, so she picked the bell up and rang it again, more robustly this time.

She heard a door slamming back in the bowels of the bakery and the sound of feet fast approaching. Her heart raced as she felt her cheeks burning and she tried to will them back to their normal color. The footsteps got closer and closer and Esme fought a sudden desire to turn and run, leaving nothing in the shop but the faint scent of Must de Cartier, which had fallen off the back of one of Charlie's father's trucks and which she saved for special occasions, wisping invisibly around the well-tanned bread *boules.*

A figure appeared in a flurry through the mesh screen door behind the counter (that slap of timber on timber again!) and Esme felt herself gasp. Could it be?

It was the same dark hair, similar black eyes, a smile that had threads of the one she had seen the night before but was nowhere near as dazzling. And all this on a face that was considerably older and a body whose circumference was perhaps double that of the one by which she had previously been transfixed.

"Bonjour, mademoiselle," the older, wider man said cheerfully. *"Qu'est-ce que vous voudrez?"*

"Oh," said Esme, suddenly unable to combine her fragments of schoolgirl French into anything remotely resembling a sentence. "Croissants, please," she said in her soft, confused British Isles accent. "I mean, *s'il-vous plait*. Four." She held up three fingers. *"Quatre."*

The man laughed. "English?" he asked as he scooped four fat pastries into a paper bag. Esme nodded. "You are staying here in Venolat?" She nodded again. "Yes," she said, "it's lovely. *C'est bon.*"

He held the bag out to her. "Anything else you would like?"

I would like to know where the younger, slimmer, sexier version of you is, Esme said to herself. To him, she said nothing, as she looked around the shop in a drawn-out overly contemplative fashion given that the shop was small and you could see all it had to offer in less than a second.

"What is your specialty?" she asked. *"Qu'est-ce que la spécialité de la maison, de la boulangerie?"* She grimaced as she tortured the wide man's language but his eyes stayed warm and friendly.

"It is plain," he said, "our specialty, but it is good. And it is certainly special." He picked up one of the round, brown loaves from the rack behind him and lifted it over to Esme. She looked at it uncertainly.

"Smell," the wide man said, shoving it under her nose. "Smell!"

Esme closed her eyes and breathed deeply. There was the warm yeasty smell that had enveloped her when she first came in. And the salt. And something else, too.

"Apple?" she opened her eyes and asked the baker. *"Pommes?"*

The little man grinned and for a moment there flared a devilish glint that Esme thought she recognized from that similar smile the night before.

"Yes, yes!" he nodded, pleased with her. "Not many guess that. We make this bread, *pain au levain,* from apple, very old apple. It's in the starter, the *chef.* A long time since. Not bad for *Anglaise!* Good. Good." He happily wrapped the bread in a sheet of bakery paper and passed it to Esme. "For you," he said. "For nothing. I mean, for no cost."

"Oh, I couldn't," she said. "You must let me pay."

"You can pay for the croissants," said the baker. "Twelve francs, thank you, *mademoiselle*—but the *pain au levain* is a gift from me. You can repay me by coming back again, yes?"

Esme fumbled in her purse for the change. What about the boy, she wanted desperately to ask. What about the boy? But the question stayed stuck inside her as she shyly gathered up her bread and pastries and, smiling at the wider, older baker, left the shop.

Every morning Esme repeated the journey. Every morning she convinced herself it had nothing to do with the boy. Every morning the question— where is he?—threatened to burst out of her like a fork of lightning but instead stayed broodily inside her head, hovering around like a dark cloud, furious and threatening.

After a week, the vision by the fountain started to quiver and become unclear in her mind. Details got lost. The beginnings of his hip bones, had she really seen them? she wondered. The glisten of his sharp pink tongue as he licked his cigarette paper—had that not been in a movie she'd gone to in London? Perhaps, she thought gloomily, the moonlight had played a cruel trick on her and nastily presented the chubby middle-aged *boulanger* as the man of her dreams, the man she was so sure was ready and waiting for her.

Stinking bloody moonlight. Who needed it, she thought crankily, as she lay in her bed yet another night, waiting for sweet sleep to put her out of her torment.

Two mornings later, though, something happened. When Esme woke up, it was not the man of her dreams who claimed her first thought. It was the *pain au levain*. She woke up tasting it, feeling its springy crumb bouncing around her mouth, its chewy crust battling her teeth. She took a deep breath through her nose to see if the smell could make its way from the bakery to her room and thought, with a tickle of her saliva glands, that it could.

She jumped out of bed, threw on an old pair of low-slung men's cricket trousers and a white tank top, and bounded down the stairs. Charlie was conked out in his ground floor pit but she knew he would be pathetically grateful to find the fresh bread ready and waiting for him when he awoke. They had given up the croissants after the first morning and concentrated instead on just the sourdough bread, which they ate with fresh home-made plum preserve Gerard at the *auberge* had given them. For lunch, they bought a slab of Brie from the Venolat corner store, which sold every-thing from fishing lines to Dickensian classics, and smeared that on the *pain,* washing it down with a bottle of Bordeaux before planning the after-noon's sightseeing or swanning about.

They fought over the crust. The crust made Esme's taste buds tingle. It was chewy and hard and had a powerful, almost cheesy, flavor. It was in the crust that the sour nature of the dough left its calling card. The crumb was spongy and shiny and almost sweet to the taste but the crust posi-tively sang with the sharp, tart notes of apple vinegar and yeast.

The thought of it spurred Esme on as she prac-tically skipped to the *boulangerie,* her mouth watering in anticipation. She flew around the corner and in through the *boulangerie* door, her eyes going straight to the happy smiling faces in their ancient wooden racks.

She opened her mouth to speak, but the *boulanger* got there first.

"Aha," he said in a voice so smooth just listening to it felt like being wrapped in warm satin. "The girl with the long red hair."

Esme's mouth stayed open, but nothing came out of it.

It was not the old, fat baker with whom she had been sharing staccato chitchat and jumbled talk of the weather for the past week. It was his younger, thinner shadow, the object of her moonlit vision here right in front of her doing all the right things in all the right places.

Up closer, in the light of day, he was even more beautiful than she had imagined, and she had been imagining a lot. Twenty-four hours a day, even. He was not tall, almost exactly her height in fact, and she was fairly sure his hips were not as wide as hers but he was wiry and strong, she could tell that, even though this time he was wearing a T-shirt.

His eyes were dark and shiny like pools of something mechanical and oily that fashionable shoes might slip on in a driveway. His skin was walnut brown and smooth on his arms, his neck, even his face, which looked as though it barely needed shaving.

"I'm Louis," he said. "Louis Lapoine."

Esme closed her mouth and gulped but couldn't think what the next normal step might be so just stood there, breathing undaintily, her heart thumping in her chest.

Louis smiled as though this happened all the time and reached for a loaf of bread, pulling out a sheet of wrap and placing it inside.

"My uncle tells me you are the only English

126

person this summer who has not asked for a baguette," he said, putting the bread on the counter in front of him and patting it.

Esme looked at the bread, then back at him. The words she had imagined saying were piled up in her throat, gridlocked.

"You are lucky to find us if it is *pain au levain* that you like," Louis said softly. "Nobody makes it much anymore."

Esme licked her dry lips and tried hard to breathe. She had not washed her face or done anything with her hair, which felt positively electric.

"The recipe has been in my family for nearly two hundred years," Louis continued, as though there were actually a two-way conversation going on. "It has not changed in all that time. That's pretty good, hm?"

Esme, appalled at her own hopeless mawkishness, nodded woodenly, for far too long, thinking as she did that she did not have on any deodorant or lip gloss and that she was acting like a complete idiot when this was in fact the moment she had been waiting for. She licked her unglossed lips again, gulped and forced herself to say something.

"It's beautiful," she finally managed in a creepy awestruck sort of a whisper, looking at the bread on the counter and thinking as the words slid off her tongue how they were totally the wrong ones to use.

Louis said nothing, just looked at her, the corner

of his mouth and one eye uniting in an expression that could have been amusement, could have been alarm. Esme couldn't bear to humiliate herself any further and so jerkily forced her frozen body into a forward lurch, grabbed the bread from the counter, let the coins she had ready in her hand bounce and clatter out of her grasp, then willed her awkward limbs to turn her around and walk out of the shop.

"If you come back at midnight tonight," Louis said coolly, astonishing her to a standstill at the doorway, "I will show you everything."

She turned and looked at him again, aware that she was having to try very deliberately not to drool. He nodded his head questioningly. Slowly, she nodded back. Then he smiled and disappeared through the screen door *(slap! slap!)*.

Esme stayed there staring for what seemed like forever. Her eyes remained focused on the spot where he had been, waiting for a sign that what she thought had happened had happened. And while no action replay ever came, Louis's velvet words still bounced around in her head telling her it was true, that he had asked her to meet him at midnight and he was going to show her everything.

It was too delicious for words.

"He's going to show you *everything*?" Charlie squawked when Esme jumped on his bed, woke him from his slumber and repeated every word of the conversation in the *boulangerie*, leaving out only the bit where she stayed tongue-tied and lumpish and deeply unsexy.

"You said, 'It's beautiful,' and he said, 'Come back and I will show you everything'? I wonder what sort of everything he means." Charlie sat up and rubbed the sleep out of his eyes.

Esme shook her head and shrugged her shoulders, biting her lip and buzzing invisibly with excitement.

"I just can't believe it," she said with a shudder. "It's like a dream, Charlie. You should see him. He is just so incredibly"—she searched for the right word—"*horny.*"

Charlie looked at her with renewed respect.

"Spoken like a real slut," he said proudly. "Details, please, mistress. Details."

"Well, if that pratty friend of yours with the cravat and the door-handle phobia was a three, Louis is a ten."

"You give Gordon a three? I say."

"I give any male with a pulse who does not vomit on me and has all his limbs a three. It's the nice thing to do," said Esme. "But probably Louis shouldn't be measured on the same scale as someone like Gordon. He's in a class of his own. Oh, he's just gorgeous, Charlie. I can't tell you! I've never felt like this about anyone before. It just feels so fantastically—aaarrgggh." Words failed her and she flopped onto the bed, her smile stretching as far across her face as it could manage.

Charlie gave her a funny look. "Don't get too carried away, old girl," he said. "It's just your hormones waking up after spending your whole entire life in hibernation, after all. You've only just met the bloke, for goodness' sake. If you even call it meeting him."

Esme snorted. "That's rich coming from you. You don't even bother meeting half the blokes you shag."

Charlie didn't laugh. "That's because I *only* shag them. I don't sit around for days mooning over them first and imagining myself walking up the aisle in a lovely white dress with a fur cape and a muff while my mother plays 'Here Comes the Bride' on a wheezing old organ."

Esme was stunned. Her invisible buzzing died away to a small but angry internal reverberation. "Don't you dare infect me with your bitter- and twistedness," she admonished, hurt and unable to hide it. "And in case you had forgotten, I don't have a mother so when it comes to wheezing old organs, you are the closest thing I possess." She got up off the bed and made as if to leave, relieved nonetheless to see out the corner of her eye that Charlie looked repentant.

"I'm sorry," he said reaching for her arm and grabbing it. "I don't want to spread my vile Charlie-ness any further than I already have; it's just that I don't want you being hurt, Es, or disappointed. Your expectations, you have to admit, are rather on the high side. But I mean, what say, for

130

argument's sake, Louis just wants to show you how to bake bread?"

"I can't think of anything I would rather see more," Esme said and she meant it. Nearly.

"Okay," said Charlie. "Okay. I believe you. I'm with you. Whatever you want me to do or say, I will do or say it."

They looked at each other and the warmth crept back into their friendship. Esme picked the loaf up from the end of the bed.

"Do you really imagine yourself in a white fur cape and muff?" she asked her friend.

"In the spring," Charlie answered without missing a beat.

By ten to midnight Esme's certainty that everything about Louis was fantastically "aaarrgggh" had given way to the deep conviction that she had imagined the entire scenario and should probably, in the interests of bakers everywhere, go on a gluten-free tour of Siberia.

Charlie had gone out in search of more (or was it less?) wayward Dutch boys, leaving Esme at home with her hammering heart, her topsy-turvy thoughts and half a bottle of Chablis, which she had taken in quick gulps between eight and nine thirty, for medicinal purposes only.

At two minutes to midnight she bolted out of the apartment feeling ridiculously Cinderella-ish and not at all sure that it wasn't the older, wider baker she was going to find whistling happily to himself behind the tantalizing bakery counter.

Rounding the corner, she saw the faint glow of the bakery inner workings reflecting off the side of the fountain. Her mouth started to dry up and her knees to tremble but she urged herself on, determined not to repeat her humiliating behavior of earlier in the day.

As she approached the yellow-and-white-striped awning, a black figure stepped out of the shadows, the red glow of a cigarette the only bit of it she could clearly make out. She stopped and the figure stepped into the moonlight. It was Louis.

Esme dumbfounded herself by laughing. The joyful sound, so light and happy, ricocheted around the little square, coming to rest neatly at Louis's feet.

"I was hoping you would come," he said in his glossy voice with its seductive lilt.

"I was hoping I hadn't dreamed the whole thing up," Esme answered, relief that she hadn't loosening her tongue. She reddened, which she hoped Louis couldn't see, and looked at his feet. He was wearing white canvas espadrilles and she could see the bones of his ankles. She suddenly felt sick with the hopelessness of never having kissed that part of him, of any man.

Louis threw his cigarette butt on the ground and crushed it with a mesmerizing twist of his hip.

"I have been trying to guess your name," he said. "You did not tell me."

"Esme," said Esme. Louis looked surprised.

"Esme," he repeated. "That's French, no?"

Esme was not equipped to convincingly lie at this point. "No, it's Scottish actually," she said. "It was the name of a highland terrier that belonged to my mother's next-door neighbor." He did not need to know this, but she did not seem able to shut up. "It was run over," she twittered. "The terrier. By the neighbor. Terribly sad, really."

Louis looked at her curiously and laughed. "Come," he said, "I will show you inside."

He held out his hand and Esme, with almost indecent haste, reached for it. At the touch of his skin against her palm she could have sworn she felt a shock, and when he tightened his fingers around her hand she feared she was going to lose it completely. The feel of him, her first feel of him, just this tiny little bit of him, left her begging, drooling, praying for more.

Inside, the front of the bakery was in darkness and the dim light shone out through the screen door. Louis pushed it aside and led her through into a narrow hallway lit with wall-mounted lanterns and smelling fragrantly of loaves past and present.

At the end of the hallway they passed a closed doorway and just beyond it turned down a set of ancient golden stone steps trodden on so often over the years that smooth dips had been worn in the middle. The stairs hugged two walls, turning a corner halfway and delivering Esme and Louis into the heart of the bakery.

For a moment Esme just stood and soaked it all in: the smell, the feel, the taste, the promise of what was to come. She licked her glistening lips, her mouth watering.

The ceiling of the basement room was curved, as if built in a giant archway, and the bricks were burned from golden brown at the bottom to chocolate brown in the middle to pitch-black at the top. The smell was tantalizing, so thick she could almost feel it, and the air was heavy and hot. She was glad she had worn just a thin white camisole and a vintage waist petticoat with her own espadrilles. The three hours spent choosing the outfit seemed now not to have been such a scurrilous waste of time after all.

The heart of the bakery was smaller than Esme had imagined. Along one wall sat a big mechanical stainless steel mixing machine, next to it a long wooden bench empty apart from a dusting of flour and an old-fashioned set of scales. The opposite wall was filled with wooden racks, and at the end of the room through another small arch Esme could see the wood-stoked fire not unlike the wood-fired pizza ovens she had seen in Italian eateries at home.

"Someone has been baking bread down here for nearly six hundred years," Louis said, his eyes following hers as she took everything in. "First it was the monks who lived in Venolat—it was once a monastery, did you know?—and for one hundred eighty-nine years it has been the Lapoine family."

Esme traced a four-finger squiggle into the flour on the wooden bench, then inspected her floury fingertips. She wanted to know more about the bakery, the bread. But mostly she wanted to know more about him.

"You speak such good English," she said.

"My best friend is English," Louis said. "The family moved here when we were both thirteen—that is seven years ago now—and we do a trade. I teach French. I learn English. It is good to share, no?"

He eyed Esme's top with a look she was sure was going to bring her out in blisters.

"It is good you wear white," he said. "You will not go home dirty."

Oh, but I want to go home dirty, Esme silently trilled. Very, very dirty. So dirty I will never be clean again.

Louis watched her watching him, then looked up at a dusty antiquated clock and clicked his tongue. "It is time for me to start," he said. "If you sit on the stairs I can see you and tell you what I am doing. Okay?"

Louis took off his T-shirt, revealing the corrugation of his ribs on his brown, smooth chest and the silky black hair of his underarms. An army of goose bumps stood at attention from one end of Esme's body to the other.

He turned his back on her and she counted the muscles and sinews shifting and changing as he reached up and opened a chute coming down from

135

the ceiling. A rush of flour hurtled into the steel mixing bowl. He closed the chute, turned on a tap sticking out of the wall and filled a tin bucket with water, which he also tipped into the bowl.

He turned the machine on and its gently rhythmic chugging filled up part of the room.

"In here," Louis said, somehow barely needing to raise his voice above the noise, "we keep our starter or our *levain*. You know what this is, no?"

Esme shook her head, her shiny, clean, twice-conditioned curls still bouncing way after her head had stopped moving. Louis turned to catch this and smiled.

"Sourdough, or *pain au levain* as you know we call it, does not use yeast the way a baguette does, the way other bread does. We make our own yeast, our own rising agent, the *levain*, from the bacteria in the air, in this air. We made it for the first time one hundred and eighty-nine years ago with the juice of three apples from my great-great-great-great-great-grandfather's only tree."

Louis laughed, a sound so sweet to Esme, despite the underlay of the mixer, that it seemed like singing.

"Great-great-great-great-great?" he said. "Do I get that right? Yes, I think so." Esme watched his shoulder blades stick out and recede again as he dipped his hand into the swirling dough. "Anyway," he continued, "we make the *levain*, or *chef* as some people call it, my uncle for one, way back then and every day we use it to make bread,

136

then leave a bit behind for the next day, and the natural yeast in the *chef* becomes stronger and stronger and after all this time, you can see, well, you know, that it makes very good bread."

Esme imagined running her fingers up his spine. "How did apple juice ever make bread in the first place?" she asked.

"The apple juice ferments, fermented with the natural yeast in the Venolat air," Louis said, turning the mixer off, pulling out the dough hook and continuing to mix with his hands. "After a couple of weeks, maybe, the many-greats-grandfather added flour and water, and every day after that he added more flour and more water, and then the *chef* got a life of its own. Finally, it had enough strength so that when he added it to more flour and water, it provided the gas to make the bread rise."

His earlobes looked edible. Esme was entranced. "How did he know when it was strong enough?"

"He just knew," answered Louis. "Plus it would have been not a good color and maybe it didn't smell so good. Sharp, like vinegar."

His elbows were exquisite. "And it never got so stinky you had to throw it away and start again?"

Louis stood up and turned around to face her, a light film of sweat shimmering on his forehead, one black curl plastered down above his eye.

"No, no, no," he said. "Stinky is not a bad thing. We would never throw the *chef* away. It is what makes Lapoine bread Lapoine bread. It is our special ingredient. The heart of the *pain au levain*. It makes us what we are."

Esme stopped lusting and felt mortified. Here he was trying to share his passion with her and all she could do was ask idiotic questions. Her face must have registered her dismay because Louis's eyes softened.

"I mean that it is what we have. And if we had something different, we would not be making our bread, we would be making someone else's. *Tu comprends?*" He smiled at her and Esme noticed a little vein throbbing in his temple, the sight of which made her lips ache.

"Now I leave that dough in the mixer for two hours," said Louis, turning toward the counter and pulling from beneath it a huge wooden box on wheels, "and I work with this dough in the *pâtissier.*"

He bent over the antiquated box and Esme's eyes traveled the length of his spine, memorizing every knob. She felt a trickle of sweat down her own backbone and lifted her hair up from her neck, a welcome breeze down the stairwell providing brief respite from the heat.

Louis pulled out a handful of the dough and half threw, half plopped it on the scales, which had they been given time to settle would have proved dead even. After he'd done this half a dozen times and gotten it exactly right, Esme laughed out loud.

"How do you know?" she said.

Louis shrugged his shoulders, an enticing gesture from behind, and kept going. "Practice makes perfect, don't you say?" he said. "I have been working down here since I was seven years old. A *boulanger* can tell these things."

When the counter was full of the right-sized dough lumps, Louis pulled out from underneath the far side of it a stack of willow baskets lined with linen inners and one by one coddled each blob into a loaf-sized shape and slipped it into the basket. Then he pulled a low-wheeled tray over from the other side of the room and stacked the baskets, four on each layer, one on top of each other, then filled another counterful of baskets and repeated the process until the dough was all gone and the stack was taller than he was.

The rhythm of it was hypnotic. No movement, no moment was wasted. He weaved and worked his way around the baskets like a wisp of smoke. His concentration was captivating. Esme was spellbound. She felt intimate with every drop of sweat on his shoulders.

They had not spoken in nearly an hour when Louis carefully wrapped the stack of baskets with a large linen sheet and turned to Esme.

"Draft is no friend of *pain au levain*," he said. "But me, I need fresh air."

He stood on the stair next to Esme and held out his hand again. She took it, panicked that this meant he was dismissing her, that perhaps he had only meant to show her how to bake bread, that

that was it. When what she needed he had not even started on. She followed him up the stairs trying not to show her reluctance. Could he really be going to send her home with just the feel of his hand to dream about?

"What's in here?" she said, in a stalling maneuver when they got to the top of the stairs by the closed door.

Louis looked at her, with those deep dark eyes, and opened the door, flicking on a light switch that bathed the room in watery light. It was full of flour. Big white sacks of the dusty white powder were stacked against all four walls and the room had the most incredible smell, almost of nothing, but definitely of something. Esme was trembling although the room was pleasantly warm. The heat of the bakery downstairs had left her sweating and the beads of sweat were now prickly on her skin. She was hearing things, feeling things, tasting things that she could not recognize, but she could have sworn she could smell the wheat the flour once was.

She turned to ask Louis where it all came from but he was standing so close she could think of nothing but what flavor his lips were. She looked straight into his eyes and saw herself in them, shaking visibly with anticipation, and when he put his hand on her arm, it was all she could do to keep from crying out.

Ever so gently, his fingers caressed the same spot on her arm until it felt like they were burning a hole in it and she thought she was going to have to pull away. Instead, she moved infinitesimally closer until just the slenderest gap separated them. He moved his fingers farther up and down her arm, circling, deliciously slowly, her elbow slightly bent as her hand lay resting on the front of her thigh.

Gradually, he fingered his way smoothly and seductively up to her shoulder, all the while their eyes meeting, their chests rising and falling in perfect time.

He wants me, Esme thought, and with it came a rush of warmth so overwhelming she nearly stepped back. She had never before wanted someone who wanted her back. It was a moment to savor and cradle.

It was also a moment to explore. And seduced by her faith in what she was feeling, it was she who leaned in toward his exquisite face and sought out his lips with her own.

He tasted of bread. Sweet and sour at the same time and wonderfully, wickedly, wantonly warm. She drank him in. Could not stop.

She felt like a fizzy vitamin tablet that had just been added to water. She bubbled. She dissolved. She was desperate for him.

Louis groaned beneath her lips and pulled her closer to him, his tongue exploring her neat white teeth and his hand sneaking up underneath her camisole and pressing against the small of her sticky, sweaty back. She pushed herself closer. She thrust her hips into his. She wanted to disappear into him. To never come back. Her yearning overwhelmed her.

His other hand moved up behind her neck and snaked under her sodden hair as he pulled her into him. She ran her fingers over the wetness on his back, frantically tugging him to her despite them already being as close as two human beings ever could be. They staggered slightly, then righted themselves, still lost in the kiss.

Louis shuffled his thighs against hers, forcing her slowly backward, and Esme let him, would have let him do anything, anything but leave. When the back of her calves hit something solid, she drew away from his lips momentarily—but died without them!—as he lowered her onto a stack of flour sacks.

Esme wriggled back and pulled up her legs so Louis could climb in between them. Then she reached for him again and pulled his warm, delicious mouth close to hers. How had she lived without his kiss all these years when now even a moment without it and she was lost? She pushed his wet hair back from his face, unsticking the curl that had been there all night, and licked the throbbing vein in his temple. He groaned again and lowered himself onto her as he buried his face in her neck.

She felt the weight of his body on hers and treasured every pound, every ounce.

He lifted his head and she licked his ear and his

neck and worked her way back to his lips again. Her kiss was drenched in a desire that went further, much further. But oh, to be kissed by this man! Esme didn't want it to stop. She wanted more. She felt his firm practiced fingers run up and down her abdomen, then creep underneath her camisole. Louis's hand ran up her rib cage and found the nipple that had been waiting for him. Slowly, he circled it so tenderly the tension in Esme's harp strings nearly pinged. How the other lonely nipple cried out for attention! Louis slid back toward the floor then looked up at her with shining eyes, but her own were closed as she relished every second of his touch. She felt her skirt being tugged below her hips, his tongue flick over her hip bone, circle her belly button and move, his hands at either side, up her chest, until his lips found that lonely nipple, standing now and begging for him.

For a moment she disappeared. Just went. Somewhere she had never been before and could not describe in words. Somewhere heavenly. When she came back, another practiced hand had slithered under her skirt and into her bikini briefs. She lifted her hips, barely breathing, so he could get them off. It was the most natural thing in the world. She knew what to do and when to do it. She had no fear, no doubt; it had all been choreographed perfectly and she knew her steps.

Louis's fingers knew theirs, too. She was dough in his hands, his breadmaker's hands. She rose beneath his touch. And while he kissed her and kneaded her she soared out of her body, the bakery, the village, the world, until she swam drunkenly around in the starry ether, feeling things she had never, ever felt before.

He wants me, she sang, as the linen of his pants melted away and his hip bones met hers, joint to joint, heat pumping ferociously from one to the other, and she groaned in a voice she had never heard before.

CHAPTER 7

When the alarm went off at six on the fourth floor of the House in the Clouds the morning after Esme's champagne and pot-smoking spree, her heart was beating far too quickly, but at least this time she could lay the blame squarely at the foot of Charlie and his oversupply of good-time substances.

Her daily panic seemed to be sitting higher in her chest than it normally was, but she tried not to think about that, pushing it back down inside herself. Bread, she thought, bread.

She slipped out of bed, wincing slightly at the throbbing in her head and saw, to her surprise, she still had her boots on—and nothing else. She glanced guiltily at Pog and pulled her shoes off, promising quietly to herself as she did so that she would never drink again, or smoke anything, nor encourage Charlie to come and stay or in fact ever speak to him again. He was lethal. She'd forgotten that about him. And she was not up for lethal these days.

Scraping around in her dresser for something suitably hangoverish to wear, she pulled out a cream cotton turtleneck that had on the one hand long since lost its shape but on the other gained a softness that she knew would feel nice next to her skin, which felt poisoned and fragile and over-stretched.

As she sat lightly on the bed and pushed her feet into her slippers a sharp snort from the other side heralded the awakening of Pog. He rolled over, snuffling, opened his eyes and attempted a smile, despite his bleariness. His face was creased with marks from his pillow and his thick difficult hair was all bunched up high on one side of his head. He looked so much like a little boy, so much like Rory, just like Rory, exactly like Rory, that for a moment Esme's entire body filled up with something hot and suffocating and she wondered if she could actually bear it.

"Are you all right?" Pog asked her, croakily in a grown-up man's voice. "Is everything all right?"

"Ssshh," she whispered, aching with the hope-lessness of her love for him. "It's just morning. It's just bread time. Go back to sleep."

Pog's eyelashes started to flutter immediately back down to his cheeks and his smile relaxed and slowly disappeared. Esme blew him a silent kiss and headed for the stairs.

"I love you, Esme," she thought she heard him say but when she turned around he was lying there, still and fast asleep.

In the kitchen, she moved silently around in just the light of her candles, which cast fairy-tale shadows off all her favorite things: the juicer, the colander, the vase of pink and white peonies, the old jug full of wooden spoons and stirrers.

It was a clear morning but windy, and the sails on the windmill next door kept catching her eye through the east window as they sluiced gracefully and quietly through the morning air.

She pulled her jar of starter out of the pantry and remembered, with a shudder, what had gone on the night before. What had been said. What had been meant. She forced the matter out of her mind with a tuneless whistle as she dragged out the bin of flour, trying hard not to let its wheatyness seep into her consciousness and poke about where her memories were hidden.

Holding the starter as far away from her nose as she could, she mixed all her ingredients into the big caramel bowl then pushed and pummeled the dough around the warm ceramic sides in an easy steady rhythm until it formed the beginnings of a loaf. She tipped it onto the counter and left it sitting, pert and plump, while she fed the starter again, wiped up any spilled flour and returned the bin and the jar to their places in the pantry.

She added the salt, then pushed up her sleeves to prepare for kneading the dough a second time. The feel of her hands on her arms as she did this, of skin upon skin, rang an ancient bell, but she stilled it. This was ridiculous! She had been making sourdough for fifteen years and it was not about Louis. It was not. It never had been. Well, perhaps a little, in the beginning but not now. There could be nothing of his Venolat starter left in her own, or at least so little as to barely count. A few tiny grains perhaps but nothing in the great scheme of things. She had not been getting up at sparrow's fart all these years just to cling to the pathetic remains of her long-lost love. That was a whole lifetime ago and so much had happened since then. So much that had nothing to do with him. Since him she'd managed a career, marriage, motherhood and a heartbreak that made the one he caused feel like nothing more than an insect bite.

So what was he doing now occupying so much of her mind?

She pressed her palm down into the dough and rolled it around the bowl, feeling it growing silky and smooth beneath her fingers. She flinched as she thought of herself wailing the night before about Louis and happiness. What on earth had possessed her?

Her arm felt tight and strong and the dough beneath her hand like naked, human flesh. Not a million miles removed, for instance, from the soft roll of her own middle. She fleetingly imagined a brown finger on her white skin. Toyed with teethmarks that did not bear her husband's signature of a wayward incisor. A tantalizing flash of past happiness streaked in front of her again.

Get a grip, she told herself, oiling the bowl and carefully placing her dough inside it to rise. Get a grip.

She felt a light film of sweat on her forehead, and as she lifted her hand to her head to wipe it away she caught sight under her armpit of Charlie leaning against the handrail at the top of the stairs wearing nothing but running shorts and clutching, if she wasn't mistaken, a newspaper. He looked unreasonably healthy.

"Work. I could stand here and watch it all day," he drawled.

"And good morning to you," Esme answered, hoping he could not tell what she had been thinking. "What have you got there?"

"Went for a run to clear the head," Charlie said, walking across the kitchen. "'Appropriated' the *Times* from outside the Tea Shop."

"Get it away from me!" shrieked Esme, waving a tea towel at him. "Throw it in the bin! Get it out of my sight!"

"Steady on, old girl," Charlie said, dropping gracefully into a chair and opening the newspaper across the table. "It's the *Times*, not the *Sport*."

From halfway across the room Esme could see Jemima's flawless face peering at her from the masthead, trumpeting the triumph of her column. Her headache returned. She felt sick.

"Remember Jemima Jones?" she asked Charlie, dully. "That conniving little madam who shafted me at *TV Now!*?"

Charlie nodded. "The pretty blonde with the legs up to her neck? Yes, I remember her."

Esme flicked her tea towel in the direction of

the glamorous photo on the front page. "Still pretty, still blond, still legs up to her neck, now spitting out perfect children and going to every la-di-bloody-da function in the land and writing about it."

"For the *Times*? Really?" Charlie was clearly impressed. "Sounds like just the sort of thing you might have done once upon a time."

If that was true, it was no wonder Esme felt so enraged. She slumped into a chair and pulled out the Style section.

"Anybody else and I wouldn't mind, truly I wouldn't," she insisted as she opened it up. "But some people just get all the breaks and it's not fair. You shouldn't be allowed to be gorgeous looking and lucky. It promotes ill feeling."

Jemima smiled out at her, wearing a gold bikini, her hip bones razor sharp, a sparkling blue swimming pool in some fancy new resort in the Maldives twinkling behind her.

The sun and a wrinkle-free visage good friends do not make, Esme read, *but when one is invited to fly first class to Toss Kroker's newest luxury hotel to party with 400 beautiful people and dine on lobster cooked fifty different ways by Gordon Ramsay, Alain Ducasse and an entire village of minions, one simply ups the dosage of Ambre Solaire and throws a thong or five in the Birkin bag!*

"Oh for Christ's sake!" protested Esme but Charlie was lost to the finance pages.

I confess, she read on, *I was a little hazy as to the*

whereabouts of the Maldives until I got there and saw Jodie Kidd, Joseph Fiennes, a Hilton or two, Bryan Ferry and Helena Christensen all sucking Perrier, or should I say Laurent-Perrier, out of tiny bottles by the pool. Why, who needs to know where you are when you know who you're there with?

Toss has done a wonderful job of throwing up this modest little 350-room palace with nine restaurants, three bars, two nightclubs and enough Philippe Starck to render the rest of the world sadly bereft of egg-shaped baths. Plus he's had the good sense to poach Christien, the foot god from the spa at Claridge's, so no tiny toenail goes unclipped or unpolished. And for just a hundred pounds you can even get your urine checked at the Matt Roberts gym to find out if you should be on the treadmill or the yoga mat. Don't ask me how that works—I was concentrating solely on ingesting fluids.

"Who says 'ingesting'?" Esme demanded. "Nobody, that's who."

And speaking of fluids, Jemima continued, *is it just me or are the cocktails on the party circuit getting more and more fruity as time goes on? I would just like to point out that a martini is a martini and there is not and never will be a substitute. If you make it with sake, it is not a saketini, it is mouthwash. And if your name is Bruce it is not a brucetini, it is something you found in the Matt Roberts "laboratory" in the Maldives. If you have the imagination to invent a new drink, for goodness' sake invent a new name as well.*

151

"What's wrong with calling a martini made with sake a saketini?" Esme wanted to know, jiggling Charlie's paper to get his attention.

"Well, if it's made with sake it's not a martini," Charlie said. "It's another drink altogether and probably not a very nice one."

"Oh, shut up then," Esme muttered crossly. "If you are going to agree with everything she says you can just go back to your stocks and bonds."

"All right then, read me out a bit and I promise not to agree with it."

"'*Mysteriously non-aging Lothario Jeffrey Timms,*'" Esme read out loud, "'*threw an extremely high energy fortieth at a friend's villa in Little Venice during the week. "It's amazing, really," a crinkled blonde slurred to me in the hallway, "we went all the way through school together yet I've just turned forty-six."*'" Charlie let out a hoot of laughter, which Esme quashed with a look. "'*Mr. Timms, fueled by nothing, I am sure, that ends in "tini," greeted guests at the door with a display of cartwheels and handstands, made all the more exciting by the fact that he was wearing a kilt, sans undergarments. Still, he was the belle of the ball until the caterers set fire to a side of beef and the local fire brigade turned up, fully dressed and oozing truly youthful charm. Next to them, Mr. Timms' offering seemed somewhat dry and withered, to say the least.*'"

Charlie could not contain his mirth.

"But it's not funny!" Esme said.

"It is so!" he sputtered. "An old wrinkly Jeffrey

Timms cartwheeling down the hallway with a dry and withered offering? Normally, you'd think that's hilarious."

"I would not."

"You would so!"

"I would not."

At that moment, Rory saved them from drawing out their childish spat by appearing at the top of the stairs, in his karate suit; his hair, Esme noticed, brushed neatly back and, if she was not mistaken, slicked down with some of the hair gel she was constantly buying Pog. She had wondered where it was going as it certainly wasn't ending up on her husband's head. "Hello," the little boy said with feigned nonchalance to Charlie.

"You're up early," Esme said, entranced by Charlie's effect even on a small boy. Was that normal? God! What if Rory was gay? She contemplated this possibility as she abandoned the newspaper and absently got her son's breakfast together. Actually, come to think of it, she would probably prefer he was gay. Little Cosmo Jones was clearly gay, after all, and that didn't seem to bother anyone. Rory could go into business with Pog as an interior designer and he would never get the neighbors' teenage granddaughter pregnant or wear dirty jeans that looked as though they were about to fall off his hips or a smelly sweatshirt or a baseball cap on backward.

The sound of her possibly gay son fishing around in the pantry brought her back to earth as Rory emerged with a blue-and-white-striped Cornish-ware jug. "Very nice," Esme said looking at it. "Fashionably modern yet authentically retro. What made you choose that one, darling?"

"It's the only one I could reach," answered Rory plainly. "Come on."

"You know what," said his mother, "I've got a fantastic idea. Why don't you take Charlie out and he can show you how to milk The Goat."

Before Charlie could finish his snort of derision, Rory had grabbed him by the hand and was tugging him toward the stairs. Charlie turned back to Esme with a disturbed look on his face. "How many steps down?" he groaned, as Rory pulled at him. "What's a goat again? Is it the one with the twisty horn on the front of its head?"

"That's a unicorn, silly," said Rory. "They don't exist."

"Help, Esme," Charlie whined pathetically.

"I'm sure your magic works just as well on the animal kingdom as it does on the human one," Esme said with a sweet smile. "Think of it as a challenge, Charlie. Now go and do your thing. Rory will help. Oh, and there are plenty of wellies by the door—I strongly suggest you grab a pair." She never had got around to poo patrol. She sliced herself a wedge of yesterday's bread, almost better than fresh with one day under its belt, smeared it with blue cheese and quince paste, poured herself a cup of tea and moved a kitchen stool to one of the tiny windows for a good view of what was about to happen in her garden.

From her position near the clouds, Esme could see The Goat tense up as she lifted her head from the newly planted nasturtiums on which she was feasting and clapped eyes on the boys coming toward her.

As Charlie and Rory moved nearer closing in on The Goat, however, Esme was amazed that instead of leaping away at great speed in the direction of whatever was handiest, more often than not a nerve-shattered Brown, The Goat stood her ground. As the familiar little boy and the strange new man approached she simply looked at them with interest, her head cocked to one side in a contemplative and not particularly combative fashion.

"Don't tell me the bloody Charlie Edmonds charm *does* work on goats," Esme said to herself as she pressed her face closer to the window and Brown, eager to stay wherever The Goat wasn't, pressed his head against Esme's knee. "Unbelievable!"

In the garden, Charlie and Rory got within five yards of The Goat before Rory's confidence clearly gave out and he stopped and handed the jug up to Charlie.

Rory pointed at The Goat's rear end and Charlie's gaze followed the little boy's finger. Esme could not see the look on his face but just imagining it gave her a thrill.

She sipped her tea as Charlie took a tentative step forward. The Goat, whose face Esme could see, seemed to be looking almost coquettishly at him. Esme could swear the ruminating bloody mammal was batting her eyelids as Charlie came right up to her and slowly, slowly, slowly, apparently taking instruction from Rory, started to bend down and proffer the jug toward The Goat's nether regions.

At that moment, the delightful creature spun around, quick as a flash, lifted both hind legs in the air and kicked Charlie so hard in the bollocks that he staggered backward, the jug flying in the air as he tripped over a spade lying in the grass behind him, and fell on his behind at Rory's feet, clutching his groin and clearly in considerable pain.

Esme, her smirk gone, leaped to her feet, the stool screeching across the floor behind her, and ran to the stairs, leaping down them and shouting in panic, "Pog! Pog! The bloody Goat's got Charlie!" Brown skittered and scampered behind her as she bounded down the stairs two at once, still a time-consuming effort, grabbed a tennis racket from the hallway and dashed outside and around the side of the house to where she could see that The Goat was now scratching at the ground with her front hoof, clearly getting ready to charge her wounded foe and his little friend.

"You evil bloody bitch!" Esme cried as she ran toward them, hurling the tennis racket in her fury as she did. Charlie was sitting up, looking pale and shaken but clearly conscious at least and Rory was crouched behind him, being brave but obviously frightened.

The tennis racket sailed nowhere near the offending animal—Esme had never been good at throwing things—but The Goat saw it all the same and did not appreciate the sentiment. Turning her attention away from the boys, she narrowed her nasty little eyes and instead launched herself with an almost balletic spring after the exposed and weaponless Esme. Esme gasped and spun around, only to see Henry coming out of the house toward her, red in the face and waving his stick. Despite her fear of being mauled by The Goat, her dread of leading the vicious animal to her father-in-law and having to live with the consequences of that forced her to half-spin again and swerve around the other side of the house. If she could make it to the gate, she reasoned, trying not to hear the rat-a-tat-tat of The Goat's hooves beating a frightening and fast approaching rumpus behind her, she could probably jump it, despite her jeans being a size too small, and leg it up the steps of the windmill to safety.

"Help!" she gasped, as the hoof beats got closer. The Goat had very pointy horns, after all, and hysteria was snatching at Esme as she imagined those horns piercing her bottom and removing big chunks. "Help!" Her bottom was not her best feature, but she was attached to it, nonetheless.

The fence lay straight ahead hardly more than ten yards away as Esme's legs burned with adrenaline and her breath tore at her lungs. She was so close! But not close enough. With an evil rent, she felt something rip at the denim of her jeans just behind her left knee, and hysterical and panicked, she stumbled and plunged forward with a desperate cry, hearing as she did a terrifying clanging followed by a spine-chilling shriek and a loud thump, none of it anything to do with herself hitting the ground.

Gasping for air and in a state of total confusion, Esme realized that she was still alive, but that it was very quiet. She twisted around to see Charlie towering, perilously close to her, over The Goat's motionless carcass, which lay near her feet. The shovel he was holding appeared to still be vibrating slightly, which left Esme to assume that The Goat had worn it around her head with quite some force.

Before she could think or speak or move, Henry limped around the corner, equally breathless and agitated, with Rory gingerly bringing up the rear.

Esme watched their faces fall at the awful sight of The Goat lying there with her tongue hanging out of her mouth and blood dribbling out of her nose. At that moment, Pog's head, wet from being in the shower, appeared out of the window on the fourth floor above them. He squinted, as if he couldn't quite make out what he was seeing.

"What on earth is going on?" he asked.

Henry had not yet regained his breath, Charlie was still stunned at the level of his own violence and Esme remained riding an emotional roller coaster between bewilderment, horror and hysteria.

Only Rory had the wherewithal to answer his father.

"The Goat's dead, Daddy," he said with much less emotion than one might have expected. "She kicked Charlie in the nuts and he killed her."

Esme grabbed at a lungful of air and looked up at Pog, who was frowning now in a strict fatherly way.

"Don't say nuts, Rory," he said. "It's not nice."

She felt a small amount of astonishment that her husband would correct her son's language, mild really in the circumstances, when a family friend had just killed their goat. It didn't seem entirely appropriate.

"Well," she said, ignoring Pog and getting carefully to her feet, examining herself for serious injury, "you know what Granny Mac would say."

She looked at Rory, who looked straight back, his face remaining blank for a few seconds until like the sun breaking through the clouds on a bleak, gray day, it lit up, transforming the entire landscape of his personality. "There's bin a murrrrrder," he cried enthusiastically in a perfect Scottish burr as he beamed at his mother, then Henry, then Charlie. "There's bin a murrrrrder."

There was a split-second's silence before Charlie

and Esme both started to laugh. Rory, thrilled with this impact, started jumping up and down around the dead goat shouting, "There's bin a murrrrder! There's bin a murrrrrder!" while Pog retreated inside the window.

Henry, shaking his head with customary disgust, ignored everybody and moved stiffly closer to The Goat, prodding her corpse with his stick.

At this, the infernal creature scared the living daylights out of the lot of them by leaping to her feet in a show of being very much alive. Esme shrieked, Rory ran behind his grandfather and Charlie's hands flew to his aching private parts to protect them from further attack.

The Goat, however, had quite lost her vicious streak. She stood wobbling on all fours, then blinked and teetered unsteadily toward them, like a nervous young hostess trying to keep her composure after overdoing it on the vodka tonics. Esme and Charlie stood aside and watched as she proceeded to walk straight into the side of the house. She remained there, her head against the wall, as they all looked on.

"Yes, well," said Charlie. "Not a murder after all, eh? Not even manslaughter by the looks of things."

Henry pushed past him, leaning heavily on his stick. It must have hurt his hips getting down the stairs so quickly, Esme realized and felt, briefly, bad for him.

"Much as you find this all terribly funny," he

said in a cold, pinched voice, approaching The Goat and reaching for her collar, "it would probably be a good idea to take the poor creature to the vet."

Pog's head popped out the window, two stories below where it had been before, placing him on the landing between his father's floor and Granny Mac's.

"Did you say the vet?" he asked. "Really, Dad. Do you think that's absolutely necessary? It's Sunday, it will cost a fortune."

"The Goat has been hit very hard in the head with a shovel," Henry said through clenched teeth, "and now appears to be blind." He looked at Charlie. "The least we can do is take her to the vet in case she needs to be put out of her misery."

Charlie thought about offering to go another round with the aforementioned garden implement but decided against it, instead going to Henry's aid and pouring on his charm.

"Of course, sir," he said, "you are absolutely right. I shall take him myself and meet the cost, of course. It's entirely my fault. I'm most terribly sorry." He patted The Goat's back, rather awkwardly, and indicated for Rory to come and help him.

Esme turned to assist her father-in-law, but he shrugged her off and hobbled unaided back toward the house. She looked up to where she had last seen Pog and saw that he was still there.

She smiled. "Don't worry, Pog," she said. "All under control."

A couple of hours later, after Charlie had taken The Goat to the vet in his Audi convertible—causing quite a stir in the village by all accounts—and the animal had indeed been proclaimed blind but in all other respects remarkably healthy, he and Esme sat in the kitchen drinking tea and reliving the event.

"Well, I can't see Nigella Lawson topping that, Es. You should really have your own column."

"Don't talk to me about columns," Esme shot back. "You *friend* of Jemima Jones."

"I don't think Jemima Jones is the problem," he said.

"God, you and Granny Mac!"

Charlie looked confused, but plowed on.

"About last night, Esme," he said carefully. "I'm worried about you, sweet."

Esme put her cup down on the well-scrubbed oak table and felt an acute attack of embarrassment. "It was all that champagne," she said quickly. "I didn't mean it. I don't know what I was talking about. God knows where it came from. It's not about Louis, Charlie. That was years ago. I probably wouldn't recognize him if I fell over him and he probably wouldn't even remember me. I was just Holiday Romance Number One-hundred-and-seventeen."

"No you weren't," Charlie said with such uncus-

162

tomary tenderness that Esme found herself pressing on.

"It's just that sometimes," she said, "when things get on top of me, I wonder, that's all."

"Wonder what?"

"Wonder what it would be like if things had been different, back then, in Venolat, if it had turned out differently. If he and I had ended up together. It's silly, Charlie, really it is, but when things are tough I just remember that feeling of being in love with him and it was such a wonderful feeling. So strong and powerful and all-consuming. Delicious, really. And I wonder what it would be like to feel like that again." Her mind started to drift into the comfort of her memories. "Nothing could permeate that feeling, Charlie. It was so strong. Nothing could beat it or ruin it. It made everything seem perfect." She stopped, suddenly feeling naked and silly. "Well, you know what I mean. You're the expert after all—falling in love every five minutes."

Charlie looked blank. "I'm not the one to talk to about love, Esme. I wouldn't recognize it if it came up and bit me in the backside. I'm more of a lust chap, really. Less complicated that way."

"There must have been someone, Charlie, somewhere along the line who was different—someone who made you feel sick and obsessed and despondent and ecstatic and crazy and all mixed up."

Charlie laughed. "Why would anyone want to feel like that? It sounds horrible. I've felt very attracted to people before, obviously, and wanted to rip their clothes off sort of thing but all that other business sounds dreadful. Why would you want to put yourself through it? I can't remember you putting yourself through it with Pog. Did you?"

"Pog was different," Esme said. "I love him plus I know for a fact that he loves me but"—and she hated the sound of that little word—"it's just not like it was with Louis."

Charlie looked at the old railway clock on the wall above Esme's head and pushed back his chair.

"Crikey, I'd better be going," he said. "Sorry to not be more help, Es, but you know I'm hopeless on the deep and meaningful stuff and much as I would like to stay and deafen your sheep or amputate your bees, I am actually pretty whacked after blinding the goat so I should head off." He came around the table to kiss her good-bye, then caught sight of Jemima in her gold bikini, still lying brazenly on the table.

"Bloody hell, is that her?" he breathed. "Nice boobs, I must say. She's looking pretty fantastic, isn't she, Es? Well, I can see why you are miffed. She looks smashing. God, look at those shoes—they must have cost her a fortune, twelve hundred quid, I'd say."

When Esme realized he was not joking, but truly impressed, she snatched the page of the newspaper up off the table and screwed it into a ball.

"Thank you for your support, Charlie," she said.

"This is the woman who is taunting me with her global success and all you can do is ogle her slingbacks and leer at her fake boobs, which are of no use to you whatsoever."

Charlie snatched the page back and unscrewed it. "I really don't think they're fake, I hate to tell you," he said, looking as close as it was possible to without seeing only colored dots. "Of course, I'm hardly an expert, but still . . ."

Esme grabbed it away from him and ripped it in half.

"I don't know what you're so put out about," Charlie said. "Jemima Jones might be bitter and twisted about not living in a giant birdhouse in the country, for all you know. It's just a matter of choice, Essie. You made yours and she made hers. It's as simple as that. She just gets better shoes."

Esme gave him a not completely playful slap on the back of the head.

"If I had wanted advice from the Dalai bloody Lama," she said, "I would have invited *him* here for the weekend, not you. And I wouldn't have such a crippling hangover either. Now, on your bike."

CHAPTER 8

I've just caught Ridge shagging the next-door neighbor!" Alice cried into the phone a week later. "In his room—at ten o'clock in the morning. Sunday morning! Mrs. bloody Miller, of all people. Oh, Es, what am I going to do?"

"Calm down, calm down," Esme soothed. "Which one is Mrs. Miller? The blowsy midmorning gin drinker or the mousy beige librarian?"

"Neither," said Alice, "she's the sexy, saucy newlywed, you know, from directly upstairs."

"Blimey," breathed Esme, "the one who married the meaty, beefy, big and bouncy kickboxer?"

"Yes," cried Alice. "What am I going to do? If the meaty, beefy, big and bouncy kickboxer finds out he will squash Ridge like the useless little worm he is."

"Well, how's he going to find out? She's not going to tell him and neither is Ridge, I imagine. And you're not either, I hope. Alice, what are you thinking?"

"I'm thinking it's too hard to be the mother of a teenager." Alice's voice cracked. "I don't feel grown-up enough. Nothing I do is right and nothing he does is right, either. It's horrible. Like being at war, or something, but without the rules. I liked it when he was little and I was all he had and he loved me. I'm sorry, Esme. I know you don't need this but I just can't help it."

"Oh, Alice," Esme said, feeling dreadful on her friend's behalf, "he still loves you, it's just hormones. It's normal to be shagging everything that moves when you're his age. You were."

"You weren't," cried Alice. "You saved yourself. He idolizes you, you know, Esme. He looks at your lovely family with your house in the country and your doting husband and your Labrador dog and he wonders why he couldn't have had all that."

Esme was staggered. "The house needs round-the-clock cleaning," she said. "The dog uses its bladder as a weapon and I did not save myself, I was a retard. I just never fancied anyone that fancied me until, you know, Louis. It wasn't a good thing. I've never been able to quite get him out of my system. I probably should have boffed Acne George from down the road when I was sixteen after all—got it all over and done with and got on with things."

Alice's sniffling got quieter. "You still have Louis in your system?"

"A bit," said Esme, wishing she hadn't said anything. What was Louis doing in her thoughts, in her conversations? She had been battling him all week. But like those invisible grains of Venolat flour still left in her jar of starter, bits of Louis remained ingrained and untraceable in Esme herself. "Well, a bit more than a bit, I suppose." She caught her bottom lip between her teeth and willed herself to stop it there. "Less than a lot, though," she continued brightly. "I'm just thinking about him at the moment because Charlie's been here and sort of raked the whole thing up a bit."

"What do you mean, raked the whole thing up?"

Why don't I just shut the hell up? Esme asked herself. "Oh, you know. Talking about Venolat and the boy I left behind sort of thing. Dredging up all those hideous old feelings. Oh, it's too silly to even talk about Alice. It's pathetic!"

"What do you mean, those hideous old feelings? You barely even mention Louis to me."

Alice and Charlie had never really hit it off and over the years continued to vie rather childishly, Esme often felt, for her friendship. At first, she'd thought the antagonism between them might have signaled a hidden attraction but she'd been wrong. It had just been antagonism and in recent years it had proved more peaceful to keep them well apart.

"It's nothing," Esme said in exasperation, "just some ridiculous middle-aged fantasy that keeps my mind off things and helps me while away the seconds between cleaning the oven, ironing the clothes, scrubbing the toilets, that sort of malarkey."

"You *fantasize* about him?" Alice stressed. "Well,

that sounds like more than thinking about him a bit, if you ask me. That's thinking about him a lot, in my book."

"Can we stop talking about this now?" asked Esme. "I am sure you have far more exciting tales of the lovelorn and heartsick than I do."

Alice, in her search for a man who could provide her son with a male role model and give her the odd roll in the hay, had become addicted some years earlier to blind dates. In the early days, when Ridge was first at school and she realized she didn't have to spend the rest of her days alone, she had expected rather fancifully to perhaps meet a good-looking, well-off, professional male about her own age to whom she might get married and with whom she could perhaps raise a family.

A decade later, all she asked was that they not lunge at her in the first ten minutes and at least buy their own drink.

She had tried dating agencies, dinner clubs, singles' nights, speed dating and answering Personal ads in the *Guardian,* the *Financial Times* and *Time Out.* She had been to more bars, cafés and pizza joints than she cared to remember and knew every kink and bend in the Thames—she had been on that many river cruises—plus she was on first-name terms with the ticket collector at the London Eye. But what Alice, and subsequently Esme, had learned over the years was that no single man that she would ever contemplate marrying and raising a family with would ever join dating agencies or dinner clubs, attend singles' nights or speed-dating sessions or place/answer Personal ads in the *Guardian*, the *Financial Times* and *Time Out*.

They were mostly already married to someone else or deeply odd. In just one memorable week a few years back Alice had dated an addictive gambler, a little person, two alcoholics, a one-armed paperhanger (seriously) and an albino with eye-watering body odor.

After five years, she realized she was never going to meet a husband. But after five years, she also realized that blind dating was cheaper than renting a movie and, most of the time, more entertaining.

Now, she just did it for fun.

"Did I not tell you?" she said into the phone to Esme. "I thought I had a normal one on Thursday. I've had three living-at-home-with-mothers in a row. Honestly, if I never see a mustard-colored hand-knitted cardie again it will be too soon. Anyway, on Thursday I go to Rockwell in Trafalgar Square—oh, I'll have to take you there next time you're down—and in walks this gorgeous-looking creature, six feet tall, full head of hair, impeccable clothes, naturally I never thought for a moment it was him."

"Shoes?" asked Esme.

"Punched leather brogues," answered Alice. Experience had taught her that if you spent one second looking at a blind date's shoes, you could generally save yourself a lot of spittle and mind-numbingly boring conversation about the inner-most workings of the Central Line.

"And?"

"And so eventually it becomes clear he is waiting for someone and I am wondering if, please God, it could be me so I go up and ask him if he's Andrew, and he just looks at me and smiles this beautiful smile, Esme, and then he says, 'Good Lord. You're not what I expected.' Anyway, then he buys me a drink, some vodka thing with coriander and mint in it, and we have a perfectly normal conversation about George Dubya Bush and I'm nearly creaming myself thinking, 'I don't believe it—he's perfect!' when he says: 'Enough small talk, let's go up to my room.'"

Esme squawked with excitement. "What did you do?"

"Well, it has been more than a year and he was gorgeous and I did fancy him like mad so I said, 'You're staying here?' and he said, 'We are all staying here.'"

"We all who?" Esme wanted to know.

"Exactly," said Alice. "So he stands up and takes my arm and starts to lead me to the lift, which is when I notice a spotty-looking geek in a bright yellow anorak carrying a bicycle seat and craning his neck around the room as if searching for a certain someone."

Esme groaned in sympathy. "Another Andrew?" she guessed.

"Another Andrew," Alice agreed. "Turns out

punched-leather-brogue Andrew is a lawyer from Edinburgh down on some big conference and he was first in line for a prostitute he and his mates had ordered up for the night and assumed I was she."

"Did you think about going through with it?" Esme asked.

"Think about it? I suggested it and do you know what he said?"

"Do I want to know?"

"He said, 'I can get it for free at home. I want to pay for it. That's the point.'"

It was an awful business, Esme had to agree. Especially as it turned out the correct Andrew was actually someone Alice had been on a blind date with once before. She didn't recognize him until he started talking about his pet hamster, Nigel, who had died when he was fourteen, leaving emotional scars that were clearly not anywhere near healed. Worse still, he had not recognized her at all.

"That's a good one," Esme had to admit. "But imagine if you had gone up and fornicated with the horrible lawyer and then he'd flung all this cash at you."

"Yes," said Alice drily. "Imagine. How terrible. Anyway, it's just as well really. One fornicator in the family is enough." She sighed.

"What are you going to do with your fornicator, then?"

Alice cleared her throat. "He is grounded for

the rest of his natural life," she said. "And I am not going to let him watch cable for a week."

"Oh, that will really show him," said Esme supportively. "And what exactly do you expect him to do with his spare time when there is a saucy neighbor upstairs just waiting until she hears your footsteps in the hall so she can put on her negligee and pop around for a cup of milk?"

Alice groaned. "I never thought of that," she said wetly. "What's the opposite of grounding someone?"

Rory appeared at Esme's knee, a frown crinkling the flawless skin above his earnest brown eyes.

"'Scuse me, Esme," he interrupted politely.

"Just a minute," Esme said to Alice, holding the phone away and pulling Rory's face toward her to give it a kiss. He smelled of dog, but it was still delicious.

"What is it, darling?" she asked him.

"We want to go fishing."

Esme looked out the window; the sea mist that had clung to the trees all morning had lifted, leaving it a spotlessly clear blue day.

"On the Meare? What a wonderful idea. I'll check on you with Daddy's binoculars, shall I? You could take your pirate flag and wave it at me."

Rory looked uncertain. "Aren't you coming?" he asked her.

"I'm just about to put the bread in, darling. It will be piping hot and crunchy just the way Daddy likes it by the time you get back. You run along and have fun." She kissed his orange curls. "Bring me back a whale," she called after him, turning back to the phone.

"She's not coming," Rory told Henry, who was waiting outside his room for his grandson.

"She's not coming," Henry told Pog when they picked him up at his shed.

"She has to put the bread in," Rory said, reaching for his father's hand.

The three of them walked to the Meare in silence. The morning mist had clearly kept the crowds away and no one was out on the water yet. Ducks huddled beneath the picnic table waiting for the crumbs to come.

Pog pulled a wooden dinghy into the shallow water and helped Henry climb stiffly into it, then hoisted Rory and his fishing rod inside, and jumped in himself, picking up the oars. Like most locals, they paid Mrs. Coyle fifty pounds a year for the right to use the rental boats whenever they wanted to as long as tourists weren't left queuing. About once a fortnight, weather permitting, they came out; but on their last few excursions Esme had been missing.

It was quiet, the bark of a distant dog and the sound of the oars hitting the water all they could hear. Rory was facing his father, his grandfather behind him. The little boy's rod lay at his feet; his attention was turned to the House in the Clouds, straddling the trees above them.

"Daddy?" He turned back to his father. "Is there something wrong with Esme?"

Pog kept rowing, didn't falter, didn't meet his father's eye.

"No, Rory," he answered. "There's nothing wrong with Esme. She's fine."

His oars dipped in and out of the water, loudly dripping fat droplets back onto the smooth surface. Henry coughed, uncomfortably.

"She's been grizzling in Granny Mac's room," Rory said.

"In Granny Mac's room?" Pog asked casually. "Whatever do you mean?"

"I've heard her," Rory answered. "Sometimes there's laughing, too. Isn't there, Granddad?"

Pog looked over Rory's head at his father and raised his eyebrows. Henry gave a shrug.

Pog sighed. "Your mother's just sad, Rory," he said. "But she'll be all right. You just have to let her be sad for a while."

"How long?" Rory asked.

"I don't know," Pog answered truthfully. "But she's baking bread again and that's a good sign, don't you think?"

Henry felt panicked by the rawness of emotion onboard the little boat. It was too close for his comfort.

"I think I just saw a carp, Rory," he said. "Do you have the bait?"

Pog stopped rowing and pulled the oars onto his lap, then passed the rucksack over to Rory.

"Esme likes bread more than anything, doesn't she, Daddy?" Rory asked, pulling out a hardened heel of sourdough, his chubby little fingers having trouble getting the hook through the crust.

"Not more than anything, Rory. It's just very important to her. Dad, could you help him with that? He's going to hurt himself." Pog dipped the oars back in the water and gently rowed them back to where Henry had seen the carp.

"Why?"

"Why is it important to her? Well, you know that story, Rory. Mummy went to France when she was just a girl and a baker gave her the magic ingredient for her special bread and she's baked it every day since then."

"Why?"

Pog had asked Esme this question himself when he first met her and on many occasions since then. And all Esme had ever done was smile her secretive smile and say, "Because it makes me feel good."

"Because it makes her feel good," Pog told his son.

"Why?"

"Oh, Rory, do we have to play this game?"

"Yes, I thought we were here to catch fish," Henry said grumpily. There was something in his tone that rankled with Pog and with a start he realized that his father's uneasiness was mirrored in his own churning stomach. Was Pog turning into a man who could fidget and bluster and ignore what was going on right in front of him? He thought he had been doing the right thing, leaving time to heal Esme's wounds, not digging deeper into them himself. But what if he was wrong? What if he had let Esme be sad for too long already? What if he was just being Henry all over again?

Pog looked up at the House in the Clouds and felt all the things he wanted to say to her float up toward the surface, stopping just short of it, like heavy logs in a busy river, lethal but invisible. No, he was different. He knew his wife. She just needed time. He was sure of it.

"I'll tell you what, when we've caught our fish we'll go and buy some of Mrs. Coyle's homemade chocolates, shall we?" he suggested, spinning the little dinghy around. "And the Sunday paper. That will cheer her up."

Esme at that exact moment was being cheered up anyway, courtesy of Charlie Edmonds, who had just rung to invite her down to London for lunch the following day.

"Time to dust the cobwebs from your glad rags, missus," he said. "Meet me at the Orrery in Marylebone High Street. Their scallops will leave you drooling."

Her good humor, however, did not last long. The chocolates only went halfway to assuaging her irritation at having Pog hand over the latest installment from Jemima, the first one of which had apparently proved so popular the paper had increased the amount of space dedicated to it.

"Oh, I am going to *vomit*," Esme dramatized later that afternoon as she sat on Granny Mac's bed, flapping her hand at invisible smoke and blanking out "The Killing of Georgie." "It's just revolting, Granny Mac, it really is. The gall of this woman. Honestly. I can't believe they publish it. There should be a law."

Granny Mac scorched her with her indifference.

"I don't know what all the fuss is about," she said. "You never got your knickers in a twist when Bridget Jones got her own Diary."

Esme threw the newspaper aside. "Bridget Jones didn't have a diary," she said, "it was Helen Fielding and that was entirely different. For a start, I don't know Helen Fielding, and for a finish, even if I did know her she would not have tricked me into hiring her then slept with my boss and turned him against me and trashed my magazine and left me lying in the gutter with only crumpled pages of the *Daily Mail* for cover while she went on to be rich and fabulous."

"And you say this Jemima has a gift for fiction. Come on, Esme, was it really so bad, what she did?"

"I can't believe you would take her side," Esme railed. "I might have ended up having her career if I had played the game the way she did, stepping on everybody with great big spiky heels and burning bridges from here to kingdom come. It just doesn't seem fair. It could be me with a fancy column in the *Sunday Times*."

Granny Mac failed to get even remotely worked up. "I didn't realize you wanted someone else's career," she said drily. "Here was me assuming you were happy with the one you had."

"Mine was hard work!" argued Esme. "I had to work my arse off for twelve hours a day to earn probably half what Jemima Jones gets for being a serial gate-crasher between seven and nine and giving little Cosmo his Balinese bloody back massage in the minutes between her facial and her hair-moisturizing treatment. It just seems to come so easily to her, Granny Mac. It always has."

"And you wanted it to come more easily to you?"

Esme could barely understand her own chagrin, let alone explain it.

"Maybe if things had come easier," she said, "if I hadn't had to work the bloody hours, to try so hard . . ."

"What?" Granny Mac asked softly. "What might have been different?"

Esme closed her eyes and tried not to think about the chaos, the turmoil, the devastation, the end of her life back in London. Her thoughts felt murky and dangerous and her head full of confusion.

She opened her eyes and concentrated instead on the photo of Jemima.

"Will you look at the size of that rock!" she exclaimed, suddenly noticing the diamond on

Jemima's wedding finger. "It must be four carats at least. It's bloody enormous."

"Well, are you going to read me what the wretched woman has written or not?" Granny Mac boldly demanded. "A person could die of boredom lying here listening to your blathering all day long."

Esme shook the broadsheet newspaper for dramatic effect and started to read.

"'*What a week—why, my feet (thanks for the pedicure, Christien!!) have barely touched the ground. It started on Monday night with an evening of thespian brilliance at the newly refurbished Court Theatre in N1. I didn't quite make it to the play itself—Marie Claire was getting her first bikini wax and needed my support—but the drinks afterward were a riot. Gorgeous leading man Lin Forbes and I spent ages sipping courtinis (!) and discussing the pros and cons of being supertalented. In fact, we'd probably still be there now if pregnant single supermodel Minty Kloss hadn't caused such a sensation by turning up in a teeny-weeny Hawaiian skirt and a bra made of coconut shells, not fully grown ones either, by the looks of them. Apparently, she had gotten her invitations muddled and a luau in Brixton was sadly minus her presence. Anyway, as if her entrance wasn't quite enough of a spectacle, offering up one of the coconuts as an ashtray some time later certainly was. She's not even going to feel that little head shooting down the birth canal it will be so small. Lucky her.*' God, she's horrible!"

"Not all sweetness and light like yourself, Esme, I can see why you find her so grating," said Granny Mac. "And anyway, what's a luau?"

"It's a Hawaiian party of some description, I believe," she said.

"In Brixton? Is that so?" breathed Granny Mac. "She leads a grand old life, does she not, your Jemima? Come on then, keep reading."

Much as she would have liked to feed the paper piece by piece to The Blind Goat at that moment, Esme found herself lured back to Jemima's drivel.

"'*Next night,*'" she continued in what she thought was a simpering tone, "'*music lovers will appreciate how lucky I was to be invited to a private concert at the London home of Lady Lucinda Grierson-Robbe, who was hosting a special perform-ance by celebrated cellist and conductor Rostrov Millopopovich. The eighty-three-year-old living treasure has been given just a few short months to live and so was making his literal musical swan song at the home of Lady Lucinda. What an event. Unfortunately, I just missed the concert as Cosmo needed picking up from Ceroc classes and Rostrov had toddled off to bed by the time I got there—he doesn't breathe too well these days apparently—but Lady Lucinda has redecorated since I was last at her home so the trip was not entirely wasted. She's so brave going back to chintz but what a palette! Her SW1 home is a veritable smorgasbord of florals. Really, it has to be seen to be believed.*'

"That is *so* rude," said Esme. "I can't believe

how rude she is. Can you believe how rude she is? It's just plain rude."

"Get on with it, will you," Granny Mac exhorted her.

"'*Sadly I had to forgo attending the celebrity premiere of the new movie by that Finnish film director who wins so many awards in favor of spending some quality time with GQ, our middle child, who's very clever, especially at mathematics. I think he'll end up in banking like his father. Anyway, the poor child is being persecuted by his schoolmates for his dedication to his studies. I won't tell you what school, that would be unfair—but all nasty little boys in blue-and-gray-striped blazers should be very careful or they'll feel the grille of the Volvo station wagon on their backs. Just joking!*'"

Esme was so disgusted by that stage, she threw the paper down on the bed for the last time and left the room. There were dirty clothes to be washed, washed clothes to be ironed, ironed clothes to be hung in closets, an oven to be cleaned, floors to be mopped, an old man to be attended to, a small boy to be entertained and a husband to catch up with. She did not have any more time to waste on Jemima Jones.

CHAPTER 9

On the train down to the city the next morning Esme wondered why she had chosen to wear her La Perla bra, from the good old days, when she was at least a size bigger than she had been when she bought it and the underwire was practically slicing her in two.

It was a stiflingly hot day and she was overdressed. At one stage, the humidity was so overwhelming that she retreated to the loo and took her nylon-mesh-and-Lycra-mix top off, letting the breeze through the window chill her armpits while she splashed her face with cold water.

However, the possibility of the train crashing and flinging her near-naked body into the countryside to be identified later by her bereaved husband got the better of her and she put the top back on.

She hadn't mentioned to Pog, in the chaos of the morning, that she was going to be in London for the day. She had simply dropped Rory around the corner to Mrs. McArthur, who looked after him sometimes when he wasn't booked in with Mrs. Monk, and then made her way directly to the station.

So far the day had been a nightmare. Rory had woken up evil with grumpiness, Henry's hip was obviously giving him trouble so he had a permanent black cloud above his head and Pog had been completely preoccupied by an early-morning phone call from Ernie Albrecht, who lived on the main road to Stonyborough and was considering adding a pergola to his dumpy little house.

As a result, her nerves were so jangled that she had nearly burned the sourdough, which never happened. After all these years she had developed a built-in timer in her head, and her nose could pick up from as far away as Gaga and Jam-jar's the scent of her bread being almost ready to come out of the oven.

She could tell, too, just by smelling the air, if one of the power surges they suffered so often at the House in the Clouds was affecting her dough, if the oven needed to be turned down four or five degrees or if one of the steam jets was clogged, thus not sufficiently hardening and crispening the crust in its area.

That morning though, she had been so busy trying to wax her own legs, get Rory out of his Spiderman pajamas, clean cobwebs and bits of orange goop off Brown, who had been somewhere disgusting, comfort The Blind Goat, who had become quite paranoid about the outside world and kept head-butting the front door trying to get inside the house, listen to Pog talking about some coach lanterns, put a load of washing on, tidy the kitchen and pick some zucchinis because another busload had pulled up the previous day and taken photos, that her nose had nearly let her down.

She'd been out in the garden when Henry of all people had opened a window and simply said in that clipped, controlled manner of his, "Bread, Esme." It was amazing how two such ripe and juicy words could shrivel and die on the wrong lips.

She'd only just caught it in time. It was a little darker than usual but on the right side of the cusp of being damaged. The crust would be extra hard and sharp and there'd be a bite, a zing to it that wouldn't be there on a perfectly cooked loaf, but the crumb would be unhindered. It would still be delicious. She had planned to freeze it, as neither she nor Rory were going to be there for lunch, but as she'd grabbed the kitchen cloth and leaned down to wipe glitter (who knew where that came from?) off her shoe, she'd seen the loaf sitting there looking embarrassed and had been unable to resist it.

After all these years, every loaf still made her mouth water and her heart hop. It was silly, really. But still, she snatched it off the bench, wrapped it in grease-proof paper and popped it in her tote bag to take to Charlie. He would probably dump it in a garbage bin on the way home from lunch, but she didn't need to know that.

Anyway, in all of this she had not mentioned her plans for the day to Pog and, sitting sweatily as the train clattered toward London, it occurred to her that she probably should have left a note. As the train pulled into Liverpool Street station, she surreptitiously patted her dampening armpits and pulled down the front of her top. High-necked but vaguely see-through, it gave her excellent cleavage, which while wasted on Charlie made Esme feel saucy again and it was hard to feel saucy these days given that she was usually covered in animal hair, up to her armpits in compost or covered in glue and sticky paper while Rory sat in a corner saying in that calm, grown-up little voice of his: "But you said you *knew* how to make a kite."

On the underground from Liverpool Street to Marylebone, her nose caught flashes of the familiar and comforting sharp, sweet smell of her bread and she was pleased she had brought it with her. Once upon a time London had felt like a comfortable old coat that could be slipped on for any occasion and went with absolutely everything, but now it felt like a leather bustier, size six: perfectly admirable, enviable even, on someone else, just not right for her.

Marylebone High Street had undergone a complete personality transplant since she'd last been there. Once a slightly dowdy, often forgotten poor relation of its fashionable neighbors Soho and Mayfair, it had become something of a spangly starlet in its own right. There were smart-looking bars and coffee shops wherever she looked and trendy furniture and clothes shops, too. There were even enough people on the street to give Esme a good jostle—whoever would have thought? She checked her watch and was slightly dismayed to find herself with twenty minutes to wait before meeting Charlie at the Orrery. The thought of twenty minutes to fill did nothing for her: her mind being full of things she could be doing, should be doing with twenty minutes at home.

She tried to start dawdling toward the restaurant but this required some skill as Esme was not a dawdler by nature. She did everything at a hundred miles an hour, she was known for it. Even before pregnancy and old people and animals, loitering had not been an option. In the magazine world, everything was done at a rush to meet, or at least not miss by too much, ridiculous deadlines, plus there had been the whirlwind of her social life to consider. She may have edited an odd hodgepodge of titles, but the invitations had come thick and fast, nonetheless, and then there was her own circle of friends to keep up with and Pog's, too.

Motherhood had slowed her down, obviously, but not that much. Not enough, anyway, Esme thought, bashing the thought away and abandoning her lingering and deciding to go to the restaurant and have a posh cocktail, a somethingtini no doubt, after all.

The Orrery did look beautiful; she could see why Charlie liked it. Beautifully understated, not much color, not much noise—the exact opposite of Charlie himself really, but the menu read so well she had to fight hard to keep herself from salivating.

"You must be Esme." A waitperson of around twelve years of age, Esme gauged, approached her, somewhat surprising her by knowing her name.

"Well, I know it's a big deal for me to go out for lunch but I didn't expect everyone to hear about it." She smiled.

The waiter smiled back. "Mr. Edmonds has called and sends his apologies but he's going to be half an hour late. Would you like to wait in the bar? My colleague Michael is in there all on his own and he makes a mean French 75."

"Is that the one with gin and champagne?" Esme asked. "Because I had six of those once before and I never did find that camisole again." With a jolt she realized what she was doing: flirting with a boy young enough to be her son. She really did not get out enough.

"You know there's a Conran Shop next door," the boy said, kindly ignoring her, "if you're not keen on a cocktail."

The Conran Shop was full of willowy wisps wafting around either shopping or working there, it was hard to tell which. Esme sucked in her stomach even though her Lycra mix was supposed to do that for her and tried her best to waft, too, although the concentration involved in wishing she had enough money to buy some of the beautiful furniture kept distracting her.

Rounding a corner on the second floor of the store, however, she happened upon a sitting receptacle of the utmost elegance, a Barcelona chair, and her stomach popped right out again as she admired it. Pog had often rattled magazines in her direction and pointed out the exact same chair, a big square combination of leather and chrome apparently designed for the king and queen of Spain, and all Esme had done was pour scorn on the cost—one thousand pounds, indeed. For a chair? That didn't even turn into a sofa? Just think of the shoes and handbags she could buy with that.

But in the flesh, the chairs were rather inviting. Deciding against the white one for fear of dirtying it, Esme sat herself grandly down in the black one, wriggling her way to the back of it and stretching her legs out in front of her, luxuriating in the feel and comfort and price.

She closed her eyes and for a moment imagined being the queen of something but almost immediately her stomach began to rumble and she was reminded that lunch was the reason she was in London, yet lunch was what she had not yet had and precisely what she needed. She opened her eyes and stood up, or tried to, but something held her back, kept her from rising.

She knew instantly what the problem was and it made her feel sick. It had happened to her once before on a bench in Clapham Common. She thought about the tube and how she had lurched

189

off it at Marylebone station. A belch of panic worked its way up from her hungry stomach. She was 99 percent sure she was stuck to the chair with someone else's gum.

Taking a deep breath, she wrenched herself sharply up and away, but unable to look at the chair, she instead swiveled her skirt around so that its back was at her front and sure enough, a great gob, even worse, half a great gob of baboon-bum pink bubble gum was smeared across the rump of her skirt, stringy tentacles hanging from it. Slowly, she turned around to inspect the £1,000 chair—the other half of the gum was there, sitting plum in the middle of the black leather and looking not very big, at least, but extremely pleased with itself.

Why did these things have to happen to her? She bet nothing like this ever happened to Jemima Jones. She must have picked it up in the train. Was that why the sweet seller at the station had eyed her rear end with such a grin? A grin she had mistaken for admiration?

A lissome brunette wearing a Conran Shop badge rounded the corner by the elevator shaft and Esme sat herself back down on the offending chair (avoiding the goop) so quickly that both her knees clicked, drawing the pale creature's attention.

"You all right there?" she asked, not stopping, as she glided by.

"Fine, fine, really. Absolutely fine," Esme

answered, recognizing the panic in her own voice and trying to counter it with a smile that felt frightening from the inside, never mind what it looked like on the outside. The assistant moved gracefully on, her eyes blank, and disappeared through a door behind the cushions.

"Fu-u-u-uck," Esme whispered under her breath as she scrabbled in her bag, looking for the Barbie manicure set Rory had given her for her birthday and insisted she take with her everywhere. "Fuck, fuck, fuck." The feel of her bread underneath its paper wrapping did nothing to calm her but she did find the pink zip-up purse, extracted the metal nail file, then slid to the floor on her knees. After a furtive glance to check for staff she leaned in over the chair and started to scrape at the splatter of gum on the soft hide with the nail file, lifting the stuck bit up around its disgusting sides as carefully as she could.

She was making good progress when the whish and whoosh of the elevator machinations distracted her. Someone was coming to the first floor! She picked as quickly as she could at the gum, relieved to see that it had not done too much damage to the leather beneath it. A small stain, perhaps, but nothing that some lucky soul with a spare £1,000 would spot without a magnifying glass.

The elevator whizzed and burred behind her as it approached, making her hands tremble. She didn't want to rush the delicate surgery at hand for fear of botching it but she didn't want to be caught doing it, either. The sticky mess was so close to being removed—so close, but not quite there.

The elevator doors clanged open and Esme again whispered, "please, please, please," under her breath as she tried desperately to get the last of the gum off the chair. Suddenly the last obstinate sinew miraculously came away, and concealing a whoop of joy, she looked up just as an exceptionally well-dressed, dark-haired, dark-eyed, dark-skinned man walked around the corner from the elevator shaft, saw her, looked away, then stopped still in his tracks and looked at her again.

The world, for a moment, seemed a strange and unfamiliar place. More like space, Esme thought afterward, where ordinary things float around in slow motion.

For a while nothing happened. They simply stared at each other in disbelief. But there could be no doubt. She knew at once that it could be no one else but him. She could feel it in the air between them. It was Louis, long-lost Louis, rising from the ashes of her past and standing there staring at her.

"Esme," Louis finally said in his voice made of melted dark-chocolate Hershey bars. "Esme, is that you?"

"Yes," Esme answered in a voice she recognized not from screaming at Brown or placating her son or discouraging her vegetables but from many, many years ago, "of course it's me."

They stared at each other again, unsure as to what to do next, until Louis took a hesitant step forward.

"You are on the floor," he said gently, reminding Esme exactly where, indeed, she was. With a hiccup of jerky movement, she stood, then made a crucial mistake. She ran her hand through her hair, which she often did when rattled. But she was not often holding a Barbie nail file complete with recycled gum at the time. On this occasion though, she was, and once the still relatively juicy blob made contact with Esme's unwieldy collection of curls, it glued itself to a hundred strands of her strong red hair and did not want to come out. When Esme realized this, she wanted to die. She stood there, her hand in her hair, knowing she only had two choices, to leave the hand there, or bring it out without the nail file. Neither seemed fetching.

"Esme," Louis said again, his voice penetrating Esme's embarrassment. "Are you all right?"

Esme looked at him, opened her mouth to speak and shut it again. Was she dreaming? Was it possible that just when her thoughts had been so cluttered with images of the French lover from her past, he should appear right in front of her?

That was when Louis smiled. It was a slow smile that started in the cupid's bow in the middle of his mouth and spread outward to the upturned corners where it crept up his cheeks and crinkled his eyes. Inside, she crumpled.

She had imagined, of course, the way she suspected many grown-up women did when it came to the subject of their first love, especially on days when they were up to their armpits in shitty nappies, that she and he would be reunited one day. Of all the fantasies in all the world she had simply not fathomed one as outlandish as this.

After all, here, standing in front of her was the man whose very name to her defined longing, defined lust, defined true, true love. He occupied a space in her head that no one else in the world had ever or could ever share, could even come close to sharing.

Of course she had lain awake at night, especially over the past couple of years, with Pog's safe, squashy body next to her purring with snores as she imagined cruising the Grand Canal in a gondola in Venice, Louis sitting opposite her stroking her feet.

Naturally she had fantasized, on the nights when Rory wouldn't settle without her there beside him, of returning to Venolat alone and finding her old lover leaning against the *boulangerie* door, lightly dusted in flour, a roll-your-own cigarette hanging from his lips and a look on his face that said, "What took you so long?"

Of course she had thought of him when she worked her bread. Who had she been kidding? Every time her pale strong hands kneaded the dough from the starter Louis had given her all those years ago, she thought about him, just fleetingly, and mostly about his skin. How smooth it felt. How salty it tasted. It was her favorite part of him and the silky dough as it rolled and shifted beneath her touch always reminded her of it. It didn't mean she loved Pog less. It just meant she remembered loving Louis. She remembered it well.

And now, after all this time, after so many dreams and imaginings, here he was standing right in front of her and a slightly soiled Barcelona chair while she had someone else's Hubba Bubba gummed up in her hair.

Her hand dropped limply to her side and she shook her head slightly, feeling the nail file wiggle and wobble above her right ear. She had not been prepared for this. She was clueless. She did not know how to get the gum out of her hair. She did not know how to confront the man who had stolen her heart, or at least borrowed it for a few wild, wonderful weeks, then broken it. And if she didn't know how to do either of those things separately, she sure as God made little green apples did not know how to do them together.

Louis's eyes soaked all this up. And then he simply took another step toward her, reached out and took her hand.

"Come," he said, and tugged gently at her. Esme felt the tingle of his flesh on hers and the years dropped away as though they had never existed.

Every cell in her body vibrated with joy at being reunited with the forgotten sensation of Louis's touch. She felt an overwhelming urge to gasp or cry or scream or something. She floated on air, she neither knew nor cared where she was going, she simply let herself be pulled by him, everything she knew about herself melting away and falling on the floor in invisible puddles behind her. Wherever Louis wanted to take her, Esme realized, she would go. Whatever he wanted her to do, she would do it. Never mind Pog. Never mind Rory. Never mind The Blind Goat and the father-in-law and the House in the Clouds. This was it. This was her destiny. Her escape. He was the one.

"Excuse me, mademoiselle," the one said, the sound of his voice extracting Esme from her trance. Louis had taken her to a counter and he was now using his mesmerizing tone to address a languid clone of the brunette she had seen earlier. "Have you some scissors I may borrow for a moment? My friend is in need of them."

He looked back at Esme and smiled again, giving her hand enough of a squeeze to nearly stop her heart. Then he took the scissors from the baleful girl at the desk, gently released Esme from his grip and moved closer, so close that she could feel his breath on her neck, and it sent goose bumps so intensely up her spine she felt each and every one separately.

Holding the scissors in one hand, with the other he lifted up the hair from the back of her neck,

196

and Esme felt the cold shock of the shop's air-conditioning tickle the sweat that her thick red curls had up until then concealed, every bead revealed sending shivers through her body.

Slowly, carefully, Louis ran his fingers up behind her ear through the tangle of her hair, inching his way gradually, his fingers firm and hard on her scalp, making tiny circular movements with his strong, clean, breadmaker's hands.

I am going to have to tell him to stop, Esme thought, fighting to keep from closing her eyes and groaning with pleasure. I am a married woman about to behave very badly in a posh shop with the man who broke my heart fifteen years ago. I am going to have to scream at him to stop. But the feeling of his fingers on her head, the smell of him, the force of him, the ecstasy she was holding at bay: She was totally powerless to fight it.

Louis himself came to her rescue. His fingers located the stuck nail file and stopped their rapturous head rub. Deftly, he isolated the curl on which the gum was riveted and in one seamless move, snipped at it with the scissors, then plainly presented Esme with the nail file, its sticky little friend and about six inches of one of her copper-colored ringlets.

It was a disgusting sight, like something left way too long at the bottom of a handbag, and Esme wished he would throw the whole sorry mess away. It occurred to her then, though, that she should probably say something. That she had said nothing since confirming that she was who he thought she was when she first saw him. But words escaped her. Words saw what was in her head and ran a mile. Words formed a picket line and refused to let her cross it.

Louis raised his astonishing eyebrows, leaned over the counter and gracefully dropped the file, gum and curl into the wastepaper basket. Then he stood up straight and looked at her again.

"Bloody hell," said Esme at last and her heart thumped as Louis smiled his slow, spreading smile again.

"My pleasure," answered Louis as though she had just thanked him, which, she realized with a clunk inside her head, was exactly what she should have done.

"Yes, yes, of course," Esme said, taking hold of her senses and lining up words in an almost orderly queue to make an entire sentence. "I'm meeting Charlie for lunch. Next door," she said, as though one and a half decades had not elapsed since the three of them last saw each other. "You remember Charlie, don't you? We were staying together in Venolat. Anyway, I'm meeting him there"—she looked at her watch—"about now actually." She was scared to stop speaking. She could not let Louis slip away. "I don't suppose . . . Well, you could always . . ." He looked at her, amused. "Louis, would you care to join us?"

She couldn't believe what she had just done.

Why? But why not? With Charlie around she felt sure she could trust herself to act normally and to go home to her family whom she loved and who loved her. It would be fine. And he would probably say no, anyway. She was certain he would say no.

"I can think of nothing better," Louis said, smiling and opening out his arm, inviting her to walk in front of him. "After you, madame." And Esme, knowing that one of the things Louis liked most about her was her bottom, walked as gracefully as she could out of the shop, thanking God and his ridiculous sense of humor for the fact that her skirt was still twisted on back to front so he would not be looking at the remains of a juicy wodge of someone else's bubble gum, which she was currently concealing with her bag.

A crisp maitre d' was on the phone when Esme and Louis got to the top of the stairs at the Orrery, but upon seeing them his face registered welcome relief.

"Mr. Edmonds," he said into the receiver, "she has just walked in. I will pass you over to her. Thank you, sir. See you soon."

Esme took the phone being offered. "Charlie?" she said. "Where are you?"

"Oh, Es," the raddled voice of her friend came back at her. "I hate to do this to you but something has come up at work and I don't know if I'm going to be able to make it to our lunch. I know you came down to London especially and

I wouldn't stand you up for all the world you know that but the Client from Hell has demanded a two o'clock meeting and I really need to—"

"You must come, Charlie," Esme butted in, trying to keep the panic out of her voice. "Louis is here."

Charlie was silent for a moment.

"I'm sorry?" he asked.

"Louis," she repeated as calmly as she could. "Louis, the baker from Venolat. You remember."

"Jesus," Charlie finally said. "Are you pissed already? You need help, Esme. You're obviously seeing things."

Esme laughed in what she hoped was a sophisticated and casual fashion given that Louis was standing less than a yard away. "No, silly," she said. "I mean it's actually Louis, the real thing. I just bumped into him in the Conran Shop. After all these years—can you believe it?"

"Frankly, no," answered Charlie. "Are you sure it's him?"

Esme snuck a look at Louis, standing at the desk next to her, looking perfectly in place the way he always had.

"I think I would know," she said. "Don't you? It's given me something of a surprise, Charlie, and I've invited him to join us for lunch."

"Well," said Charlie, clearly flabbergasted. "What a bugger I shan't be there to watch the whole lovely thing unfold."

Esme stood on her toes and squeaked into the

phone with the exertion of not unleashing a string of Granny Mac's most venomous invective on him.

"Look," Charlie said calmly, obviously enjoying her discomfort. "I think the two of you should take the booking and I'll pay for the lunch. How's that for a deal? I have an account there and—"

"Oh, we couldn't possibly," Esme interrupted loudly, aware the maitre d' was tapping his pen on the desk and trying not to look agitated.

"Bollocks," said Charlie. "You could possibly. You will possibly. Listen, Es, I really have to dash but say hello to Louis from me and I want details, darling, *details* when you are through so ring me later and tell me everything. Oh, and have the foie gras." With that he hung up and the line went dead.

Esme handed the phone back to the maitre d' and smiled wanly.

"Table for two as guests of Mr. Edmonds?" he asked, and she nodded, afraid to look at Louis but aware, somehow, that he was smiling at her again. She had never wanted to eat anything less in all her life.

Seated at their table overlooking a pretty, leafy park across the road and the hustle and bustle of Marylebone High Street, Esme wondered how long she could keep staring out the window and saying nothing. She snuck a look at Louis, who had never felt the need to fill silent spaces with unnecessary words and so was sitting there, cool as a cucumber and perfectly happy to be sneakily looked at.

His hair, Esme could not help but notice, was just as black as it had been when she last saw him, but perhaps it was receding a little at the front. This suited him though, she thought. How typical! He still wore it unfashionably long at the back but this, too, was right for him. Those black eyes must have held a thousand more secrets by now but little about his face had really changed. The dark skin was still smooth as satin—maybe there was more stubble, but maybe not.

He was wearing a very dark gray Saville Row suit and a very pale gray business shirt and matching silk tie. He looked positively edible and it made her feel sick. How could she possibly be sitting here opposite him? It was like being in a dream.

A suited waiter appeared at her elbow with all but the click of his heels.

"Bread?" he questioned, proffering her a basket. She looked across the table at Louis, whose faint left dimple appeared.

"Have you any sourdough?" Louis asked.

"No, sir," the waiter replied. "Just the kibbled wheat slice and our chef's own fresh-made rolls."

"We will both have one of each," Louis said, and Esme's heart quickened for the hundredth time in the past half hour. If she got through this lunch without a coronary, she promised herself she would find a religion, join it and go to church or temple or synagogue or wherever the hell she had to every day for the rest of her life.

CHAPTER 10

After nineteen years of being flat and dull, once Louis added his starter to Esme in the hot salty flour store of the Venolat *boulangerie*, she rose. The bits of herself that she had never been sure of before suddenly all made sense. Her pieces fell into place. She felt like a black-and-white drawing, abandoned for years in a tatty book by some spoiled child, then discovered, dusty and dirty, and colored in perfectly, without one single stroke going over the lines.

"If you tell me he completes you I will seriously have to slap you," Charlie told her, but Esme laughed aside his cynicism. She felt happy, truly, deliriously, deliciously happy, for the first time in her life and nothing could change that. Nothing could turn her back into the old colorless Esme of before.

She had been Louis-ed and she was never going back. Without him she might have gained fifty pounds and ended her days as an ancient stand-up comic cracking jokes about being ginger and never getting laid. Without him the suspicion she had that she was too odd for most men might have turned into a mean streak a mile wide and manifested itself with a short unattractive haircut and steel-capped boots. Without him she might never have discovered the pure and glorious sensation of knowing, knowing deep down inside at the most intimate level, with absolute certainty, that the man she loved loved her straight back.

It was different from knowing that Granny Mac loved her, or Charlie, or her distant father in his own peculiar way, or her dead mother, for that matter. They had to love her. That was how families, how best friends worked. But Louis—he could have just scuffed his toe outside the *boulangerie* that night and never so much as looked her way, let alone felt her desperate longing from across the square and eventually plugged, so to speak, that hole.

What Esme loved most about him was what he loved about her.

He loved her hair, especially where it was kinkiest and reddest, down where it had been viewed by spectacularly few people. He adored her freckles, was forever counting them and giving them names, in French, as he kissed them separately and succulently. He noticed straightaway her perfect feet. Her bottom fitted perfectly in his two hands, nestled expertly in his lap. He treated her breasts like crown jewels, lifting and holding them with reverence and kissing the nipples as though they were rings on a fat pope's finger. Just hearing him say her name made her tingle all over. He made her feel like the ridiculous fairy-tale princess she had always wanted to be. She couldn't get enough of him nor he of her.

After deflowering her in the dusty upstairs room that first fantastic night, Louis had taken her back down to the bakery and refloured her on the counter. The scales had fallen, clattering, to the ground as her foot caught them when Louis rolled her underneath him, the weights bouncing loudly on the stone floor and spinning away in different directions. It was a sound she would never forget.

Then, momentarily sated, he had taken the linen sheet off the stack of bread baskets and wrapped it around her, and she had sat naked beneath it on her favorite stone step and watched him work.

First, he stoked up the fire, then, reaching above his head to a rack hanging from the ceiling, he pulled down a paddle with a handle long enough to reach the back of the oven. Swiftly but carefully he upended the baskets of dough that he had stacked earlier two at a time onto the paddle, then expertly sliced a flowery *L* into the top of each one with a little razor-wheel contraption that he held between his teeth as he slid the loaves two at a time into the oven.

The dough, spongy and floury and so ready and willing to head into that fiery furnace, had reminded her of herself, only moments before. So full of promise! So teetering on the brink of becoming something much, much better, something it was made to be.

When every last *boule*-to-be had been safely tucked in the crackling oak-fired oven, the well-worn wooden paddle lifted back into its ceiling rack, the floor swept, the scale weights retrieved and the baskets stacked neatly under the bench, Louis slipped up and sat on the step behind Esme, wrapping himself around her. They sat like that, his lips nuzzling her hair, her cheek, her ear, for a long, lovely time, until Louis lifted his head, sniffed the stifling air, and excused himself to bring the perfect loaves out, two at a time, and place them on the waiting empty racks.

"It's all in the rise, see?" he told Esme, holding up a pair of fat happy *boules* in front of her. "Look, see the gloss on the crust? Perfect."

How he loved his sourdough. And how Esme loved that about him. He emptied the oven, wiped the sweat off his brow with his discarded T-shirt, then pulled Esme to her feet and kissed her deep and lazily as the sweet, sweet smell of the cooling bread embraced them like a warm blanket.

Finally, Louis pulled away and whispered that his uncle would soon be arriving, that she should go home and he would see her again at midnight or later, if she preferred. He led her naked and glowing upstairs to the flour room, where he retrieved her clothes and dressed her, lingering over the tiny buttons on the ancient, delicate camisole. He kissed her hip bones as he knelt and gently pulled up her Marks & Spencer bikini briefs, then ran his tongue lightly around her belly button, tickling her.

She slipped out the door just as the sun snuck its first pink and yellow fingers over the village ramparts. The world was a far more colorful place as Esme walked home than it had been when she had slunk hesitantly out hours before. Everything looked different. But then, everything was different. At least, nothing would ever be the same.

That day, after she'd slept the sleep of the very recently enlightened and completely exhausted, bits of the night kept wafting in and out of her consciousness, making her feel dizzy with desire.

Charlie, of course, had insisted she regurgitate every second, and while she kept the truly intimate details to herself, she only too willingly poured out the rest.

"He really said that?" Charlie asked, looking revolted as he lay next to Esme on her bed. "He said he had been waiting for you all his life?"

Esme squirmed. "Oh, it sounds so corny when you say it but when Louis said it, Charlie, oh my God! It's just what every girl wants to hear."

"You really are a strange bunch," Charlie said, reaching for a juicy peach from the nightstand beside Esme's bed. "I'm so glad I'm not relying on you lot for my jollies."

But he did agree that it was a perfectly romantic way for Esme to be relieved of her virginal status and much more interesting than having some spotty git from high school give her one in the back row of the Swiss Cottage movie theater.

That night though, Esme was fearful as she sidled up to the *boulangerie*. What had happened the night before had awoken so much in her that she was now forced to consider life without it and it hurt.

But Louis was there, the red glow of his cigarette dancing in the dark as he discarded it, ready to take her in his arms, which he did.

"I wait all day for this kiss," he said, after drinking from Esme's lips for what felt like forever. For the first time in many hours, she felt her heart relax. It was not going to come crashing down around her. It was really happening. They made long, languid love straightaway on the counter of the shop, Esme using a *boule* from the day before as a pillow. Afterward, Louis heated croissants in the oven downstairs, which they ate hungrily with Belgian chocolate he had bought for her. Their appetites were insatiable.

"You're going to wear it out!" Charlie scolded her two weeks later when Esme slipped into the apartment as the sun rose for the umpteenth morning in a row. "It's like you've never had sex before in your life." He rolled over and threw a pillow across the room at her. "Oh, that's right . . ."

"Shut up, you grumpy old shit," Esme said without an ounce of venom, unable to keep a grin from swallowing up her whole face. "Your evil black magic no longer works on me, remember?" She tried not to swivel girlishly but failed, and Charlie sat up, groaned in an exaggerated fashion and patted the bed beside him. She flew across the room and launched herself at it.

"And what magic did the baker's fingers work on you last night, pray tell?" he said.

"Oh my God, Charlie," Esme prattled, "he is just such a gloriously divine specimen I can hardly contain myself. He's just so completely, fantastically—" She flailed. Words simply did not do him justice.

"You have got it bad," Charlie said with a strange steely tone in his voice. Esme turned to look at him, a wiggle of worry crinkling her brow.

"Why do you say it like that?" she wanted to know. "If this is having it bad, bad is how I want it!"

Charlie laughed humorlessly and unnecessarily rearranged himself in the bed. "I didn't say it like anything," he said snippily.

"Ooooooh," teased Esme, "don't tell me you are jealous because I have finally got a boyfriend." Her worry disappeared, chased away by the hot flush that swept over her at the sound of that last word.

"Well, if you are sure that is what he is," said Charlie. Esme's hot flush sank to her toes.

"Of course that's what he is," she said quietly. "I've seen him every night for a fortnight. He's told me he loves me. I'm going to see him every

night for the next fortnight, maybe for every fortnight of my whole entire life. If he's not my
boyfriend, Charlie, what else would he be?"

Charlie picked at the top sheet. "So you're going
to stay here in Venolat for the rest of your life? Or
is Louis going to come back to London and live
with you and Granny Mac?"

"Well, thank you very much, Captain Bring
Down," Esme said. "Actually, we haven't really
talked about it." Once she heard this out loud,
she wished she'd kept her mouth shut. They hadn't
talked about it. They hadn't talked about much.
She had just assumed that because she was mad
about Louis and he was mad about her, they
would find a way of being together. That was what
happened when people were in love, wasn't it?

But of course she could not leave Granny Mac
behind in London and was not sure if her grandmother would want to come and live permanently
in Venolat, despite the foie gras and the snails.
And anyway, it had only been two weeks. It was
too early to talk about the future. The present was
too enticing. But she had never been more sure
of anything than she was of the way Louis felt
about her. All the things she had ever dreamed of
someone saying to her, he said. All the ways she
had ever imagined being touched, he discovered.
It was so perfect. So completely perfect.

That night at the bakery, the smell of warm
bread seducing her all over again, Esme tried but
could not bring up the subject of what lay ahead.

Every time she opened her mouth to speak, Louis kissed it closed again. He told her he loved her, not once but a dozen times, and the sound of his words was so intoxicating that Esme could not bear to change their tune.

She started trying to hide her hopelessly-in-love status from Charlie when they were both in the house together, and for a while, a week or two, this worked out quite well; but one morning, as she slid in through the double doors and headed for the stairs after a long, luscious night with her lover, Charlie's voice cut through the silence.

"Don't you think it's strange," he asked, "that Louis never invites you to his house, Esme? That all this torrid lovemaking of yours takes place at his work?"

She came around the corner and saw him sitting up in bed, chewing on his lip, black rings under his eyes, and a gray pallor to his face. She barely recognized him. He did not look at all like the carefree Charlie she knew and loved.

"That's not true," Esme answered. Twice they had snuck away while the dough was rising and made love in the moonlight in the fields above the village. And once they had sped down the hill in the bakery van and skinny-dipped in the river. These details she had not shared with Charlie. "He lives with his uncle and aunt," she said. "They're French."

Charlie ignored this last morsel of irrelevance and continued in a careful tone. "Well, doesn't his uncle come to work during the day, Es? Couldn't you see Louis at his place, then?"

Esme felt a niggle of something that could have been fear. "Are you trying to get rid of me?" she asked. "Are you up to something?"

Charlie's usually worry-free face looked at her with uncustomary solemnity. "No, Esme," he said. "*I'm* not up to anything." He was silent for a moment. "I'm worried about you, that's all. It's just that . . ." He petered out.

"It's just that what exactly?"

"It's just that as someone who shags a lot of men, Esme, and not all of them readily available, I have to say that if you are not being invited to Louis's house there is probably a very good reason."

Esme was furious. "What is the matter with you?" she cried. "Why do you always have to be so bloody mean? Is it really so hard for you to believe that Louis might be madly in love with me?"

Charlie tried to hush her but she was unhushable.

"Just because you bonk anything that moves and don't care if he's the happily married father of three or a Catholic bloody priest doesn't mean the rest of us are all twisted and unhinged," she raged. "Just keep your bitter horrible thoughts to yourself, you great big gay bastard."

She ran out of breath and took a lungful of air, which started to calm her down. "Maybe some of us," she said more evenly, "are lucky enough to find the one person in the world who is right for them, Charlie. And just because you personally find that such a thoroughly abhorrent proposition doesn't mean it can't happen. To me, even."

Her heart was hammering in her chest. She felt sick with regret. She never fought with anyone and loved Charlie to death. He was staring at her, slightly stricken, but with a steely glint of non-repentance still shining in his eye.

"I am so sorry I called you a great big gay bastard," she said, then turned and ran upstairs, collapsing face down on her bed, fists clenched and eyes shut tight.

The truth was that while her body had been asking nothing of Louis other than his own flesh and bones over the past few heavenly weeks, her mind did have tiny vents of doubt. Why didn't he ask her back to his house? she had wondered. It was on the other side of Venolat, he had told her already, halfway to the next town, too far to expect her to walk to and from. She had wanted to insist, to make more of a fuss about it, but something had stopped her and instead she had simply leaned into him for another taste. But that didn't mean the little niggle that may or may not have been fear went away. It didn't.

That night she stayed at home, had an early night for which her desperately tired body was truly thankful, and at daybreak slunk downstairs and across to the *boulangerie,* where Louis was just taking the *boules* out of the oven.

"Esme" he said, instantly dropping the paddle on the ground and coming to meet her at the bottom of the stairs. "What happened to you? I was so worried. I did not know . . ." He looked so unhappy and fretful that she cursed herself for having doubts and for depriving herself of him for all those extra hours.

His hand where she could feel it on her waist felt blisteringly hot and all she wanted to do was savor his beautiful, bare skin next to hers again as soon as possible.

"I fell asleep," she lied sheepishly. "I've only just woken up."

He rubbed the dark rings under her eyes with his thumbs and looked at her quizzically. "Esme," he said. "I missed you. I thought perhaps . . . perhaps you do not want me."

"I want you, Louis," she answered him, her voice husky with longing. He pulled her close and sank his face between her breasts, kissing the cotton of her top.

"Thank you," he whispered. "Thank you."

"Your uncle must be nearly here," Esme said, feeling treacherous. "Why don't you come to see me when you're finished? At my place."

Louis pulled away from her, something, she couldn't be sure what, flickering in his eyes. "I fancy a bed, for a change," she joked.

"You don't like the *boulangerie*?" Louis asked her.

"I love the *boulangerie*," she replied, "but I have

flour stuck in bits of me I didn't even know existed and I have a very nice bed just a hundred yards away from here. Is there any reason why . . . ?" She let the question trail away to nothing.

Louis looked around the room. "I love it here," he said simply. "It is like being inside one of our Lapoine *boules*, no? Safe from the outside world."

"Until someone cuts it open and eats a slice," Esme pointed out. "Which is, after all, what bread is for."

"Yes, yes," agreed Louis looking slightly bashful, "of course. That is what bread is for."

"So I will see you in an hour or so?" Esme prompted him. "First door on the right through the brick archway next to the *auberge*? You'll have to knock loudly so I can hear you from the top floor."

Louis smiled at her suggestion and her heart melted. "Maybe two hours," he said, then reached for the rack and pulled out a fresh loaf and handed it to her. "To eat. That's what it's for, *oui*?" She clutched the *boule* to her chest and its warmth made her feel like a better person.

She skipped home, stopping at the end of Charlie's bed to inform him that Louis would be arriving some time later, and as his room was not cordoned off from the entranceway, could he please keep a civil tongue in his head if he felt moved to use it at all but pretending to be asleep would be better.

A muffled answer came from underneath the

pillows. "That's what great big gay bastards are best at, I believe."

Esme gulped, chose not to take the matter any further and went upstairs, where she promptly fell asleep to be woken some time later by the distant rapping on the front door. She collected a sheet around her shoulders and danced down the steps to receive the love of her life, who was bearing a small bowl of fresh and juicy strawberries, one of which he popped straight into her mouth as soon as she opened the door to him.

She shushed him quiet, pointing at Charlie's allegedly sleeping form, and drew him upstairs, where they stayed in bed all day while Louis made sure all her crevices were completely flour-free. In the late afternoon they both draped themselves in sheets and Esme watched Louis create the most delicious omelettes out of the rotting components of the refrigerator vegetable bin. They drank cold white wine and toasted each other on the patio overlooking the Dordogne, and Esme wondered what she had done to deserve being so happy.

Charlie even emerged and joined them for a drink as Esme had hoped he would. She wanted Charlie to see what sort of a person Louis was. How he was different from other men. How he loved her so obviously.

"Right, better dash," her friend said after making uncustomarily stiff conversation and quaffing a glass of wine. "Hot date over in old Lalinde tonight, you know. Better make myself presentable and all that." He stood up as if to go. "Esme tells me you live over that way, Louis," he said, looking exaggeratedly casual.

Esme imagined getting up and smashing him over the head with the nearly empty wine bottle. But instead she kept staring, unflinchingly, at the river below.

"In that direction, yes," Louis agreed.

"You must tell us where. Esme and I were thinking of hiking over that way at the weekend. We could drop by and say hello," Charlie gushed.

Louis was nonplussed. "I am not there at the weekend," he said with a shrug. "I deliver the bread to other villages at the weekend."

"Maybe one evening before you go to work, then?" Charlie suggested cheerfully.

Louis shrugged again. "Sure, if you want to," he said. "When do you think you will come? I must check with my uncle first."

Esme felt sick. She was scared but she had to admit to herself—although never to Charlie—she also wanted to know how this was going to play out. She held her breath.

Charlie laughed, not cruelly—he wasn't cruel—but not nicely either.

"You have to ask your uncle if you can have visitors? Poor chap. And you look so grown-up!"

Esme could bear it no longer. "For God's sake, Charlie!" she said in as light and airy a fashion as she could manage. "Leave him alone."

"No, no," Louis agreed, "it is not usual, you are

right. But my family is not usual, not normal, if you like. I live with my uncle Louis, I am named for him, and my aunt. But she is very ill, she has been for many years. Arthritis." He stumbled over the word. "She is bedridden. We take care of her. And work in the *boulangerie,* too, of course."

The smirk had been wiped off Charlie's face. Louis turned to Esme.

"That is why my uncle works during the day and I am the baker," he explained. "In most *boulangeries,* the baker's wife runs the shop. But *Tante* Marie has been unable to work since I was very young. And my uncle he is good with the customers and he needs to be at home at night."

"Oh, Louis, I am so sorry," Esme said, pulling her togalike sheet tighter around herself. Charlie had the good grace to look ashamed. But not for long.

"What about your own parents?" he asked.

A dark cloud passed over Louis's face.

"What about them?" he asked back, the first signs of aggression in his voice.

"Where are they?" Charlie persevered. Esme wanted him to shut up but she also wanted to know the answer. She had been so busy letting Louis explore her, she had done a poor job of investigating him.

"They live in Paris," Louis said tersely. "But I am not in communication with them."

"Louis," she couldn't help herself saying. "Why ever not?"

"I am sorry." Louis clearly was not happy talking

about it. He looked at Charlie. "You say you have a date in Lalinde. You should be going, *non*?"

"Oh, a few more minutes shouldn't make any difference," he said, settling back into his chair. "So, about Paris."

"My parents move there four years ago," Louis said darkly, "when I am just sixteen but I do not wish to go with them so I stay here with Louis and Marie."

"Oh really?" Charlie asked. "I imagine most lads your age would die to live in a big city like that. All those bars and nightclubs and pretty girls and bakeries."

"Please," spat Louis, "you call them bakeries? Monkeys could make bread the way they do in Paris. All those baguettes with their flimsy little crumb and flaky crust? That is not bread. Those are not bakeries."

"You're *angry* about baguettes?" Charlie teased and Esme loathed him for it. Could he not see that this was important to Louis, that this was what Louis was about?

"Of course not," Louis said, smiling now, willing his even temper to return, "but I am angry about what bakers, especially in Paris, pass off as bread these days because it might be made from flour and water but it is not bread as we know it, as we make it."

"You have to admit," Esme said to Charlie, "that Louis's bread tastes better than any you have ever eaten in your whole entire life."

Charlie shrugged but did not disagree. Louis smiled at Esme. "That is because we make it the way it was meant to be made. With the ingredients from the air and the fields and the river and the touch of our hands, hands that have been making it this way for nearly two centuries."

"So what about your parents, then? Why aren't they still here making your delicious bread with their hands?" Charlie was keen to return to the subject of Louis's family.

"My uncle and I agree exactly on the principles of the *boulangerie,*" Louis said, his face darkening again, "but not so my father. When the *boulangerie* passed into his hands Papa was keen to make changes, many changes. My uncle and I were not."

He stopped, his lips remaining thin and pursed.

"What sort of changes?" Charlie persisted.

"You probably do not understand," Louis said rather dismissively to Charlie, "but Esme does." Esme glowed beneath his sentiment. "To bake *pain au levain* the way we always have, the way we do, is"—he searched for the word, frustrated in his passion—"it is honorable if that is what I mean. The baker has always been at the center of village life in France. He feeds people. And he puts his honor and his love and his skill into every single *boule,* separately, that is what makes him an artisan. He does it with his hands. That is what makes him different from a machine. That is what makes him want to go to work at midnight and not leave until there is enough bread for everyone and he has left a little bit of himself in every loaf."

Charlie looked confused, but Esme reached for Louis's hand and unclenched it, taking it in her own.

"Your father didn't want to do it that way?"

"My father wanted to borrow money for a machine to cut dough into the right size for baguettes, and for another machine that would roll the dough into the right shape, and for an electric oven that would cook ten times more baguettes than the oak-fired oven we have been using all this time. He wanted to stop making *boules* and just make baguettes and buy in frozen pastries from a big factory. He wanted to have nothing to do with the bread but the money."

Charlie was obviously struggling with the concept that this was unacceptable. "Isn't that why most people work?" he said. "For the money?"

"Most people are not artisan bakers," Louis said, and Esme squeezed his hand tighter.

"So your father is a baker in Paris?"

"My father is a businessman in Paris," Louis corrected him sharply. "He owns a factory that mixes and rises and refrigerates baguette dough and then delivers it through tubes from big tankers to *boulangeries* throughout Paris. I want nothing to do with it."

How Esme loved him in that moment, his face fierce with passion for his work. Her heart swelled with pride.

"Yes, well, I had better get going," said Charlie, clearly not as impressed. "Lovely to finally meet you, Louis, and I'm sure we'll meet again."

"Your friend does not like me," Louis said when he had gone.

"Oh, he does," cried Esme. She could not bear the thought that the two most wonderful men in her life might not get on. Plus, she thought the meeting had gone much better than it could have. "That's just Charlie," she added lamely. "He's very, you know . . ."

"Suspicious?" Louis suggested, which sent a shudder down Esme's spine.

"I was going to say English," she said, and they both laughed.

That night—she could not keep away—in the bakery, she was so in love with him she wanted to explode. She just couldn't get close enough, he couldn't get deep enough, her tongue, her fingers, her secret caverns could not contain him enough for her liking, her loving. It was almost unbearable but deliciously so. And as she watched him weigh out the dough, upend the baskets and carve his swirly signature into every single loaf, leaving a little bit of himself behind him in each one, she was desperate to have more of him.

"I want to make some myself," she announced, swathed in linen, from her spot on the stairs. "Sourdough. At home. For you. I want to know what it feels like."

"Truly?" Louis asked, his body glistening with sweat and his eyes with interest.

"Truly," nodded Esme.

"But no one in France makes their own bread. Never! Why would they?"

Because no one has ever wanted to please anyone else this much before, Esme thought to herself. No one has ever loved anyone this much before. No one ever will.

"Go on," she wheedled. "Please let me. I want to do it."

"You know, the *levain* has never left the *boulangerie* before," Louis said as he kissed her goodbye at dawn, handing over a willow basket, a bag of flour and a stone jar of his family's precious starter. "I hope it brings you luck."

"It already has," Esme said, leaning in to him again, his lips soft and supple against her own.

"To think," he murmured, "there will be some of you *and* me in the bread you bake, Esme."

"Like a child," she said without thinking, then blushed at her foolishness. Couples in the first flush of true love did not talk about babies, even she knew that. But Louis seemed unfazed. He brushed a curl away from her neck and smiled at her so kindly she wanted to cry.

"Yes," he said, "I suppose. Like a child. Made with love." She could not for a moment imagine Gordon from Charlie's work being able to say something like that. Louis's French romantic streak made it possible to hear things from him that would have her wetting her pants with laughter should they be delivered in an English accent. He kissed her again and went back inside.

Esme floated through the rest of the day, her faith in her lover fully restored. And she baked. For the first time, she baked. One beautiful, brown, slightly lopsided *boule* of sourdough bread just the way Louis had taught her. Next to the joy of sex, it was the most satisfying discovery she had ever made. She loved the feeling of flour and water under her fingers and the way the texture changed as she mixed it and mixed it until if she closed her eyes she could almost believe it was Louis she was kneading. She slept deeply and untroubled on both three-hour occasions she left her mixture to rise. And despite the unreliable and in fact unknown nature of the apartment's little oven, she watched through the glass door as her *boule* turned perfectly from dough into bread.

What possessed her to deliver her first offering in person to Louis's house that afternoon, she would never know. She must have realized as she looked up his uncle's address in the phone book that in the circumstances it was a foolish thing to do. She must have known as she took her first ever *boule* out of the tricky little oven that delivering it to Louis was not necessary. She could have taken it to him at the bakery at midnight. There was no reason to go to his house. To surprise him. To catch him.

Or had she known all along he was too good to be true? Had Charlie's constant scratching away at her certainty triggered more doubt inside her than she had realized? Esme was to ask herself these and similar questions over and over again in years to come, but in the stifling heat of that summer afternoon as she walked up the dusty road toward Lalinde carrying her wonkily shaped slightly flat but sweet-smelling loaf of home baked bread in a linen dish towel, she asked herself nothing.

When she got to the modest house hidden in the cool shade of half a dozen leafy trees partway to Lalinde she was hot and sticky and tired. Her legs were covered in dust and she had sweat patches under her arms. The pale pink silk shirt she had chosen and tied at the waist above her baggy white shorts seemed like a poor choice now.

She knocked at the door and it was opened almost immediately by a pretty, tired-looking woman a little older than herself, carrying one child on her hip and another in her belly. The woman had straight brown slightly disheveled hair and a peaches and cream complexion.

"Hello," she said. She was English. "Can I help you?"

Esme stared as a dark-eyed, dark-haired toddler ran up the hallway behind the woman and hurled itself at her legs. Her heart had sunk through her body and was now rolling down the hill up which she had just climbed, leaving big fat splodges of blood in cartoon puddles behind it.

"I'm sorry," she said. "I think I must have the wrong house."

"Oh yes?" the woman said. "Who are you looking for?"

"I'm looking for Louis," Esme said uncertainly, peering behind the woman and clutching on to the glimmer of hope that she was indeed at the wrong house.

"Oh, really?" The woman raised her eyebrows. "What for?"

"I wanted to give him this," Esme said, the horror of her situation claiming the pale skin of her cheeks as its own and brightening them radiantly. She held up the bread and the woman opened the dish towel and looked at Esme's *boule*, then closed it again.

"If there's one thing Louis doesn't need, trust me, it's more bread," she said tiredly. "Who are you?"

"I'm Esme," said Esme, the saliva disappearing from inside her mouth as her happiness spiraled downward. "I've been helping"—the lie stuck in her throat—"Louis at the *boulangerie*." Any pretense of helpfulness slid off the woman's face. "I'm learning to bake sourdough."

The woman hitched the baby up on her hip and looked the dusty, silly young girl on her doorstep scornfully up and down.

"Who are you?" the dusty, silly young girl asked in a quavery voice.

"I'm Diana, his wife," said Diana, his wife. "Did

227

he not mention me?" Her eyes had hardened to a frightening shade of icy ocean blue. She turned and yelled over her shoulder. "Louis!" Esme tried as hard as she could to believe that the man this woman was hailing—her husband, of all people— was not her Louis, the Louis who had told her he loved her a hundred times over the past few weeks. The Louis who knew her body better than she knew it herself, who purred when she whispered what she loved about him in his ear, in whose arms she fitted so perfectly. But as he rounded the corner into the hallway, tucking a white T-shirt into the front of his faded blue jeans, jeans she could unbutton in her sleep, possibly even had done, there was no doubt at all that her Louis and this other woman's husband were one and the same.

He looked up and saw her and seemingly without even flinching came to the door and stood behind the woman. His wife. His English wife. The best friend who had moved here when Louis was thirteen? "It's good to share, no?" How could Esme have been so stupid?

"Hello," Louis said. "So, you try the baking yourself?" The mild hiccup in his English was the only sign he was at all unnerved.

"Who is she?" his wife asked rudely, shifting the baby on her hip again and shushing the toddler behind her.

"I told you," Louis answered, "she is the English girl who wants to learn about *pain au levain*. Tante

228

Marie needs help in her room, Diana. Can you go?"

"You told me no such thing," his wife snapped back. "I'm not completely stupid, Louis."

Ignoring her, he leaned over toward Esme and lifted the dish towel, raising his eyebrow and shaking his head in a mildly approving fashion. "Not too bad," he said, looking at her and meeting her eyes as though he had not stared into them just hours before professing his deep and undying devotion. "I say you need to work a little on your mixing technique. Maybe leave the dough a little longer in the basket."

Esme struggled to keep breathing. Louis's wife was looking at her with such contempt she was surprised her skin wasn't breaking into welts.

"Come back tomorrow," Louis said casually, "and we can work on your kneading."

Esme tried to smile but the muscles that were usually so easily at her beck and call had frozen in fear and panic. "Thank you," she found her voice saying politely, if not a little shakily, "but I am just about to leave. For England." Louis gave a little lackluster shrug and Esme wondered how she was expected to keep on living. "I just wanted to say," she fought on, even though tears had actually sprung from her eyes now and were trailing down her cheeks, "thank you," she whispered. Then she turned and fled.

"You bastard!" she heard his wife spit behind her. "You filthy little bastard."

Louis started to protest but Esme was running as fast as she could away from him, his wife and his children and did not care to know what he was saying. His shrug of indifference at the news she was leaving had told her everything she needed to know. As if the fact he was married and the father of two, nearly three children was not enough on its own. She had been sleeping with a married man! Louis had given her something that was not rightfully his to give. The contemptuous look on his wife's face kept flashing in front of her as she ran all the way back to Venolat. She felt guilt and disgust mixing in her gut as her feet kicked up mushroom clouds of dust where they pounded the road. Charlie had been right, she was a fool; a clueless, hopeless, silly little fool.

Her tears formed streaks through the dust on her cheeks as she pushed open the door of the apartment and ran up to her room, pulling her suitcase from under the bed and clumsily throwing her clothes into it, her ribs aching with the sobs that racked her.

She pulled the case down to the kitchen and, barely able to think, to breathe, started scratching out a note to Charlie.

"You were right," was all she could manage in the end. "He's married. Gone home. Esme."

The words "He's married" pounded in her head as she searched the kitchen for her tote bag. How could she have been so wrong about him? It didn't seem possible. How could her feelings have let her down, betrayed her, lulled her into thinking she deserved a love like that? And if she hadn't been wrong, if he really had loved her, well, that was even worse because his love could never belong to her anyway. It belonged to his pretty wife and their black-eyed children and she had nothing to show for it, nothing, nothing but this awful black bottomless feeling.

Her eyes fell on the stone jar of *levain* sitting on the kitchen counter and she picked it up and pressed it, cool as the waters of the river below, against her burning cheek. Her eyes closed and her sobbing slowed. So, Louis had lied. So, he had tricked Esme into handing him her heart. So, nothing about him was real. Nothing except his bread. That was real. She had seen it, she had smelled it, she had tasted it. She had made it. She slid the stone jar into her tote bag and slipped out of the apartment. So, she would have something to show for it after all.

CHAPTER 11

A decade and a half later, sitting across a crisp white linen tablecloth from each other on the opposite side of the Channel, Esme and Louis agreed, with fewer than a dozen words between them, that the bread was as good as you could get at any restaurant in London but not as good as Lapoine's.

After a glass of Bollinger, which she downed with indecent haste, Esme concentrated on trying to stop worrying about the implications of meeting in secret with her old lover, even though it had been a secret even from herself.

She watched Louis's slim brown fingers gently crumble his olive roll onto his plate as he looked at her and smiled his comfortable smile.

"I suppose I should stop acting like such a bloody jessie and ask you what you are doing here," she said rather brightly, although up until she heard the words out and about and clanging around her own ears she had assumed she was only thinking them.

"I suppose you should," Louis agreed.

Esme's hands flew to her hot cheeks. She was

mortified, afraid that her blush was going to spread to the tablecloth and the Orrery's white walls and the street outside and take over the whole of London until it made the six o'clock news and Pog would know it was her and wonder what the hell she was doing there.

Louis let the breadcrumbs fall away from his fingers.

"Esme," he said with such kindness that she felt it in her toenails. "It's all right. Relax."

Her hands fell back down into her lap. She was suddenly tired of being herself. She didn't want to get gum in her hair. She didn't want to blush and stutter and stammer and keep the things she really wanted to feel, to know, at arm's length. It was exhausting. It was pathetic. It was a habit so ingrained that she had begun to think it came naturally, but sitting here with Louis she realized how bloody hard it was. She relaxed.

"How could you do that to me, Louis?" she asked him. "How could you tell me all those things—that you loved me, that you wanted to be with me forever, that I was special—when you were married to Diana, when you obviously loved her, when you had children with her? I didn't understand it, Louis, I still don't understand it. I thought I was the one. I was sure I was the one. You certainly made me feel as though I was. How could you say all those things without meaning them? How could you possibly do that?"

At that moment Louis turned seamlessly to the

waiter, who appeared just then for their order. "I will have the foie gras and the beef and madam will have the soup and the salmon," he said. The waiter nodded and retreated and Esme continued as though they had never been interrupted.

"Do you know what that did to me, Louis?" she asked, aware that she was opening the floodgates yet feeling strangely detached from the flood. "It took years to let anyone love me again. Years! I'm only just managing it now. I could never believe a word anyone told me after Venolat. I assumed everyone was like you, unbelievably good at lying and totally heartless. What you did to me was cruel, Louis. It was unspeakably cruel. And yet I don't think you are an unspeakably cruel person."

Louis looked away from her for a moment, but when he looked back his eyes were far from weak or apologetic.

"I meant everything I said to you, Esme. Everything," he said with a passion disguised by the smooth low timbre of his voice. Yet for the first time he seemed slightly flustered and Esme felt a flutter of something but couldn't work out whether it was satisfaction or fear or something completely different. "But the time was not right," Louis said. "I apologize for that but not for what I said to you. I mean every word, Esme." He stopped, and shook his head. "I *meant* every word."

"But you had a wife, Louis, and little children. How could you possibly have meant every word?"

"Just because I did not act the way a gentleman should does not mean that I was not being honest with you, Esme."

"Well, you were certainly not being honest with one of us, Louis."

"Yes, but I am not the one who ran away in the night, Esme, never to come back," he said.

"Louis, you had a wife, a beautiful wife," hissed Esme. "I met her. I was humiliated by her, and rightly so, too. You turned me into a slut, Louis! And you shrugged at me. After everything we had done together, you shrugged at me!" She knew the shrugging was the least of his wrongdoing but oh how it had hurt.

"That was not the time to tell Diana, Esme. I would do that, I would have done that when the time was right but instead you turn up like that at our house and everything is ruined. If only you had waited."

Esme's skin prickled at what she was hearing. If Louis was telling her that they could have had a future together, she did not want to hear it. He was telling her fifteen years too late.

"And then," Louis said, gaining momentum in her silence, "what was I to do? You knew how to find me, Esme, but how was I to find you?"

Their waiter slid in between them and gently placed their food.

"You could have tried," Esme continued, amazed that the things she had kept in her head for so long were sliding out so loud and easily.

"You could have got it out of Charlie, for God's sake. All you'd need to do was tickle him. He was there for another two days."

The calm in Louis's reflective pool rippled.

"Charlie?" he hissed, although anyone looking from another table would have just seen a beautifully handsome man smile. "Did he not tell you, Esme, about the night I came to find you? About the night you went away?"

Esme's heart stood still as she shook her head.

"I came to find you and he tells me that you have gone and when I beg him, *beg* him to tell me where you are he beats the living *shit* out of me, Esme." His voice was growing louder although he was trying to control it. He leaned urgently in toward her. "I needed five stitches under my nose, Esme," and with that he stuck his neck even farther forward, and she leaned in herself and could see the faint scarring from an old wound that had not been there when she had explored every inch of his body in her youth.

She wanted to reach out and touch it but instead tried her soup. It was delicious. Yet what he'd said made her feel ill and uneasy. What if he had tried to find her? What if Charlie had stopped him? What if the last fifteen years of her life had been the wrong ones?

"You could still have come to fetch me back," she found herself saying.

"But, Esme," Louis said, calmer now but still clearly agitated, "I did come. I came to St. John's

Wood in London and looked for you for one week"—he shook his head as if unable to believe it himself—"for one whole week but then I ran out of money and have to return to the *boulangerie*. And then," he added, his eyes lighting up as he remembered, "I advertised in the *Evening Standard* for you, but nothing. *Nothing.*"

Esme felt another stirring deep down below. Louis had come looking for her and failed? As she had lain in a dark room crying with her grandmother, who didn't believe in evening papers, sitting beside her consoling her, her lover had been combing the streets outside trying to find her? "But that's terrible," she whispered, unable to respond in any other way. "That's terrible, Louis."

"You are right," he said, sitting back. "That is terrible. I waited for one month, six months, a year for you to reach me, Esme, but you did not."

"But why would I, Louis? You had a wife and two little children with another one on the way. I wasn't the sort of person who would break up a family. I'm still not. *You* were the one in the wrong, Louis. If it is anybody's fault, it is yours."

Louis sighed and his shoulders slumped in a gesture of total desolation. "Is it about who was right and who was wrong, Esme?" he asked her quietly. "Is that what you really think? That it was some sort of a competition and one of us won and the other one lost?"

"How is she?" Esme asked, holding his gaze and

slurping back the last of a glass of Sauvignon. "Diana?"

Louis looked wretched.

"Do you think I could have gone back to Diana after you?" he said so quietly she wasn't sure for a moment if she heard him properly. "For even a moment? I could not live like that, Esme. Do you not know me at all?"

At that moment, something inside Esme unzipped itself and spilled violently out into the no-emotion zone where she required, for her sanity, nothing of the sort. With a clang of cutlery and glassware she rapidly stood, excused herself and dashed to the ladies' room, where she sat on a lavatory seat lid and shook so violently she thought she was going to throw up. All this honesty was hard for her to handle. The answers she was getting were not necessarily the ones she wanted to hear. She concentrated on her breathing, trying to get air deep into her lungs instead of sucking at it, panicked.

After five minutes she started to feel calmer. She held her hands out in front of her, and though she could see them quivering, she thought she could probably hold a knife and fork without disgracing herself. She left the stall, splashed her face at length with cold water, reapplied her makeup, sponged the last of the gum off her skirt and turned it the right way around, then returned to the table.

Louis half rose out of his chair as she approached, looking tormented.

"I am so sorry," he said as she sat to find her main course sitting and waiting and, despite her inner turmoil, looking rather gorgeous. "These are old wounds and I have no business opening them again."

"Shall we eat?" Esme suggested with a calm she got from she didn't know where. She let the delicacy of her lightly spiced fish fill all the corners in her body that were otherwise buzzing with anger and regret and sadness and guilt. Food was good like that. And when she felt she had control of her emotions enough to speak properly, she did.

"So you are not with Diana, then?" she asked.

"No," answered Louis emphatically. "She lives in Venolat with Emily and little Marie and Jean, he is eighteen now, but I see them only maybe two or three times a year. I live in Paris," he added. He returned to his food.

"She was the best friend, wasn't she?" Esme asked. Louis looked perplexed.

"The best friend who moved to Venolat when you were both thirteen? Who taught you English? Who you taught French? 'It's good to share'?"

Comprehension dawned on Louis's handsome face.

"Yes," he said. "Yes, she was once my best friend but truly we never should have married. When my father fought with my uncle and moved with my mother to Paris, well, I made my own way. Diana was my family just as much as Marie and Louis.

And when she fell pregnant with Jean . . . I was just seventeen. We were too young."

"So, did you marry again?" Esme asked casually.

He stopped, a forkful of food halfway to his mouth and shook his head. "No," he said. "I never married again. Never, never. There have been others of course but nothing, nobody . . ."

"What do you do in Paris, then?" she asked, amazing herself at how normal the conversation was sounding. They could be any two old friends catching up, not a heartbreaker and his heart-broken. "Don't tell me you went to work for your father?"

"But no, of course not," Louis said, disgusted at the suggestion. "Although you might like to know that his fleet of tankers has increased a hundredfold and delivers tubes of baguette dough all over France now." He shook his head as he chewed his food. "I am still not in communication with him," he said. "I work for the federation of master bakers. I travel around the world teaching people how to bake *pain au levain,* you know, the old-fashioned way, just like I taught you, Esme. The tradition is almost completely lost in this world of *supermarches* and fast food. Even in France I am teaching the art of baking sourdough bread. It seems silly, no?"

"It would seem silly to do anything else," Esme answered with fervor. How she had always loved that passion of his. "Your uncle must be so proud of you, Louis. How is he?"

Louis stopped eating and let his knife and fork collapse on his plate as his eyes dulled and fell on a spot in the middle of the table between them.

"My uncle died," he said quietly, "six weeks ago today."

Esme felt a sharp pain, like a spear or a long knife being thrust somewhere near her heart. Six weeks ago? She looked at Louis across the table as he lifted his melancholy face to look back at her, and in that moment Esme realized that the years might have passed and their lives might have gone on without one another but she and Louis were inextricably linked and always would be.

His sadness at losing his uncle would have coincided with her own black, breadless hole. The loss of his uncle with the slow shake of Dr. Gribblehurst's jowls and all that followed.

A glimmer of possibility floated into Esme's future. Maybe it would not be poisoned by what had happened to her in Notting Hill. Maybe it would be saved by a past much sweeter. Despite what had happened back in Venolat, despite what had occurred in the intervening years, perhaps Louis really was her destiny. She realized, suddenly, that what she felt for him now, sitting across the table in a smart London restaurant, was exactly what she felt all those years ago on the unforgiving sacks of unbleached wheat flour from the pastures of Dordogne.

And if Louis were to stand up now and reach for her, she knew that she would go. In fact, parts of her were tingling in anticipation of that very possibility. Parts that should know better. Parts that should be reserved for the attentions of her husband, Pog.

His name clunked in her brain. Pog. His kind, dear, uncomplicated face hovered into her consciousness, despite the chasm the past two years had dug between them, and grinned at her. She closed her eyes for a second and cleared her head. What had happened in Notting Hill had not just happened to her. It had happened to him. It had happened to all of them. She could not escape it alone.

"I am so sorry," she said to Louis, "about your uncle. I really am. I know what it feels like and you must be devastated, Louis, especially as you were so close. It must be like losing a limb." She pushed her plate away from her and moved her chair back, as if to stand and leave. "The thing is that I really have to get going."

Louis was looking at her, confused. "But why?" he said. "Esme, please."

But Esme was flailing around on the ground in search of her bag. "I have to fly, Louis. I'm sorry. I can't tell you what it has been like to see you again—"

"Yes, you can," Louis said, leaning forward in the same urgent fashion as he had before. "You can stay here and tell me. We can have cheese. They have beautiful French cheese here, Esme. All your favorites."

Esme shook her head and wondered for a moment if the rest of her body was shaking with it. She was becoming transfixed with the way his lips moved, with the moistness of them, the color, the texture, the memory of their feel.

"The thing is," she said, finding her bag and plonking it on her knee to form a comforting extra barrier between herself and him, "I just feel extremely sort of thrown by bumping into you today. I mean I have thought about it for years of course but I never thought it would be like this. I always imagined that I would yell at you and call you a bastard and tip crème brûlée on your head or something."

Louis stared at her. "Esme," he said, "I cannot believe you have changed so much you would waste a crème brûlée."

It was a joke, but not entirely funny.

"That's what I mean," said Esme. "I feel as though I haven't changed a bit. I feel like that same silly young girl who fell in love with the village baker and just assumed she was the woman of his dreams as much as she assumed he was the man of hers. And it's ridiculous because I am really not that person anymore."

Louis's smile had spread across his face once more.

"You were the woman of my dreams, Esme," he said. "You still are."

Esme cleared her throat and pushed away thoughts of lying naked with him.

243

"Louis," she said, "I am not. I am happily married. I am a mother. I live in the country and grow rude vegetables. I dye my hair. I am nearly fifteen pounds heavier."

His smile spread even further. "I like you better with more roundness," he said. "It suits you."

Esme was suddenly aware of every extra inch of her roundness and felt supremely uncomfortable with it. Not for the first time, she silently resolved to join the Seabury yoga group even if they were twenty years older than she yet still, no doubt, twice as bendy. The thought of Seabury brought a lump to her throat and she stood up.

"I am taking my roundness back home to the country now," she said, fishing in her bag for her sunglasses and finding, well, how could she miss it, the loaf of bread she had brought for Charlie. Her heart skipped a beat and she pulled it out of the bag and handed it to Louis.

He took it, delighted, lifted it to his nose and sniffed it, then tapped the base with his finger, his eyebrows rising (how she wished they wouldn't do that!) at the wonderful hollow sound.

"Perfect *pain au levain*," he breathed. "Well, a little overcooked perhaps but still, you bake bread!"

"Every day, nearly," she said, "since back then. With your great-great-great-great-grandfather's starter. I took it with me, you know."

Louis raised the loaf to his face again and closed his eyes, pressing it to his cheek, inhaling deeply.

His smile appealed to her hormones in a way she could not fathom and she tried as hard as she could to not wish herself in the *pain au levain*'s place. Louis opened his eyes again and must have read something like this on her face because he put the *boule* on the table and stood up, moving in so close to her that she could have leaned into him and put her lips on the smooth brown skin of his neck.

"Esme," he urged into her ear. "This cannot be coincidence, you and me, the *pain au levain*, today after all this time." He pulled back a bit. "Someone," he said, raising his eyes skyward, "is trying to tell us something."

Esme pulled back slightly. "Yes," she said, "and that someone is me. I am trying to tell you that I have to go." She put her sunglasses on her head and turned toward the door, but not before she saw Louis's smile crawl across his lips.

"You are trying to tell me something, yes," he said, "but it is not that."

She turned back to him for one last look.

"I will be here next Thursday at one o'clock," Louis said. "And I would like to see you here, too, Esme."

The way he said her name, lingered on it, savored it, nearly brought her to her knees there and then, but instead Esme smiled what she hoped was a smile that said she would not be there the following week—although in truth she did not know that for a fact. She did not, at that particular point, know very much at all. She floated out of the restaurant, smiling and thanking the Orrery staff. In a cloud of bewilderment, bedazzlement and deep, dark thought, she turned to go down the stairs, but was halted in her tracks by a high-pitched tinkering laugh that came around the corner well before its owner, who by the click-clack that echoed in the stairwell was wearing a pair of exceptionally high heels.

Because of the sort of day it had been so far and because she recognized those two sounds, especially together, Esme knew she was about to come face-to-face with none other than Jemima Jones. But of course! Why wouldn't she? Clearly, there had not been enough surprises in the day. With astonishing speed she veered into the Orrery's tiny bar, at the top of the stairs just opposite the entrance to the restaurant, and plonked herself into a big wingbacked chair.

Unfortunately for her, Jemima Jones came through the door not long after. She was dressed in white and surrounded by a collection of twenty-something men and women all wearing black and elbowing each other out of her wake.

Jemima did a theatrical double take when she saw Esme sitting in her thronelike seat on her own trying to pretend she hadn't been in the throes of shoveling down a handful of salted almonds.

"Esme MacDougall?" she trilled across the small room. "Is that you, Esme MacDougall?"

"Stack," said Esme, to her great embarrassment

spitting out little bits of chewed up nut as she did so. "It's Stack."

"What did she say?" asked a whippet-thin girl criminally negligent in the hip department.

Esme's blush ate up the city of London all over again.

"Esme Stack," she said, croakily. "My name is Esme Stack."

After a moment's silence the people in black all turned away and started as one to rearrange the furniture away from her so they could sit together without having her in their sights.

Jemima, however, seemed entranced.

"Stack, of course," she said, laughing. "I heard you got married and things."

Esme said nothing. She wondered which "things" Jemima had heard.

"You've moved to the country, haven't you?" Jemima continued, flicking her long golden hair over her shoulder. "So what brings you to a place like this, darling? It's media types and business boys from floor to ceiling as a rule."

She turned and shone a dazzling smile at the barman. "Champagne, darling," she ordered him. "All round." She looked at Esme. "You'll have some, of course," she said.

"A French 75," Esme said with an authority she was delighted to find roaming around free for the taking.

The tiny golden arch that was Jemima's eyebrow raised itself minimally, given the restraint it was under by virtue of, as Alice had so correctly put it, being "Botoxed for Africa."

Her face was beautiful, as it always had been, but as animated as your average Louis Vuitton steamer trunk, Esme thought. Her eyes moved inside their sockets, and her mouth opened to speak, but her face remained glassily smooth, like the rest of her.

She stood in front of Esme's chair looking as long and silky as Esme felt short and frumpy.

"I'm writing a book," lied Esme suddenly, "about hair-clips." It had been such a strange day.

Jemima seemed to barely listen. "I'm having a meeting," she said, throwing her hair again in the direction this time of the people in black, who were murmuring among themselves, "about getting my own talk show on television. Can you believe it?"

Esme smiled encouragingly.

"Perhaps when your book is published," Jemima said, her expressionless face leaving Esme no clue as to whether she was being facetious or not, "you could come and talk about it."

The waiter delivered Esme her French 75, which she snatched with a nervousness that could have looked like greed.

"That would be brilliant," she said, smiling winningly and gulping back half of the lethal drink. "I'll let you know closer to the time."

The people in black started murmuring louder on the other side of the room and Jemima rolled her eyes. "I'd better go," she said. "Work, work, work!" And she twirled to give Esme a perfect eyeful of her tiny Stairmastered-within-an-inch-of-its-life butt. Not a hint of baboon-bum gum in sight. Esme gulped down the rest of her cocktail in one second flat.

"Do keep in touch," Jemima said, over her shoulder, before accepting a cigarette from one of her adoring crowd and getting down to business.

Esme stood, ever so slightly unsteadily on her feet, collected her bag and her thoughts and teetered across the room.

"Thanks for the drink," she said timidly to the group of backs and slid out the door.

"We paid for her drink?" she heard one of the men in black say, and her embarrassment was so acute that she forgot until she was at the bottom of the steps that the scab of her unrequited love for Louis Lapoine had not two hours ago been ripped off and left open and sore and bleeding.

She looked at her watch. She was just, as she stood there, missing the 2:30 to Ipswich and would have to ring Henry to get Rory from Mrs. McArthur, which he would count against her all week if not all month.

It was too hideous a prospect to contemplate.

CHAPTER 12

Well, I'll be jiggered," Granny Mac said, impressed, the next morning, when Esme slid into her room smelling so strongly of fresh bread that the stale cigarette stench hardly got a look in. "If there's not more than the merest hint of young Louis Lapoine in the air I'll eat my hat!"

Her hat sat on top of her wardrobe and looked extremely unappetizing. She had bought it in 1949 when it looked like an enormous pink hydrangea, and age had not improved it.

Esme had not breathed a word to anybody about her lunch the day before and as far as she knew only Charlie and a handful of waiters knew anything about it.

"What do you know about Louis Lapoine?" she asked briskly, pulling the bedclothes straight and whistling unwittingly to the inevitable Rod Stewart.

"I know as much as you do," her grandmother said. "And I know that no matter how much you might try to love again, Esme, the first cut is the deepest."

Esme thought about closing down, disagreeing,

arguing, but it seemed pointless. "I had lunch with him yesterday," she said evenly instead, taking up her position on her grandmother's bed.

"I knew it!" roared Granny Mac. "I bloody well knew it! And????"

"And he had hardly changed a bit except that now he wears a posh suit and travels the world spreading the good word about sourdough."

"And????"

"And we had a very civilized and delicious meal and I missed the two-thirty train and Henry had to get Rory from Mrs. McArthur so I am up there with Adolf Hitler in his books today and even though I've done nothing wrong I feel sick about Pog and I've found a roll of fat I am sure I didn't have a month ago and—"

"Oh, please, enough," Granny Mac demanded in her usual straightforward manner. "Cut to the chase, why don't you? Tell me more about the Frenchman."

"What do you want to know?"

"Don't trifle with me, Esme. Is there still something there?"

"What do you mean?" Esme asked in a small voice, knowing it was asking for trouble but stalling for time nonetheless.

"Does he still do for you what Sean Connery still does for your grandmother?"

"What are you on about?" She was pleading innocence but feeling the heat of her grandmother's disdain.

"Do you have to skip over and dance around everything that's even slightly tricky, Esme? Let alone the big stuff?"

She sat there, listening to her heartbeat, wondering what was happening to her.

"You have to start somewhere, you know, lassie." Granny Mac's voice seemed to soften. "It's not going to get easier, do you realize that? It is never going to get easier. You have to start letting it go."

The room fell silent and heavy with words unspoken from either end of the cozy single bed.

"I miss him," Esme finally whispered into the darkness.

"I know you do," her grandmother said. A tiny crevice of candor infiltrated the black air between them, and Esme realized with something that could have been a gasp, could have been a sob, that she felt like a woman whose very tight corset had just been loosened the tiniest bit, letting her breathe easily for the first time in a long, long while.

At just that moment the doorbell rang and she instantly felt the black boot in the small of her back of someone tying her corset tighter again. She straightened up. "The door," she said. "I'd better . . ."

Moments later she was staring aghast at Jam-jar standing on her doorstep and holding a scabby-looking donkey with what seemed to be a broken and badly splinted back leg. She wished fervently she had ignored the doorbell and stayed on her grandmother's bed, with perhaps her grandmother's pillow over her face, permanently.

"Well, I'm really not quite sure what to do with a donkey," she said to her neighbor, whose enormous eyes googled out at her, terrifyingly oversized, from behind his ancient Coke-bottle lenses.

"It's a he," said Jam-jar and to back him up the donkey chose that moment to drop his organ, also terrifyingly oversized, from wherever he had been keeping it up to that point and, appearing to stand on tiptoes, if donkeys even had them, urinated gushingly on Esme's doorstep.

Jam-jar seemed not altogether surprised and stepped niftily aside, missing the worst of it, but Esme got such a fright she shrieked and jumped backward. As she did the poor donkey also took fright and reared clumsily sideways, managing to spray huge jets of donkey pee through the open door and directly into Henry's brand-new Wellington boots. He had gone to Stonyborough three days before, on the bus, to get them. He would not be happy.

"Oh, no! Not again," she cried as Jam-jar grabbed at the donkey's halter and it retracted its enormous protuberance, steam still rising enthusiastically from the puddles on the ground and in her hallway.

The *tap-tap-clomp* that always preceded Henry heralded his imminent arrival, and Esme, panic-stricken, grabbed the Wellingtons and slung them inside Granny Mac's room just seconds before her father-in-law hove into view.

"What on earth is going on?" he demanded, taking in Esme's flushed face, the elderly neighbor and the lame donkey. At least he seemed oblivious, Esme thought thankfully, to what she was pretty sure was Granny Mac's version of "Do Ya Think I'm Sexy?" leaking out from her bedroom door.

"For God's sake, don't give the poor thing to her," Henry said over Esme's shoulder to Jam-jar.

Esme felt a little catch at the back of her throat which she recognized as hurt. "Don't be silly, Henry," she said as kindly as she could before turning to Jam-jar. "The Goat was really not my fault. Apparently they go blind quite often without anything to do with spades."

Jam-jar looked at her as though she was speaking a foreign language, and Esme realized that perhaps he hadn't known about the goat-blinding incident.

"I wasn't aware I was being silly," Henry harrumphed. "Have you seen my Wellingtons?"

Oh God, thought Esme. Does it really always have to be like this?

"She put them in the—" Jam-jar started to say before Esme leaped outside, shutting the door and Henry behind her.

"He's only just gotten over Brown peeing on his brogues," she hissed. "Please, I need time to explain the boots."

Jam-jar started to look scared and glanced

nervously back to the safety of his windmill. "Gladys from the bookshop in Seabury brought us the donkey," he said in his usual expressionless tone. "It's been hit by a van, I should think, or perhaps a small lorry and patched up by the receptionist at the vet but no one's claimed it and we can't keep it at ours as we've no fencing."

The donkey looked so gloomy Esme couldn't bear it. She didn't need another handicapped creature on her hands, but then again, who else would take care of the poor thing? Besides, despite telling herself she didn't care what Henry thought, she did care what Henry thought and she wanted to show him that she could do more with animals than repeatedly diminish their capacities.

"I'll take him," she said, and Jam-jar turned immediately and without a word started to shuffle away. "Come on, Eeyore," said Esme, using barely a sliver of imagination to christen the donkey. His big dark eyes looked at her glumly and she led him slowly past the house and through the willow fence into what had once been a grass tennis court, where she untethered him and watched him hobble toward a patch of dandelions.

God knew what donkeys ate, she thought. Or drank. And the poor thing was probably gasping for a drink after emptying his bladder so spectacularly. She headed back to the house, thinking she would get a bucket, but as she approached the front door, it flew open, and there stood Henry with a face like thunder holding up his dripping gum boots.

"I suppose you find this amusing," he challenged her.

"Of course not," Esme tried to reason. "I just put them in there because I thought I could clean them up before you found them."

Henry quivered with rage. "I am perfectly capable of cleaning them myself."

"Well, I'm sure you are but I just thought I could save you the bother since it was me who opened the door to the donkey."

"Oh, so it should have been me opening the door, then?" Henry fumed, catching the wrong cog yet again.

"For goodness' sake, Henry," Esme sighed, exasperated. Her father-in-law was acting as if she'd peed on his boots herself. She held out her hand. "Give them to me. I'll use the hose to clean them."

Henry snatched them away. "Your grandmother's room smells revolting," he said. "And you shouldn't be spending so much time in there."

Esme blushed. "That's none of your business," she said quietly.

"My son is my business," Henry said. "And your son is my business. And they both need you out here."

Esme gasped at the hardness in his eyes and Henry instantly tried to recant.

"Esme," he said, his old, craggy face collapsed with regret. He had not meant it to sound cruel but saw that it had. He held out a pleading hand to her but she whirled around and disappeared into Granny Mac's room again, slamming the door behind her, throwing herself on the bed and howling tears of rage and misery that had been pent up so long they barely knew what they were there for.

"Och," Granny Mac said soothingly, "there, there." She made no attempt to stop her grand-daughter's tears. She was glad to see them.

"Henry hates me," Esme sobbed. "Things keep weeing on him. It's not my fault. Everything's too hard. And Jemima's got my life."

"Oh, Esme," her grandmother sighed. "How can you be so blind?"

"I've had to be blind," wept Esme. "If I open my eyes and start seeing everything, I will die."

"Well, if you keep your eyes closed, you can hardly consider it living," Granny Mac said. "Say his name, Esme. Just say the wee boy's name."

"I can't," wept Esme. "I just can't. I can't think about him or hear about him or talk about him. I just can't. Oh, Granny Mac, what shall I do? Everything's such a mess. Of all the times to meet Louis, now just seems so wrong. What's to become of me? And Pog? And Rory? What's to become of all of us?"

"Oh, now's not such a bad time," Granny Mac said soothingly.

"How can you say that?"

"Well, has seeing the Frenchman again made you feel better or worse?" Granny Mac asked.

"What's that got to do with anything?"

"Just answer me, Esme. Better or worse?"

Esme closed her eyes and tried to take control of her sobs and think about the true answer to that question.

"It felt good yesterday," she said honestly. "But it feels bad today."

"And why did it feel good, do you think?" her grandmother inquired politely.

"Because," answered Esme, "he made me feel like the girl I used to be."

"Well," Granny Mac said softly. "Maybe, finally, we are getting somewhere."

Upstairs, the phone rang. Esme wiped her eyes and leaped up the stairs, grateful, in a way, to be safe from having the blatantly unhealed wounds of her distant and not-so-distant past poked at by the interfering specter of her grand-mother.

It was Charlie on the phone, wanting to do a bit of poking of his own.

"Was he still gorgeous?" he pestered her. "Was he still sexy? Did he make you horny, baby?"

"What is it with everyone?" Esme grumbled. "Why do you all want to know about that?"

Charlie was surprised. "Who else wants to know? Did you tell Pog?" he asked. "I thought you might have kept your little tryst to yourself, Es."

"No one," she said. "I didn't. It wasn't a tryst."

"Well, whatever it was I bet it spiced up your life, eh?" Charlie plowed on, hounding her for details. "Did it take you back to the sweltering bakery days of yore?"

"He told me he came to find me the night I left Venolat, Charlie," Esme told him. "You never mentioned that."

A small silence traveled uncomfortably down the phone line. "Well, why would I have told you that, Es? And what difference would it have made, anyway? It didn't make him unmarried."

"No, but it means that I wouldn't have spent the last fifteen years thinking he was a complete and utter shit who never gave a toss about me when it turns out that actually he did."

"Steady on, old girl."

"Did you know he came to St. John's Wood to find me and he stayed for a week looking but then gave up?"

"Really?" asked Charlie with a cough. "Do you suppose that's true?"

"Why wouldn't it be true?" Esme asked incredulously. "What would be the point in lying after all this time?"

"Well, I don't know," Charlie said awkwardly. "He wasn't exactly the most trustworthy fellow in the world, was he?"

"You are so bloody cynical, Charlie," Esme said angrily. "He's got stronger principles than you or I. He is still turning his back on his family fortune and teaching people how to bake sourdough. I mean you could hardly say the same about our careers, could you? You don't give a tinker's cuss about yours and I don't even have one."

"Calm down, Esme." Charlie was rattled now, too. "It was just a chance meeting. It's not like you are going to up and run off with him."

The very suggestion gave her a tremor of excitement.

"Actually," she said, "I could just up and run off if I wanted to. He isn't married anymore, he doesn't live with his kids, he travels the globe making the world's most delicious bread. It certainly seems a pleasant enough alternative to standing ankle-deep in donkey pee worrying about what a crappy mother you are."

"Essie"—Charlie's concern was clear—"are you all right? I would have thought lunch with Louis would have been a little surprise pick-me-up not a cat among the pigeons."

"Yes, well, lunch with you might have been a pick-me-up but with him it has unleashed a whole—"

The feel of someone's lips on the back of her neck sent a jolt of fear up her spine. She gasped.

"Unleashed a whole what?" Pog asked behind her, before moving over to the stove top to put the kettle on. "Sounds exciting. Is that Alice?" He must have come home for lunch and she'd not heard his footsteps on the stairs.

"I'd better go," Esme said into the receiver. She felt guilty and grubby. "I'll talk to you later."

Pog slumped down at the kitchen table and

smiled at her and Esme's heart swelled with love and confusion. What the hell was the matter with her? They may not have had the romance of the century, she and Pog, but she had never doubted for a moment how much he adored her. She could see it now in his eyes, despite the baggy black cushions underneath them and the thin veil of things he never told her lurking in front of them.

She sat down opposite him. "Is everything okay?" she asked.

"It's fine," he said with what she thought could have been a slightly forced smile, "although my father seems to be doing something very strange outside with the garden hose and if I'm not mistaken a wounded wildebeest of some description."

Esme rolled her eyes. "Don't ask," she advised, her heart racing inside as she examined her feelings for this gorgeous man and wondered how there could be room left to entertain thoughts of Louis.

"I thought I might go into Stonyborough this afternoon," Pog said, "and see if I can drum up a bit more work. Something a bit more challenging, perhaps. Mrs. Murphy is clicking her ballpoint pen to the point where I may have to do her some serious bodily harm so I thought I might get out of the office for a bit. Apparently that falling down old pub at the end of the High Street is up for sale so whoever buys it might be looking for an architect of my supremely outstanding skill. What do you think?"

In their old London days the thought of Pog trolling the high streets for renovation work would have had them gurgling derisively into their Chardonnays. Was it worth it? Had they made the right move?

"What about doing up Seabury—when will you hear about that?" she asked helpfully.

Pog looked surprised and she realized that he already had heard. She felt instantly mortified at having been too preoccupied with herself to think about him and got up and went to his side, cuddling him and kissing his head, sniffing his Pog-smelling hair.

"Oh, darling," she said. "You got it? Congratulations. I'm so sorry. That's wonderful news. When did you find out?"

"Oh, not long ago," he said brightly. "Don't worry about it. It doesn't matter." This was not true and they both knew it. But who between them would be the first to open the Pandora's box of what really mattered? Pog, though, thinking of Rory's sad little face and inquiring eyes out on the Meare and feeling suddenly reckless, decided on the spur of the moment to at least wriggle the lock.

"Esme," he said. "I've been thinking."

"About what?"

"About counseling."

"Oh, really?" Esme's voice was light but her shoulders had frozen. "For whom?"

For us, Pog wanted to say. For you and me and

our two darling boys. He eyed his wife and her square, frightened shoulders across the canyon of grief between them.

"Esme," he said quietly. "We can't go on like this."

"Like what?" she whispered.

"Like two normal people constantly tiptoeing around this great gaping puddle, terrified of stepping in it in case we bloody drown."

"Don't," she pleaded. "Please, Pog, don't."

"I miss him, Esme," Pog said, and his voice caught. "I want to talk about him."

He expected her to flee, but she didn't. She stayed there, stiff and square, looking straight at him.

"I'm not ready," she finally whispered, barely audible.

"But I am," Pog answered her, the strength almost back in his voice. "I am."

"Then *you* talk about him," she said. "*You* get counseling."

She looked so frightened then, so lonely and small and lost and hunted, that Pog's bravery abandoned him.

"Silly idea," he said, shaking his head. "You're right. Forget I mentioned it."

Her shoulders stayed tense, her face rigid with fear. Pog felt cruel. He knew she wasn't ready. But like Rory, he wondered how long they would all have to wait.

After two years of sidestepping the puddle, however, they were both surefooted.

"Any chance of a sarnie?" he asked, abandoning the dreadful subject and watching her shoulders slowly relax. He'd already had a bag of chips and two doughnuts since breakfast, but the kitchen was ringing with the sweet smell of freshly baked sourdough, and if there was one thing that would give Esme back her equilibrium, move them away from the torture of his failed attempt at progress, it was slicing into a freshly baked loaf.

Her face collapsed with relief and she jumped up and pulled out a bread knife.

She wasn't ready, but she was closer. He knew that. Those weeks when she had stopped baking he'd been worried, but since her return to sourdough there had definitely been a change, a lift, in her spirits. Without that early-morning ritual life had been torturous in the House in the Clouds. Without the rhythm of Esme's breadbaking it had been hard to recognize the place as his own. Practically every routine they had, from folding the washing to paying the bills to fitting in a quick shag, in the good old days, had been introduced around the various stages in the process, and once Esme abandoned her bread, nothing fell into place anymore.

The jams and chutneys and preserves had stopped her from taking to her bed entirely, something Granny Mac, half delirious with her pneumonia, had warned him could one day happen, but her heart had not been in them. Her heart

264

was in her sourdough. And then, after those few bleak weeks, she had started making it again and Pog had just about collapsed with relief because it heralded the beginnings of a return to normal, if life could ever be considered normal at the House in the Clouds. For once he felt he had done the right thing in his despair by feeding the starter despite Esme's insistence that she would never need it again.

So it hadn't bubbled and burped the way it did when Esme mollycoddled it, but it had smelled vinegary and sharp and had not turned its nose up at the healthy meals of flour and water he fed it.

And when, for whatever reason—Would she ever tell him? Would he ever know?—Esme returned to it as he had prayed she would, it had turned itself into a perfect *boule* and hurrah, they were back in business again. So his wife's behavior had been slightly odd since her return to bread-baking—it was her slightly odd behavior that had attracted him to her in the first place.

He had spotted her across the room: a life raft of color in a sea of black-clad architects. Her hair had been piled on top of her head so that her red curls were like an eccentric fountain cascading down over her shoulders and back. She was wearing a citrus green wraparound top that hugged her curves, a black full skirt with matching green embroidery of some sort winding its way around the bottom, red platform boots and a tiny red leather backpack, and was picking at a tray of smoked salmon canapés. When he got closer, Pog saw that she was taking capers off some of the soggy little pancake things, and placing them on others, which she was then popping in her mouth.

"We're a perfect match," he said to her from across the catering table as he reached for a de-capered snack. "I don't care for the little green balls myself." She looked up at him, her big emerald eyes slightly horrified at having been caught, and he fell in love with her there and then.

She looked like a fallen angel.

A blush that matched her backpack crept up her chest and onto her face and she opened her mouth to speak but, realizing it was still full of food, shut it again. Pog felt an urge to snatch her into his arms, which as it turned out was pretty much what happened. The capers in Esme's mouth, confused by being interrupted during their journey to her stomach, became confused and went down the wrong way. Esme choked.

Pog then leaped, fast as lightning, around the table, and reaching around her from behind, her backpack buckle scratching his belly as he did so, crushed her with such force that a mouthful of munched up blini and sour cream spotted with half-chewed caper shot out her mouth. They gazed, aghast, as the creamy-looking clump flew straight back onto the catering table where it landed in the middle of a plate of cheese-and-walnut balls.

Before either of them could move a muscle, a hand belonging to the extremely fat convenor of the judging panel—who was standing right next to the platter boring a young architect's wife rigid with stories of rambling in the Cotswolds—reached, unseeing, and popped Esme's regurgitated snack into his own phlegmy mouth.

Pog was frozen in fascination, Esme in horror. Yet nobody else seemed to have seen. The fat judge merely licked his fingers and reached for more canapés.

"I think we should get married," Pog said when his paralysis evaporated and he held out his hand to introduce himself. "I'm Hugo Stack."

"Esme MacDougall," reciprocated Esme. "I think we should have a sit-down meal at the wedding, don't you? Bite-sized snacks can be dangerous."

The first night they stayed up talking and laughing and watching old Peter Sellers films. The next day they walked in Kew Gardens, ate at the River Café—how he loved to watch her eat!—listened to jazz until the wee small hours and then the next day she took him home to Granny Mac and fed him her homemade sourdough. Sitting in her warm little flat eating cannellini bean and pesto soup with his first ever inch-thick slice of Esme's *pain au levain*, it seemed to Pog that the missing piece of the jumbled jigsaw puzzle he had long felt like had been found.

Every minute he had spent without her ever since had been a minute he didn't care for. He thanked his lucky stars every morning he woke up and smelled her there in the bed beside him. Without her he was like old lemonade. Flat and tasteless. She provided the bubbles that made his life worth living, worth loving.

He doubted, often, from the very beginning whether he was exciting enough for her, whether he was anything enough for her, although she laughed off these suggestions as completely ridiculous.

"Wearing fawn-colored corduroy is not the worst crime in the world, you know," she had said in the early days of their courtship.

"Corduroy is a crime?" Pog had asked her, bewildered. "How am I supposed to know these things?"

He had loved Granny Mac from the word go, too. She was just the opposite of everyone in his family. Totally outspoken, insatiably curious, straightforward to the point of irascibility. He loved it and she loved him. She thought he was perfect for Esme and told him so within a minute of meeting him. Esme, who blushed at everything, simply smiled and laughed at this, unembarrassed. The bond between the two women was awe-inspiring.

Pog, who knew his parents loved him but had spent his lifetime wondering if they liked him, found being at the MacDougall flat in St. John's

Wood unbelievably comforting. Henry and Grace had been adept if aloof parents. Milo and Pog had both been sent to boarding school at seven and neither had lived permanently at home ever since. Visits, short or lengthy, were pleasant but formal affairs. Feelings were never discussed or displayed. Conversation revolved around Henry's work, Grace's garden, the boys' careers, the weather. At Granny Mac's place, though, emotion ran wild and free and the small, cozy rooms echoed with laughter and Rod Stewart. There, Pog need never wonder how anyone felt, he just knew. It was as plain as day. And as Pog had never been one to poke or pry, just knowing came as a blessed relief.

He bit into the bread and felt it surrender to his tongue, the sharp tartness of the apricot jam hitting the back of his throat just as the sour crust of the bread met resistance from his teeth. There was such joy in eating, thought Pog. He watched his wife watching him as he ate his lunch. He felt happiness and he felt despair. It was a combination he was used to. He wiped the crumbs from his face and kissed Esme good-bye, then went back to work.

Esme too felt happiness and despair, for the same and for very different reasons. She was consumed with what Pog had said, what Granny Mac had said and with heart-thumping silent reenactments of the day before's lunch. Had she really just out and out asked Louis why he had broken her heart? Why had she done that? The damage had long been done and there was nothing to be gained by stirring up the past. The present was enough of a hornet's nest after all.

She twice got all the way out to the washing line before remembering that the basketful of laundry was sitting on the kitchen table and then got a run in her favorite tights on the hideous gargoyle that had been at the front door of the house when they bought it and which Pog had been too scared to discard in case it came back to haunt them. Hah! Fat chance, she thought, glowering at the wretched thing. Then, to top it all off, Rory greeted her at nursery school tired and grumpy and full of loathing.

"I hate those shoes," was the first thing he said to her when she turned up to collect him. "They stink. I want Granddad." Esme smiled wanly at Mrs. Monk, who in turn looked indulgently at Rory as though he had just said the cleverest thing in all the world.

Mrs. Monk's own shoes where battered brown lace-up Hush Puppies, worn down on the soles and doing nothing for her stumplike ankles. Esme's, on the other hand, were strappy Louis Vuitton boots bought at a seconds shop in London several winters previously. Esme loved them with all her heart.

"Well, they're Mummy's favorites," she said more kindly to her son than she felt, flinching internally at the cross little frown that ran across his round baby face. "So I guess that's what counts."

"Other mothers wear proper ladies' shoes, Esme," Rory said, turning to his teacher for backup. "Don't they, Mrs. Monk?" The old dragon's smirk added another thousand lines to her already wrinkled face.

"Well, it takes all sorts, Rory, isn't that what we say?" counseled Mrs. Monk. "And I'm sure Mother has other shoes at home she can perhaps try wearing tomorrow."

The cheek of the woman, thought Esme, her emotions running too high to contemplate a retort that might not see her run out of town by good Christian women.

"Come on, darling," she said, holding out her hand to her son.

"Go away. I can walk by myself," Rory said meanly, and started toward home without her, earning another approving look from his adoring teacher.

Esme's skin felt stretched thin. She was sure that if one more piercing arrow was pointed in her direction she would explode, leaving bits of her shattered self hanging from the light fittings like dough mixed too wet and flung out of a mixing bowl.

Rory, to her great relief, seemed immensely cheered by the sight of the gammy-legged donkey in his backyard. He dropped his bag and his pinched expression and went with his grandfather to examine the creature's fecal matter for signs, apparently, of worms.

CHAPTER 13

"What the hell have you been up to?" Alice barked from the phone on Sunday morning as Esme looked out the window at eye-level clouds. The weather outside was gloomy and dull, which matched just how she felt.

"Nothing," she answered her friend. "Except laundry, polishing the stairs, making the beds, stewing apples, polishing more stairs, ministering to the donkey, trying not to strangle my son, polishing more stairs. You get the picture."

"It sounds far more exciting the way your friend Jemima puts it," Alice said crisply, rustling the *Sunday Times* as loudly as she could manage while holding the telephone under her chin. "I didn't realize she still had it in for you to quite such a degree. Is there something I should know?"

"Jemima?" Esme was bewildered. "What does she have to do with anything?"

"You only feature in her column this morning, Esme. In startling Technicolor."

In the hurricane of thoughts that had whirled around her head in the aftermath of her lunch with Louis, Esme had quite forgotten she had seen Jemima.

"What on earth are you talking about?" she asked Alice, but as she did her bewilderment curdled and turned to dread, the contents of her stomach appearing to slither down six flights of stairs and land on the cold flagstones of the bottom floor far below her.

"'*Which slightly disheveled-looking former fag mag editor,*'" Alice read out, "'*was spotted during the week sucking back champagne cocktails all on her lonesome in the bar of posh Marylebone High Street eatery the Orrery?*'"

"Oh, my God!" whispered Esme.

"That's nothing," said Alice, reading on. "'*The sad little Ginger-No-Friends has been hiding away deep in the Suffolk countryside for the past few years but obviously needs to pop her head up for air and a sip of Taittinger every now and then and who could blame her?*'"

She paused to gauge Esme's response but there was none. Shock had rendered her speechless.

"You didn't know this was coming?" Alice asked. "Blimey. You'd better brace yourself for the next bit, Es." She had started out the conversation piqued at being left out of the lunchtime cocktail-loop but was now having second thoughts. Trying to end up in the Sunday papers was one thing, but being there unexpectedly was another.

"'*All those warm lagers and porkpies down at her local pub,*'" Alice read out as quickly as she could, "'can obviously play merry hell with a girl's waist-band. No wonder this once-rising star of the London publishing scene needs to escape back to the big city every now and then. And for the one or two of you who may have been wondering what project the rumpled little creature is working on now? It's a book about hairclips.' My God, where does she get this drivel from? 'And I don't know where she's doing her research but it's certainly not on her own head. I guess the perm is still alive and well and living in the countryside!' And in case you weren't sure about how sarcastic that is supposed to be, Es, there's an exclamation mark."

Alice, finally, was silent. "Are you still there, Es?"

Esme felt too anesthetized with humiliation to speak. How could that unspeakable woman embarrass her this way? Whatever had she done to Jemima?

"She called me a Ginger-No-Friends?" was all she could finally manage.

"Well, were you sitting there all on your own swilling champagne or not?" Alice demanded. "And if so, why wasn't I invited?"

"I was supposed to be having lunch with Charlie," Esme said, her lips white with dismay. "But he never turned up. Is she saying I looked fat? Is the bit about the porkpies meant to say I looked fat? Because if she's saying I looked fat I think I might seriously have to kill her."

"You think that's worse than calling you a once-rising star?" Alice wanted to know. "When after all it was she who shot your rising star down in the first place. You're right, though. She is evil and she must be destroyed. And I think she *is* saying you looked fat but you don't."

Esme collapsed into a chair and tried to sort out in her mind what was the worst thing about appearing in Jemima's column. For a start, neither her husband nor her best friend had known she was out for lunch that day. She should have told Pog, she knew that, but she hadn't and then it had been too late. She'd been unable to come up with a way to make her meeting with Louis seem innocent, even though it was, and so had fudged the details of what she'd done with her day. As for Alice, if she'd told her she had met Louis, she would have also told her that he wanted to see her again and Alice would have insisted she stop being so bloody stupid. She supposed she had been avoiding that.

"Oh, Alice," she said. "What am I going to do? Pog doesn't know I went down to London for the day, nor does—oh my God—Henry! They will jump to all the wrong conclusions and how dare she call me sad and little. Did she really call me sad and little? And rumpled? And a creature? Oh, it's too hideous for words."

A slight frostiness chilled the phone line. "You didn't tell Pog? What's going on? Is there a wrong conclusion to jump to?"

"No. Nothing. No," Esme said hastily. "There's

absolutely nothing going on. I just stupidly, for no reason, didn't tell him. You know how he is about Charlie. He's probably the person Pog likes least in the world, which is not really saying much because he still likes him and everything but, oh shit, I'm all over the place at the moment, Alice, you know that. It wasn't on purpose. I didn't mean it. And now to be ridiculed publicly by that long streak of, of, of—" She struggled to come up with an apt description.

"Weasel's piss?" suggested Alice.

"Yes, weasel's piss. It's just too much. It feels like just too much." The wind, indeed, felt taken out of Esme's sails, and Alice could tell.

"Nobody will know it's you," she said assertively, deciding to be supportive. "And anyway, Pog doesn't read the *Sunday Times* and Henry wouldn't bother with Jemima's column and to be honest, you should be thankful that she didn't come to your house. You should hear what she has to say about Primrose Beckwith-Stuyvesant's new place."

"Really?" Esme asked without interest. Her own troubles seemed too many and varied to contemplate anyone else's.

"Get a load of this," Alice started. "It's right under the bit about you. *'I had heard that poor dear Primrose had decided to do the decorating herself but nobody had quite prepared me for her spectacular lack of skill let alone flair in this department. You'd imagine that someone with a name like Primrose*

277

would know the difference between caramel and brown, would you not? Between chartreuse and lime green? Between cerise and shocking pink? Anyway, I am sure that somewhere in Morocco lurks a second-rate seventies bordello owner who is seriously wondering what happened to all his furnishings. Try Belgravia, Achmed! That's my advice. All eyes were supposed to be on Juniper Smythe, the stepniece of the hostess, who has recently announced her engagement to PR king Lance Silverspoon, but frankly it was hard to make the poor girl out among the kaleidescope of garishness that is Primrose's drawing room. Let's hope the wedding will be held somewhere more demure. In the finger painting room of the local nursery school, for example.'"

Esme's own misery was left bobbing, temporarily, in a sea of sympathy for poor Primrose.

"She is a complete and utter cow," she breathed, astonished at the level of Jemima's bitchery. Whatever had poor Primrose done to deserve such a public lambasting? "It's like a horrible nightmare."

"I won't read you the bit about little Marie Claire's first piano recital then," suggested Alice, "because it may give you a duodenal ulcer. And compared to poor Primrose, you didn't do so badly really."

"No, I'm just a fat, lonely has-been with ginger hair in need of clips that looks permed but isn't," said Esme. "I'm just swell."

"God knows where she got the story about the

278

hairclips. The woman is obviously completely deranged."

"Yes, well," coughed Esme, "I did see her at the bar in the Orrery and we had a perfectly pleasant conversation. In fact she bought me the drink, or the nine-year-old TV producers who were courting her did, much to their own horror. Oh, God, what a mess!" Her head raced with illegal thoughts of the bar, the restaurant, Louis.

"Don't tell me she is getting her own TV show," shrilled Alice. "If she gets her own TV show you won't have to kill her because I will have done it for you. Did she look good?"

"Gorgeous," Esme said dully. "A little masklike in the face obviously but very tall and slim and blond and—"

"Ridge!" Alice pulled away from the phone and called to her son. "Ridge! Wait a minute! Esme, I have to go. Ridge has just come in and it's been three days since I've seen him. Hold on," she called to her son. "I'll ring you back later," she garbled to Esme, "to tell you about the Armenian with the extra nipple. Disastrous. Don't worry. Talk to you soon. Ridge!" And she was gone.

For the rest of Sunday Esme felt so close to tears or a nervous breakdown or a full confession (even though she hadn't really done anything, she kept telling herself) that Pog put her to bed, like Peter Rabbit, with a cup of chamomile tea at 7:30. Every time the phone rang, her heart dropped down to the pit of her stomach and churned.

The next day she stumbled through her chores convinced that her husband was going to storm into the house at any moment waving the newspaper and shouting, "What is the meaning of this, you filthy hussy," which, of course he never did. Pog was not a stormer and anyway, the House in the Clouds was probably not an ideal place to storm. If you were still full of bluster and huff after six flights of stairs you were most likely not someone who liked chocolate sauce on their cornflakes and who preferred eating homemade bread with your wife to watching football with the lads down at the local.

By the end of the next day Esme had started to relax and think that maybe Alice was right, that no one would ever know it was she that Jemima was talking about, and that although she didn't really have anything to be ashamed about, she could stay privately not ashamed of it without any dreadful consequences.

By the end of the day after that, however, her relief was verging on something that seemed to approach resentment. She had even gone so far as to get Alice to fax a copy of the hideous column up to her—she had definitely not bought the paper herself—so she could read it to Granny Mac once "I Was Only Joking" faded away to a reasonable level.

"It's bloody hilarious," her grandmother roared. "Oh, she has spunk, that one. 'Ginger-No-Friends,' I've not heard that before, Esme. I've not laughed so much in a long, long while. Thanks. Thanks a lot. Och, read it again will you?"

"No, I will not!" Esme answered. "It's not funny, it's horrible. She's humiliated me."

"In front of whom?" Granny Mac asked her. "As Alice says, no one would ever know it was you. I mean in the first instance most people would presume that a fag mag is something subscribed to by homosexuals, not cigar smokers. And who would ever imagine that you would be sitting in a fancy bar in Marylebone swilling cocktails on your own in the middle of the day? Nobody, that's who. It's a ridiculous notion."

Granny Mac had, as was her wont, hit the nail on Esme's head. Who *would* ever imagine that she would be sitting in a fancy bar in Marylebone drinking cocktails on her own in the middle of the day?

Nobody. That's who. It was a ridiculous notion. They, whoever they were, would be too busy imagining her running up and down a thousand stairs in her hideaway hole in the country with her head in the clouds like the rest of her house. They would be imagining her trying to tighten the splint on her donkey's broken leg, milking her blind goat, taming some mad bees, kowtowing to her difficult father-in-law, wrangling her recalcitrant son, pouring all her leftover love and ancient desire into fat, brown, round loaves of bread, hiding from the tragedy about which others still spoke among themselves with words that stayed choked up and constipated in her own throat.

"It hasn't always been a ridiculous notion," she told her grandmother. "Once upon a time nobody would have been surprised to find me swilling French 75s in swanky surroundings in the middle of a weekday. Quite the opposite—they would have been surprised if that wasn't what I was doing. And now, you're telling me not one single reader of England's most famous Sunday newspaper has put two and two together and come up with four? Am I so much of a has-been bloody hausfrau these days that no one could be surprised by me? When did I get so pathetic? So predictable?"

Her grandmother looked at her. "Is a French 75 the one with the gin or the one with the cherry?" she asked.

"Granny Mac," Esme said as calmly as she could, fixing her eyes on the hydrangea hat atop the wardrobe. "I am in trouble here. Please help me."

"The problem is not that you are a has-been bloody hausfrau," Granny Mac answered her eventually. "And the problem is not Jemima Jones."

The room was deathly silent. The temperature seemed to have plummeted. Esme felt cold with dread. She started to shiver.

"The problem is you, Esme. You and your loss." The words came painfully slowly and cut right through her. "The worst loss a woman, a mother can suffer."

"It's not that," Esme said, her teeth chattering.

"You can't keep pushing it away and not feeling

it, Esme. It's not working. Especially not now with me the way I am."

"It's not about that," whispered Esme. "It's not about him."

"Oh, Esme, aren't you tired of this?"

She was tired, unbelievably tired. Too tired to deal with what her grandmother wanted from her. "It's about Louis," she insisted, feeling cowardly but determined. "It's all about Louis."

Her grandmother's displeasure was palpable, the air in the dingy room clanged with it. "Have it your way, then," Granny Mac said finally. "But if it is Louis stirring you up, for God's sake at least have the guts to let yourself be stirred."

Esme sat stock-still on the end of her grandmother's bed.

"He wants to meet me for lunch again tomorrow," she said.

"I know," answered Granny Mac.

"I want to go," said Esme.

"I know," answered Granny Mac.

Silence filled the room and left Esme with nothing but the pounding of her heart and the contents of her head.

"Because even though it is vastly complicating matters, it feels"—she sought out the word from the carnival in her head—"good. Like the end of something. Or"—she was loath to even think such a thing—"heaven forbid, the beginning."

"I know," said Granny Mac. "Just not like you're stuck forever in the bollocking middle."

"That's right," agreed Esme. "Is there anything you don't know?"

"I know everything you do," said Granny Mac. "It's just that sometimes I know it sooner. I'm good like that."

"You don't think I'm wicked?"

"Oh, don't flatter yourself. You're just a girl in the world, Esme, trying to get through life without killing someone or having a nervous breakdown just like the next person. You truly think you're the first person to suffer a loss so enormous you can't get your head out of the sand to confront it? You think no one else has ever tried to escape the reality of their life with the fantasy of another? It's nothing new. It's all been done before."

"Is that supposed to make me feel better?"

"You tell me what it's supposed to make you feel."

"Honestly, times like this I don't know why I bother, Granny Mac," Esme snapped, straightening her soft pink lamb's-wool jumper, and standing up to leave.

"Oh, aye," Granny Mac said rudely. "Silly me. Pants down, bottom smacked."

Esme left the room and started the climb up to the kitchen. She had soup to make, a pair of Pog's pants to mend and afternoon tea to prepare for Henry and Rory plus the oven was horribly overdue for a clean and the windows in the sitting room were so filthy she could barely see out of them. She had a lot of housework to get through if she was going down to London the next day to meet the love of her life.

"The *first* love," she corrected herself out loud.

"What was that?"

Unfortunately, she had corrected herself out loud while passing Henry on the first floor landing.

"Oh, nothing," she smiled. "Just talking to myself."

"Yes, well, there would seem to be an awful lot of that going on around here lately," he said gruffly. "And in my day that thing out there would have earned itself a bullet between the eyes, not a lot of fussy mollycoddling by a bunch of ignorant city people."

It took Esme a few seconds to work out that he was talking about poor Eeyore.

"I thought you liked the donkey," she said, surprised. "And Rory certainly seems to. It's good for him to have another friend about the place." She smiled brightly but Henry shot her a look of such inexplicable contempt that she simply turned and traipsed up the stairs.

She defrosted some chicken stock, chopped a pile of carrots and parsnips, hand-stitched the pants Pog had split bending over at Enid Entwhistle's house to inspect a blocked drain, then rang Alice at work to see what was happening with the wayward Ridge.

"He's got a job at some restaurant in the West End," Alice garbled into the phone. "And I think he is spending the nights with Mrs. Miller. He barely speaks to me, just grunts as he comes and goes, and I seem incapable of doing anything about it. It's such fun."

"What about Mr. Miller?"

"He's off on an oil rig for six weeks at a time, I do know that much, but not from my hulking ingrate of an offspring. From Olive upstairs."

"The blowsy midmorning gin drinker?"

"No, the mild-mannered mousy librarian. Oh! And she's not a librarian. She's a hostess at some private drinking club in the City all full of ancient old relics in fancy suits sipping cognac and wetting their pants. Who'd have guessed? Anyway, she says it's not the first time Mrs. Miller has 'entertained' during her husband's absence and that I should not be too worried and that, get this, Ridge is such a nice young man. He picks up her shopping from the supermarket and brings it home for her. Every week. Has done for nearly a year. You could have knocked me over with a feather. The things you find out!"

Esme heard the pride in Alice's voice and felt thrilled for her.

"We always knew he would turn out well in the end, didn't we? How could he not have, with you as a mother and a procession of three-nippled psychopaths with bicycle clip issues as 'uncles'?"

Alice groaned. "Don't talk to me about 'uncles.' I swear, if I don't have sex soon I am going to explode in an unsightly fashion all over Nose Hair's shredder. It's not fair that I am approaching my sexual peak and there is no one for me to peak on. I'm considering going into one of those shops in Soho to buy a big pink rubber thing with multiple attachments and a key pad of instructions."

"Considering it?" Esme asked. "I thought you would have a cupboardful by now."

"I've been resisting it on the grounds that if I find something to have sex with, why would I bother with an actual man?"

"Well, I think you deserve points for optimism and perhaps a medal from Prince Charles."

"Ooooh you are nasty," Alice squawked. "Fancy mentioning Prince Charles when you know I am all fizzy down below."

"Alice, I thought we had a rule about the Royal Family."

"Sweetie, he isn't married, has his own car and a big lump in his jodhpurs, of course I fancy him. And at least it keeps my mind off Prince William."

Esme shrieked. "That's illegal!"

"Well, I may even have to jump the bones of one of the poor pathetic wretches I am dating this week," Alice said matter-of-factly. "That is what it has come to."

If Alice was considering actually seeing one of her heinous microbes without his clothes on, Esme knew she was in a bad way.

"But there's more to life than sex, Alice," she said supportively. "We have talked about this before."

"You have talked about it before, Esme, because you are having it. I just listen and wish I had someone like Pog to curl up in bed with at night and make mad, passionate love to in the morning."

"I could loan him to you like what's-her-name did with Kevin Kline in *The Big Chill*," Esme offered. "Although I would be scared he might not come back to me."

She realized that this was true. Their dwindling, or rather dwindled sex life was just another thing that she and Pog chose to ignore, but she had not discussed this with Alice. It seemed mean to have it all on tap and not be thirsty.

Her mind turned to Louis and his tongue on the curve of her belly.

"I thought I would come down to London tomorrow," she said, reining in her imagination, "and we could catch up for a drink in town after work. Do you fancy it?"

"Do I what!" said Alice.

When Esme woke up the next morning, she felt an excitement she could remember from the Christmas mornings of her childhood. If she closed her eyes she could almost smell the pine needle spray Granny Mac had gone to town with in the absence of a real tree with real pine needles.

Pog, in his sleep, snorted, rolled over in their bed and flung one arm over her middle. Esme looked down at his floppy hair and his sleep-squashed face and wondered how she could love him so much but have a stomachful of butterflies fluttering in anticipation of a different man altogether.

When had she turned into this person who could lie and keep such dangerous secrets? She gently removed his arm, got dressed and went up to the kitchen to get her bread started. Even high up in the sky she could smell the rain that had fallen on the grass overnight and, if she was not mistaken, there was a hint of donkey in the air as well. Her senses were on red alert, just as they had been all those years ago in Venolat.

As Esme dragged the flour bin out of the pantry, she was sure she could smell wheat, in the fields, and maybe a wisp of the water used to turn the wheel at the mill in Pakenham where she bought it.

Her own tap water jumped excitedly into the jug before she poured it in with the flour, and her starter seemed more wildly exuberant than usual. She could swear that it smelled of that little *boulangerie* by the fountain. Esme lifted the jar to her face and breathed it in. There was definitely something special in the air this morning.

She plunged her hand into the bowl and swirled the wet mixture between her fingers, then squeezed it against the palm of her hands until all the ingredients were mixed together. Again and again she danced around the bowl until the floury, watery mixture turned into dough and started to feel like skin against her hand. She was getting hot. She threw the salt into the bowl and kneaded it into the dough, feeling every grain resist disappearing into that luxurious blend but pressing and pushing and ever so gently pummeling until the crunchiness was gone and the dough was silky and skinlike again.

She rolled it out of the bowl and started working it on the counter. With the heel of her hand she pushed it away from herself and with the curve of her cupped fingers she pulled it back, again and again and again until she could feel sweat trickle between her shoulder blades.

With every pump of her arm she thought of Louis. Her teeth on his skin, her lips on his neck, his fingers in her—

"Bloody hell, Essie, you'll do yourself a mischief!"

The sound of her husband's voice gave her such a fright that for a moment she was completely lost. She felt so utterly, embarrassingly caught in flagrante delicto that she could barely believe it was only bread she was making.

Pog came up behind her and wriggled into her.

"You're going at it hammer and tongs, Esme," he said. "What's all that flour and water done to deserve that?"

He kissed her neck and she felt ill with artifice. She turned in his arms and kissed him, pushing all thoughts of Louis deep down inside.

"Delicious," Pog said, pulling away and looking at her. "It's not right that anyone should look as good as you at this ungodly hour." He scratched his stomach. "Couldn't go back to sleep," he added, yawning. "Anything I can do to help?"

Esme shook her head and went back to her bread, listening to him scrabble around in the pantry for his breakfast cereal.

"I have to spend another twenty-six hours talking to Ernie about his 'loggia,' as it's now called," he said as he mooched about the kitchen. "And I think I have a meeting today with an Ipswich developer who might be keen on that Stonyborough pub. Shady-sounding bloke, though. Shouldn't imagine it will come to much. Not that it needs to with all the work Mrs. Murphy has piling up for me. What about you? Anything exciting planned for today?"

Esme tried not to stop the rhythm of her kneading.

"Actually, I thought I might go down to London for a spot of shopping and to meet Alice for a drink. She's got the dimwit blues," she said lightly.

"Oh, that's right," Pog said. "Henry mentioned you'd asked him to look after Rory. Good on you, darling, say hello to Alice from me."

"Anything you need?" she asked. "Anything I can get for you? Books? Magazines? Little tidbits from Fortnum and Mason?"

Pog's spoon stopped clanging against his bowl and she turned around to see him looking at her.

"What?" she asked him.

"You are amazing," he answered. "That's all.

Simply amazing. Whatever did I do to deserve you?"

All the way to London she thought about his adoring face and what he had said and she kept thinking about it as she sat at the same table in the Orrery, fidgeting with her table napkin and waiting for Louis.

She had a wonderful husband, a healthy child, a lovely home. Why the hell was she risking all that for some duplicitous little French baker who had broken her heart a hundred years ago and without whom she would happily have kept on living had not fate brought them together over a bubble gum disaster next door?

But when Louis walked into the room and saw her, all her doubts disappeared, to be instantly replaced by nothing but the certainty of chemistry. His effect on her was pure and physical and no amount of debating the appropriateness of the situation could change that. He walked across the room, late but not rattled, then leaned in and kissed her on each cheek. They burned. He looked into her eyes. They swam. He reached across the table and took her hand in his. She let him.

The bread came and went, their appetizers were demolished; their main courses sat in front of them tantalizing their taste buds with their rich, delicious smells. She could not remember, afterward, what they talked about over the scallops and wild mushrooms and crispy skinned duck. All she knew was that right there and then she felt an over-whelming hunger that she knew food would not sate. She felt empty from the nails on her toes to the hair on her head and as her eyes feasted on Louis, she knew that somehow he held the key to filling her up.

She could see nothing but the dark intense features of his face in front of her, the hustle and bustle of the busy restaurant moving behind him, blurred and out of focus like a modern-day cooking show. She was not really even listening to what he said, what she said, just transfixed by the barely perceptible hook in his nose, the smooth-ness of his cheeks, the roll of his wrist bone, the arc of his eyebrows, the length of his lashes, the little lines under his eyes that were new to her.

But the things she was keeping to herself were groaning and growing inside her. And there were a lot of them. And they were in desperate need of escape.

A silence grew between them.

I want you, she wanted to say to him. *I want you now. Over there. On that banquette.* But even as she opened her mouth to speak she knew she wouldn't. She shut her mouth again. Instead, it was Louis who spoke.

"Tell me about your children," he said quietly.

"Child," said Esme. "Child. I have a son. Rory. He's four-and-a-half."

Louis looked at her, slightly quizzically, as though he somehow knew otherwise. He did not speak, just kept looking straight at her, a funny wriggle in his eyebrows.

She felt suddenly icy cold and boiling hot at the same time and her chest started to rise and fall too quickly. The toxic fumes of her inner demons were dancing close to a naked flame and she could feel it so dangerously it took her breath away.

Something deadly was trying to escape the constraints of her heart and for less than a split second Esme pictured, just glimmeringly, the relief of letting it go, and in that fraction of a second it bolted for freedom.

"I have one son," she said again before she could taste the words on her lips, "but he had a twin brother."

It was out now, floating in the space between them.

"Ted," she said. "Teddy." How strange the feel of his name was on her tongue. How lonely and lost. How long had it been since she had said it out loud?

Actually, she knew.

It had been two years, two months, thirteen days, twenty hours and forty-seven minutes.

Esme floated up to the ceiling of the restaurant and looked down at herself about to tell this heart-stoppingly handsome, perfect almost-stranger about the day, the hour, the minute, the second she stopped being herself and became a mother of one.

And the tears that she had found so difficult, so

impossible, to shed for her poor little Rory-Pog clone suddenly presented themselves for the inspection of Louis Lapoine, her long-lost lover, and the waiting staff and patrons of the Orrery restaurant.

Oh, but they had been such a long time coming.

CHAPTER 14

Life had been going well for Esme and Pog until that cruel spring day in Notting Hill. Their prospective careers, in which they had both managed to spend quite some time up until then floundering, had finally clicked into place and they were both charging full-steam ahead.

The previous year, through an old college friend, Pog had won a modest contract to refurbish a small investment brokerage in the City and had done such a good job that when the company had been bought out by a big German firm, they engaged him to do a similar job, only ten times bigger, in another empty shell near St. Paul's. More recently his company had been contracted to design a new thirty-story building, and after years of scratching away virtually unnoticed by his employers, Pog had been asked to manage the project. It was the stuff of which major awards were made, and while being a daunting task of quite some proportion, Pog reveled in the responsibility. He wasn't the sort to push himself forward but once out front, had all it took and more. He had blossomed.

Esme's career, too, had finally stopped hitting potholes and seemed to be running along smoothly. When she had been deposed by Jemima and lost her job at *TV Now!*, the road back from ruin had been bumpy, to say the least. Humiliated by her ousting and—typically for a London girl in her mid-twenties—short on anything so helpful as savings, she'd accepted a job running an old men's smoking magazine published by a company that made pipes and cigarette papers.

Vogue, it wasn't. But Sebastian Goodhart, the elderly publisher/pipemaker, was an old-fashioned gentleman who adored Esme from the moment she whirled into his office with her ginger curls and slash of red lipstick, and under his gentle and bemused patronage, she and the funny little magazine flourished. In less than a year it doubled in circulation, partly due to Esme's hard work and sheer dedication and partly due to the newly fashionable trend toward cigar-smoking: a bandwagon on which she had been quick to jump.

Sebastian Goodhart, naturally, was delighted and, on the strength of her success with *Smoke*, picked up an industry title much ignored by the rag trade called *Apparel*, which Esme similarly turned around for the better.

Both magazines, however, were subscription only, and Esme's dream was to find herself as editor of a successful newsstand magazine. Sebastian, who had recently given up smoking so had little interest in his first magazine and only ever wore the same tweed suit so clearly had even less in his second, was with her all the way.

The one she had her eye on was a little-read tome called *Baker*, which languished, its edges usually ripped and curling, in small amounts at the back of the magazine racks behind the glossies at all good and many extremely average book-stores.

Soon she was the editor of three magazines and her feet barely touched the ground as she flew between her home in Notting Hill and her expanding office off Oxford Street.

"Och, look out, here comes Rupert Murdoch," Granny Mac would say rudely when Esme rushed in the door after work, usually just to change and bolt out the door again to some industry function or other.

Granny Mac lived with Esme and Pog in a crumbling Victorian terrace house in probably the least salubrious part of Notting Hill: All Souls Road, famous for its drug dealers, who hung about the street in Rastafarian colors waiting for rich white boys in convertible cars to come and pay large amounts of money for small blocks of what they thought was hashish but was usually licorice.

Granny Mac had moved in with Pog when Esme had. It was inconceivable that she should do anything but, and Pog, bless his heart, had not only never said anything about it, but barely thought about it.

The odd jibe at work made him realize it wasn't

exactly commonplace to live with one's grand-mother-in-law but then his workmates treated Pog as an oddity anyway. He dressed differently—that is to say not in the requisite young-architect-about-town black—but also worked solidly and seemed to like it more than nipping down to the pub at lunchtime for a few swift pints of lager and a look at the latest *FHM* magazine.

He had bought the house with next to no deposit when he was in his early twenties, which his mates also ribbed him about—homeowning was a mug's game at his age, they said—but as the years passed the area became more and more populated by people just like him and Esme, the scungy flats and studio apartments converted back into single residences for the well-off or heavily mortgaged.

Following Henry's financial collapse, Pog convinced his father to invest what little he had left in the top flat of the All Souls Road house and eventually drew up plans to renovate its three poorly conceived separate dwellings back into one house with room for all the generations.

Granny Mac was very skeptical about this. She had not taken kindly to Henry moving into the house but had kept her tongue in her head on the grounds that as long as he had a different front door key from her then he was strictly really nothing more than a neighbor. Upon finding out that he was to be more of a flatmate in the new version of the house, her eyes hardened to tiny dark raisins and her mood plunged into darkness.

"It's not natural," was all she would say. "If I wanted to live with another cranky old bastard, I'd send Esme out to find me a husband."

Esme, however, was in her element. Her magazines were going brilliantly, her publisher loved her and while not a scratcher or clawer in the ambition stakes, she could hold her head up high among her peers and did.

Pog's rise from blahdom meant the Stacks were also socializing with the Bright Young Things on the architectural scene, and through contacts of her husband's Esme even had her eye on a flailing design digest that she knew Sebastian would buy at the snap of her fingers if she wanted him to.

She absolutely loved Notting Hill, always had. She'd been shopping at the markets in Portobello Road for as long as she could remember and had on more than one occasion, it had to be said, been in the other side of Charlie's convertible in the illegal exchange of licorice on the very road where she found herself later living.

She was happy to leave the redesign to her husband, it was his domain, after all, and she trusted him completely. The landscaping, however, she undertook herself.

The house, like every other one in the street, had a long leafy backyard to which you would, when the house was finished, step out from the kitchen or dining room. Pog had pretty much left it alone apart from mowing the lush green lawn occasionally, and its perimeter was clogged with mature trees and overgrown shrubs.

Esme had big plans for this luxurious outdoor space. But its pièce de résistance had come to her in a blinding flash as she worked her sourdough on the scratched stainless steel bench obscenely early one morning, obscenely early being the only time she could squeeze it in. Her mind had drifted while working the dough back to that little village square above the kinky Dordogne with its graceful little fountain trickling water into its bowl and throwing sunlight around the surrounding surfaces like a benevolent emperor dispersing gold coins to his crowds.

"You have got to be kidding me," Granny Mac breathed when Esme showed her the plans she had drawn up for a tiled courtyard of her own, complete with boxed topiary olive trees and the crowning centerpiece of a two-meter fountain that wept extravagantly into an elaborate circular pond. It was as close as she could get to the one behind which she had hidden when she first saw Louis, given that so many years had passed in between. She had found an artisan stonemason in Cornwall who had been just as enthusiastic as she, if not more, about creating the water feature and was already working on it in his chilly not-quite-converted barn near Padstow. It was costing a small fortune and worth, Esme thought, every penny.

"You don't like it?" Esme had asked her sour-faced grandmother, dismayed.

"Oh, sure, I like it," Granny Mac answered sarcastically. "Me and the Count of Monte bloody Cristo."

"But this is our dream house," protested her granddaughter.

"More like a bloody nightmare if you ask me," Granny Mac said. "What in God's name are we going to do with a fountain?"

"You don't do anything with them. You look at them and admire them and they add ambience and interest."

"Oh, well, if it's ambience and interest you're after, fine, right, a fountain's the very thing."

They agreed to disagree. Well, that is to say, Esme agreed to disagree. Granny Mac agreed to no such thing and ridiculed the fountain at every possible opportunity.

"Perhaps we could have a bubbling brook," she suggested politely to Pog on one occasion with an evil glint in her eye, "or a waterfall. Had you thought about a waterfall?" Pog, as always, refused to take the bait, just smiling and shrugging his shoulders.

"If Esme wants a fountain . . ." he replied.

"You great jessie," Granny Mac scolded him. "You let her get away with murder."

"Come on, Granny Mac," Pog argued gently. "She works bloody hard, you can't blame her for wanting somewhere nice to come home to. She deserves it."

But Granny Mac would not, could not be

swayed. Henry agreed with Granny Mac for once, in opposing the fountain. Normally, Granny Mac would have run a country mile rather than have Henry agree with her on anything, and might even have changed her stance just to avoid having anything in common with him. Yet she was so against the fountain that in this one case she welcomed Henry's agreement. The subject of the fountain stopped being discussed, Esme choosing to whisper her reports on its progress to Pog when her grandmother was in bed.

In the month before the renovations were to begin, however, life in the Notting Hill house was turned on its head.

Esme fell pregnant.

It had been an accident. That is to say, they had always wanted children but had planned on waiting another couple of years. Mother Nature of course put babies before fountains and so gave Esme a dose of gastroenteritis, which upset the rhythm of her contraception long enough for the reproductive fairies to do their bit.

The house in All Souls Road fair hummed with happiness when they broke the news to their elders. Henry was actually seen to smile at Granny Mac and not be hissed at in return.

"There may," Esme joked in bed that night, "even have been voluntary bodily contact."

Henry and Granny Mac, however, were also joined in horror at the punishing schedule Esme kept up despite her pregnancy.

"But the baby's smaller than a peanut," Esme wailed as she packed to go on an overnight press trip to Paris while the two "Crumblies," as she and Pog called them, loomed over her like the shadow of doom. "What harm can a quick flit across the Channel do?"

"They have cheese over there," Henry rumbled. "Unpasteurized."

"Well, I won't eat it," said Esme, who loved unpasteurized cheese and thought that actually she probably would.

"They have French people," Granny Mac glowered. "From France."

A mean little silence hung in the air between them and Esme felt a hole in her happiness for the first time since she had found out she was pregnant.

"I shall wear a bodice made of kryptonite to protect my unborn child from French infiltration," she said, and then she looked at her grandmother in a way she only employed once every year or so when she really seriously needed shutting up.

The plans for the house and the garden were shelved in the sideboard in the sitting room while talk turned to all things baby, and after the twelve-week scan, all things babies. At the news they were having twins, the assorted householders could have been shifted into the proverbial cardboard box in the middle of the road and still been delirious with happiness. Esme had thought her husband was going to explode with pride and joy and Granny Mac attempted the Ghillie Calum sword dance, such was her excitement.

Esme, despite having ankles swollen like fence posts, worked like a Trojan to make sure no one could accuse her of abandoning her career in favor of motherhood, stopping work just two weeks before the babies were due.

Granny Mac and Pog were at either end of her when she brought the little boys into the world and it was without doubt the happiest day of all of their lives. Ted emerged first at five pounds one ounce and Rory twenty minutes later at five pounds two.

"Ginger Megses, the two of them," Granny Mac cried delightedly as Pog looked into his wife's tired eyes and loved her so much he thought he might burst.

"Perfect," the midwife announced as she placed the redheaded babies on their mother's chest.

And so heralded a new arrival of Stacks into the tumbledown house in All Souls Road. Even Henry forgot his own private bitterness and entered into the spirit of calming and soothing and to Esme's surprise playing with the babies, who grew fat and happy under such devoted love and attention.

Esme had never truly believed it when fresh parents waxed lyrical about the love they felt for their newborns and doubted that she could ever really explain the feeling to childless people herself.

"It's like a whole new emotion," she told Pog

as they lay in their bed gazing adoringly at their beautiful children one cozy Sunday morning. "It's like a combination of crying and laughing and something else completely different. Remember the time we tried to go camping and ended up driving over our picnic and sleeping in the car and we drove through the night to get home and ate a whole loaf of *levain* when it was so hot I kept dropping it? Remember the taste of biting into that flesh when we were so *so* hungry?"

"It was the best feeling in all the world," Pog said, tears lapping in the pools of his eyes, Teddy's tiny hand curled around one of his fingers. "Until now."

They were fascinated by the twin-ness of their sons. From their very arrival each seemed secretly, silently aware of the other. Take one away and the other would go on alert, eyes wide and ears almost pricked for any sound that might help identify the twin's whereabouts.

At first, Esme allowed herself a glimmer of envy that each had the other and always would, and that even as their mother it would be a link she could not share or break.

"We should be grateful, Es," Pog said, kissing her nose. "It's something special. Something extra. Wouldn't you have wanted another you when you were growing up? I know I would have."

"Oooh, Daddy!" Esme squealed. "What is it with men and two girls?" But his words comforted her.

Her boys were more blessed than most, she came to believe, and loved them all the more for it.

Being the mother of twins carried a certain cachet. Esme could not move the double stroller out of All Souls Road without an army of gray-haired old biddies in raincoats and ill-fitting shoes reaching in to pinch cheeks and chuck chins. Teddy loved it, stretching his legs out and wriggling with pleasure but Rory loathed it and would squirm as if trying to escape out of reach.

"He's got a redhead's temperament, that one," the old biddies would crow, stepping back, and Esme would smile demurely in a way she hoped demonstrated that while she was a redhead herself, she was not one of the bad-tempered variety.

The boys may have looked identical but their different personalities emerged very early on and were a constant source of fascination. Teddy was impatient and loud while Rory seemed more tolerant and self-contained. Teddy would suck greedily at Esme's nipple, always hungry for more, while Rory's attention would wander and he needed encouragement to feed. When they moved on to solids, Teddy only ate egg yolks while Rory only whites. Teddy liked crusts, Rory discarded them. They were matching halves of the same little entity.

And how those boys were loved!

Alice, of course, cherished them as well as, to their surprise, did Ridgeley.

"He's so good at playing," Esme marveled as

she and her friend sat on the sofa sipping Chardonnay one Sunday afternoon while Ridge assembled a very unusual construction with the boys' blocks. "I can read books and tell stories and cuddle and kiss but honestly I am hopeless at playing. It's just not in me. But I swear that Ridge has got more patience and imagination than even Granny Mac and Henners."

"He's always desperate to get here," Alice smiled. "It's the only thing he ever shows any enthusiasm for."

"Well, he's practically old enough to father his own children," Esme said. "Better get your knitting needles out, Nanna!"

Alice swatted her with a cushion. "If he takes after me he'll be as old as Methuselah before he can find anyone to father them with."

"If he takes after you," Esme reminded her, "he has only six child-free years left."

"Mum's been seeing a bloke from Ghana," Ridge said solemnly from the floor where he was kneeling, carefully placing a block at eye-height while the babies looked on. Esme raised her eyebrows at her friend but Alice shook her head.

"He had potpourri in his bathroom," she said. "It would never have worked."

Of course, it wasn't all plain sailing, far from it. In the first few months Esme, like many a new mother, suffered the worst excruciating doubt and terror and heart-wrenching regret of her entire life. There were more than a few nights when she fell into bed so numb with exhaustion she silently begged to die in her sleep. There were days when she felt so out of her depth that hysteria was the only emotion she recognized. There were moments when she felt so alone, so responsible, so scared, it was almost unbearable. Plus, a month after the twins were born she was asked when they were due, a low moment that led to so much weeping and wailing and inspection of her post-baby body in the bedroom mirror that Pog feared for her sanity.

Eventually, though, her convoluted road map of stretch marks began to fade and so did her fear that motherhood was too hard, that she couldn't do it. She could. It was hard work but Esme was used to that, and soon enough tiny pockets started appearing in the chaos of her bustling day where her mind strayed away from bottles and nappies and sleep patterns and back to the innermost workings of Goodhart Publishing.

When the boys were a little over nine months old, she went back to work, leaving her babies in the care of a sunny, outgoing Australian nanny called Tracey. She had thought she was ready for it, had looked forward to it even. But on her first morning back she had felt physically sick with guilt, was crying in the loo by lunchtime and at two concocted a business meeting in Chelsea, lunged for her bag and ran out the door to get home to her boys.

They were pleased to see her but had survived

the day better than she had. As Pog said, their twin-ness was a huge help. They were never alone. They always had each other. And now they had the irrepressible Tracey and, lurking in the background, Granny Mac and Henry, who watched like hawks for signs she was an alcoholic or a slave trader.

She was neither and the boys loved her. Granny Mac was not convinced, saying she reminded her of a horse rustler she once met in Gretna Green, and Henry was similarly unimpressed. He didn't think it was a good idea, he told Pog, for the boys to be minded by someone with a voice like fingernails on a chalkboard.

Esme trusted her, though, and as the days passed into weeks and months, her enthusiasm for her work returned in spades until mixed with motherhood there was barely a second in her day left unspoken for. Her schedule was so grueling that she had to have details written in three different places just to keep track. She moved her planning meetings from ten in the morning until nine, just to fit them in, which meant two early departures from the house a week. She worked till nine on a Thursday so she could have Friday mornings off to take the boys to a neighborhood coffee group. She held a conference call with her editors from home on a Sunday evening to smooth the way for her Mondays (Rory famously throwing up down her cleavage during one of them). Her Wednesdays gave her shivers just thinking about them.

Sebastian had asked her to actively court the architectural magazine, which meant endless phone calls, lunches and meetings, and Wednesdays she dedicated to this.

She felt pulled in a thousand different directions but somehow managed to hold it all together and even allowed herself to believe—in the rare moments she had to indulge in such thought—that perhaps she could be a career woman and a mother and be good at both.

Through it all, she baked. It was another tug at the restraints of her time but no one, nothing, could persuade Esme to give up her sourdough.

"We could always buy bread, Esme," Pog said gently one night as he watched her, eyes sliding closed as she sat on the sofa waiting to knock back the bread before refrigerating it, a trick she had learned, which meant she could start the bread at night and slow rise it. "There is an organic bakery in Chalk Farm now, you know. We could get Tracey to go there or send one of the Crumblies on the bus."

Esme felt suddenly and sadly overemotional.

"No, no, it's fine," she said, a tremor in her voice. "I adore it, Pog, you know I do. It's just a bit tricky at the moment with the babies this age and work and everything but it's the only thing that ever stays the same. If I ever stop doing it," she said, heaving her body off the sofa, "you'll know I've lost the plot and you might as well just take me outside and shoot me."

Pog looked worried.

"We don't have to do this, you know," he said quietly, following her into the kitchen. "You could stop work or go freelance and have more time to do the things you like doing."

"I like working," objected Esme. "And we want to get enough money together to sort the house out, don't we? Make it a lovely big home for the boys to grow up in? We do. You know we do. Now Pog, does anything need ironing for tomorrow?"

The childcare arrangement, however, threatened to come horribly unstuck when Tracey's sunny personality began to recede behind a cloud. Nine months of being at home with Granny Mac and Henry Stack could do that to a sweet-natured young thing from the colonies.

"They're just so mean," she wailed to Esme, who came home one day to find her sitting outside on the front steps crying. "They sent me to put the rubbish out and locked the door behind me. And that was at three o'clock. I've been trying to get in all afternoon but they just keep holding the babies up at the window and waving."

"It's like having four children in the house," Esme complained when she fell into bed, exhausted, that night. "And the littlest ones are the least trouble of all. It's those old ones causing all the trouble."

"What do you think we should do?" Pog asked her, hating to see her tired and worried.

"Maybe the boys would be better off in a nursery

during the day. That way Henry and Granny Mac can fight it out on their own during the day and we'll let natural selection do its bit."

"That's not fair," Pog said. "We may have to draft in some extra senior citizens to give Granny Mac some real competition. Too easy for her otherwise."

Esme laughed and burrowed in as close as she could to her cuddly husband. Despite being exhausted, despite being worried, despite trying to split herself in too many directions, she had never felt happier. Everything she had ever wanted was in this house and as long as she had her boys and her Granny, she was okay. More than okay.

But she had perhaps underestimated what an important part of the equation Tracey was. When the still-distraught girl rang the next morning at seven o'clock to say that she was not coming back it ripped something of a hole in the fabric of the happy household. But before Esme could even look into nursery fees Granny Mac and Henry formed a seemingly united front and insisted that between them, they could look after the twins.

"Was this the evil old menaces' plan all along, do you think?" Esme asked Pog over the phone during the day. "Did they torture that poor girl all this time just so they could get the boys to themselves?"

Pog refused to see the dark side. "Look at it this way, Es," he enthused. "Without paying the nanny, we can probably afford the renovations."

"My fountain!" squealed Esme.

"Yes and the relining and new stairs and carpet and kitchen and bathrooms," Pog said. "It's major, Es. Do you think we can cope?"

"Yes, yes, yes," said Esme, not even stopping to really think about it. A full-time job, boisterous babies, two evil old people—what was there to cope with?

And so, at eighteen months of age, the twins were left at home with their grandfather and great-grandmother who, while abhorring each other, adored them.

Despite any doubts anyone had about this new regime, the twins thrived. Teddy walked in the first week—they were late developers when it came to moving—with his not nearly so curious twin following in his footsteps a fortnight later, miraculously on a Saturday when his parents were home and at that exact moment watching him.

Teddy embraced his mother's exotic palate and devoured pâtés and spicy chutneys and anchovy pizza and on one exceptionally greedy occasion caviar, while Rory's taste leaned more toward his father's preference for eggs on toast and baked beans.

Teddy remained cuddly and kissable while Rory squirmed and squiggled out of arm's reach from the moment he could crawl. Esme loved their differences. She loved that most people could not tell them apart yet she could point out, with her eyes shut, the seventeen physical dis-similarities that made them Rory and Ted, not "the twins."

She was the only one who never (apart from on one occasion) got them mixed up. And how could you, she often wondered, when Rory had that little freckle just below his left earlobe and Teddy's eyelashes were at least two shades paler than his brother's?

Esme was intrigued by the boys' connection with each other. They had almost never, even as tiny babies, cried at the same time, as though they had silently secretly worked out that it was better to have all their mother's attention than half of it, even if it meant starving or putting up with a wet nappy for a bit longer.

Teddy also kindly waited until Rory's chicken pox had cleared up before getting his own walloping case of them, and despite their genetic ties they teethed at completely different times, meaning Esme and Pog could spread their sleep-lessness around a little.

They were slower than most toddlers to talk, which Esme, at first concerned, read was quite common with identical twins; and one magical afternoon when everybody else in the house was out or resting she watched her babies share a secret silent joke for the first time ever and it made her feel something so deep and strong in the pit of her stomach that she thought she was going to faint. It thrilled her that Rory and Ted would always have each other. That there would always be the two of them. The leader and the led. The loud and the quiet. The happy and the sad.

CHAPTER 15

Both Louis's arms were stretched across the table now, holding Esme's hands in his, his handsome face etched with dismay at the tale his lost love was telling.

"I am so sorry," he murmured softly. "You do not have to tell me, Esme."

But it was too late. The dreadful details had been kept too long in the dark and could not help but pour out, into the light of the Orrery dining room.

"I should have known," Esme said, staring into Louis's eyes and seeing only their blackness. "How could I not have known?"

The day Rory became an only child had not started like any other and afterward Esme could not believe she had not seen disaster hanging heavy and horrid in the air.

For a start, she had slept in even though it was a planning meeting morning and she had to be out of the house by 8:30 or her day went to pieces.

She had been up in the night twice to see to Rory, who had a streaming cold, and she was grumpy even before she stubbed her toe on a large power tool left lying in the dusty hallway by one of the builders.

The house was in ruins. The floorboards had been sanded but not polished, baseboards replaced but not painted, walls framed but not lined and bathrooms plumbed but not completely. The kitchen was all but finished and so was the living room and the boys' bedroom, thankfully, so that the children had somewhere to play when the builders were working, but it was far from ideal.

And in an idiotic burst of wanting to get it all over and done with as quickly as possible, Esme had brought the landscapers in at the same time. The backyard was only partially tiled and spotted with large pyramids of dirt, and she had not been able to work out whether these were coming or going.

In the midst of this sat her fountain, or the pieces that would eventually become her fountain. The bowl had been sited by the stonemason himself and bolted to a concrete pad but the centerpiece lay on its side, providing a leaning post for two spades, a large sack of compost and the assorted unidentifiable detritus of half a dozen laborers.

It did not look remotely gorgeous. It looked like a bomb site and a week of depressingly wet weather had not helped.

On top of this, though, and far more worrying, Granny Mac was not her normal self. Pog had actually been the first to notice it and had mentioned to Esme that her grandmother had twice failed to bite back when Henry was obnoxious. Esme had hardly given it a thought until she followed her grandmother up the stairs a few days later and had to slow herself down to avoid overtaking her. She could not remember a time when she had not had to run to keep up with the woman.

She kept an eagle eye on her grandmother over the next little while and although there was nothing glaringly obvious, she thought she detected a subtle slowing down, as though Granny Mac's batteries were running out.

"Are you all right?" Esme had asked her after seeing her grandmother obviously think twice about picking up Teddy, then wince with the exertion.

"Och, what are you doing sneaking up on me like that?" Granny Mac had grumbled. "Can an old woman not even be an old woman these days? No, that would be right, I suppose. We're all supposed to be Sebastian bloody Coe. Makes perfect sense that does, oh aye."

But the morning that Esme slept in, she was astonished to find that Granny Mac, who'd been an early riser since Adam was a cowboy, was still in her bed, too.

"There's no need to look at me like that," Granny Mac said croakily. "You don't need to call MI5 just because I took an extra twenty winks. What's good for the goose is good for the gander, you know."

"I'd better call in sick," Esme said, hopping

around in her grandmother's room trying to get a pair of opaques on. "I can't leave you at home like this and Pog has a huge meeting with the Germans so he can't stay home either."

"You'll do no such thing," Granny Mac said, leaping out of bed in a fashion very sprightly for someone whose batteries were running out. "I'm not at home 'like this' or any such nonsense. Now leave me alone to get dressed."

The kitchen, to Esme's relief, was a relative oasis of calm, with Henry quietly feeding the boys their breakfast. He gave his daughter-in-law the barest of glances.

"You'll be out again this evening, I take it," he said in his clipped way.

"Who, me? No," Esme said, shoving a bit of bread in the toaster and attempting to run her fingers through the bird's nest that was her hair. She poured not quite boiling water onto a tea bag in a dirty cup and, sipping it down, peered at the calendar on the refrigerator.

"Oh, shit," she said, then bit her lip because Henry hated her swearing in front of the boys and even if he didn't, she shouldn't do it anyway. "I forgot. I said I would go to Ridge's parents night with Alice tonight." Ridge was not terribly academic or sporty or charming and Alice hated going to meet the teachers on her own. Esme had promised she would go with her and wouldn't think of pulling out.

She didn't need to look at Henry to know he was

glowering at her and reached into her bag for her diary, flipping it open to the day's date. She had a lunch with the executives of a major hosiery manufacturer on the brink of placing an advertising contract with *Apparel,* then she had page proofs to check for *Smoke,* her fortnightly meeting with Sebastian and the official opening of the *Baker* test kitchen at four. It was going to be a difficult day.

Teddy smiled at her from his high chair and blew a snot bubble out of his nose, which gave Esme what she realized in retrospect was probably the last truly happy moment of her life. A snot bubble.

She got up, kissed both her sons on their curly ginger heads and turned to Henry. "Could you keep an eye on Granny Mac for me?" she said in as low a voice as she could afford for fear her grandmother would hear her. "She seems a bit off . . ."

Henry spooned porridge into Teddy's open rosebud mouth. "There are homes for people like your grandmother," he said.

"Yes," she said, "homes like this one."

Henry harrumphed and Esme bristled but then reminded herself that he was just a lonely old man who needed love and attention like anyone else.

"Please," she said, appealing to the good nature she was sure he must have but kept so well hidden. "I'll take tomorrow off and see if I can trick her into going to the doctor but today I just need your help a bit more than usual."

"You're taking me for granted," Henry said. "And I don't much care for it."

Esme pulled a run in her tights, which she had been straightening, in frustration. This was the man who had begged to be able to look after his grandsons? Who thought at home with their elders was the best place for them? He really was impossible.

"I'm sorry," she smiled sweetly. "It won't happen again. Tomorrow, I promise, I'll make up for it." A crack of thunder ended the conversation and she swore quietly to herself again as she looked out the new (unpainted, handleless) glass doors at the courtyard, where fat raindrops were pinging hysterically off the tiles.

Pog trampled down the stairs, his floppy hair still wet and his cheeks flushed as he nodded and listened to someone on the other end of his cell phone.

"See you tonight," he mouthed, rolling his eyes, and then kissed Esme on the forehead and went into the kitchen.

"Bye, Granny Mac," Esme called up the stairs, jumping from foot to foot as she waited for an answer even though she was now impossibly late.

"Granny Mac? Are you—"

"For God's sake!" her grandmother roared, appearing around the corner onto the landing. "Will you get about your business and leave me be!" And she marched robustly down the stairs pushing Esme out of the way as she headed for the kitchen.

Esme took a deep breath and opened the front door. Three burly builders with a kaleidoscope of differently tattooed biceps simultaneously blew full strength Marlboro smoke into her face but she just smiled, did her best to rise above it all and scuttled to the tube station, her umbrella blowing inside out on the way.

The day passed in a blur. She hadn't even had time, she realized as Shonel from the art department hurried her up about the test kitchen do, to go to the bathroom. It was five past four already and she was supposed to be making the key speech in ten minutes.

"Come on," Shonel urged her from the door, "everyone else is already there."

Esme took a quick glance at her phone before deciding—realizing more than deciding really—that her bladder needed attention before she checked in at home. She had picked the damn phone up half a dozen times to ring and check on her grandmother but had been interrupted on every occasion.

"I'll ring in the taxi," she said to Shonel. "You go and grab one while I go to the loo. I'll get kidney blowback at this rate."

Sitting in the back of the cab, Esme rummaged around in her bag, eventually finding her phone only to discover its battery was flat. "Oh, bollocks," she said. "Shonel, can I borrow yours?" Her art director looked sourly at her boss then down at her own hairy legs and Birkenstock sandals.

"They give you brain cancer," Shonel said. "They're worse than cigarettes."

Arriving at the test kitchen in Portland Street, Esme was immediately swamped by well-wishers, staff members and advertisers availing themselves of the free pinot gris, Irish cheese and freshly baked breads—sourdough not among them, she could tell, just by sniffing the air. She would have to talk to someone about that.

"Is there a phone here?" she asked Jenny Gibson, a truculent teenager with a wicked feel for pastry whom she had taken on to help in the kitchen.

"Not bleedin' likely," Jenny answered her. "You try telling British Telecom you're in a hurry and see how far you get."

"Shit, shit, shit," Esme muttered before turning on her energetic smile and calling for everyone's attention, the formalities about to begin.

Afterward she grabbed a glass of wine from a passing waiter and, as she gulped desperately at it, happened to notice that a lanky-looking man dressed in black and looking very disinterested was slipping a phone into his pocket.

"Excuse me," she trilled. "Could I borrow that?" And before the greasy article could respond, she had whisked it out of his hand and punched in her home phone number.

After eight rings it clicked on to the answering machine. Esme felt a clunk of worry in her stomach. She checked her watch. It was five thirty.

The boys should be having their tea. Why was no one answering?

She dialed the number again—still it rang and clicked on to the answering machine. Then she tried Pog but his phone was turned off, no doubt during his meeting.

"Do you mind?" the lanky man asked her, reaching for his phone, which at that moment Esme realized was the same outdated model as her own. Despite the thumping of her heart, she smiled at him. "I'm sorry," she said, clutching the phone as she slipped through the crowd and out the door, ignoring his surprised whining behind her.

Hailing a taxi she jumped in and slipped his battery into her phone. She would get it back to him somehow. That wasn't important. For a full minute she stared at the tiny LCD screen as her own phone flickered into life, telling her it was on, then telling her it had a signal and then, with a series of loud terrifying beeps, informing her that she had one, two, three, four, five, six messages.

Shakily, Esme pressed the button to reveal the contents of the first message. "Henry rang, please call home," the first one read. "Henry says call home," read the second. "Call home asap," read the third, fourth, fifth and sixth.

Esme felt the glass of warm pinot gris rise up in her stomach and hit the back of her throat. She tried to tell herself that probably nothing major was wrong but still she could not rid herself of the taste of fear. Her breathing quickened and she felt a film of sweat on her forehead despite the chill in the air.

"Please," she said as loudly as she could as she knocked on the cabbie's window and dialed home again. "Please, could you go faster?"

The phone rang eight times and clicked on to the answering machine again.

"Henry," she said, her voice sounding foreign and frightened. "It's Esme. Are you there? Please pick up." Her plea disappeared emptily into the phone. "I'm on my way home. I didn't get your messages. I'm so sorry. Is everything all right?" Still, silence. "Is Granny Mac all right?" She bit her lip, wondering if the pounding of her heart could be heard on the tape. "I'm on my way. I'll see you soon. I'm sorry, Henry."

The house in All Souls Road was still standing, which at least allowed Esme to breathe again as she threw a twenty-pound note at the cabbie and raced up the stairs to the front door.

"Hello!" she shouted in the hallway. "Henry!" The kitchen was empty, as was the living room. "Granny Mac!" she called again, panic rising, as she saw the message light pulsing on the answering machine. Her words were getting swallowed in gulps of fear.

"Henry," she called again as she made for the stairs.

"I'm up here." His irritated voice bounced down

the stairwell. "In the bathroom. Where the hell have you been?"

His crotchetiness assuaged her panic. She felt the blood rush through to all its rightful places again. She breathed deeply as she pushed the half-closed bathroom door open.

Henry was sitting on the edge of the bath holding a naked Rory wrapped in a towel on his lap. Before she could get any closer, the little boy heaved and Henry gently rolled him toward the lavatory, where he vomited a trickle of clear fluid into the bowl.

"Oh, my poor baby," Esme cried, kneeling beside them and kissing Rory on the foot that was the closest bit to her. "How long has he been like this?"

"He's been going at both ends since two o'clock," growled Henry, and Esme looked at his wrinkled scowl but saw in his eyes that he was worried and scared, not cross. "I can't imagine the poor devil has anything else to get rid of but it's still coming."

Esme put her hand on Rory's head; it was hot, but not dangerously so. His body was limp, and he opened his eyes to look at her but did not raise his head.

"Where's Teddy?" she asked.

"With your grandmother," Henry replied. "In her room."

"Should we take Rory to the doctor, do you think?" Esme asked her father-in-law. "Or the hospital?"

"I rang the surgery," Henry answered her. "And they said it's just a virus. They've had a waiting room full of it for the past two days and it should pass in twelve hours. I expect Ted will get it, too."

A wave of guilt pulsed through Esme but she pushed it away. She should have been here. She should have rung the surgery. She should be worried that Teddy would get the bug, too.

"Are you all right with him?" she asked, nodding at her poor sick son as she stood up.

Henry shot her a look which she knew meant, "Haven't I been up until now?"

Esme's relief that all was well was short-lived. The moment she walked into Granny Mac's room it was clear that something was wrong. Her grandmother lay on the bed fully clothed but seemingly awake, and as Esme approached her, she did not move or even look her way.

"Granny Mac!" Esme chided. But there was no response. And as Esme leaned over her she realized with horror that one side of her grandmother's face had collapsed downward as though the puppeteer controlling her had gone off for a cup of tea and left her hanging from the back of a chair.

"Granny Mac!" Esme cried again, this time taking her grandmother's thin shoulders in her hands and pulling her slight body toward her own.

Her grandmother gurgled and Esme held her tighter, too many terrifying thoughts crowding her mind. Why had she gone to work? Why had she ignored the warning signals? How could she have been so careless, so heartless, so selfish, so stupid? "Don't leave me," she whispered, rocking her grandmother awkwardly back and forward. "Please, please, please don't leave me."

Granny Mac gurgled again, louder this time, and Esme, suddenly afraid she was hurting her and aware that she should be doing something other than holding her and pleading with her, lowered her back onto her pillow.

"Eegggggghhhh," her grandmother moaned, saliva drooling out the dropped side of her mouth. "Eeeegggghhhhyyyyyy."

"I'm going to call an ambulance," Esme said as soothingly as she could yet she felt nothing but terror and turmoil. If Granny Mac died then she would surely die, too. "I'm going to get some help."

"Eeegggghhhhh," her grandmother groaned again, seemingly more agitated this time. "Eeeeggggghhhhhy."

She fixed Esme with her bright black eyes and despite her incapacitated state held her grand-daughter's distraught gaze.

"Egg," she said almost clearly. "Eggy."

Ted, thought Esme. Teddy. She immediately started to pant and stood up. Where was Teddy? Her grandmother's eyes were still fixed on her and Esme knew in that moment she had something to fear.

Teddy was supposed to be in here with Granny

Mac, Henry had said so. Idiotically, she looked under the bed.

"Is he in here somewhere?" she asked, even though she knew her grandmother could not answer her. She checked the closet knowing that he probably wasn't there either, and despite the dreadful feeling that she should not leave Granny Mac alone like this, she took one last look at her and stumbled into the hall.

"Henry!" she called. "Have you seen Teddy?" She checked the twins' bedroom, not allowing herself to fly into a fully fledged panic, then slipped out into the hallway again. Henry was standing in the bathroom door, still holding a floppy Rory, whose head was turned to look at his mother.

"Teddy is not with Granny Mac," Esme said. "I think she has had a stroke, Henry. When was the last time you saw her? What did she say?"

"He's not in her room?" Henry was confused. "I sent him in there, not long ago. Just before you came home. Are you sure?"

Just before she got home. Esme breathed out. It hadn't been long. He would be fine.

"You check our room, I'll check downstairs again," Esme instructed. He may have slipped downstairs when she was in the bathroom with Henry or in with Granny Mac. Granny Mac!

She leaped downstairs and picked up the phone, punching in 999 and asking for the ambulance service.

"Thirty-nine All Souls Road," she said, as she

330

checked the cupboard under the stairs and the space behind the sofa where the boys often hid. "Morag MacDougall. She's never been sick a day in her life but she seems sort of paralyzed and one side of her face isn't working properly. Is that a stroke? I mean it sounds like a stroke. Do you think it's a stroke? Will she be all right?" She was gabbling, she knew, as she moved back into the kitchen and checked the pantry. How would this woman on a headphone based in God knew where know if Granny Mac would be all right?

"Thank you," she said as the woman repeated the address. "How long—" but the words dried on her lips as she suddenly saw what she had missed before—that one of the paintless, handle-less doors from the kitchen into the courtyard was slightly open. She dropped the phone and raced outside. There were lethal tools and probably dangerous poisons lying willy-nilly all over the place. A little boy could come to terrible harm out there.

"Teddy!" she called, not noticing that the rain still fell hard and cold on and around her. "Ted!" There were few places to hide and she knew the seven-foot-high brick wall around the garden was impenetrable. Where was he?

She trod across the damaged lawn, mud sucking at her shoes, to check the shrubs and foliage around the perimeter. "Teddo!" she called as she pushed sodden branches out of the way. "Baby boy!"

There was no sign of him. Thoughts of child molesters and kidnappers tried to niggle at her brain but she pushed them away. He must be somewhere. The front door was deadlocked. Henry's room!

She turned and ran as quickly as the sticky ground would let her back inside, sliding as she passed the fountain bowl on a bit of black polyethylene that had been draped over it and spilled down the side and across the ground.

Henry was in the kitchen, still holding Rory, who was crying now, his face twisted with pain and distress.

"Your room," Esme said.

"I've checked it," Henry told her over Rory's howling. "I've checked everywhere upstairs."

The doorbell rang, making him start.

"It'll be the ambulance," Esme said, pushing past him and skating down the hallway to open the door. "She's upstairs," she told the two paramedics. "I'll show you."

But then she stopped and spun around. "My son," she said. "We can't find him." He wasn't upstairs and he wasn't downstairs. She turned again and started to lead the ambulance men up the stairs. Well, he must be outside. She stopped yet again. "She's in the room at the end of the hall. On the left." How could she leave Granny Mac alone with these men? Her grandmother would kill her. "Henry!" she called down the stairs, plainly distraught.

"It's all right," one of the ambulancemen said, reaching for her arm and giving it a pat. "We'll sort out your gran. You find the nipper."

Esme bounded down the stairs again, bumping into Henry, completely gray in the face now and still holding on to a roaring Rory as he emerged from the cupboard under the stairs.

"I've checked there," Esme said. "I've checked everywhere. I've looked in every nook and cranny and hiding place and hole I can think of. There's nowhere outside he could be. Nowhere that we can't see—"

As if in slow motion she and Henry turned at the same time and looked out through the kitchen door again. Out to the fountain bowl, with its sloppy black plastic covering.

"Who put that there?" Esme asked as she floated toward the door. Her wet feet slid on the slippery tiles as she scrabbled toward the fountain, falling over on her knees just short of her little bit of Venolat. Clawing blindly at the overhanging polyethylene she pulled it away and dragged herself up to the lip of the fountain.

Teddy's chubby, toddler body lay there, face down, his arms outstretched, his ginger curls indelibly brilliant against the murky darkness of the bowl. Did she scream or not? Certainly her mouth was stretched open in a dark raw hole as she frantically clawed at the icy water, reaching for him, turning him over, but she knew by his touch that she was too late. She pulled him from the water then sank back onto the ground, clutching his limp, sodden, freezing-cold little body to her chest, her mouth stuck in a frozen howl, her eyes staring into a future she did not want to contemplate.

The rain fell on the two of them, plastering her hair to her head and darkening it to the exact shade of her son's, brilliant still against the blackness of everything else.

Esme's eyes focused briefly on the sight of Rory, in the open kitchen door, struggling to get out of his grandfather's arms and screaming at the sight of his twin, his eyes burning a hole in his mother that would never, ever be filled.

The bright yellow vest of an ambulanceman pushed past Henry and his grandson and was at Esme's side in a flash. He took Teddy's body from her—forced her to give it up—and then placed him gently on the soaking tiles, rain pinging off them as he tipped back his head, held his nose and blew into his twenty-six-month-old lungs.

It was into this tortured scene that Pog, having canceled his meeting after clearing his phone of similar messages from Henry, walked.

Esme looked over the body of the hopeful ambulanceman breathing into her lifeless son and met the eyes of her husband. He was wearing a red anorak that was blurred and out of focus, but not so the look on his face. She saw that perfectly clearly and what she felt then she knew she could never feel again. Like Rory before him, Pog emptied Esme with his pain. The world stood still. She wanted it to end.

And, in a way, it did.

A sleepy numbness started at Esme's toes and crept slyly up her body as her brain registered what the rest of her could not: that Teddy was gone. The numbness crawled cleverly in and out all of the pockets of her mind, clutching her in its dark embrace, squeezing her heart so subtly that it could keep on beating but would never feel the same way about anything ever again.

CHAPTER 16

Esme walked into Rockwell cocktail bar on Trafalgar Square to find her friend sucking already on a watermelon and basil daiquiri. "You look bloody gorgeous!" squawked Alice. "Whatever you're having," she said, clunking her drink down on the table, "I want some, too."

Esme hid her blush by rummaging in her bag, taking off her coat and getting settled on the chaise next to Alice. The truth was, she felt different.

Being with Louis, talking to Louis, had changed her. She had left him, reluctantly, in Marylebone High Street after sharing the kiss she had dreamed of all these long Louis-less years. Her heart, so scrubbed raw by relieving herself of the buried memories of losing Teddy, her beautiful baby Teddy, had swelled up with hope and desire as Louis had reached for her at the bottom of the stairs and pulled her into him.

"My poor Esme," he had said, kissing her ear, her eyebrow, her cheek, the remains of her tears. "My poor Esme." And it had been such a small movement, tilting her head back and making her lips available. She had had no doubt he would

336

accept her offer of them. It was all unfolding so naturally in front of them. It felt like Louis was sloughing off the heavy, rotten layers that had built up over the past two years and the old fresh, shiny, brilliant Esme was emerging from underneath. She had groaned beneath the weight of his kiss, felt those hip bones once more against hers, tasted the salty sweetness of his mouth, felt his hand cupping her breast, thanked God her La Perla had stood the test of time.

Louis had drawn back, his eyes dark and wet, his lips glistening.

"I must go," he said. "But I feel wrong to leave you like this."

"No, no," she said quickly. "I'm fine. Perfectly fine." And it was true, she was. She truly was. She felt light with the relief of unburdening the terrible tale of her darling Teddy, of saying his name, of picturing his face, alive and happy, of remembering the curve of his tiny fingernails, his throaty chuckle. These details that she had been incapable of sharing with her husband, her friends, even her grandmother, had come tumbling out of her like Grand Prix champagne as she stared into the deep, dark eyes of Louis Lapoine. She had poured out memories of her lost boy, sometimes crying, sometimes laughing, but never choked or gridlocked. She felt drunk and weightless and liberated by the delight of being able to repeat his name, Ted, Teddy, Teddikins, without the air being sucked from her lungs and a fog clouding her head. Louis had done that. Louis had set her free.

"I do not know what it has been like for you since Teddy—" Louis had dropped his gaze yet Esme felt nothing but warmth now at the sound of that name. "You are a brave and remarkable woman, Esme."

"I'm nothing of the sort," Esme murmured, but she basked in his praise nonetheless. She felt more tied to him now than ever, but he was behind schedule and she had to meet Alice.

Alice. How was she going to keep Louis to herself? she wondered as she messed about, putting off the moment when she had to look her best friend in the eyes. How could she not spill the beans to her best friend, the one from whom she had never before held anything? How would Alice not notice that everything about her was different now?

"So," Alice prompted, interrupting her thoughts, "are you going to tell me or do I have to guess?"

Esme was momentarily confused.

"Is it something that comes in a bottle or is it something Pog does to you before slipping on his Y-fronts and going to get your breakfast cuppa?" Alice persisted.

Confusion turned to understanding and at the mention of Pog slithered away to become shame and remorse. Of course, she could not tell Alice about Louis. What was she thinking? She might feel shiny and new but she was sailing in murky waters.

"I've changed my moisturizer," she said brightly, caressing her cheeks dramatically and scaring herself with the smoothness at which the lie plopped out. "Some natural thingie with no greeblies in it from Neal's Yard."

"Stick with it, sweetheart," Alice said, handing over the cocktail menu. "You look positively glowing." Another obvious possibility occurred to her. "Hey, you're not—"

Esme shook her head, thinking her friend couldn't be more wrong if she tried. She looked away from Alice knowing that she would take this as a sign that no matter how much time had passed, she still did not want to discuss the subject of pregnancy. After Teddy died, people couldn't be quick enough to suggest she conceive another baby to replace him. As if that were possible. As if she could stand to think about not having him, let alone replacing him. A wave of unadulterated grief cut through her euphoria.

Alice put down her drink and reached over to squeeze Esme's hand. "I'm sorry, darling," she said, and the sympathy in her voice made Esme feel sick with duplicity. How could she have just shared the contents of her heart, of her unmentionable loss with Louis, whom after all she hardly even knew, when she could not, had never been able to, with Alice, her soul sister? The subject of Teddy had been out of bounds since his funeral, a day so bleak and painful and raw she still could not conjure up its memory. Esme had been unable to speak her lost son's name to anybody, even Pog, even Granny Mac, for goodness' sake, until today. Until Louis and his big black searching eyes and strong brown breadmakers' fingers.

Something in their shared history had made her able to unburden the awful details of Teddy's loss in a way that she had found inconceivable up till now, and the truth was, the frightening, horrible truth was, that she felt on top of the world. Yes, it hurt. It hurt so deeply it was like burning in hell. And it would probably always hurt like that but at least now she could *feel* it. She could really, truly feel it. She had been numb for so long but now there was pain, and with it, pleasure.

Louis had unleashed—yet again—something in her that nobody else had been able to tap, and Esme felt so light with happiness and relief and horror and fear that she could barely even think about the fact she had agreed to meet him again the following week. At his hotel.

Despite the fireworks exploding in her head, she managed to trade the usual gossip and girl talk with Alice as they put away another cocktail.

Louis made her feel, she realized as Alice burbled about a failed singles' dance, like the Esme she really was: the Esme he had discovered back in that salty little bakery so many years before. That's why she could talk to him about Teddy. Because she was nothing to him apart from that collection of skin and flesh and juice that had so enraptured him despite the complication of his marriage. She was not his wife or his daughter-in-law or his granddaughter or his mother. She could not upset him or blame him or hurt him or herself by digging up the events of that terrible day in his presence. She did not have to be the person that terrible day had turned her into. She was Esme, plain and simple. So, in real life she had molded herself into another shape and added preservatives—she'd had to—but to Louis she was still Esme, plain and simple as sourdough.

"You are a million miles away today, missus." Alice interrupted her thoughts. "That moisturizer certainly has sunk in. What's the name of it again?"

"Do you know, I can't remember," Esme lied, again easily. "I'll ring you when I get home. Speaking of which." She gathered up her bag and her coat. "Do come and visit soon will you, Ali?" The thought of being home, in the House in the Clouds, suddenly scared her. Everything seemed different now.

"You know I'm allergic to the country," said Alice, standing up to leave as well. "I need dirt and grime and rude people and men with not the right amount of testicles and appalling breath and vulgar tattoos or I just fall apart."

Esme must have looked dismayed, although she had hardly even been listening to her friend, because Alice leaned in to kiss her good-bye.

"All right, all right," she said. "I'll come but you had better set me up with that gorgeous hunk next door or I'll break out in a rash."

"Jam-jar?" Esme marveled, repelled. "You are deeply disturbed," she told her best friend as they parted.

In the train on the way home she replayed Louis's kiss a thousand times in her mind, clawing at the memory of the way his lips felt on hers, of the way his hands felt on her ribs, his thumbs below the underwire of her bra. But her buzz of delight kept giving way to waves of dread and remorse. She thought of Pog and how much she loved him. But then she thought of Louis and the way he made her feel and there was so little comparison between the two that it frightened her. Then she thought of the photo albums she had been unable to look at since Teddy's death. They had disappeared after his funeral from the second-floor living room, but with a hot flush Esme knew instantly where they were. She thought of Pog's guilty face when she first infiltrated his shed, of the stack of redundant paperwork camouflaging the folders. Suddenly she could not get home quickly enough. She wanted to see those two little redheads lying on her breast at the hospital, peeing on their sheepskin rugs, sitting in their blow-up paddling pool, walking with Granny Mac before the stroke rendered her bedridden. A lump rose in her throat at the picture of a healthy Granny Mac, and Esme shook her head. What a day it had been. She was not ready for anything more.

* * *

The next couple of days passed in a whir of such domestic chaos that Esme barely had a chance to think about what had happened in London. Even when she wasn't wrangling recalcitrant animals or cooking or cleaning, her head did not know whether to be full of her stolen kiss with Louis or of her mental home movies of Teddy, so long forbidden that now, when she let them, they played over and over and over again.

Deep down though, beneath the rubber gloves and cleaning fluids and flour, she felt a little burr of happiness that permeated everything. Pog sensed this immediately and put it down to going to London and meeting with Alice.

"You should do that more, you know," he said the next night in bed in the few minutes he was still conscious before exhaustion claimed him.

"Do what?" Esme asked, wondering if it was shame she felt, or something else.

"Go for girlie drinks with Alice," he said. "It's done you the world of good."

Esme was awake long after Pog had drifted off. Her hum of happiness waned and left guilt in its wake. She wondered how long it would be before she could say Teddy's name to his father, this warm and precious man who slept such a deep, sound sleep beside her. She tried to imagine bringing it up, after everything they had been through, but could not see a way. Her heart pounded with love as his snuffles echoed around the room, then it ached, then it pounded again. She would not go to London and see Louis, she decided, as she tossed and turned. He had given her a precious gift that she was coming to see would clear the way to a real life, a real future, with her family here in the House in the Clouds. But she could not give him anything in return. One kiss would have to do. But by the time she got up to make her bread, she had changed her mind again, and again, and again, until she could not remember if she was going to see him or not and was so tired that she didn't consider it would matter either way.

On Sunday Esme walked to the shop and got the paper herself. She didn't even bother pretending that she wasn't going to.

"Another gorgeous photo of the silly cow," she said, settling herself on the end of Granny Mac's bed, coughing at the ghosts of a thousand cigarettes. "The liposuction pipes of Harley Street will be well clogged this month, I'll be bound."

"Never mind you with your petty resentments," Granny Mac said. "Tell me how little Cosmo is getting on with his nuclear physics lessons."

"'*What a whirlwind!*'" Esme started. "I can't believe the *Sunday Times* allows so many exclamation marks. There should be a law."

"Get on with it," grumbled Granny Mac.

"'*My Manolos have barely had a chance to touch the ground and my diary is positively bulging with invitations. Please!*' Exclamation mark. '*Enough!*' Exclamation mark. Do you see what I mean? It's like there is no other punctuation in the universe."

"For God's sake!"

"'*The week started not terribly auspiciously,*'" read Esme, "'*with the opening of Grayson McFadgeon's much heralded art exhibition in some dreary, drafty loftesque space in Pimlico "borders." I am astounded at what these smelly little ingenues get away with these days. I mean, I am sorry, but who is it that decided that three toenail clippings on a piece of whole-meal toast is art? It's not good enough to look at, let alone eat. And if we could all charge two thousand pounds for a bottle full of our own saliva, I'm sure we all would. And it would probably taste better than Grayson McFadgeon's, too, although might not have the alcohol content. By the look of him he's not spending any of his easily earned cash on a square meal (or a deodorant, for that matter) but you should see the spotty little wretch put away the cabernet/merlot blend. I suggest he leaves the likes of Ear Wax on a Tampon well and truly behind him and concentrates on performance art instead. By the end of the evening his white shirt (no natural fibers there!) looked like something Jackson Pollock would be proud of.*'"

"What?" Granny Mac interrupted. "No exclamation marks?"

"Oh, actually there was one," Esme said, "after the natural fibers bit."

"You sound put out, Esme," Granny Mac said casually. "I believe you and Jemima have similar opinions on the matter of modern art, do you not?"

"Well, I wouldn't say similar," Esme said. "Shall I continue?

"'*It was my great pleasure to be invited to the wedding of disgraced supermodel Evangeline Lithgow and her latest catch, Lord Lachlan Highfield, to be held in his family castle near Oxford this weekend. Evangeline has had such a difficult time since giving birth to her daughter, also Evangeline—the poor woman must have racked her tiny brain for weeks coming up with that name. Anyway, it was obviously as much of a shock to Evangeline as it was to her former fiancé, something-or-other heir Geordie White, when Young Evangeline emerged from her mother's slender hips bearing an unmistakable resemblance to a certain premier league midfielder of a shall we say decidedly dusky persuasion. Geordie with his snowy blond hair and dull blue eyes only took a week or two to figure that one out and, naturally, headed for the hills. And it was but weeks before Old Evangeline was seen teetering around town on the arm of Lord Lachie, a confirmed bachelor, in every sense of the word I would have thought, of many years' standing. Of course, like most people invited to the nuptial festivities, I did not exactly rush down to Versace and pick out a little something strappy. So while it was a great pleasure to be invited, it was no great surprise to get a phone call from a Highfield minion on Monday to say the wedding had been canceled due to, reading between the lines, lack of interest. Oh, the shame!*'"

"Exclamation mark?" guessed Granny Mac.

"Exclamation mark," Esme confirmed.

"'*As for the mobile phone launch at the Serpentine, I am sorry, but Princess Ferguson simply does not cut the mustard these days. And if you say you are going to serve Moët et Chandon, for God's sake, serve it. If it comes in a thimble it just does not count.*'

"I bet there was an exclamation mark there but the sub-editors took it out," Esme said meanly, but only to deflect Granny Mac from pointing out that she had often whined herself that there was nothing worse than schlepping across town in rush hour traffic only to find your hosts had employed a mean-spirited drinks pourer.

"'*I was gasping for a drink by the time I got to GQ's Japanese night. He is taking to the language like a duck to water and his father is thrilled. Apparently we would all be learning Japanese if we knew what was good for us. His tutor is a delightful little chap with a name that sounds just like a motorcar and no idea about canapés. That wasabe sure does clear a girl's sinuses!*' Yes!" Esme answered before the question was asked.

"'*Cosmo and I, along with half the gay population of London and a good proportion of the nuns, are going to* The Sound of Music *sing-along off Leicester Square this afternoon. Cosmo is going to go as a bee, we have the most gorgeous costume from a dear little place in Knightsbridge—I'm sure he will get lots of wear out of it—and I am going to go as Leisl, wearing a dress I had made for a fancy dress party when I was sixteen going on seventeen!*'

347

"Aaarrrgghh," Esme threw back her head. "Is there no end to it?"

"But you like *The Sound of Music,* too," Granny Mac said wickedly. "Haven't you been saying you'd like to take Rory down to London to see it?"

"In a dress I had made when I was sixteen going on seventeen—I don't think so."

She threw the newspaper on the bed. It was indeed distressing to find herself agreeing with so much of what Jemima had to say.

"So," said Granny Mac, "are you going to see him again?"

Sometimes Esme wished Granny Mac wasn't privy to her innermost thoughts.

"I don't think I can stay away," she sighed, "even though it is probably the most foolish thing I could possibly do, but he just unlocks something in me that I can't even get to myself, Granny Mac, and I feel like I have to pursue it. After talking to him, you know"—she dropped her voice because it still seemed such foreign territory—"about Teddy, I just got this glimpse of what I used to be like and it felt so good I just have to get more of it. We'll just, you know, talk. It's just talking."

"Oh aye? Is that what they're calling it these days?"

"Don't be so disgusting!" Esme retorted. "It's not about that." But she wasn't so sure and she knew it. And if she knew it, Granny Mac knew it. And if Granny Mac knew it. . . Well. There was nothing more to be said.

The next few days slipped by with Esme lurching from woeful remorse and self-flagellation to a giddy light-headedness of long-gone proportions. She hugged the secret of Louis close to her chest, and with it, stolen thoughts of her angel baby. It was heavenly and hellish, all at the same time.

Pog, who had been monitoring her every shoulder slump for the last long while, was aware that she was battling something, and while the low moods worried him, the highs brought joy to his heart. She had started humming again in the happy, thoroughly tuneless way she had done before. Her bread was tasting so sharp and zingy it made his mouth water just thinking about it. At night though, in their bed, she still turned her back on him. Nestled into the space his soon-to-be-sleeping body made, she would hold his hand around her waist and snuggle, but at any suggestion of anything more, she would straighten up or shrink away.

He could wait though. He would wait. Forever, if he had to.

"I thought I might go down to London again today," Esme said casually on Thursday morning over breakfast. Until she opened her mouth to suggest it, she had not been sure she was going to go, but Pog beamed at her over his bowl of porridge sprinkled liberally with brown sugar and home-preserved peaches, and she was so encouraged she forgot for a moment why she was going.

"Be sure and give Alice my love, won't you," Pog said. "How's the love life?"

Esme glossed over his wrong conclusion. "Hope-less, as usual," she said. "The last one hadn't changed his socks since his A levels. Alice said his feet smelled like the stuff you floss out of your teeth."

Pog kissed her good-bye and headed off down the six flights of stairs to consider Meg D'ath's plans to convert her pint-sized potting shed into a granny flat for her mother-in-law.

Esme then spent nearly two hours getting show-ered and dressed, and dressed again, and dressed a third time before finally settling on a pale green agnés b suit with a seriously short skirt. Then she felt embarrassed about parading in front of Henry, so put her trench coat on over it before she went to find him and check it was okay for him to look after Rory.

"Actually," Henry said, when Esme found him in his sitting room, "it's not."

"I'm sorry?" she asked sweetly. Why hadn't she thought of this before?

"I am going to play bridge in Stonyborough with Dr. Mason and his wife," Henry said briskly, closing his book and dusting his trousers. "They've been asking me for some time and it felt impolite turning them down yet again."

She looked out the window where Rory was in the garden, attempting to brush poor Eeyore down with a broom. The pathetic creature seemed to be enjoying it.

"Never mind," Esme trilled. "I'll ring Mrs. McArthur."

Earlier in the week, when she had thought about booking Rory into nursery school for the day, she had decided not to, reasoning that this would keep her from going. Clearly, that was not the case and now there was no way Mrs. Monk would take him at such short notice. It was Mrs. McArthur at five pounds an hour or nothing.

The House in the Clouds seemed to have grown extra stairs. She clattered up to the kitchen to retrieve her address book, stopping outside her bedroom door to kick off her high heels. She really should have organized this sooner, she knew that, but then she would have been forced to admit she was going. It was like the difference between manslaughter and murder.

Mrs. McArthur proved to be annoyingly engaged. Esme tried her number four times in a row, all the while keeping an eye on Rory out the window and trying not to look at her watch more than once every fifteen seconds. She had to make the eleven o'clock train if she was going to meet Louis at his hotel at one and it was already ten past ten. The thought that she might not be able to make it shattered her in a way that made her think perhaps there really had been no doubt as to her motives. Perhaps it was murder after all.

"Shit, shit, shit," she said under her breath as she quickly made a sandwich for Rory using deliciously mature cheddar and that morning's sourdough. She scoured the pantry, finding a bashed-up little bag of chips and a squashed chocolate bar, and then tripped down the stairs again, grabbing his little day pack out of his room and putting in a warm jumper, his raincoat, a hat and his hastily prepared lunch.

She slipped into her high heels, then continued down to the bottom of the house and out the door, where she removed the broom from her small son's clammy little hands and informed him they were off to the babysitter's.

"But I haven't got a hankie," Rory said, panicked. He had a cold and Esme knew that Mrs. McArthur had a pathological fear of snot but would only wipe it with paper towels, which her delicate son found, rightfully so, too abrasive.

"Ooooh," grumbled Esme. "You hold your bag and I will go and get you one."

She ran into the house, nearly breaking her ankle in the process. It was useless trying in Granny Mac's room; she had always used toilet paper if her nose had run. Not for her the extravagance of a handkerchief or tissues! Despite the pulling in her calves, Esme declined to ask Henry yet another favor and so ran up the extra flight to her and Pog's room, only to find the box of tissues empty. It wasn't until she went through all the drawers that she remembered there was a whole week's worth of ironing sitting in a corner in the kitchen. That was where the handkerchiefs would be.

By the time she got back down to Rory, it was twenty to eleven and she merely grabbed his hand

and pulled him straight down the lane to Mrs. McArthur's. The door was open, which it almost always was, and Esme went straight in to find the woman in all her Sunday finery fussing about a little lace-covered table laden with garishly colored cakes.

"Oh!" she said, when she saw who it was with what Esme felt was some disappointment.

"I'm in a terrible spot," Esme gabbled. "Could you take Rory for the day? I have to go down to London and Henry's playing bridge with the Masons so he can't watch him."

Mrs. McArthur's lips pursed significantly. "Bridge?" she sniffed. "With the Masons?"

Esme nodded and jiggled Rory's hand.

"Well, I am actually hosting the inaugural meeting of the Seabury Mah-Jongg Club this morning, in fact I thought you were one of my girls, so I'm sorry but I can't help you. Bit of a cold, Rory? Poor lamb. Here, have a rice cake."

Rory reached out and clutched the crunchy dry cake while Esme looked at her watch. She had less than ten minutes to find someone to look after her son and get to the station to catch her train. She had no choice.

"Right-oh," she said in a jolly voice. "We'll be off then." She turned and walked as quickly as her heels would let her down the drive and across the road. She could make it, she could, if she took Rory with her. Her son scurried along at her side.

"What's happening, Esme?" he asked.

"You're coming to London with Mummy," she answered.

"Why?" He broke into a trot to keep up with her.

"Because a man said so," came her reply. It had answered many a question in the past and would have to do for this one as well.

It wasn't until they were seated, sweating and steaming, on the train as it pulled out of Seabury Station that it occurred to Esme that while she was now indeed going to be able to make her rendezvous with Louis, it was going to be with the added complication of Rory present and able.

Getting there was only half the battle. It was simply too sordid for words.

"Are we going to see Alice?" Rory asked, looking out the window as the countryside whisked by.

Esme felt wretched at what she was doing and decided then and there that she would take him to Hamleys toy shop then somewhere smart for lunch and perhaps they would meet up with Alice or even go to a movie, and she would forget the ridiculous prospect of rediscovering her lost love even though the opportunity had been handed to her almost on a silver platter and the prospect of not snatching it away made her feel sick to her heart.

But over the course of the next ninety miles she changed her mind, and changed it again, and again, and again until once more she was completely confused about her intentions and could only decide as far as going to the general area of Louis's hotel, which after all was not far from Hamleys, and where she also knew many a fine lunch spot, having worked in the area and its surrounds for most of her adult life.

It was the sensible thing to do, she told herself.

CHAPTER 17

An hour later, standing in the street, wind lashing at her ankles and a fine rain starting to fall as her son whimpered beside her, she wondered if she would ever see sense again.

She had found Louis's hotel and walked past it three times before dragging Rory to the corner and stopping there, flustered and frayed. Her thoughts were having trouble collecting themselves, as though the unseasonable city wind was gathering them up like fallen leaves and blowing them every which way, mixing them up with other city debris like dog ends and chocolate wrappers.

It was just so far from what she had imagined this past week, these past weeks, these past years. She had always fantasized that Louis and she would meet again but that it would be something windswept and wild and hopelessly romantic. Something blurred around the edges and misty like an old black-and-white Katharine Hepburn movie. And in just the past few days she had seen herself so many times knocking on the door of Louis's room and having him open it, sweep her into his arms and carry her to a four-poster bed where he would make love to her in a way that would put those ancient sacks of flour to shame.

Never had she seen herself standing in the rain outside a grotty bistro with a small snot-faced boy whining desperately that he wanted to do wees.

She had never felt less like Katharine Hepburn in her life. Here she was, her shoes splashed with rain and quite possibly ruined, dark sweaty stains under her armpits and her coat wearing the best part of a puddle from a number 17 bus bearing the wrinkle-free visage of Jemima Jones, which had swept past her just seconds after they had emerged from the Underground.

She had lost three pounds over the course of the past week but could still feel her waistband cutting into the flesh around her middle. Her crotch felt sweaty as well. She felt crumpled and ruffled and grubby and cheap.

The gods, she had to accept, were conspiring against her. No matter how much she wanted to feel Louis's smooth nut-brown skin pressed hotly against hers, it wasn't going to happen.

She looked at her son's damp ginger curls. Had she really thought she would take Rory with her to meet Louis? Or had she brought him to keep herself from doing just that? Was Rory ruining her chances, or saving her life? Her marriage? Her bruised and battered heart?

"Come on, Ror," she said finally, blocking out her thoughts and making her decision. "We'll find a loo and have a nice cup of tea somewhere." She took his hand and started back down the street.

Rory perked up instantly. "Can I have one of those little cakes that's half brown and half white?" he asked enthusiastically, trotting along slightly behind her. "And a pot of tea all to my own self?"

"Of course you can, darling." Esme looked at her watch. She had kissed her chances with Louis good-bye. Her feelings, at that moment, as she pulled Rory along were so complicated she could barely identify them. Her insides roiled with conflicting thoughts. Did she want to be a woman who cheated on her husband, anyway? Did she have it in her? Was that who she was? A cheat? An adulterer? A slut? The part of her that hoped she was not felt relief as she left Louis behind. But what if he truly was the big love of her life? Would she ever find happiness by walking away from him? A second time? The part of her that lusted after whatever it was he awoke in her felt anguish and resentment.

"Esme," Rory wailed, adding to her turmoil. "You're going too fast. I want to do weeeeees." His little face was red with exertion and he was clutching at his trousers in desperation. Esme felt dreadful. On top of everything, she was a bad mother. She was still a bad mother.

She stopped and looked around the street. It was just three blocks from where she had worked at Goodhart Publishing and she knew there was no public lavatory nearby, just offices and a few furniture shops and her old gym, Body Works, which was just across the road. Of course!

"It's okay, Rory," she said. "We'll go where Mummy used to do her exercises," and she dragged him across the road and up the stairs to the front desk, where the same yappy receptionist who had been there when she still frequented the place, albeit sporadically, before their move to the country, was filing the same old nails and reading what looked like the same old magazine.

"Blimey, we haven't seen you in donkey's ages," she said.

"Don't mention donkeys." Esme smiled, she couldn't remember the girl's name. "But I have a little boy desperate to go to the loo. Could he . . . ?"

"'Course, but you'll have to send him into the Gents'. We get complaints, you know." She rolled her eyes and Esme nodded sympathetically, then shuffled Rory toward the men's changing rooms, pushing him in the door and telling him to find the toilet as quickly as he could, use it and come straight back out.

Waiting outside the door, she was straightening her coat and attempting to run her fingers through her frizz when she was distracted by the sound of children laughing and clapping their hands. As it dawned on her what the sound was, a plot hatched so virulently in her mind that she was powerless to stop it.

The gym had a day care. She knew that. For a

fiver an hour, you could leave your children under expert supervision while you did your thing in the weights room or the aerobics studio. Esme, with two ancient child-minders built in for free at home, had never used the day care herself but other women she used to work with had.

The part of Esme that did not want to be a woman who had an affair told her to not give it another thought, to stay right there and wait for her son. The part that cried out for Louis told her that if she tried she could still make it to the hotel. He might still be there.

Esme teetered on the brink of her options. She could do nothing and go home to her husband and the rest of her life, complete with the complications of the past, or she could follow her pheromones and rekindle the intoxicating, over-powering, awe-inspiring, all-consuming passion she had discovered with Louis before the rest of her life had happened.

Esme shuffled on her heels. Everything up until this point had been conspiring against her, or conspiring against Louis. Yet here she was with a child who needed minding and a facility to do just that. Was it fate?

Of course, she was no longer a member of the gym but her friend (whatever her name was) on reception might overlook that. Perhaps that could be the deciding factor.

"You wouldn't do me a favor," she said, sidling up to the reception desk. "I've a couple more hours' shopping to do and my son is already dead on his feet. I couldn't possibly . . . ?"

The receptionist quickly checked that no one else was close enough to hear them. Esme was obviously not the first person to make this request.

"Twenty quid," she said. "And you'd better be back in two hours or I will sell him to the Gypsies."

Rory emerged from the bathroom with a big happy smile on his face and Esme tucked him in and explained what was happening. He was more than happy with the arrangement. Like his father, he was not a shopper, and while he sensed the change of plan meant his very own pot of tea was no longer just around the corner, he was happy to avoid an afternoon of shoes and handbags. Gluing colored things onto other colored things and biffing Play-Doh around a room was a pretty good alternative as far as he was concerned.

Esme ruffled Rory's hair and smiled at the smattering of other children in the playroom, but her hand shook as she wrote his name on a name badge and for a moment she considered throwing the lurid bit of cardboard in the bin, snatching her son and running for home.

But she did not. She stuck his name badge on his little chest, kissed him good-bye, told the daycare supervisor she would be back in an hour or so and dashed out into the street and back toward Louis's hotel.

"Stop thinking," she said out loud. "Just do it."

And so she found herself not five minutes later

staring up at the Excelsior Hotel on the brink of entering into something she knew could change her life forever.

In truth, the Excelsior was not what she expected. It was a slightly dilapidated Victorian building of the type often converted in this part of London to private hotels or guest rooms. The paint was peeling off the façade and the blinds in the bay windows on either side of the door did not match, but then boutique hotels came in so many different shapes and sizes these days, Esme reasoned.

Inside, however, she was forced to wonder if it *was* a boutique hotel. The reception area was dimly lit and sadly underfurnished and had a nasty stale odor about it. Esme rang the bell and a greasy little man with thick glasses and a terrible case of comb-across hair came out licking his fingers and smelling strongly of vinegar.

"Is there a Louis Lapoine staying here?" Esme asked him, suddenly sure that she had the wrong hotel and that her plans to meet up with him were seriously being mangled by unknown forces.

"Oh, yes," whined the greasy little man. "*Monsieur* Lapoine. Room sixteen. Up the first flight of stairs, love, and third on your left."

The Excelsior did not stretch to an elevator. Why would Louis stay in a place like this? Esme wondered as she climbed up the narrow staircase, noticing that the smell did not get any better as she ascended.

The six of room sixteen had fallen sideways and made a whole new number.

Esme rapped on the door and waited. Could there be some mistake?

But it was Louis's face that looked into hers when the door flew open and she knew from the look on it that he had given up on her.

"Esme!" he said, catching her by surprise by throwing himself excitedly in her direction to kiss each check, pushing her slightly off balance. She staggered backward into the hallway but Louis grabbed at her, apologizing profusely, and drew her into the room.

"I thought you were not coming," he said, his eyes bright with renewed anticipation. "I wait for an hour, which in London, you know, is usually enough, and when you didn't come, I think . . ." He shrugged. "But now, here you are!"

The room was tiny with a double bed—not of the four-poster variety—one ratty chair and a tatty dresser. It fell sadly short of her imaginings.

"Do you stay in places like this wherever you go?" Esme asked, looking around, trying not to sound stuffy. "I imagined that you would be in something slightly more, um"—she searched for the word—"midmarket."

Louis pulled her down beside him on the bed. It creaked rather rudely and its overstretched springs left her sitting awkwardly on its edge.

"We do not waste money on fancy hotel rooms at *la fédération*," Louis said dismissively. "We have better things to think about. Take off your coat, Esme. You are wet."

He watched her greedily as she struggled out of her trench coat, feeling shy and silly even though there were many layers to go and she could be proud of her matching underwear.

She looked up and met Louis's eyes.

"Do not be afraid, Esme," he said, in his hypnotic soft voice, understanding her doubt. "You were right to come."

And he leaned in and gently kissed her so lightly it was like drinking champagne. The bits of her that weren't loyal to her husband raced with excitement and she felt her blood heat up and heard a groan escape from her throat. Louis pressed her slowly back on the bed and she felt his lips on her neck and his tongue on her collarbone. She pushed thoughts of Pog out of her head. This was so much more treacherous than a stolen kiss in a restaurant doorway. This was it. There would be no going back. And already, her body was showing signs of being unstoppably on the track to Louis Lapoine.

He was exploring the neckline of her agnés b, his lips moving covetously over her skin. She was starting to feel hot, indescribably hot, deliciously, dangerously, undeniably hot. He moved, slowly, up her neck, along her jaw and across her cheek until his lips met hers and she nipped at him like a hungry foal, desperate for the bliss he could unleash in her, had unleashed in her, all those years ago and again here and now.

They kissed for an age. Her eyes were closed and her mind was locked in the past, where if she breathed in deeply enough she could smell the wood-fired oven, feel those golden well-worn steps beneath her back, taste that first crumb of sourdough, the crumb that would introduce her to the delights of which before she had only dreamed.

Her pleasure was indescribable. She writhed with it. And all from a kiss! Louis drew back and looked at her, drinking in her enjoyment. Then, still looking, his hand traveled too slowly (no, not slowly enough!) down her rib cage, forgiving the indent at her waistband and continuing to her hips. His thumb flicked against the softness of her belly and he dived into her again.

He tasted different, she realized then, from the way she remembered him. Different even from the Orrery doorway. But his flavor still sang to her. She lapped him up. She devoured him. She had waited so long.

He was panting when he pulled back from her again, his eyes glazed with pleasure, a light film of sweat on his forehead.

"Esme," he groaned in his chocolate-covered accent, and he knelt up, astride her, running one hand through his hair as though trying to slow himself down. Oh, the joy of being loved back! Esme felt it all over again.

She reached up and traced the line of his neck with one finger from the corner of his mouth, back to his ear, his edible ear, then down to the collar of his shirt. Over his exquisite Adam's apple her fingernail trailed, then she started to pull at his tie, already loosened, noticing for the first time that it was the same one he had worn when they last met. And when they first met, in Marylebone High Street. In fact, it was the same suit and perhaps the same shirt, which, now that she looked closely, was slightly grubby around the neckline.

Sensing her hesitation, he ripped the tie off himself, then unbuttoned Esme's jacket and brought his mouth down to her silk shirt, biting at her nipple through her new bra and rendering her unsure whether to scream for more or for him to stop.

Her body was working on its own now. She tugged at Louis's shirt buttons, undoing them to his waist then pulling the shirt away from his delectable shoulders. She rose up and bit into him, savoring his taste. He was salty and sour, like bread. He wriggled downward and ran his hands up her rump underneath her skirt and he tugged at her bikinis, flicking his finger inside them against that soft, doughy skin.

Esme groaned and wriggled farther into the middle of the bed. Something beneath her was digging into her shoulder and making her remember herself, which she did not want to do. She wanted to forget herself. She wanted to know nothing but this, but him.

"Ouch," she cried as Louis pressed down on her and whatever she was lying on bit into her shoulder.

Louis was on top of her now, fumbling with his belt, his erection pressing into her thigh.

"Esme," Louis moaned. "Oh, Esme."

She twisted around and grabbed at what lay underneath her. It was in Louis's suit-jacket pocket, and she would never know what made her dip into it but dip into it she did. It was the dusty track up to Louis's uncle's house all over again.

She pulled out a hard plastic baby pacifier. Pink and slightly gooey. Aghast, she felt her phero-mones spiral back into control.

"But, Louis," she said, looking at him, and wondering how his black eyes could still sparkle like that. Louis's children were teenagers now. And he did not even live with them.

"It's not how you think," Louis said breathlessly, his erection nonetheless withering. He leaned down onto one elbow and ran the other hand through his hair. The cut was wrong, Esme suddenly noticed. It was too long at the back. And he had missed a few spots on those smooth nut cheeks when he shaved.

She pushed him off her, then sat up and looked around the room. There was no suitcase. No brief-case, even. The bathroom door was open and there were no toiletries by the sink. Her heart was starting to thump in her ears, and not in the way Louis usually made it.

Something was wrong. There was a hip flask of brandy, open and only half full, and two plastic triangles of chain-store sandwiches sitting atop the Bible on the bedside table.

"Oh, my God," whispered Esme. Chain-store sandwiches? She pulled at her blouse, which was open and exposing most of one ripe breast and a morsel of soft white stomach. Her skirt had twisted around and come unzipped and her tights were halfway to her knees. She felt sick.

She looked at the pacifier in her hand.

"Whose is this?" she asked, trying to keep her voice steady. "Whose baby does it belong to?"

Louis, his shirt still off, his trousers unbelted and unbuttoned, reached for her.

"Esme," he said in his bewitching voice. "Does it matter?"

Esme closed her eyes to the sound of half a lifetime of dreaming being flushed gently down the toilet.

"How can I have been so stupid?" she asked herself as she slid to the side of the bed, stood up, slipped into her shoes and started to right her skirt. She was shaking.

"No, no, no," groaned Louis. "Please, Esme. We should do this. We are meant to do this. You and me. Come on."

But her rose-colored spectacles were off for good. Her fairy tale had disappeared. All she could see was a tatty little man in a tatty little room and a married woman, every bit as tragic, who was trying to go somewhere that no longer existed.

"So let me guess—you're not married to Diana

anymore but you are married to someone," she said, more amazed than angry as her fingers bumbled over buttoning her shirt. "And I suppose she is waiting in the nice hotel or shopping at Harvey Nicks or back in Paris with the ladies who lunch."

She straightened the ankles of her tights but did not want to expose her thighs to right them in the crotch. Louis watched her, his shoulders slumped.

"It doesn't have to be like this," he said.

"It already bloody isn't!" Esme said vehemently. "How could you do this to me a second time? After everything? After we talked about how much you hurt me last time and how I couldn't love anyone for ages and how you meant every word but the time wasn't right? I told you about Teddy, for God's sake. I have not been able to talk about him with anyone. Ever! I trusted you. Again. I trusted you and you could have ruined my life."

Louis looked sad. "Your life seems ruined already, Esme," he said.

"That's not true." Esme was horrified. "I have a perfectly good life."

"Oh, yes," Louis hit back. "Then what are you doing here?"

"I thought you could save me," Esme replied, realizing as she spoke the words that it was true. "I thought you could make me feel the way I did when I met you. Like nothing else mattered. Like nothing in between had happened."

Louis, sensing a gap in her resolve, leaned

toward her. "I can, Esme," he said earnestly. "I can."

She looked at him in wonderment as she reached for her coat and struggled into it. "You can't," she said. Oh God, this was not what she wanted! He was not what she wanted. "Nobody can save anybody else," she said. "And certainly not me."

"That's not what your friend Charlie thinks," Louis said, standing up and pulling himself together. Esme froze. What did Charlie have to do with this?

"What do you mean?"

Louis shrugged. "Nothing," he said. "Forget about it."

"What does Charlie have to do with any of this?" Esme insisted, her heart, already low, sinking further.

Louis shrugged again. "Maybe meeting you this time was not such a coincidence, Esme. That is all."

She thought about the lunch, the phone call from Charlie, meeting Louis while she waited. What was Louis saying?

"Charlie *arranged* this?" she asked, her voice barely a whisper.

Would Charlie really do that to her?

A hardness stole into Louis's eyes as he zipped up his pants and threaded his belt through the loops.

"I met him in a bar one night not so long ago and he was sorry for the stitches in my nose and tells me you still think of me, that you think a lot of me, and he offers to buy the lunch. At the Orrery. He thinks it will cheer you up and make you happy. He is a good friend, no? He even sends me this suit. Not really my color, but still."

Esme collapsed slowly into the ratty chair as her head spun. The whole thing had been a setup. She had not been meant to meet Louis and rekindle their passion. It had all been engineered behind her back. Destiny had nothing to do with it. It was all design.

Louis, she noticed, was slipping his feet into badly scuffed shoes. He wore brown socks. He drank during the day. He ate chain-store sandwiches and he had a baby young enough to need a pacifier.

"Do you even work for the bakers federation?" she asked tonelessly.

"Oh, Esme, you are such a romantic."

Esme sucked back a sob.

"There is no such thing as the bakers federation," said Louis. "The artisan bakers of France are a small group and getting smaller. No one cares about them! No one cares about *pain au levain.* You would be lucky to find it in Paris let alone in the country where it came from, where it belongs. There is nothing magical about sourdough, Esme. Once, maybe, I thought there was but not anymore."

"You can't mean that, Louis. You of all people. What happened to the *boulangerie*? What happened to your starter, the starter your great-great-, your many-greats grandfather began two hundred years ago?"

A dark look crossed Louis's face. "My uncle was offered a lot of money and so he sold the bakery." His voice was bitter. "I could not afford to buy it myself and he could not afford to keep it so that is that. Now it is an Internet café."

"And your uncle, is he, did he really die?"

Louis was shocked.

"But of course! I could never lie about something like that."

"Well, you can lie about everything else, Louis. Did you really come looking for me after I left Venolat?"

She could tell from the look on his face that he was tossing up whether to lie again, in itself providing the painful answer.

"No," he said. "Diana was very angry. My aunt was unwell. I could not leave then."

"But you do live in Paris now? You are still a baker?" She was desperate for something about Louis to be right.

"I live in Hounslow, Esme," he said tiredly, his skin looking gray and dull in the dingy light of the awful room. He had no life left in him at all. She could see that now. "I live with my girlfriend, Katarina, and our baby, Eleanor. I am the manager of the high street Pret a Manger."

Esme was too stunned for tears. She suddenly understood what people meant when they said the rug had been pulled out from under them. She felt like she was skittering on air above a bottomless canyon. She felt sick to her stomach.

"Your *girlfriend*? Pret a Manger? How could you do this to me?"

"Nobody is perfect, you know," Louis told her, looking small and pathetic. "No matter how much you want them to be."

He reached for her but she shrank away.

"But how could you, Louis, how could you? After your family had been baking in that building for all those years. It was you who said that the secret to sourdough was sticking with it but then you just let it go!"

Louis shrugged again. He looked pitiful.

"You are foolish if you think it is anything more than just bread," he said, and in that moment Esme knew he was not the Louis he had once been, just as she was not the Esme she had once been, and that there was no going back for either of them.

He picked up the brandy and drank from the bottle.

"Your friend Charlie thinks he is doing us both a favor but I think not." He wiped his mouth with his sleeve and looked at her. "I have paid for the room," he said. And he walked out the door.

But instead of closing it behind him, he turned to her.

"Your bread, your *pain au levain*, was good," he said, and she detected a wistfulness she did not think he could manufacture. "Different from Lapoine, of course, but good." And with that, he was gone.

Esme sat on the bed, speechless, her head reeling until she realized that the feeling that was surfacing above all others was one of relief. "Thank God, thank God, thank God," she breathed. She might have teetered but she had not fallen. She was not a cheat or an adulterer or a slut. Close. But not close enough.

How could she have fallen for him a second time? How could she have been so stupid? Thoughts still whirred in her head but made more sense than they had in a long time, and all, at least, pointed in the same direction: home.

She looked at her watch. It was nearly four. She would pick up Rory, maybe go to Hamleys and then go back to her family, where she now knew she belonged.

Louis, she would forget. Charlie she would deal with later. Charlie! Did he really think he had been doing her a favor? Was that his idea of helping? Pog she could not wait to wrap her arms around. She had saved him from her betrayal and she would never do that to him again.

She hurried through the streets—it was still, of course, raining—and took the steps to the gym two at a time. Her receptionist friend merely raised her eyebrows as Esme headed for the day care, trying to pick Rory's orange curls out in the kaleidoscope of color.

"Forget something?" the day-care supervisor, Felicity, asked.

Esme laughed. "No, I'm back," she said. "For Rory."

Felicity's face paled. "But he's gone," she said. "Your driver picked him up. Not long after you left him here. He's been gone for more than an hour."

Esme hit her head on a tiny little table as she fell to the floor. It wasn't a faint so much as a collapse. She had lost a child before. She knew what it felt like. And it felt like this. Like being lost yourself. With no chance, ever, of being found.

This time, though, she deserved it. And the pain was unbearable.

CHAPTER 18

The policeman who arrived in the gym manager's office less than ten minutes later had trouble making sense out of what Esme was saying.

Hysteria had her firmly in its grip and showed no signs of letting go.

"We don't have a car," she sobbed. "And my son Teddy died two years ago."

"I'm terribly sorry," the policeman said. "But I'm going to have to ask you some questions."

Panic gripped every nook and cranny of Esme's body. Her son had been taken while she had been acting like some two-bit hooker in a D-grade porn film. He was gone. She had lost both her sons. And yet again there was no one to blame but herself. Her heartbreak had taught her nothing.

She trembled as she tried not to think of what else she was about to lose. It was about Rory, of course it was about Rory. But also, her own foolishness and treachery were about to be laid out on the table for all to see and try as she might she could not ignore this. Rory would end up in the papers as the little boy whose mother was having a secret rendezvous in a seedy hotel room while he was being—

"Oh, God!" she cried, dissolving into more tears. The policeman squirmed uncomfortably in his chair and cleared his throat.

"Mrs. Stack," he said gently. "If you could just give me a few moments."

Esme tried to calm herself down. She was not helping Rory like this. She would talk to the policeman, help him find her little boy and then she would kill herself. She took a deep, wobbly breath.

"I'm not even a proper Catholic," she told him. Yet she knew her son—her only son, her only child—had been taken to punish her for almost cheating on Pog. She was wicked and it was what she deserved. But oh, not what he deserved!

The policeman looked at her as though she had just said something terribly sensible and nodded.

"Has Mrs. Stack seen a doctor?" he then asked the gym manager, a mother of two herself, who while furious that the day care had been so flagrantly abused with such dreadful results, could not help but sympathize with the distraught Esme. She shook her head.

"I think it might be a wise idea," the policeman said. "Would you mind arranging it?" He then turned back to Esme. "Now, Mrs. Stack. I know this is hard for you but it's important we think very clearly. That we don't jump to any conclusions.

Is it at all possible that your husband arranged to have your son picked up?"

Esme shook her head. "He doesn't know," she said. "I'm not even a member." Her hands, trembling in her lap, started clawing at each other. "Who would do this?" she cried. "Who?"

"Well, that's what we have to try and think about," the policeman said calmly. "But we should find out from Mr. Stack, just to make sure, that it was nothing to do with him. Most cases like this, Esme—can I call you Esme?—turn out to be little communication hiccups. You thought you were going to come back and pick Teddy up but your husband—"

"Rory," Esme corrected him, bleakly but loudly. "It's Rory." She was stuck in a deep, dark hole and she was never going to get out.

"Of course," the policeman said, feeling wretched. "Rory." Teddy was the other son. This poor woman. He started to feel a lump in his throat. It might be a communication hiccup, but then it might be worse.

"So if you would just like to ring him," he said gently, "your husband?"

Tears spilled down Esme's cheeks. "I went to meet a friend," she said, "at a hotel."

The policeman instantly understood. "I see," he said, some of his sympathy draining away.

"Rory was supposed to stay home but he had a cold and his grandfather was angry with me so I had to bring him," blubbed Esme. "I came in here

378

and saw the day care and, well, I thought there were rules," she sobbed. "I thought only I could pick him up."

Even the policeman had to agree that should have been the case. That it had been a terrible mistake on the day-care supervisor's part. She too was distraught and had been taken to a separate room for questioning and to try and give the police an Identikit picture of the kidnapper.

"Young Felicity says your son seemed to know the man," the policeman said, looking at his notebook. "A black man in his twenties."

Esme wept uncontrollably. What would this do to Pog? To lose his second son and his unfaithful wife in what would basically amount to a single phone call? It would kill him. And he was such a dear, sweet, gentle soul. She wanted him then, desperately, helplessly, stupidly. How cruel that the only person she wanted to reach for when she was in this kind of trouble was the person she had betrayed to get in it in the first place. But Pog was the rock she clung to, not perfect, yet safe and secure.

Of course they suffered their own dysfunctions: What couple didn't? She should have talked to him about Teddy, had known that all along, but as time went by it got harder, not easier, to bring up that lost and lonely name, and he had never talked to her, either. They were just two little lost peas bobbing about in a giant ocean of misery, each keeping an eye on the other to make sure

379

they stayed on course, yet stopping just short of throwing a line in case it sucked them both underneath the surface. It was all they could do in those dark desperate days to put one foot in front of the other and keep breathing, in and out, in and out, these past two years, being parents, a son, a daughter-in-law, a granddaughter. Who had room for the added angst of dredging up the details, raking through the pain? Who could bear it? There was the fresh pain, too, of Granny Mac to consider and avoid. Esme should have reached for her husband these past few weeks, not pushed him away and instead resurrected her past.

Sitting in the manager's office, her son lost, her lover a fraud, her life in tatters, all Esme wanted was Pog. But he would not want her. Not after this. Her sordid, sad little secret had cost them everything.

"We didn't even do anything," Esme sobbed wildly at the policeman. "It was a trick! Charlie set the whole bloody thing up."

The policeman, who was tired and slightly confused, perked up at this. "Charlie?" he repeated. "Are you referring to the kidnapper, Mrs. Stack? Is he known to you?"

"Louis," cried Esme. "In the hotel. We didn't do anything. I don't love him. I love Pog. I just wanted to come and get Rory and go home and live happily ever after. That's finally what I wanted! I only just found out, what? Half an hour ago? And now what chance do I have? Do any of us have?"

The policeman, who had soiled his own marital reputation not so long ago with a one-night stand on a boys' weekend in Amsterdam, culminating in a nasty rash and some quick explaining a week later, cranked up his sympathy again. He could see that Esme was not your average careless caregiver. And he did not wish himself in her shoes.

"I am sure it's just a misunderstanding," he said. "We all make mistakes, Esme. Could it have slipped your mind that you mentioned the day care to someone else?"

"But I didn't even know we were coming here," Esme said. "We just came in to use the loo and then I saw the day care—" Her heart stopped. "Could someone have seen him in the changing rooms? I didn't go in. People complain. He went in on his own. Oh please, please, please . . ."

The policeman's heart sank but he tried not to let her see it.

"Well, the front desk will have a record of everyone who was here at the time so we shouldn't have too much trouble tracking him down if that is the case," he said. "Now, I know that in the circumstances it is a delicate matter and perhaps not the easiest thing for you to do but I am going to have to insist that you ring Mr. Stack."

More than two hours had passed since Rory had been snatched and still her perfectly blameless husband was blissfully unaware. Esme knew the policeman was right.

"I'll go and check on the Identikit picture," he

said, and placing a kindly hand on Esme's shoulder, he left her to it.

The silence was unbearable. Esme's mind flicked from one frightful scenario to the next. Where was Rory now? What was happening to him? Why did he go with this black man in his twenties, this driver? How could he know someone that she didn't know herself?

She refused to allow herself to dwell on where he might be and what might be happening to him. Her heart couldn't bear the pain. It was all her fault. Her precious son was in the worst danger in which a four-year-old boy could possibly be. And why? Because his wretched, foolish, frivolous mother had wanted to recapture the pathetic drama of her long-lost youth.

How could she call Pog? How could she tell him what she had done?

She couldn't. But she had to do something to help Rory. And she couldn't do it on her own.

Wiping her eyes, then her nose, Esme lifted the phone and slowly, shakily, dialed Alice's work number. To her horror, Nose Hair himself picked up.

"Alice," Esme whispered into the phone. "Alice."

"Not here," Nose Hair barked. "But should you find her, please inform her I'm currently interviewing her replacement." And he hung up in her ear.

Esme stared, weeping, at the phone. Her brain

was all muddled. Her thoughts were mashed together and she couldn't separate one from the other. It was like fishing in dark and soupy waters. She poked around for thoughts that made sense but could find none. What should she do next? She couldn't find the answer. And time was ticking away, taking Rory farther and farther from her.

At this realization, she knew she could not wait any longer.

She was in such trouble, they all were. And Pog needed to know.

She picked up the phone again and, still weeping, punched in his work number. Mrs. Murphy answered almost straightaway.

"Is Hugo there, please?" Esme asked, trying hard not to hyperventilate with fear.

"I should be so lucky," snapped his assistant. "Gets a phone call from London and hightails it down there quick smart," she said. "Left me here to hold the fort entirely unaided, I might add. No respect, that's what's wrong with people these days. No respect."

"London?" Esme echoed. "Whatever for?"

"Don't ask me," Mrs. Murphy said. "It's not like he tells me anything. I'm just chief cook and bottle washer, me. Wouldn't tell me if the building were burning down, I expect. But come time to photocopy plans for the new one and it'll be muggins here who—"

Esme hung up. She felt like a cartoon character who had been hit on the head. Birds tweeted around her. Sense could not get in. The door behind her opened and a tap on her shoulder alerted her to the return of the police officer, behind him the Identikit artist.

"Ludkin here thinks he has a fairly good image," the policeman said cheerfully. Felicity, it seemed, had taken a shine to the kidnapper, flirted with him by the sound of things, and while quite distraught and totally ashamed, had provided Ludkin with more than enough detail for a good likeness. Ludkin indeed looked pleased with himself as he sidestepped the policeman to show Esme his image.

"Reckons he's about six feet tall, just a bit taller than myself," said Ludkin, who was five feet eight if he was lucky. "Quite well spoken, plainly dressed in clean, sport-style street clothes, and as you are aware, known to the victim." He realized his gaffe immediately. "That is, known to your *son*."

But Esme was not listening to him. She was staring at the line drawing in front of her and it was staring back.

The soup in her head suddenly started to clear as the straight lines and subtle shadings emerged from a stranger's blur into a frighteningly familiar face.

All was not lost. It had been a hiccup of some description.

Esme's tears dried as she burped out something approaching a laugh. She looked at the policeman, her eyes shining, and pointed at the picture.

The kidnapper was someone she knew. And he was not a kidnapper. Nor was he a black man in his twenties—rather a coffee-colored boy of sixteen.

It was Ridge.

Ridge had taken Rory.

Relief flooded through Esme like intravenous Valium. Rory was fine. He was with Ridge. Why, she couldn't fathom, but she also knew that her little boy would be safe. There would be an explanation. The police could go home. So could she. So could Rory. So could Pog.

Moments before, her life had lain in ruins at her ankles and now bits of it had risen up into the air, and although all were currently floating just out of her reach, she knew that if she could just grab them and join them all up together again, it would be all right. Everything would be all right.

Esme allowed herself a further injection of guilt at the way her relief, while almost entirely over Rory, was yet tinged with traces of her Excelsior secret. Her marriage was not lost. Her secret was safe.

The policeman understood all this and forgave her. Nobody wanted to think of a little kid being kidnapped by some nasty piece of work so the time wasted could not really be considered so.

"So you know how to get hold of this Ridgeley, then?" he asked.

Esme had not thought that far ahead, but at this snatched up the phone again and stabbed in

385

Alice's home number. It barely rang before she heard her friend's anxious voice on the other end.

"It's Esme. Is Rory there?"

"Yes," Alice cried. "He's fine. He's absolutely fine. I mean I don't know what the fuck is going on but Rory is fine, Esme."

"Thank God," Esme cried. "He's okay," she said to the policeman who, seeing the look of joy on her face, could not muster up a trace of annoyance. Sometimes, he thought, he bloody well liked his job.

"Who's that?" Alice asked. "Where are you, Esme?"

"It's the police," Esme told her. "I'm at the gym with the police. We thought Rory had been kidnapped, Alice. I've been going out of my mind."

"Well, he was kidnapped," interrupted the Identikit artist, who was peeved at barely being congratulated on his contribution to recent events.

"Oh, Esme! They won't press charges, will they?" Alice was panicking. "It will ruin his life and he only did it because—well, because he loves Rory so much and he's just a bit screwed up and he would never, ever hurt a hair on his head, on anyone's head and I know you probably need me to be your friend right now but honestly, I could kill you, Esme. I could just throttle you. Ridge has told me about the Frenchman. How could you? Behind Pog's back. Behind all of our backs. I'm so angry, Esme. I know it's been hard for you with Granny Mac and everything but it's hard for all of us, Esme. And even harder now. Why didn't you tell me? Oh, Esme, please don't let them press charges. Please!"

Her punishment, Esme realized, was far from over.

"Ridge knows about Louis?" she asked, lowering her voice.

"He saw you, Es. In Marylebone High Street, snogging. And then outside the hotel. He works right next door, I told you, didn't I? At the bistro. He followed you to the gym. Oh, Esme, it's not his fault. He's just a confused kid. Please don't ruin his life. He knows he did the wrong thing. He rang me as soon as Rory started asking for you."

With a downward beat of her heart, Esme realized that her own foolishness and treachery were not out of the woods just yet. Her little boy was safe, but she was not. And as for darling damaged Ridge: Of course she would protect him. From what, she didn't know, but there were enough ruined lives in the offing as it was.

"I won't," she said quietly. "I wouldn't, Alice."

"Of course," breathed her friend. "Of course. I just had to make sure. He shouldn't have done it, Es. He knows that. He shouldn't have done anything."

"Does Pog know?" Esme asked, knowing that her husband fleeing to London was unlikely, the way things were going, to be a coincidence. Silence.

"He does," Alice said eventually. "Ridge rang him first. I think he told him everything and then Pog called me. He assumed I must know what you were up to with Louis. I mean, you've never not told me anything ever before, Esme." Alice started to cry. "I'm so sorry," she wailed. "You and Pog always seemed so perfect, despite everything." Esme was feeling sicker as every minute passed. "How could you do this?" her friend sobbed into the phone.

"Nothing happened," Esme intoned blankly. "With Louis. I bumped into him in town, the day Jemima saw me at the Orrery. We had lunch, twice, and I talked about Teddy and then nothing happened. Absolutely nothing. It was all a mistake."

We all make mistakes, the kind policeman had said to her. Yet hers felt bigger than most. And of what had she been guilty? Chasing dreams and being stupid. For that she had nearly lost her treasured son and would surely lose her husband.

"Pog is on his way here," Alice said. "You'd better come."

Esme nodded wordlessly and slid the phone back into its cradle, the policeman watching her as relief and happiness slid off her face into a puddle on the floor.

"I'll give you a lift," he said, shaking his head and waving away a flustered doctor who had appeared at the door with the gym manager. "Probably best you avoid the tube after a day like today."

Esme stared at him blankly. She had forgotten his name, wasn't sure if she ever knew it.

"How can I face them?" she asked him, as though he could truly help her. "I've only gone and cocked up my whole life. I mean, it's like some horrible nightmare only I know I am awake because my waistband is too tight and it's digging into me and I can feel it. But is it normal to not know whether you are alive or dead?"

The policeman, who had gotten up to leave, sighed and sat down again.

"I thought I had it all under control," Esme continued. "I thought I had found a way just to goddamn carry on and for nearly two years, I bloody well did. You know? I really bloody well did. Then Granny Mac goes and has another stroke. And then she gets pneumonia."

She was gazing at the floor, shaking her head. "And everything goes to pot. I go to pot."

A silence, surprisingly lacking in awkwardness, grew between them.

"It can't be easy," the policeman eventually said, "going on with your life when you've lost a little one."

Esme nodded, miserably. It hadn't been. Life after Teddy had barely been life at all. It was like pretending to live, really. Why hadn't she seen it at the time? She'd been so determined for everything to return to normal, for everyone to return to normal, to cover up the hole left by the loss of their little boy, that she had simply gone through the motions, keeping the outside world happy, yet all the while she'd been shriveling up inside, relishing her numbness. The memory of her son had become a hard, dry, nasty little nugget inside her and for some reason, Louis had been able to nourish it. Granny Mac had seen that. But then, she would.

"Would mess up your head," the policeman was saying, "make you do mad things, I imagine. Grief does that to a person. I've seen it a thousand times." He stopped and waited for Esme to look at him. "I expect the same goes for Mr. Stack," he said, with an encouraging raise of his eyebrows.

"Why are you being so kind to me?" Esme asked him.

"Because you look like a woman who could do with a break," the policeman answered, with a smile, and he stood and nodded at the door. "Shall we go?"

Esme's future lay cold and harsh and flat in front of her. But could it be worse, she asked herself as she let the policeman lead her out of the gym, than the soft and slushy murk of her fairly recent past?

CHAPTER 19

A very fat man dressed entirely in purple stretch cotton was sitting sprawled on the steps of Alice's building when Esme arrived, her face streaked with tears and her mind cluttered with possibilities.

The policeman, whose name, he'd sheepishly told her on the way, was also Ted, had done his best to calm her fears by reminding her that her son, after all, was safe and sound and that was what really mattered.

But when she had asked why it was that people had affairs all the time and got off scot-free yet hers had not even started before her son was for all intents and purposes kidnapped and her secrets exposed to all and sundry, he had been unable to think of anything to make her feel better.

"You've got to have it out," he advised, although he had lied to his wife about his poxy Amsterdam whore. He did not like himself for it, though. "Get it all out in the open."

"Thank you, Ted," she said, when he dropped her at the curb.

"I should come up and make sure the boy is all

391

right, really," he said. "You go ahead and I'll park the car and be right up." He wanted to give her a moment on her own. She had been humiliated enough without turning up on a policeman's arm.

The purple vision on Alice's steps, however, was far from similarly sensitive to her needs. In fact, he seemed not to see her at all.

She lunged to the left of him before realizing there was not enough room down that side, so then attempted to get past him on the right but it, too, was a squeeze.

"Could you please excuse me," she said as politely as she could. "I need to get past."

"All right, all right," the fat man wheezed, wiping at his forehead with a pudgy purple arm but not moving. "No need to get your knickers in a twist."

Esme was repelled by the thought of her knickers, which had only a few long hours ago indeed been twisted nearly right off her in that god-awful hotel room. She had never in her life felt so low-down dirty and despicable as she did at that moment.

"Oh God!" she cried in anguish. All she knew was that she did not want to be looking at the rolling silvery skin that poked out between the fat man's too-small zip-up top and equally challenged elasticized pants. Turning on the step as much as his bulk would let her, she lifted her knee and kicked him neatly in the side of his arse. "Get out of my bloody way," she cried.

The fat man looked at her with surprise and

scrunched up his face so all his features landed in the middle. "Steady on," he said, his sausage-like fingers rubbing the spot where she had booted him but shuffling sideways nonetheless to make enough room for her to pass. "All you had to do was ask, you silly ginger cow."

But Esme was past him and already desperately pressing the buzzer to Alice's apartment.

"It's me, it's me," she cried into the speaker and the door was buzzed open.

By the time she reached the third floor she was gasping for breath, her trench coat flapping around her body, her hair stuck to her neck as she pounded on Alice's door.

Her friend, her face pinched and unfamiliar, opened it wide and looked toward the front room. Her anger radiated the space between them but Esme's guilt glands were already full and over-flowing.

She walked into the room and there was Rory, sitting all on his own on the sofa, surrounded by cushions, in perfect health, and pretending to read his favorite book, *Madeline,* the words of which he knew by heart.

Stifling a sob, Esme knelt on the floor, feeling, disgustedly, her opaque tights tugging at her crotch where she had failed to pull them up properly. How could she have exposed her family, her little boy, to her sorry, sordid mistakes? How could she live with what she had done? She pulled Rory to her, hugging him close and smelling his innocent little boy smell as she nuzzled his neck and kissed him.

"I'm so sorry, darling," was all she could say. "I'm so, so sorry."

Rory put up with this for a few moments but then pushed her gently away. "It's okay, Esme," he said. "I made a giant panda out of Play-Doh and then Ridge came and got me. We went on the bus and the tube and he bought me some chocolate and an orange drink." He looked guiltily at her. "I had to do wees again," he said. "I think it was the drink."

Ridge stood by the fireplace fidgeting and looking dangerous in a way she would never have guessed he could. She started to say something but the angry teenager interrupted her.

"You don't bloody deserve him," he cried. "You've got everything right in front of your own bloody face and you can't even see it. You make me sick!"

Esme was stunned. Ridge was shaking with rage.

"I'm so sorry," Esme started to say, even though Ridge was just as much in the wrong as she was, more, possibly, but his anger could not be contained.

"You have this husband who worships you," he seethed, "and this little kid who thinks you're the cat's pajamas and you'd throw it all away on some stupid lying little French git who just wants to get into your pants. It's disgusting!"

"Ridge!" Alice spoke sharply from the door.

"It's true, Mum," her son answered, and he sounded so young and so hurt that Esme could not hold back her tears. That she could damage her own family so badly was one thing but to hurt Alice's was incomprehensible.

"You're out there year after year trying to find someone to love you," Ridge continued, looking distraughtly at his mother, "going out with all these utter dead-shits and she's got someone perfect right there and she bloody well craps on him. It's not fair!"

"Ridge," Alice said again, but there was a softness in her voice that made Esme feel even worse. "Don't. It's not your business."

"You're my business," Ridge said to his mother, and his voice cracked, giving way to tears.

"Please," Esme bawled at him from the floor, her face awash. "Please forgive me, Ridge. I am so sorry."

"Yeah? Well, maybe it's too—"

"I've been stupid," Esme cried. "But I didn't mean to hurt you or Alice or anyone. I just—"

"You just never thought about anyone apart from yourself," roared Ridge, his embarrassment at crying in front of them fueling his rage. "You're nothing but a—"

Thankfully, for everyone in the room, the intercom rudely heralded the arrival of Pog.

"You don't deserve him," Ridge hissed as Alice buzzed him in.

"You think I don't know that?" Esme said

quietly, sitting up on the sofa next to Rory. How she was going to get through the next few minutes, let alone the rest of her life, she did not know.

Alice opened the door and Pog walked in, barely acknowledging her as he strode straight toward his wife and son.

"Oh, Esme," he said with no trace of rancor and Esme could not even look at him. Pog knelt down and hugged his son to his chest but Rory was sick of being hugged and quickly resisted.

Pog, then, put his hand on his wife's knee. "Esme," he said again, even more gently, which only made her cry.

"Why are you being so bloody nice to her?" Ridge shouted, his tears making his voice mean and throaty. "She's only been shagging some slimy little frog behind your back."

"That's enough!" commanded a new voice. Henry's voice. Esme looked up just long enough to see his miserable face attached to his miserable body, standing by the doorway next to a distraught Alice. Esme's hands flew up to her face to cover the tears she could not stop and disguise her shame. Why had Henry come?

"But you're just—" Ridge started to say.

"Enough!" It was Pog this time. "Stop it, Ridge. Esme has enough going on without you having a go at her, too."

He turned to Esme and put his other hand on her other knee. Still she could not meet his gaze.

Rory shifted ever so slightly closer to her on the sofa.

"But you shouldn't—" Ridge started again, tears and anger mixing on his face.

"Please," begged his mother. "Just stop."

"You don't know everything there is to know, Ridge," Pog said tiredly. "You don't know what Esme has been through. Nobody is perfect."

"I do know," insisted Ridgeley. "I've known her since I was born, haven't I? I've known her for longer than you have."

"Yes, but the past couple of years, the last couple of months, have been hell for her and you're not—"

"So her son died and her grandmother—"

"THAT'S ENOUGH," Pog roared again. It was such a rare sound, his voice angry and raised. "Let's not forget the part you have played in all this today, Ridge."

A silence so thick with secrets and regret hung over the sad collection of friends and family so suffocatingly that Esme wished Ridge would start shouting again.

The buzzer rang again, giving them all a fright, and they waited in painful silence until Alice opened the door to Ted, who simply took in Esme and the little boy, asked a simple, "All right?" and excused himself again at her unhappy nod.

"Alice, why don't you take Ridge to the pub," Pog suggested in a bright, sensible voice after the policeman had gone. "I hate to toss you out of your own home but I think we need some time alone here."

Alice nodded and looked relieved. Watching her favorite family disintegrate in front of her very eyes was hardly pleasant viewing. And her feelings about Esme were mixing in her stomach like too many cocktails and a late-night kebab. She loved her and felt sorry for her but felt angry and vengeful as well.

"We'll take Rory," Alice said, reaching her hand out for him, but Rory scooted right over so that he was squashed up against his mother and shook his head.

"I'm staying with Esme," he said.

"Do you want him to see all this? Hear all this?" Alice asked Pog.

"I'm not going," Rory pouted. "I'm staying with Esme."

"He shouldn't hear all this, Pog," Alice said gently.

"Oh, Alice," Pog said, and he sounded so sad that Alice's own eyes filled with tears again, "he has to hear it. We all do. Really, it's time."

Alice grabbed her own angry son and hustled him, protesting, out the door of their flat.

After they left, nobody said anything, and the room was filled only with the sound of Esme's sobbing. She had no idea how she was going to resurrect her life and knew that it would probably never be the same again, but what she had caused others, she swore as she sat there on the sofa, she was prepared to repair, no matter how hard and no matter what the sacrifice.

When she could bear to, she raised her eyes to meet Henry's. He was sitting now on the chair by the window, turned sideways to her.

"I'm so sorry, Henry," she said before dissolving into great hiccupping sobs again. "I know I've always been a disappointment to you and that this only proves that you were right all along but I really, truly am sorry."

To her added distress, she felt a small clammy hand through the fabric of her coat and looked down to see that Rory, who was pretending to read his book again, was rubbing her leg with his milky, soft hand, comforting her.

She watched the bone-colored fabric grow fat dark dots as her tears fell on it. When the dots got smaller, she looked up at Henry, ready, with the help of her little boy and his chubby caress, to take her punishment.

To her horror, Henry, far from steaming at the nostrils, was also weeping, his hand, red and purple with his old man's veins, shaking as he brought it up to wipe a string of mucus from his nose.

"No," he said, his voice thick with grief. "It is I who should be sorry." He sobbed with a shudder that racked his whole body. "I have been cruel," he said, "and unreasonable. And I have been a coward." His voice splintered, unable to string words together any further.

Confusion interrupted Esme's own unhappiness. "Don't be silly, Henry," she said. "A coward? You haven't been a coward. What do you mean?"

Henry allowed one more deep, raw sob to shake him, then he took a big breath, drew himself up in his chair and looked at Esme with bloodshot, heartbroken eyes.

"It was me," he said. "It was me who pulled the plastic over the fountain."

Esme sat completely still.

"Your grandmother told me to do it first thing in the morning," Henry continued wretchedly, "when it first started to rain, but I didn't. Just to be blessed contrary, I didn't. I did it at lunchtime after she had asked me twice more and by that stage the bowl was already full of water." His shoulders shook as he fought to keep control. "I should have emptied it out but I thought covering it would keep the boys from harm. I never dreamed that anyone would, that Teddy would—" His lips trembled and his eyes blinked rapidly to ward off fresh tears.

"If it wasn't for me, Teddy would be alive," he exploded, his mouth thick with the glue of grief. "He would be alive and none of this would have happened."

Hearing Henry say his name shocked Esme completely tearless. The sound of it ricocheted around the room.

"Teddy," she said out loud. Nothing happened. She took Rory's little hand in her own, and rubbed it. "Teddy," she said again. Rory looked at her and smiled.

"Teddy," he repeated. "Rory and Teddy."

Her heart was bleeding but her mind suddenly, strangely calmed. She looked at Pog, whose unfathomable blue eyes were there, ready and waiting, to return her gaze.

"Why couldn't I talk about him?" she asked her husband. "Why was it so hard for me to say his name?"

"It wasn't just you," said Pog. "It was all of us."

"But I'm his mother," Esme said. "I'm the one who was opening a test kitchen while he was"— her mouth was as dry as a bone—"at home, in need of me. I'm the one who took too long to find him. Who never thought to check the fountain. Whose idea the bloody wretched fountain was in the first place."

"But I was there," Henry said. "I was there and in control and I could have stopped it happening from the very beginning. It's my fault and you've had every right to hate me for it."

"Nobody hates you, Dad," said Pog. "Even though you often give us reason to and not because of Teddy but because you can be rude to Esme and ungrateful when she is one of the sweetest people alive."

"Esme hates me," Henry said. "She's blamed me all along and she's been right to. It was my fault."

"I've done nothing of the sort, Henry," Esme

exclaimed. "Do you think I had a moment spare from blaming myself? It was not your fault. I'm his mother and I should have been there looking after him and I should have found him before it was too late. It's not about the plastic. Bugger the plastic. It doesn't matter whose idea it was. It was a good idea to cover the fountain. It was the right thing to do, the sensible thing to do. It was just—"

"It was just bad luck," Pog said, getting up off the floor and squeezing in on the other side of Esme on the sofa. He leaned forward and put his head in his hands. "It was just one of those terrible things that happens: that you think will happen to someone else but in this case happened to us."

Esme closed her eyes and saw Teddy's ginger curls floating in a shiny black slick.

"It's true, Esme," Pog said quietly. "I know you think it was bad management on your part, on my part, on our part, but other people work hard and have busy lives in the city and their children don't die."

Behind her closed eyelids, Esme lifted Teddy out of the water and held him to her chest again.

"I think we did the right thing leaving London, leaving that life behind, moving to the House in the Clouds and starting again up there. I really do. It's been good for Rory and it was good for Granny Mac, too."

Esme's remaining secrets scrabbled around the corners of the room searching for an escape.

Henry sniffed in the silence that ensued, and although her eyes were closed and her head was resting back against the sofa cushions, Rory climbed into her lap and snuggled into her neck.

"Sometimes, Esme," he said in a matter-of-fact voice, "I talk to Teddy."

Tears slid down Esme's cheeks as she wrapped her arms around him.

"I know he's not here," Rory continued, "but I still talk to him."

Pog cleared his throat, for the first time seeming to struggle with his emotions. "Now, now, Ror," he said.

"Esme?" Rory tugged at her and she opened her eyes and looked into his, finding in them something she hadn't known she needed but wondered how she could ever have missed. She kissed her son and drew strength from him.

"Yes, darling," she whispered. "I know."

"It can be our little secret, if you like, about Granny Mac," Rory whispered back, snuggling up against her, and she treasured him more in that moment than she had treasured anything ever before.

"I've not been myself these past few weeks," she finally said to the room. "I've had trouble. I've been struggling. Everything seemed wrong. Nothing fit properly. I felt wretched on the inside. All messed up and horrid."

She thought of the turmoil that clawed at her innards all the time and wondered, dimly, if perhaps now that everything was out in the open, she would be free of it.

"You're always so damnably cheerful," Henry said, "no matter how dire the circumstances. How are we supposed to know when there is something wrong?"

Esme almost laughed. "Well, you're not," she said. "That's the whole point of me. It always has been. You can always rely on me to make you laugh and feel better. It's actually one of the things I like most about myself. I'm the feel-good girl."

"But Esme," Pog said, the pain clear in his voice, "you can't go through what you've been through and still bear that responsibility. It's too hard."

This was true, Esme knew, but only to a point.

"But, Pog—if I climbed into bed with a vat of gin and cried myself to sleep for a year, what would you do?" He knew the answer as well as she did.

"I would climb in, too," he said. "To be with you."

A faint whistling from Esme's lap told her that their son, after saying his bit, after sharing a little magical drop of himself with her, had nodded off to sleep. She smoothed his curls off his forehead.

"Well, I couldn't bear that," Esme said softly, so as not to wake him up. "I don't want to think anyone else could feel the same deep, dark, horrible, awful bloody pain that I do. And I certainly don't want to see it. It would be the end of me."

"Don't say that," Henry said, with some of his old fierceness. "He would never let that happen. He loves you too bloody much. For better or worse."

"It's true," said Pog. "I love you so bloody much, Es." And he exploded into tears so loaded with grief that Esme thought she simply could not bear it. Her aching heart rendered her silent.

Henry, at this, pulled himself out of his chair, took the sleeping Rory off her lap and wordlessly limped out of the room.

Then out into the air between them, so full of unspoken thoughts and raw, ragged feeling, burst the pent-up declaration Pog had long been holding and hiding.

"I love you so much," he exploded again. "You'll never know how much, Esme." Tears pinged off his cheeks and onto the carpet. "I just—" His voice shook but he took a stuttering breath and plowed on. "Talking about it doesn't do it justice, Es. I don't know the right words, what to say to make you feel better. I just know that I have adored you since the moment I first saw you and that if you were to leave—" The thought brought with it fresh tears but he brushed them away. "If you were to leave it would be devastating—but that's not even the word. It would be, God, living hell, Esme. Absolute living hell."

He tried to curb his emotion before he continued. "But I've thought about it all after-noon, I mean I've thought about the possibility for years, and if you want to go off with Louis," he said, "and live in some bloody bakery in the middle of France, well, part of me wants to shake you till your head drops off, Esme. How could you do this? To me? To us? But part of me only wants you to be happy because you bloody deserve it, you truly do, no matter what, so if you want to go to Louis I will help you pack your bags, Esme. I will fold your clothes and brush your hair and rub lavender moisturizer into your legs before you go. I might die afterward, or at least never live properly again, but if going with Louis is what will make you happy then I will help you, Esme. I will. I swear I will."

He had a lot to get off his chest as Esme sobbed silently next to him.

"But will he ever love you the way I do?" he burst out again, his face wet with sorrow. "Will he love the way your hair springs out one side of your head first thing in the morning, or the way you smile in your sleep, or the little fold of skin near your armpit? Does he know that you can't stand marmalade but eat apricot jam out of the pot with your fingers? Will he understand that you always keep in touch with your friends even though they neglect you and take advantage of you and don't take care of you and will you tell him that you need to take painkillers an hour before a bikini wax or it makes you cry?"

Esme had never heard anything so clearly in all her life.

"I know he's a baker. I know he bakes bread. I know that's what you love about him, Esme, but there's more to life than bloody bread, you know. Man cannot live by bread alone, Esme. Everybody thinks you're so strong, so capable, so funny, so amazing and you are, my God, you are, but I understand you like nobody else ever will. I understand that you needed to wait to talk about Teddy. I understand that you can't look at Rory without wondering how being half a twin for the rest of his life is going to affect him. I understand that Granny Mac was more to you than a guardian, she was an angel, a crotchety old angel, and everyone else came second and I love that about you, Esme, I really do. And if you go with Louis and I never see you again I will still wake up every day and thank God that I knew you and understood you as well as I have because every day with you has been a marvelous bloody gift and I treasure each moment."

What have I done to deserve this man? Esme thought as she watched him pour his heart out into a puddle on the middle of Alice's swirly orange and brown carpet. How could she ever have doubted that where she belonged was with him?

Esme slid off the sofa, sank to her knees in front of Pog and took his hands from his head, which had sunk into them again. She placed his precious arms around her shoulders.

"Nothing happened with Louis," she said softly.

"I had lunch with him twice, Pog, and I went to his hotel today but nothing happened, I swear to you." She stopped. How could she hold anything back from Pog when he had just bared his own battered and bruised soul so bravely to her? "I thought it might," she said, sniffing as her tears dried, "happen, I mean. With him, Pog. With Louis. I talked to him about our baby, our Teddy, and it just felt like such a huge bloody release that I thought it must mean something, that there was more to it. But once I got there and saw him for who he really is, I just . . ." She thought about the pacifier and how it had saved her from making the worst mistake of her life. Without it, she might not have seen who Louis really was until she had already betrayed her husband. Maybe destiny had played a part after all. She cleared her throat.

"I don't love Louis," she said and the words tasted far from sour in her mouth and gave her courage. "I've been lost and scared and I thought meeting him again was a sign that I could find the sort of happiness that I knew when I was young and uncomplicated and pure, not the screwed up, heartbroken mother of a dead little boy."

Pog clasped her tightly and wept into her curls.

"But I was wrong, Pog," she continued. "I don't think I can ever have that happiness back. I think it's a once-in-a-lifetime thing." She felt her husband shudder with anguish as she realized she had not put it the way she meant it.

"Shhh," she hushed him. "I don't mean it like

that. I mean that I don't want it again. I think I can have a new kind of happiness. I have had a new kind. A better kind. With you."

She pulled away and lifted Pog's face so his waterlogged eyes met hers.

"I've loved you from the moment I spat up the regurgitated cheese ball, Pog. You're my best friend in all the world, I'd trust you with my life—I *do* trust you with my life. You're the kindest, sweetest, most patient, adoring husband any woman could ever hope for and you are the father of my son, my sons. There is no other man in the universe I will ever want for that job. You've loved me and taken care of me and made me feel like a beautiful princess all these years, and I can't believe that I have even got close to messing that up, Pog, and if I could wind back the clock I would but I can't, you know that, because you know just when I would wind it back to."

Pog nodded as his eyes filled with tears again.

"We have to move on," Esme continued, a path clearing in her mind, "we have to look forward not backward. I haven't really understood that until now because the future seemed so grim, so Teddy-less, but we can do it, with each other, I know that now. Oh God, Hugo Stack, I love you! With all my heart. I truly, truly do. I know I've bungled it, I know I don't deserve it, but do you think you can ever, will ever be able to forgive me?"

Pog looked at her with his steady, unwavering

gaze. "It's not about forgiving you, Esme, it's about being sure you love me as much as I love you because if you don't, I can't bear it."

"But I do!" cried Esme. "I do! That's what this whole horrible mess has taught me. Honestly, Pog, I've never been more sure about anything in all my life."

He was silent for a moment and when he spoke, his voice did not need to be chocolate-coated. "I know you think you're plain old flour and water, Es," he said, "and that Louis was your starter, but that's not true, it's never been true. We're the flour and water and you're *our* starter.

"You're the best thing that ever happened to any of us," he said, and she leaned in, raised her face and kissed him, tasting the salt of his tears and the promise of their future.

It was delicious.

CHAPTER 20

Esme and Alice both sat on Granny Mac's bed but the *Hello!* magazine they had snuck in to ogle was discarded between them.

"You have been *what*?" Alice was asking Esme, aghast.

"I have been talking to her," Esme answered, her cheeks turning pink. "I know it sounds nutty but I have. She told me to start baking bread again and she told me to go and meet Louis."

"But Esme, sweetie, Granny Mac is dead," Alice said. "She died two months ago."

"Well, I know that. That is why it sounds nutty that I have been talking to her," Esme returned, as though Alice were the crazy one. "But I found her in here, sort of sitting up large as life, the day that Brown peed on the quince, and she started talking to me and I started talking back."

Alice was stunned. She stared at the ceiling and wriggled her jaw, uncertain what to do or say.

"Oh, don't go all thingie on me, Alice," Esme pleaded. "You wanted me to tell you everything from now on so I'm telling you. And I haven't gone all crystal-gazing or psychic phone number

411

or anything. I mean, I don't believe in ghosts, either. But I don't think that was what she was. She just hadn't quite finished with me. Or with here. Or something."

Alice's face crumpled into an expression of hopeless worry. "But, Esme," she groaned. "That's loony! People don't come back from the dead in real life. It only happens in films."

"I know," her friend sighed. She was silent for a moment. "It's just that if you take away the whole not actually being alive and well and, you know, *here*, thing then it almost makes sense."

"It does? How can it?"

Esme had thought about this long and hard and had a theory that she believed enough to know that she had not gone mad.

"You know, when Teddy died," she explained, "I thought that as long as I had Granny Mac everything would be all right. That was all that kept me going, Alice: the thought that she was with me. And I know I had Pog but Teddy was his son, too, and he was going through everything I was, whether he showed it or not, and I couldn't bear for him to have to grieve for me as well as himself, but Granny Mac was there for me. Just for me. She was mine. She would never let me crawl into a hole and not come out again. And you know that's a real possibility with MacDougall women, but we had a sort of secret unspoken pact about saving each other from that particular fate. It's just that I never let myself contemplate a life

412

without her so when she went with so little warning, I think a switch flicked in my head that I couldn't unflick myself without a little bit of help."

"Esme, you mustn't say things like that."

"But it's true, Alice! There's no blueprint for surviving the loss of your child, you know. You bloody well grasp on to whatever you can to stop yourself from drowning and for me it was Granny Mac. She was my life support, she always had been. It's not as though we talked about him, Teddy, I mean, but she was just there, my life raft, keeping me afloat. And I thought I would know when I had to let go and that I'd have the chance to prepare for it, but instead Dr. Gribblehurst just steps out of her door after his regular visit and tells us to make arrangements, that it's a matter of hours, and it was."

"Esme, she'd been bedridden for two years. She could barely speak. You must have known."

"I couldn't bear it," Esme said. "I just couldn't bear it, Alice. I just couldn't let her go."

"And so," Alice said, rather skeptically, "she came back, from the other side, from beyond."

"From wherever," Esme said. "Don't laugh at me! I know it's losing your marbles territory, my God, you think I don't know that? And now I sit in here like I did before and think perhaps I was just imagining her. Perhaps I was only telling myself things I already knew, suggesting things I really wanted to do. But the room felt different,

413

Alice. It felt full of her. It smelled of her, too. You know, Embassy Regal. And Rod bloody Stewart was always playing. Constantly. You know how she always loved to sing along. He seeped from the walls, Alice."

She looked around at the walls, now freshly painted a gentle spring yellow. The smell of smoke was gone. The handbags were gone. The hat was gone. Rod was gone. The curtains were open and sun streamed into the room in which she had shared such a strange, spirited time with her grandmother.

"You have to admit," she said to her friend, "when hasn't Granny Mac been here when I needed her? She's always been my guardian angel."

The hairs were starting to stand up on the back of Alice's neck.

"She's not here now, is she?" she asked, her skepticism fading.

"If she was," Esme answered, "you would be sitting on her and dead or not you would know all about it."

"Well, when she was here," Alice wanted to know, "could you see through her and was she all blurry around the edges and did things float around the room?"

"No! It wasn't like that. It was just that when I came in it was as though she was sitting up in bed and so I would snatch a few minutes to myself and talk to her. It wasn't spooky or anything like that."

"But could you see her?"

"I never opened the curtains. She liked it in the dark."

"But was she really here?"

"I can't explain it, Alice, to you or to myself but yes, she was definitely here."

"And you could hear her."

"Yes. I think so, anyway."

"And does Pog know about this?"

"I've told Pog everything."

"And what did he say?"

"I've told Pog everything *but* this," Esme clarified. "And I will tell him. I just thought I would test it out on you first to see what happened, and I have to say I don't know that I would consider it a raging success."

"Well," conceded Alice, "I don't think that you shagging Louis was the best idea Granny Mac ever had but then technically you never actually did, and along the way the little slimeball did seem to clear your pipes on the, you know, Teddy front." She bit her lip. She was so used to dancing around the subject that it still felt unnatural to broach it.

Esme smiled, sweetly, sadly. "I miss him," she said, and Alice breathed again. "But I can think about him now without hating myself. And I can remember more than the snot bubble he blew out his nose that last morning." Her voice faltered. Alice scooted closer and hugged her. "But it feels better," Esme whispered. "Better than before when I could hardly bear to look at Rory without seeing that same little face, never growing up, just staying two and a bit forever."

"Oh, Esme, I'm so sorry."

"It's all right," wept Esme, "really it is. I'm much happier now." Her shoulders shook with grief but instead of fighting it, of pushing it away, she let it embrace her, and with that, as she had come to learn, came a warmth, a calmness.

"He was a gorgeous boy, wasn't he?" Alice said, gently rocking her friend.

"Yes," sniffed Esme, her tears subsiding. "He was. Remember the night you baby-sat and he ate the contents of his nappy?"

Alice laughed. "How could I forget? I had to clean it out of his teeth, for goodness' sake. And what about the time Ridge swapped their clothes and the Crumblies never noticed and it wasn't until you gave them a bath the next night that you realized what he had done and swapped them back?"

"Oh, don't," Esme cried. "That makes it sound like I was such a crap mother!"

"You are the best mother a boy could have," Alice said robustly. "And Teddy might not have had you for long but he couldn't have had anyone better. Don't shrug me off, Esme, it's true. And I know you worry about Rory and who wouldn't, in the circumstances, but he is actually one pretty cool little bloke and he is going to be all right. He might have lost his brother but he's still got two wonderful parents, a doting grandfather, adoring friends and a donkey with the biggest dick I have ever seen in my whole entire life."

Esme laughed and the sound bounced around and around the sunny room, chasing away, once and for all, the spirit of the past.

Alice squeezed her again and they sat there, quietly staring at crumpled Elizabeth Hurley squashed on the cover of *Hello!* magazine between them until Esme sniffed at the air and sat up.

"Time to put the bread in," she said to her friend. "Come on, clench those buttocks."

"Unfurl the flag, sherpa," Alice grumbled as she heaved herself off Granny Mac's bed and headed up the stairs.

Up in the kitchen Esme's dough sat proud and floury in its linen-lined basket. Esme loved this last raw look at it. She opened the oven door and pulled out the baking stone she used to even out the temperature and give her bread a crispier bottom and chewier crust.

Gently but quickly, she upturned the basket just millimeters off the heated stone and out plumped her *boule,* making an almost imperceptible sizzle as it hit the heated ceramic surface. Swiftly, she took the waiting razor and cut a few clever lines into the skin of the dough, then shut the door and flicked the steam jets on three times in quick succession.

Although she had done this a thousand times before, she could not help but crouch down and watch her bread through the glass door of the oven. She still saw the magic in every single bake and she was sure she always would.

"Esme," Alice said, from her position at the kitchen table, "you never finished telling me about what happened with Charlie."

Esme put the kettle on. Yes. Charlie.

Obviously Esme's intention, once she got her family back to the House in the Clouds that awful, wonderful day two weeks before, had been to take out a contract on Charlie and get him killed, stone dead.

He had risked so much, and none of it as his own expense, in his little turn at playing God, that Esme doubted she could ever look at him again let alone speak to him. But it had been Pog, kind, gentle, remarkable Pog, who had finally talked to him at length on the phone and then suggested that maybe Esme should go and meet him and listen to what he had to say.

So it was that the previous Friday Esme had found herself looking at Charlie over a very expensive glass of Reisling, his treat, and wondering how much of a fuss it would cause if she choked him then and there. It was lunchtime and they were sitting upstairs at Assaggi in Notting Hill, as far away from the pitfalls of Marylebone High Street as Charlie could manage in a busy working day.

"Darling, I'm so glad you finally agreed to have lunch with me," he was saying. "It's been awful these past two weeks. If you'd hung up on me one more time I swear I was going to have to—I don't know—not top myself but do something pretty drastic. I've been quite distraught."

Esme took a sip and thought how terribly Charlie this was.

"Yes," she said demurely, not ready to let him off the hook, "it must have been dreadful for you."

"Oh, Esme," Charlie said, pushing his wine away, and missing her sarcasm. But she had to admit he did look awful. The glow that normally illuminated the air in front of him had vanished and he looked quite ordinary, which was not a Charlie state at all. "Please, please forgive me, Esme. I never meant to hurt you, of course I didn't. I would never do that. I would rather, what? Stick needles in my eyes? Wear synthetic boxers? Reveal my natural roots? Oh please don't freeze me out, Esme, I can't bear it."

Esme swirled the rich straw-colored wine in her glass. Of course, she hadn't come all this way to ignore him, and she wanted him to know that before they ordered their food so she could order up large and not feel bad that he was paying.

There were things she had to say to him, though. Questions she had to ask.

"Why, Charlie?" This was the main one. "Why did you do such a terrible thing?"

"Well, I would have told you on the phone if you hadn't kept slamming it down in my ear," Charlie answered, but the color returned to his cheeks. He could sense progress. He sighed and

419

took a deep breath. "It's the most terrible cock-up. Really. I was in some Spanish bar off Tottenham Court Road one night," he said, "not long after I came to stay with you in the country, and there the little turd was, propping up the bar and sniveling into his Rioja."

"He was sniveling?"

"Well, no, but he was pretty bloody miserable. Anyway, I recognized him straightaway. I suppose I had been thinking about him after what you said that night, you know, about him being your one big chance at happiness. Oh, don't look at me like that, Esme! What do I know about these things? You said that when things were rough—and things have been rough, haven't they?—that you wondered what it might have been like if you'd ended up with Louis. And there the little shit was sitting right in front of my nose. Well, the idea just came to me. What if you could see him once again? Naturally, I assumed that just one look and you'd realize that the life you've been living has been the right one after all. I just wanted to give you a slice of your happiness back, Es. I thought you could have a lovely romantic lunch at my expense, perhaps a bit of a snog in the lavs and then go your separate ways. I thought it would cheer you up."

"But you bought him a suit, Charlie. You turned him into someone he wasn't," protested Esme.

"He was already someone he wasn't!" Charlie argued. "He was *always* someone he wasn't." He took a gulp of his wine. "Okay, look, to be honest, the suit was a bit of a mistake, I agree. I've had it for a while, actually bought it for someone else but, oh, never mind. Anyway, it was you who turned Louis into the handsome prince, not me. And I am incredibly sorry for what I did and when I think of how much worse it could have been I cringe, darling, I honestly cringe but I didn't do it to hurt you. I thought I was doing you a favor. Adding a bit of spice to your life. I was trying to be nice."

"Well, why couldn't you tell me that he was working in a sarnie shop in Hounslow and let me go and find him the way he really is?"

"Yes," Charlie agreed. "I can see now that would have been better but at the time I wanted you to have your little dream, Es. You love all that romantic stuff. You always have. You know I don't understand it myself but I love how you love it. And I thought how marvelous to meet this man looking all dashing and international and saving sourdough all around the world. Of course he was supposed to tell you that he was still happily married and that he hoped you were too but the cretin obviously got one look at you and decided he wanted a piece of that for himself."

"But can you see what a dreadful thing it was to do?" Esme asked him. "Charlie, what if Rory really had been snatched? What if Louis had turned nasty? Or Pog had left me?"

"Yes, yes, yes," Charlie said. "I have been

421

torturing myself with the same possibilities, I told you, I have been cringing. But that part of it is really not my fault. I mean, the slimy little bastard was supposed to disappear after the first lunch. I had no idea he was going to hoodwink you so badly, Esme. To hurt you all over again. Good Lord, that's the last thing I would ever want. You are precious to me. You are my oldest friend. I love you more than my new Rolex. Have you noticed it, Es? Twenty-four-carat gold. Anyway, if I ever see the lying, cheating, sneaky little toad again I will box him in the nose all over again, I promise you."

"Well, if you are ever in Hounslow and feeling peckish," Esme told him, "don't hold back on my account."

The waiter approached and Charlie looked at her, worry creasing his brow in a way she knew would have him shrieking for forehead-smoothing surgery should he catch sight of the wrinkles in a mirror. The damage had been done. And repaired. And with one smile they put their angst behind them and ordered vast quantities of food and another bottle of wine.

The truth was that Charlie was precious to Esme, too. So, he would never understand what true love was, or what her idea of true love was, but then her idea of true love had completely changed. And she could not in all honesty stay angry with Charlie. The whole sorry mess had been her own fault.

She had stupidly told him she thought Louis was the key to her happiness, and in the bleakness of losing Granny Mac she had truly believed that to be the case. She had reached into her past and plucked out the most vivid uncomplicated happiness she could find and dreamed of recreating it. An impossible task, as it turned out. Not to mention a foolish one.

"The funny thing is," she said sheepishly to Alice as they sat nursing their second cup of tea high in the Suffolk sky, "despite all the, you know, terribleness, the drama, the upset I've caused, everything is better now."

Better than it had been in two long, awful years. She knew now how much she loved Pog. She knew how much he loved her back and it was a thousand times more than Louis, than anyone else, ever could. Henry, finally trusting that she did not blame him, was a changed man and while not exactly a delight to have about the place, not a curse, either. And Rory, well, Rory: Her heart simply swelled with adoration. Something about relieving herself of the silent, secret ghost of Teddy had allowed her to love Rory in a way she had not thought possible before. And free of the blame for taking his twin-ness away from him, she was able to see, as clear as day, that just like his father, Rory loved her back, too. It was simply euphoric.

Pog, looking blissfully boyish, Alice thought, clattered into the kitchen, his nose sniffing the air.

"Am I on time?" he asked as he kissed his wife and smiled at her friend.

"I swear," said Esme, "you are getting almost as good as I am."

She moved over to the oven, put on her mitts, and opened the door, letting the heat and strength of the sourdough aroma engulf her. Reverently, she lifted out the *pain au levain* and set it on the countertop wooden rack she had for just that purpose. It sat there, fat and crisp and brown, radiating warmth and good taste.

The kitchen filled instantly with that moist, sweet, salty smell. Pog and Esme's eyes met above the *boule* and they smiled at each other. Their sadness aside, all seemed right with the world.

Even Alice licked her lips. "What's that?" she asked, peering over Esme's shoulder.

Sliced into the loaf was not the E that Esme had so deftly carved all these years, but an impression of the house in which they now stood.

"It's Bread from the House in the Clouds," Pog answered her, getting a jar of apricot jam from the pantry, a dish of butter from the fridge and a breadboard and bread knife from the kitchen drawers.

"What are you on about?" Alice asked, sitting down again, as Esme brought the bread to the table.

"You tell her," Esme said.

"Tell me what?"

"Tell you to make the most of Granny Mac's

room while you can," said Pog, handing the knife to Esme. "Because in a month or two right where you were just sitting and gossiping will be a roaring oak-fired oven."

Alice was confused. "I don't follow," she said, looking at Esme for guidance. "Is that an exorcism thing?"

"I told you we had a lot to catch up on," Esme said. She took the knife and expertly sawed through the thick, solid crust, the sound tickling her ears, a new, luscious, more-honeyed smell releasing into the air. The gorgeous gassy holes of the cream-colored crumb glistened with health.

"We're opening a bakery," she said, "right here at the bottom of the stack of Stacks. Bread from the House in the Clouds. What do you think?"

"I think I need a lie-down before Granny Mac's bed is chopped into a thousand pieces and fed into the furnace," Alice answered. "You're going to bake at the bottom of your house and have people come here and buy the bread?"

"People come here anyway," Pog pointed out. "To marvel at Esme's vegetarian protuberances and offer incontinent animals."

Esme laughed as she slathered a thick slice of her bread with homemade jam.

Alice chewed on her own unseemly chunk of sourdough. "I thought your bread was just for you, Esme," she said wickedly. "Not for everyone. That you couldn't mass-produce it. That it's personal."

Esme just smiled. "Why, Alice," she said. "It's

bread. It's the staff of bleeding life. People put butter and jam on it and eat it."

"Seriously, Esme, you are going to do this for a job?'"

"Yes, she is," answered Pog. "No one cares more about sourdough than Esme and artisan bread-makers are a dying breed these days, even in France, hey, Esme?"

"Hey, yourself." Esme grinned back, her cup overrunning with love for him.

"You two!" Alice was disgusted. "Get a motel! You've got a sad, sorry singleton in your midst, let's not forget."

"I shall leave you to it, then," Pog said. "I'm sure there's a lot of girl talk still to be had. Have you told her about you-know-who?"

Alice looked confused. "I thought you hadn't told him?" she said to Esme.

"I haven't."

"Haven't told me what?" Pog wanted to know.

"Nothing, Pog. Something Granny Mac said. Some things Granny Mac said. I will tell you later."

Pog disappeared down the stairs.

"What is going on here today?" demanded Alice. "Who is you-know-who?"

"Jemima Jones," Esme announced, swallowing the last mouthful of her bread and missing it as soon as it was gone. "I banged into Jemima Jones again."

It had been the same day she'd lunched with

Charlie, she told Alice. He'd had to get back to work and she had decided to walk to Portobello Road and have a coffee at the Electric before heading to the station to make her train.

But no sooner had she sat down with her low-fat latte, than who should fly in the door but Jemima, her cream Armani coat flapping at her sides and her stilettos screeching across the floorboards.

"Vodka tonic, double, and be quick about it," she slung at the barman as she collapsed in a chair at the table right next to Esme. She flung her tote bag on the chair next to her and scrabbled around in it until she pulled out a box of tissues and loudly blew her nose.

Esme pressed herself back into her own chair and twisted slightly away from Jemima, in the hope she would disappear. She did not.

"Oh," said Jemima Jones looking up and noticing her. "Esme."

Esme nodded, dumbly.

"How's the book coming along?"

Esme opened her mouth to speak but nothing came out.

"If you're worried it's going to end up in my column," Jemima said, "don't be. They've dropped it. I've been given the arse. Fucking Primrose Beckwith-Stuyvesant. How was I supposed to know her uncle is apparently the patron saint of all newspaper bosses and godfather to half of News International?"

The barman delivered her drink, which she knocked back in almost one gulp. "Same again," she said, then put one bare pretty ankle on her knee and took off her shoe. "Bloody corns are giving me hell," she said, rubbing her toes. "What kind of demented homosexual woman-hater would design shoes like these, anyway?"

And to Esme's amazement and alarm, the gorgeous Jemima burst into loud, wet tears.

Esme and the barman stared at each other for a moment, then he quietly put Jemima's drink down beside her and slithered away, leaving the two women alone together. In the absence of knowing what else to do, Esme went and sat beside the weeping woman and cautiously gave her a rub on her bony little back. The coat felt beautiful.

"Gregory's leaving me," wept Jemima. "And this time, it's for good. I'm not 'adventurous' enough for him, apparently, and he's found some eighteen-year-old eastern European model-cum-waitress who doesn't mind if he soils her underwear—while he's still in it—so he's going to live with her. GQ hasn't come out of his room since he found out—Christ only knows what he is doing in there with that sodding computer of his, porn I expect, he is such an odd boy—and Marie Claire is eating us out of house and home. A home we won't even have for much longer." Her mascara had done scary things to her flawless face. Tears swept unfettered by wrinkles down her smooth cheeks. "It's all gone horribly wrong and I don't know what to do about it," she sobbed.

"What about your television show?" Esme asked feebly.

"Those twitty nine-year-olds!" Jemima cried. "They wanted me to bankroll it. Dropped me like a hot potato when they realized that wasn't going to happen. It's so unfair! The world is a horrible place."

Esme kept rubbing.

Jemima stopped crying.

"I'm sorry," she said, blowing her nose again. "I really am sorry."

"Don't mention it," Esme said brightly. "I'm constantly blubbing into my vodka tonics."

"No," said Jemima, sniffing. "I'm sorry about stiffing you at *TV Now!* You were always very nice to me and it was a rotten way to pay you back."

"Oh, that," Esme said, as though she could barely remember it. "That was nothing, really."

"And I'm sorry for writing about you like that in my column."

"Oh, was that me?" Esme asked wetly.

Jemima cleared her throat. "Somebody at the *Sunday Times* told me about your little boy. I didn't know that's why you left London and put on the weight and everything. I would never have said anything in that stupid bloody column if I had known about that. I'm a mother. I can't imagine how awful that must have been. I felt like a real shit, I can tell you."

She burst into tears again. Put on the weight? Esme repeated in her mind, her fingers itching to give Jemima a pinch.

"My life is such a mess," Jemima wept. "I wish I lived in the country and wrote books about hair-clips like you do."

How long would that blessed lie come back to haunt her? Esme wondered. She looked at the sorry sight in front of her and marveled at the way the world worked.

"Actually," she said, deciding then and there to set the record straight, "there is no book about hairclips, Jemima. Please, stop crying. Look, I'm sure everything's going to be all right. Do you think we should have a cup of tea?"

Upon hearing this part of the story, Alice lost her cool. "You asked her if she wanted a cup of tea? You were nice to her? You bloody well *have* lost your marbles, Esme. Truly!"

Esme was prepared for this.

"She was a wreck, Alice. A total disaster area—it was terrible." She picked up a tray she had prepared for Henry and Rory and started down the stairs, indicating for Alice to follow her. "She's just another one of us, you know, trying to muddle through and make sense of it all without having a nervous breakdown or killing someone. She's not so different from you or me."

She could feel her friend's eyes boring into her back. "Oh God," said Alice. "There's more, isn't there?"

Esme nodded, as she negotiated the next flight of stairs. "I think you will find that we are having little Cosmo to stay next weekend."

"I give up," Alice said behind her in disgust. "I seriously give up." But before she could say anything else, they were distracted by a loud and very nearly tuneless singing coming from somewhere below them.

As they approached the ground floor they came upon Rory, sitting on the front doorstep pulling on his Wellingtons and rasping in a decidedly Celtic tone.

"If we want his body," Alice echoed him, "and we think he's sexy?" She turned to look at her friend. "It's the body of a small boy," she said in astonishment.

"But the voice of an old Scottish woman?" suggested Esme. "Now do you believe me?"

"Now," Alice answered, "I believe anything."

SOURDOUGH BREAD

⅓ cup rye flour
3¾ cups strong white flour
¾ cup starter
1 T salt
1½ cups + 1 T water

Mix all ingredients except the salt in a large ceramic or glass bowl, by hand, for five minutes. The mixture will be quite wet but if you are having trouble mixing it (if most of it is ending up on your fingers or around the bowl), try using just 1½ cups of water. Rest for five minutes, then add salt. Mix for another 5 to 10 minutes on a countertop, without adding any extra flour, until mixture is smooth and elastic, then put into a slightly oiled container (this can be the same bowl) and leave for 3 to 4 hours loosely covered, so air can still get in.

Knock back or punch down with a gentle fold, then leave for another hour.

Tip the dough out and gently premold the loaf by folding it in on itself and turning it over; let sit for 10 minutes. Then give it a final mold, dip it in flour and put it in a basket (approximately 10 inches diameter) lined with a heavily floured linen dishtowel. Rub the flour well into the dishtowel and don't wash it in between uses. If it's not floured enough, the dough will stick when you try to upend it for baking.

At this stage you can leave the dough for half an hour, put it in the fridge overnight, then bring it out and let it sit for an hour before baking.

Or:

Leave for 3 hours in the basket, then tip out, preferably onto a preheated pizza stone. With a very sharp knife or razorblade, cut some quick slashes in the top of the bread so the gases can escape and bake at 500°F for 20 minutes, and then 425°F for 10 minutes, remembering to steam the oven when you put the loaf in. (Do this by spraying the sides of the oven with one of those squirty waterbottles and quickly shutting the door.) This makes the crust crunchier.

When the loaf is baked it should be a nutty-brown color and should sound hollow when you tap the base.

Note: The bread Esme bakes is based on the recipe used at the famous Poilâne bakery in Paris, however this one was given to me by baker and sourdough aficionado Dean Brettschneider. Of all the recipes I have tried, it is by far the most consistent.

SOURDOUGH STARTER

Day one: Juice three fresh organic apples, strain and leave the liquid in a partly covered jar or jug.

Days seven to ten: When the juice is obviously bubbly and fermented, add it, in a glass or ceramic bowl or plastic container, to 1½ cups flour and ¾ cup water and leave, covered with Saran wrap poked with holes or in a loosely tied supermarket plastic bag.

Day eleven: Add another 1½ cups flour and ¾ cup water and leave.

Day twelve: Discard half the mixture and add another 1½ cups flour and ¾ cup water.

Day thirteen: Repeat the above, and do so every day until you know your starter is alive and kicking because it will rise up the sides of the bowl or container in between feeds and will be bubbly and smell sharp and cidery. If you want to get your starter going more quickly, feed it twice a day.

When you think it is active enough, try the recipe

for a deliciously delectable loaf of homemade *pain au levain.* As the starter strengthens, the bread will rise more, gorgeous shiny holes will appear in the flesh and the crust will take on a tart, almost cheesy flavor.

The starter will keep in the fridge unfed for up to 2 weeks but you will need to bring it out, get it to room temperature and feed it for a couple of days before you use it. The starter is best used in the bread dough 8 to 12 hours after its last feed.

Another Note: The active ingredients in your starter are the natural bugs in the air where you live so some will get going more quickly than others. Don't let your starter get too hot or too cold and make sure it isn't in a draft. Most of all, remember to feed it and persevere. My starter took more than two months to get going after a lot of trial and error. And flour and water. The end result is worth it, though.

Sarah-Kate Lynch lives in New Zealand in a lakeside alpine town that, it turns out, has very dry, clean air not particularly conducive to getting a sourdough starter going. In the early stages of researching this book, she had eight different bowls of festering flour and water littering her kitchen counter and her clothes were permanently splattered in paste. Perseverance, however, paid off and now she bakes a mean *pain au levain* which on occasion she even shares with her husband.

ACKNOWLEDGMENTS

I've always liked eating bread—well, I need something for the cheese to go on—but before starting this book I was far from an expert at baking it.

And without the help of baking aficionado Dean Brettschneider I would still be rubbing floury hands through my hair going, "Why won't it work?" Dean has done everything from lending me reference books to taking panicked late-night phone calls from Provence to spending an afternoon actually teaching me, step by step, to make sourdough. He is a man who cares about ingredients and methods and the beauty of *pain au levain* and I simply cannot thank him enough.

Similarly, Joan Richardson at the famous Poilâne bakery in Paris was instrumental in transforming my understanding of the traditional French bakery. At a moment's notice she made it possible for me to camp out in the Rue du Cherche-Midi bakery and her generosity was overwhelming. And Felix, the baker, deserves a medal for putting up with my schoolgirl French. He's probably still wondering what I meant when

437

I said the flour is on the bicycle. Just a few months after I warmed those ancient stone steps watching Felix at work, Lionel Poilâne lost his life in a helicopter accident and I can only imagine the devastation his dedicated team must have felt. May his memory live on in his *pain au levain*, the best you are ever likely to taste, still baked just the way it always has been with his daughter Apollonia now at the helm of the company.

And for those who think I am terribly clever for inventing the House in the Clouds, I am not. It exists pretty much as described in the village of Thorpeness on the Suffolk coast, although in real life the kitchen is, rather sensibly, on the ground floor. It is a truly eccentric and wonderful place and I couldn't have made it up if I tried.

To Jamie Raab and everybody at Warner Books, a big hurrah for your patience, and to Stephanie Cabot, Ginger Barber and Tracy Fisher at William Morris, heartfelt thanks.

Much appreciation also, for help along the way, to Lauraine Jacobs, Rachel Scott and, for reasons of an entirely different nature, Simon Barclay, without whom none of this might have been possible.

As those close to me know, writing this book has been something of a mission with more than the usual number of obstacles littering the path and I want to thank my friends and family for helping me every step of the way. To my mum, my sisters and my brothers, I love you all and am lucky to have you. And to my husband, Mark, well, words truly, madly, deeply aren't enough.